THE MASTERPIECE

FRANCINE RIVERS

THORNDIKE PRESS
A part of Gale, a Cengage Company

GALE
A Cengage Company

Farmington Hills, Mich • San Francisco • New York • Waterville, Maine
Meriden, Conn • Mason, Ohio • Chicago

Copyright © 2018 by Francine Rivers.
Scripture quotations are taken from the *Holy Bible,* New Living Translation, copyright © 1996, 2004, 2015 by Tyndale House Foundation. Used by permission of Tyndale House Publishers, Inc., Carol Stream, Illinois 60188. All rights reserved.
Thorndike Press, a part of Gale, a Cengage Company.

Thorndike Press® Large Print Christian Fiction.
The text of this Large Print edition is unabridged.
Other aspects of the book may vary from the original edition.
Set in 16 pt. Plantin.

LIBRARY OF CONGRESS CIP DATA ON FILE.
CATALOGUING IN PUBLICATION FOR THIS BOOK
IS AVAILABLE FROM THE LIBRARY OF CONGRESS.

ISBN-13: 978-1-4328-4672-5 (hardcover)

Published in 2018 by arrangement with Tyndale House Publishers, Inc.

Printed in the United States of America
1 2 3 4 5 6 7 22 21 20 19 18

THE MASTERPIECE

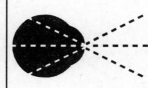 This Large Print Book carries the
Seal of Approval of N.A.V.H.

TO MY HUSBAND,
RICK RIVERS.
Thank you for a life full of adventure!

ACKNOWLEDGMENTS

One of the great blessings of being a writer is the opportunity to interview people who are experienced in arenas I have not entered. I've had a great deal of help on the winding road of writing *The Masterpiece.* I want to thank the following people for the information and encouragement they gave me:

Gary LeDonne shared his knowledge of the juvenile court system and group home referrals.

Heather Aldridge of the Sonoma County Sheriff's Office forensics department and Christopher Wirowek, deputy director of the San Francisco Medical Examiner's Office, told me about policies and practices of departmental record keeping and finding identities of Jane and John Does.

Ulla Pomele gave me daily scheduling information for a group home program structure and activities.

Debbie Kaupp gave me an extensive list of the various duties of a personal assistant.

My brother, Everett King, told me about his experience with silent heart attacks, heart surgery, and the installation of a defibrillator implant.

Ex-cartel gang tagger and graffiti artist "Allude" shared some of his street adventures and misadventures in the Bay Area.

My friend Carolyn Dunn invited me to brainstorm my characters with a group of certified, professional family counselors. Thank you, Uriah Guilford, Candace Holly, Terri L. Haley, Laurel Marlink Quast, Gary Moline, and Rebecca Worsley for your insights into the realities of bonding issues in traumatized children and how they might play out in adulthood. Laurel Quast also gave me much-needed information on working with women in crisis pregnancy and child placement.

Ashley Huddleston and Tricia Goyer shared heart-wrenching insights into the psyche of traumatized children, as well as the struggles of foster and adoptive parents who love them and strive to help them heal.

Antanette Reed, Kern County assistant director of CPS, gave me essential information about the foster care system.

When I got lost in my story and couldn't find my way around, I called story doctor Stan Williams. He asked the right questions to get me on track.

Holly Harder, my dear friend, has awesome

navigational skills on the Internet. Whenever I got lost in cyberspace or couldn't find details on any given subject, I sent out a distress call to Holly, and she found in minutes the exact information I needed.

A huge thank-you to my Coeur d'Alene brainstorming friends: Brandilyn Collins, Tamera Alexander, Robin Lee Hatcher, Karen Ball, Sharon Dunn, Gayle DeSalles, Tricia Goyer, Sunni Jeffers, Sandy Sheppard, and Janet Ulbright. All amazing women of God who pray, plot, and know how to play. Whenever I hit a wall, these remarkable women helped get me over or through it.

Colleen Phillips, kindred spirit and missionary in Chile, was in this project from the beginning. Thank you for "listening" to all the variations of Roman and Grace's journey and for being the first one to read, comment, and make corrections on the manuscript — not once, but twice — before I dared submit it.

I also want to thank my brilliant agent, Danielle Egan-Miller, for her insights and long hours of work in managing my writing career. It's a blessing to be able to leave all the complex details of business to someone I trust so that I can concentrate on writing.

Thank you also to Tyndale publisher Karen Watson, who always has the questions to get my creative juices flowing. I'm grateful to Cheryl Kerwin, Erin Smith, Shaina Turner, and Stephanie Broene, who handle the lion's share of my Facebook author page. Robin Lee Hatcher manages my website, and my daughter, Shannon Coibion, posts my blogs and helps me with incoming mail.

Finally, I am indebted to my longtime editor, Kathy Olson, who understands my process and story. Without her expertise in cutting, restructuring, and slipping in scenes from previous drafts, this book would not be in your hands.

Blessings to each of you in your future ventures. You are all God's masterpieces.

1

Roman Velasco climbed the fire escape and swung over the wall onto the flat roof. Crouching, he moved quickly. Another building abutted the five-story apartment house, the perfect location for graffiti. Right across the street was a bank building, and he'd already left a piece on the front door.

Shrugging off his backpack, he pulled out his supplies. He'd have to work fast. Los Angeles never slept. Even at three in the morning, cars sped along the boulevard.

This piece would be seen by anyone driving east. He'd be at risk until he finished, but dressed in black pants and a hooded sweatshirt, he'd be hard to spot, unless someone were looking for him. Ten minutes. That's all he needed to leave a parade of characters dancing on the wall — all looking like the top-hatted businessman from the Monopoly game, the last one leaping toward the street. He'd stenciled the figure laden with money bags going into the bank across the street.

The paper stencil hooked on something and tore. Swearing under his breath, Roman worked quickly to tape it. A wind came up, pulling a portion away. It was a long stencil and took precious minutes to secure. He grabbed a can of spray paint and shook it. When he pressed the button, nothing happened. Cursing, he pulled out another can and started spraying.

A vehicle approached. He glanced down and froze when he spotted a police car decelerating. Was it the same one that had come by an hour ago, when he'd been heading for the bank? He'd walked with purpose, hoping they'd think he was just some guy heading home from a night shift. The car had slowed, checking him out, and then moved on. As soon as it disappeared down the street, he'd done the work on the glass door of the bank building.

Roman went back to work. He only needed a few more minutes. He kept spraying.

Brake lights glowed hot red on the street. The police car had stopped in front of the bank. A white beam of light fixed on the front door.

One more minute. Roman made two more sweeps and started the careful removal of the stencil. He'd had to use more tape than usual, so it took longer. The last section of paper peeled away, and he added three small black interlocking letters that looked like a bird in flight.

One officer was out of the car, flashlight in hand.

Roman crouched low, rolled the stencil, and stuffed it into his backpack with the spray cans. The beam of light rose and moved closer. It flashed right over him as he started moving across the roof. It traveled down and away. Relieved, Roman shouldered the pack and rose slightly.

The light returned, silhouetting him against the wall. He bolted, face averted.

The beam of light tracked his escape across the roof. He heard voices and racing feet. Heart hammering, Roman took a flying leap onto the next building. He hit hard, rolled to his feet, and kept going. The police department probably had a file on the Bird's work. He wasn't a teenager anymore, facing community service for doing gang tagging on a wall. If he got caught now, he'd do jail time.

Worse, he'd destroy the budding reputation Roman Velasco was earning as a legitimate artist. Graffiti earned street cred, but didn't help in a gallery.

One officer had returned to the squad car. Tires squealed. They weren't giving up.

Roman spotted an open window a couple of buildings over and decided to climb up rather than down.

A car door slammed. A man shouted. Must be a slow night if these two cops wanted to spend this much time hunting a graffiti artist.

Roman swung over the edge of another roof. A half-empty can of spray paint fell out of his jostled pack and exploded on the pavement below.

The startled officer drew his gun and pointed it at Roman as he climbed. "LAPD! Stop where you are!"

Gripping a ledge, Roman pulled himself up and went in through the open apartment window. He held his breath. A man snored in the bedroom. Roman crept forward. He hadn't gone two steps before bumping into something. His eyes adjusted to the dim light from the kitchen appliances. The occupant must be a hoarder. The cluttered living room could be Roman's undoing. He left his backpack behind the sofa.

Opening the front door quietly, he peered out and listened. No movement, no voices. The man in the bedroom snorted and stirred. Roman slipped out quickly and closed the door behind him. The emergency exit door was stuck. If he forced it, he'd make noise. He found the elevator, his heart pounding faster as it took its sweet time rising. *Bing.* The doors opened. Roman stepped inside and punched the button for the underground parking garage.

Just stay cool. He shoved the hood back and raked his hands through his hair. He took a deep breath and let it out slowly. The elevator doors opened. The basement parking lot was well lit. Roman held the door open and waited a few seconds to scope the area before he stepped out. All clear. Relieved, he headed for the ramp leading up to the side street.

The police car sat at the curb. Doors opened, and both officers emerged.

For a split second, Roman debated inventing a quick story for why he'd be heading out for a walk at three thirty in the morning, but somehow he knew no story was going to keep him out of cuffs.

He bolted up the street toward a residential neighborhood a block off the main boulevard. The officers followed like hounds after a fox.

Roman went down one street, along a paved driveway, and over a wall. He thought he was home free until he realized he wasn't alone in the backyard. A German shepherd leaped to its feet and gave chase. Roman raced across the yard and over the back fence. The dog hit the fence and clawed at it, barking fiercely. Roman landed hard on the other side and knocked over a couple of garbage cans in his haste to get away. Now every other canine up and down the street was sounding the alarm. Roman moved fast, keeping low and in the shadows.

Lights went on. He could hear voices.

Inquiries would slow down the cops, and they'd be less likely to go over fences and trespass. Roman moved fast for a few blocks and then slowed to a normal gait to catch his breath.

The dogs had stopped barking. He heard a car and slipped behind a privet hedge. The police car crossed the next street, not slowing as it headed back toward Santa Monica Boulevard. Maybe he'd lost them. Rather than push his luck any further, Roman waited another few minutes before venturing out to the sidewalk.

It took him an hour to make his way back to his BMW. Sliding into the driver's seat, he couldn't resist driving east to check out his work.

The bank would have its front door cleaned by noon, but the high piece on the wall across the street would last longer. The Bird had gained enough notoriety over the past few years that some building owners left the graffiti untouched. He hoped that would be the case with this one. He'd come too close to getting caught to have the work buffed and forgotten in a day or two.

Freeway traffic had already picked up. Fighting exhaustion, Roman turned on the air-conditioning. Cold air blasted him, keeping him wide-awake as he drove up into Topanga Canyon, feeling drained and vaguely depressed. He should be reveling after his successful night raid, not feeling like an old man in need of a recliner.

He slowed and turned onto the gravel drive down to his house. The push of a button opened the garage door. Three more cars bigger than his 740Li could fit in the space. He shut off the engine and sat for a few seconds as the door whirred closed behind him.

As he started to get out of his car, a wave of weakness hit him. He sat still for a minute, waiting for the odd sensation to pass. It hit him again when he headed for the back door. Staggering, he went down on one knee. He anchored his fist on the concrete and kept his head down.

The spell passed, and Roman stood slowly. He needed sleep. That's all. One full night would fix him up. He opened the back door to dead silence.

Unzipping and removing the black hoodie, he headed down the hallway to his bedroom. He was too tired to take a shower, too tired to turn the air conditioner down to sixty-five, too tired to eat, though his stomach cramped with hunger. Stripping off his clothes, he sprawled across the unmade bed. Maybe he'd get lucky tonight and sleep without dreaming. Usually, the high he got from one of his night raids earned a payback of nightmares from his days in the Tenderloin. White Boy never stayed buried for long.

Morning shot spears of sunlight. Roman closed his eyes, craving darkness.

■ ■ ■ ■

Grace Moore got up early, knowing she would need plenty of time to cross the valley and arrive on time for her first day as a temp worker. She wasn't sure the job would pay well enough to get a small apartment for herself and her son, Samuel, but it was a start. The longer she lived with the Garcias, the more complicated things became.

Selah and Ruben were in no hurry for her to leave. Selah still hoped Grace would change her mind and sign the adoption papers. Grace didn't want to give Selah false hope, but she had nowhere else to go. Every day that passed increased her desire to be independent again.

She'd sent out dozens of résumés since being laid off over a year ago and only received a few calls back for interviews. None had produced a job. Every employer wanted a college graduate these days, and she'd only completed a year and a half before putting her education on hold so she could support her husband, Patrick, until he graduated.

Looking back, she wondered if Patrick had ever loved her. Every promise Patrick had made, he'd broken. He had needed her. He had used her. It was that simple.

Aunt Elizabeth was right. She was a fool.

Samuel stirred in his crib. Grace lifted him

gently, thankful he was awake. She'd have time to nurse him and change his diaper before handing him over to Selah. "Good morning, little man." Grace breathed in his baby scent and sat on the edge of the twin bed she'd just made. She opened her blouse and shifted him so he could nurse.

The circumstances of his conception and the complications he'd added to her life ceased to matter the moment she first held him in her arms. He hadn't been an hour old before she knew she couldn't give him up for adoption, no matter how much better his life might be with the Garcias. She'd told Selah and Ruben as much, but every day brought its own anguish as Selah took over his care while Grace went out looking for a way to support herself and her son.

Others do it, Lord. Why can't I?

Others had family. She had only Aunt Elizabeth.

Father, please let this job work out. Help me, Lord. Please. I know I don't deserve it, but I'm asking. I'm begging.

Thankfully, she'd passed the interview and tests with the temp agency and been added to their list. Mrs. Sandoval had a job opening. "I've sent this man four highly qualified people, and he rejected every one. I don't think he knows what he needs. It's the only work I can offer you right now."

Grace would have agreed to work for the

devil himself if it meant a regular paycheck.

The sound of chimes pulled Roman up out of the darkness. Had he dreamed he was in Westminster Abbey? He rolled over. His body had just relaxed when the chimes started again. Someone had pushed the doorbell. He'd like to get his hands on the owner who installed the blasted system. Cursing, Roman pulled a pillow over his head, hoping to muffle the song that could be heard from one end of the five-thousand-square-foot house to the other.

Silence returned. The interloper had probably gotten the message and left.

Roman tried to go back to sleep. When the chimes started again, he shouted in frustration and stood up. A wave of weakness surged again. Knocking over a half-empty bottle of water and the alarm clock, he caught himself before he pitched face-first onto the floor. Three times in less than twenty-four hours. He might have to resort to prescription drugs to get the rest he needed. But right now, all he wanted to do was unleash his temper on the intruder who was ringing his bell.

Pulling on sweats, Roman grabbed a wrinkled T-shirt off the carpet and headed barefoot down the hall. Whoever stood on the other side of his front door was going to wish they'd never set foot on his property. The chimes started in again just as he yanked open the door. A young woman glanced up in surprise and then backed away when he stepped over the threshold.

"Can't you read?" He jabbed a finger at the sign posted next to the front door. "No solicitors!"

Brown eyes wide, she put her hands up in a conciliatory gesture.

Her dark, curly hair was cropped short, and her black blazer, white blouse, and pearls screamed office worker. A faint recollection flickered in his mind, but Roman dismissed it. "Get lost!" He stepped back and slammed the door. He hadn't gotten far when she knocked lightly. Yanking the door open again, he glared at her. "What is wrong with you?"

She looked scared enough to run, but stood her ground. "I'm here on your orders, Mr. Velasco."

His orders? "Like I want a woman on my doorstep first thing in the morning."

"Mrs. Sandoval said nine o'clock. I'm Grace Moore. From the temp agency."

He spit a four-letter word. Her eyes flickered, and her cheeks filled with color. His anger dissolved like salt in water. *Great. Just great.* "I forgot you were coming."

She looked like she'd rather be any place but here, not that he could blame her. He debated telling her to come back tomorrow, but knew she wouldn't. He was up now. He might as well stay up. Jerking his head, he let the door drift open. "Come on in."

He'd gone through four temps in the last month. Mrs. Sandoval was losing patience faster than he was. "I'll send you one more, Mr. Velasco, and if she doesn't work out, I'll give you the name of my competitor."

He was looking for someone to field calls and handle the mundane details of correspondence, bills, scheduling. He didn't want a drill sergeant, a maiden aunt, or an amateur psychologist to analyze his artist's psyche. Nor did he need a curvy blonde in a low-cut blouse who pushed papers around, but didn't have a clue where to file them. She had ideas about what an artist might want besides a woman with office skills. He might have taken her up on her offer if he hadn't had enough experience with women like her. She lasted three days.

Not hearing any footsteps behind him, Roman paused and looked back. The girl was still standing outside. "What're you waiting for? An engraved invitation?"

She entered and closed the door quietly behind her. She looked ready to bolt.

He offered an apologetic smile. "Long night."

She murmured something he didn't catch, and he decided not to ask her to repeat it. He felt the onset of a headache, and the click of her high heels on the stone-tile floor wasn't helping. He was thirsty and needed caffeine.

He went into the kitchen adjoining the living room. She stopped at the edge of his sunken living room and gaped at the cathedral ceilings and wall of glass overlooking Topanga Canyon. Sunlight streamed through the windows, reminding him most people were serving time on their nine-to-fives by now.

Opening the stainless steel refrigerator, Roman grabbed a bottle of orange juice. He removed the cap, drank from the bottle, and lowered it. "What'd you say your name was?"

"Grace Moore."

She had the right look for the job — cool, calm, collected. Pretty, midtwenties, trim and fit, but not his type. He liked voluptuous blondes who knew the score.

Feeling his perusal, she looked at him. Women usually did, but not with her guarded expression. "You have a beautiful view, Mr. Velasco."

"Yeah, well, everything gets old eventually." He put the bottle of orange juice on the counter. She looked uncomfortable. Understandable, considering his less-than-friendly greeting. He smiled slightly. She looked back at him without expression. Good. He needed a worker bee, not a girlfriend. Would she take offense at his first request?

"Do you know how to make coffee?"

She looked over at the one-touch automatic coffee-and-espresso machine that could grind beans, heat milk, and make a latte in less than sixty seconds with the press of a pinkie.

"Not a cup. A full pot of real coffee." He left the kitchen to her. "Use the regular coffeemaker."

"Do you like it strong or weak?"

"Strong." He headed down the hall. "We'll talk more after I get cleaned up."

Roman stepped into a shower big enough for three. Lathering himself, he added side jets to the overhead waterfall. If he hadn't made such a bad first impression on Grace Moore, he'd let her wait while he had a twenty-minute, full-body water massage. Shutting off the tap, he stepped out, kicked aside used towels, and grabbed the last clean one off the cabinet shelf. Clothes spilled over the hamper. He had one pair of clean jeans left in the armoire. Pulling on a black T-shirt, he looked for shoes. He found the sneakers he'd worn the night before. No clean socks in the drawer.

The coffee smelled good. She was rearranging everything in the dishwasher. "I didn't tell you to clean the kitchen."

She straightened. "Would you rather I didn't?"

"Go right ahead."

She opened the lower cabinets and straightened again, perplexed. "Where do you keep your dishwashing soap?"

"I'm out."

"Do you have a grocery list?"

"You're the personal assistant. Start one." She'd already cleaned the granite counter. He hadn't seen it that shiny since he moved in. "Where's the OJ?"

"You said you wanted coffee." She filled a mug and set it in front of him. "If you use cream or sugar, you'll have to tell me where you hide them."

No sarcasm. He liked her tentative smile. "I take it black." He took a sip. She'd passed the first test. "Not bad." Better than Starbucks, but he didn't want to hand out compliments too soon. There was more to the job than making coffee — a lot more. He hoped she'd be more amenable to a variety of duties than the others Mrs. Sandoval had sent. One told him he could make his own coffee.

"I'll show you where you'll be working." He led her down the east wing and opened a door. "It's all yours." He didn't have to look inside to know what she faced.

The other temps all had something to say about it, but none seemed capable of knowing where and how to start. Would this girl be up to the task?

Grace Moore stood silent for a few seconds, then carefully stepped past him. She picked her way to the center of the room and looked around at the stacks of papers. The closet doors were open, revealing cardboard storage boxes, most unlabeled.

Roman debated leaving, but knew there

would be the inevitable questions. "Think you can bring order to my chaos?" The girl was silent so long, he felt defensive. "Are you going to say something?"

"It'll take longer than a week to organize all this."

"I never said it had to be done in a week."

She looked back at him. "That's the longest you've kept a personal assistant, isn't it?"

The staffing manager must have warned her. "Yeah. That's about right, I guess. The last one left after three days, but then she thought all an artist needed was a nude model."

Grace Moore blushed crimson. "I don't model."

"Not a problem." Roman gave her a swift once-over and leaned against the doorjamb. "That's not what I'm after." She looked nervous again. He didn't want to scare this one away. "I need someone detail-oriented."

"Do you have a specific way you want your —" her gesture encompassed the mess — "information sorted?"

"If I did, the place wouldn't be such a mess."

She frowned slightly as she surveyed the room. "You'll want some kind of easily maintained system, I would imagine."

"If there is such a thing. Think you can do it?"

"I don't know, but I'd like to try. I'll have a

better idea of what you need after I go through all this."

Roman relaxed. She was frank and honest. He liked that. He had the feeling this girl would know exactly what to do and how to get it done quickly. The sooner, the better. "I'll leave you to it, then." He finished his coffee. "You might last longer than all the rest." He gave her what he hoped was an encouraging smile and headed down the hall.

She came out of the room. "Mr. Velasco, we need to talk about a few essentials."

He stopped, hoping nothing was about to spoil his sense of relief. "Essentials?"

"A desk and office chair, for starters. Filing cabinets, a phone, and all the other supplies for any normal office."

He had said *detail-oriented*. "I'm an artist, in case you weren't told. I don't do normal. And that's a lot of stuff you're asking for on your first day on the job."

"I can't sit on a folding chair eight hours a day, five days a week, and I'll need something more than a card table to work on. There's barely open space on the floor." She peered back into the room. "Is there a phone in there somewhere?"

"Yes. And a computer, unless the last temp girl walked off with it."

"I'll find them."

"Do you really need all that?"

"Yes, if you want your stuff filed properly,

not jammed helter-skelter into cardboard boxes or piled up like a beaver dam."

Things weren't looking as good as they had moments before. "There are contracts, sample sketches, letters of inquiry, the *stuff* of my business." If Roman didn't know the staffing manager would hang up on him, he'd tell Grace Moore where she could shove her list of essentials. Unfortunately, he knew what Mrs. Sandoval would do. He'd be right back to square one in this endless hunt for an assistant who was willing and able to do the job. Talia Reisner had planted the idea of hiring someone to take care of what she called "the mundane minutiae of life" so he could concentrate on his art.

Grace Moore stood silent, not offering an apology. Did he have the right to expect one?

"Get whatever you need."

"Where do you buy your office supplies?"

"I don't." He lifted the mug and realized he'd already downed the coffee. "Find the computer and figure it out." He needed another cup of coffee before he did anything else.

"And you'll be . . . ?"

"In my studio!"

"Which is where?"

"Down the other hall, up the stairs on the right." He paused and looked back at her. "Take a self-guided tour of the house and get your bearings." He left her standing in the hall. Grabbing the thermal pot from the coffeemaker, he headed for his studio.

Roman didn't see his personal assistant for two hours. She tapped lightly at the doorframe and waited for permission to enter. She'd found the laptop. "I have the list and prices. If you have a credit card, I can place the order and have everything delivered by tomorrow afternoon."

"Let's get it done." Tossing his pencil down, he dug in his back pocket and found it empty. He muttered a four-letter word. "Stay where you are. I'll be right back." His wallet wasn't in or on the armoire or his bedside table. Angry now, he fished through his dirty laundry, checking pockets until he remembered he'd left it in the glove compartment of his car last night. Cursing loudly, he went to get it.

Grace Moore stood exactly where he'd left her. She held out the laptop rather than taking the credit card he offered. "If you approve of everything I've listed, you can put in your credit card information."

"You do it!"

She flinched and let out a soft breath. "It's your financial information."

"Which you're going to know if you do your job." He took the laptop from her. Looking at the order total, he swore again. She headed for the door. "Where are you going?"

"I'm sorry. I can't work for you." She

sounded apologetic, but uncompromising.

"Wait a minute!" He dumped the laptop on his drafting table and went after her.

She hurried down the stairs.

"Just hold on." He followed her to the office, where she picked up her purse and looped the strap over her shoulder. She was pale, her eyes dark when she faced him. Had he scared her that badly?

She stepped forward, her hand clenched around the leather strap. "Please move."

Roman saw she'd already cleared work space on the card table and made neat piles. He didn't want this girl to leave. "Give me a hint why you're quitting already."

"I could give you a list."

"Look." He lifted his hands. "You're catching me on a bad day."

"Mrs. Sandoval said you don't have any good ones." She took a shaky breath and met his gaze.

She clearly regretted speaking so quickly, but he couldn't argue. "Yeah, well, the people she sent weren't a good fit. The whole process has been frustrating, to say the least."

"That's not my fault, Mr. Velasco."

"I didn't say it was."

She took a step back. "I'm not trying to make you angry."

Was that it? "I'm not angry with you. I'm just . . ." He muttered a foul word under his breath. "I don't know what I want, but I think

30

you're what I need."

She probably came from a nice tidy life. Two parents, nice home in a nice suburb, private school, college. A class act. He hadn't said anything worse than what she'd hear in a mall, but clearly, she found him offensive. He'd have to be more careful if he wanted to keep Grace Moore around. "You'll be working in here. I'll be in my studio. We won't be around each other that much."

"A personal assistant has to work in close contact with her boss. It's the nature of the job."

"*Personal* is a loaded word." He let his smile turn rogue. Seeing that didn't go over well, he removed any hint of innuendo. "Maybe I should call you something else."

"You can call me Ms. Moore."

She was unbending a little, but still setting boundaries. Okay. He'd honor them. "Ms. Moore it is." He could be respectful . . . when the situation called for it. She frowned, studying him like a bug under glass. "At least give me two weeks before you quit."

Her shoulders drooped slightly. "Two weeks." She made it sound like a lifetime, but she let the purse strap slip off her shoulder. "Please don't swear at me again."

"If I swear, it won't be aimed at you. But I'll try to be careful when you're around. Deal?" He held out his hand. She bit her lip before she accepted the gesture. Her hand

31

was cold and trembled slightly before she withdrew it.

"I'd better get back to work."

He got the hint. If she proved to be as efficient as she looked, things might just work out this time. He found himself curious. "Why a temp agency?"

"It's the only thing I could find." She blushed.

He felt on firmer ground. "Good to know you need this job as much as I need an assistant." She didn't say anything. He tilted his head, studying her. "Where did you work before the temp agency?"

"At a public relations firm."

"And left because . . . ?"

"I was redundant, as the British would say." She glanced at him. "I have a letter of recommendation, if you'd like to see it."

"I'm sure Mrs. Sandoval vetted you."

She took a deep breath. "I do need this job, Mr. Velasco, but I'm sure you understand I'm looking for something better than temp work. I'll give you my best while I'm here." She gave a slight shrug, as if not holding much hope that her best would be good enough. "You're a far cry from my last boss."

"A Philistine?" There was that blush again. He couldn't remember having met a girl who blushed at all, let alone three times in a few hours.

"He was a gentleman."

Meaning Roman wasn't. He'd been taught to play the role when necessary. "Why aren't you still with him?"

"He retired and turned his business over to another firm. They were fully staffed."

Roman looked her over again. He wasn't sure he liked anyone making rules in his house, but then this one had done more in two hours than the combined efforts of the other four. And he liked her. He didn't know why. Maybe it was her complete lack of interest in him. Might be nice to have someone who did the work and didn't ask too many questions.

"So, we're good?"

"For two weeks."

He gave a soft laugh. "Okay. We've both got work to do. Let's take care of the order so you can get going on yours."

2

On the long drive home, Grace wondered if the temp job was a gift from heaven or more trouble on the rise. Mrs. Sandoval had told her about the temperamental Roman Velasco. He was an artist, after all. Mrs. Sandoval had neglected to tell Grace the man himself was a work of art. Even unshaven, barefoot, and wearing wrinkled sweats and a T-shirt, he could model for *GQ*. Long dark hair, café au lait skin, all muscle, not an ounce of fat on him. The minute he'd opened the door, her defenses had gone up. Patrick was handsome, too.

Her hands shifted on the steering wheel. It didn't do any good to dredge up memories best left buried.

Day one. A rough start, but a start, nonetheless. Five minutes in Roman Velasco's house had confirmed his need for a personal assistant. Her first task of making coffee hadn't been much of a challenge, other than hunting down the coffee and filters he'd put in a drawer meant for pots and pans.

The self-guided tour was an eye-opener. The bathroom off the office was lovely with cream-colored marble, polished nickel fixtures, and white crown molding. The fancy toilet with a heated seat and the luxurious shower made it clear the house had never been meant for a bachelor.

The rest of the five thousand square feet was equally gorgeous and echoed with every step. One large room was furnished with a torturous home gym contraption to keep the man in shape. Another contained an unmade California-king bed, armoire, nightstands, and dirty clothing and towels on a red marble floor. The other bedrooms were large white cells without furniture or window treatments, each with a private bathroom with expensive polished nickel or burnished bronze fixtures.

Roman Velasco's studio had been the biggest surprise. He'd turned what must have been the master suite into a cluttered work studio. Light streamed in from the bank of windows, undoubtedly the reason he'd chosen the space for work. He'd splattered paint all over the beautiful hardwood floor. Crumpled papers looked like monstrous dust bunnies scattered about the room. Didn't the man own a wastebasket?

The air smelled of paint, oil, turpentine. A cheap bookcase held dozens of volumes on art and biographies of famous painters, as well as sketch pads. Brushes of various sizes stood in Yuban coffee cans. Tubes, spray cans, and jars of paint lined makeshift shelves constructed of boards and cinder blocks. He had several easels set up, each painting senseless and modernistic. She hadn't seen any work framed or hanging anywhere in his house. Even if she didn't like what he painted, he should be proud of his work.

And why would an artist use mud-colored paint to cover whatever he'd been doing on the back wall? A five-gallon bucket sat in the corner, along with a tray with a dried-up roller. He hadn't bothered using a tarp.

He'd received three personal calls. All from women. He didn't want to talk to any of them. One hung up; two left messages.

The first business-related call came from Talia Reisner, a Laguna Beach gallery owner who wanted to know if Roman was working or playing around.

"Mr. Velasco is in his studio."

"Thank goodness you're on board. I've been after the boy to hire an assistant for months!"

Grace almost laughed. The "boy" looked thirty, and all man.

Talia rushed on. "He's been buried under minutiae. We don't want anything slowing down his momentum. He's hot right now and getting hotter. In my opinion, he's just begun to tap his talent. I sold his last painting yesterday, and I've had two calls already this morning asking when he's doing a show. Is he painting? I keep telling him he should be painting!"

Grace had walked to the studio while Talia talked. There must be an intercom system in a house that size, but she didn't know where it was and doubted Roman knew either. She'd suggest a new phone system where she could put someone on hold and call him. He'd glanced at her when she entered his domain. "One moment please." She held out the phone. "Talia Reisner. She says she's your business associate."

Roman took the phone, punched the button ending the call, and tossed it back. "I'm not her employee. If she calls back, tell her I'm working. That'll make her greedy little heart happy. If Hector Espinoza calls, I'll talk to him. Everyone else can go to —" He broke off abruptly with a sheepish smile.

What a first day on the job!

Traffic slowed to a crawl. Grace had gotten off at five, but it would be well after six before she made it to Burbank. She'd have to fill her Civic's gas tank twice this week, which wouldn't leave much to save toward a deposit on an apartment. How was she ever going to afford a place of her own? Fighting tears, she tried not to let emotions take over. She'd cried enough in the last year to float a ship.

Grow up, Grace. You live with the mess you make.

Maybe God was punishing her. He had every right, considering how she'd behaved after the divorce.

Ruben, eyes fixed on the television news, raised a hand in greeting as she came in the front door. Alicia, a freshman in high school, and Javier, a senior, were in their rooms finishing homework. Selah had already put Samuel to bed.

"He was fussy, so I put him down at six." She smiled as she placed the last glasses in the dishwasher. "Your dinner is in the oven, *chiquita,* still warm. How did it go today?"

"Fine." She'd stick with him until something better opened. "I'm going to see Samuel."

"He's sleeping. Best to leave him alone."

"I'll only be a minute."

"Sit. Eat dinner."

Grace pretended not to hear. She'd been away from her son all day. She just wanted to hold him for a few minutes.

Samuel lay on his back, arms spread. He looked so peaceful, she didn't awaken him. Adjusting the soft blanket, she leaned down. "I love you, little man. I missed you so much today." She kissed his warm forehead and stood at his crib, just watching him sleep. Wiping tears away, she went back to the kitchen. Selah had set out a plate of rice, coleslaw, and a thick, cheesy enchilada. Grace thanked her as she took a seat at the kitchen table. Selah went into the laundry room.

Grace ate alone, cleared and washed her dishes. She joined Selah and started folding Samuel's clothes. Selah plucked a onesie from her and waved her away. "I can do it, *chiquita*. Go sit and talk with Ruben."

It wasn't the words that stung, but the implication that Selah wanted to handle everything that had to do with Samuel. Grace watched her fold Samuel's onesie and press it onto a pile of other outfits she had bought. Ignoring Grace, she picked up a small T-shirt.

Grace didn't want to feel resentful. The Garcias had been kind and supportive for months. When Grace told them she'd changed her mind about giving up Samuel, Selah told her she had time to think things over. Selah was never unkind, but she seemed intent on showing Grace she was a better mother for Samuel.

Lord, I'm grateful. I truly am.

Ruben looked up when she came into the living room. "How did the temp job go? Will it work into something more permanent?"

"Rocky. He's an artist. He lives in Topanga Canyon."

"No wonder you were so late getting home tonight." He glanced at the news program. "Alicia has a volleyball game Wednesday night. We should leave by six."

Grace got the message. If she couldn't make it back in time, they'd take Samuel with them, and she'd miss another evening with her son.

Roman's days became easier with Grace Moore on the job. She arrived promptly at nine, made his coffee, and went to work in the office. He'd already informed her to hold his calls. He told her which to ignore, which to answer. People called frequently, wanting murals. He debated taking on any more, finding them time-intensive and less lucrative than his work on canvas.

He felt pressed, but undirected. Did he want his work hidden away in a private home, or displayed for all to see? Murals gave Roman Velasco legitimacy, even though he was being commissioned to fulfill someone else's vision rather than his own. He still occasionally spoke his own mind through the Bird's simplistic graffiti, but with growing risk. It had become a game, more dangerous as time went by.

Rubbing his forehead, Roman tried to fix his mind on the mural. He had a deadline, and it was fast approaching. *Don't think. Just do the work and get the check. Concentrate on that.*

Hiring Hector Espinoza had taken the pressure off doing all the work himself. The man was set to begin Roman's mural for the lobby wall of a new hotel near the San Diego Zoo. Management had hired Roman to create an African savanna scene complete with migrating animals. Roman had almost finished drawing the design on transfer paper, which Hector would use to start the painting. Once Hector finished the transfers, Roman would drive down and do the fine detail work to bring life to the mural.

Roman dropped the pencil and flexed his cramping fingers. When had he last taken a break? He'd been working since sunup. Pushing the stool back, he stood and stretched while walking to the windows. He looked out at the canyon. Movement caught his eye, and he spotted a jackrabbit making its cautious way across the path down to the cottage the previous owners had built for an aging parent who didn't live long enough to move in.

He'd been inside the cottage only once, when the Realtor took him on a final walkthrough before he signed all the papers. It had the same square footage as the Malibu beach cottage he'd sold for an astonishing amount of money, most of which he'd sunk into this fortress.

Bobby Ray Dean couldn't get any further away from the Tenderloin than this. He didn't know who he was anymore. Somehow, Bobby Ray Dean had gotten lost between the Bird and Roman Velasco.

Grace had put the office in order by the

end of the second week. She liked to stay busy. She was an active but quiet presence in the house, and he liked that. But this morning, she said she wanted to explain the new filing system. He had a feeling he knew where she was going with that. He'd said he didn't have time.

A light tap at the studio door made him turn.

"Do you have time to talk now, Mr. Velasco?"

"Depends on what you want to talk about." He faced her. "Don't even think about quitting."

"I told you I'd give you two weeks. You don't really need a full-time personal assistant."

"I like the way things are working."

"I have a lot of downtime."

"There are other things you could do for me." He saw the wary look back in her eyes. She still didn't trust him, but then, how well did they know one another? Everything had been strictly business since day one. Just the way they both wanted it. "Cooking, laundry, a little housecleaning."

"You eat frozen meals. A cleaning service comes every Wednesday to pick up your laundry. And I'm sure you could easily find someone to change your sheets and make your bed."

He sensed the innuendo. "I don't usually

invite women up here." It was easier to leave a woman's home than ask one to leave his.

"I'm not interested in your private life, Mr. Velasco."

And yet she knew more about him than anyone else. Not that his paperwork told the whole story. "Can we cut the *mister*? Call me Roman." He'd liked the formality at first. Now it annoyed him. "How about making a grocery run for me? I can't spare the time right now. I'll reimburse you for gas."

"I'll need a list."

He gave a soft laugh. "You live by lists, don't you?"

Her shoulders relaxed, and she smiled back. "You did say you wanted someone detail-oriented."

"You probably know better than I do what I need." He gave her two hundred dollars and told her the closest supermarket was in Malibu.

The phone rang several times while she was gone. He didn't bother picking up. He ignored the front door chimes, too, until he realized it might be Grace. Opening the door, he took the two bags of groceries. "Any more?" She said she could manage and headed back to her car.

Sitting at the kitchen counter, Roman watched her empty the reusable bags. She stacked pizzas and frozen dinners in the freezer and put packaged salad mixes in the fridge. She'd bought orange juice, eggs, cottage cheese, and two jars of peaches, though he'd forgotten he needed them. She seemed to know what he liked.

Glancing at the clock, she quickly folded the bags. "I have to leave. I'm going to hit traffic."

"Some calls came while you were gone. I let them go to voice mail, but —" She looked stressed, and it was almost five thirty. "They can wait until tomorrow."

"Are you sure?"

"Go."

She did. As the front door closed behind her, Roman felt the silence fill the house.

3

Bobby Ray, Age 15

Girls developed quick crushes on the new boy with dark hair and eyes, the skin tone that announced his mixed-race parentage. Boys noticed their girlfriends watching Bobby Ray Dean, but learned quickly that he never backed down from a fight — or lost one. He followed his own set of rules: don't start a fight, but hit hard if one comes to you; knock your enemy down until he stays down; watch your back.

He was drawn to gang kids. They broke rules and had their own law. No one bothered them, and they always had money in their pockets. They looked and acted like family members. When Reaper, one of the older boys, offered him fifty bucks to deliver a package to a club on Broadway, Bobby Ray didn't think twice about saying yes. He knew this was a test, a way in, a chance to belong somewhere.

Bobby Ray realized before he'd gone a

block the whole job had been a setup. Someone had called the cops. Rather than dump the package, Bobby Ray did what he'd always done. He'd been running through the streets of San Francisco from his first nights in foster care. He knew every street, alley, and park. He knew how to get from one rooftop to another, go down a fire escape and scale a cyclone fence, swing over the top and drop to the other side. He delivered the package.

At school the next day, he found Reaper and demanded his fifty bucks. Respect crept into Reaper's eyes. He paid up and invited Bobby Ray to a party, where he met the brotherhood. Wolf was sixteen, a Denzel Washington look-alike with two girls hanging on his arms. Lardo weighed over two hundred pounds and had a nervous laugh. White Boy gave a nod of greeting without looking away from a computer game. Bouncer rocked on the balls of his feet and looked ready for a fight.

It didn't take long to get hooked on what the gang had to offer. The problem was, Bobby Ray didn't like carrying what had killed his mother. Every night after he made a delivery, he'd dream about Mama in a cheap motel room. She'd be sitting on rumpled sheets, her body emaciated, her face ravaged by guilt and shame. She'd cry and hold her hands out to him. *You know I love you, baby. You know I'm gonna come back.*

Don't you? He'd wake up in a cold sweat, heart pounding, tears still wet on his cheeks.

The fourth time it happened, Bobby Ray raked his hands through his hair and sat on the side of the bed, fighting down nausea. If he said no now, Reaper would see it as a challenge to his authority. Reaper had earned his name by getting away with murder. Bobby Ray knew explaining his aversion would reveal his weakness, something he couldn't do with the guys he hung out with now. He wanted their respect. But he wanted it on his own terms.

He needed to think, and he did that best when he was out wandering the streets after dark. Pushing the curtains aside, intending to climb out the window of his foster parents' apartment, he spotted a guy dressed head to foot in black, tagging the wall across the street. Bobby Ray sneered. One letter and a number? That was the best he could do?

Bobby Ray stared at the tagger's work, his mind flashing with ideas of what he could have done with a couple cans of spray paint.

The adrenaline rush came along with the ideas. Heart racing, he started making plans. He saw a way to stay in the gang while steering clear of the drug trafficking.

Bobby Ray hugged the wall and inched along the narrow ledge on his toes. He reached the drainpipe and climbed, hand over hand. When he could grip the edge of the roof, he pulled himself up and swung over. He got a running start and leaped the narrow alley, dropping and rolling onto the neighboring roof.

A fire escape took him down the other side. He spent the next few hours checking out graffiti. Most was messy, clearly done in haste. A few pieces impressed him, though Bobby Ray knew he could do better.

He had ideas that would blow minds, make people talk. It would have to be a high place, a risky place, a place where the piece couldn't be easily buffed by city workers.

All Bobby Ray had to do was get his hands on a few cans of spray paint, and he could show Reaper what a real gang tagger could do. Bobby Ray's delivery days were over. He'd be in the gang with all its assets, without taking part in the gang's real business.

Suspended in a climbing harness, Bobby Ray hung over the side of the building. He pulled a can of red spray paint from his pack and worked fast. Lardo paced on the roof, keeping watch on the streets below. He swore. "Did you have to pick a place where anyone and his brother can see you?"

Bobby Ray laughed. He had to take risks to establish his reputation. The higher, the better. "Another two minutes."

"Cops! Two blocks down!" Lardo hauled on the rope.

Bobby Ray gasped and swore as the harness cut into his groin. "Wait!" He swung to one side and grabbed hold of a pipe. Pressing against the brick wall, he went still. He had dressed in black for a reason. No one would see him unless they looked up. Cops usually kept their eyes at street level, not four stories. He calculated how long it would take to have Lardo get him to the roof and then to stow his gear and paint supplies in the backpack. He stayed flush with the wall and looked down without moving. The squad car slowed, shooting a beam of light against the wall.

Bobby Ray spit out a profanity. "Pull me up!" He gritted his teeth against the hard pinch of straps as Lardo yanked on the rope. A can of paint fell out of his backpack. It exploded in front of the squad car. The beam of light swung up. Turning his face away before the spotlight pinned him, he felt Lardo yank hard, and he grabbed hold of the wall and swung onto the flat roof.

Unsnapping the harness, Bobby Ray reached for his backpack. "Forget it!" Lardo groaned. "Come on!" He ran for the stairs. He stopped and looked back.

Bobby Ray told him to be cool. "They didn't see you, bro." He stuffed his gear into the backpack and tossed it onto the roof on the other side of the alley. He moved back far enough to get a running start and sailed across, hit hard and rolled to his feet.

Halfway down the block, he ducked down and watched two officers questioning Lardo on the street. They let him go. They hung around another minute or two, checking the alley with flashlights. When they finally returned to the squad car and left, Bobby Ray went back. He didn't have Lardo teaming with him, so he had to tie the rope and walk down the wall. He worked for another few minutes and used the black marker he'd made from PVC pipe to write *BRD.*

"I knew you wouldn't be able to leave it alone," Lardo snarled from below.

Bobby Ray hauled himself up to the roof and stuffed the rope in his bag. The piece was big enough to draw attention, small enough to be precise, and positioned where volunteers wouldn't be in a hurry to risk life or limb to cover it.

He spotted someone in the apartment house across the street. Was the guy reporting him or viewing the graffiti as an improvement? Bobby Ray shouldered his pack and climbed down the fire escape to meet Lardo on the street.

The whoop of a police siren made Bobby Ray's pulse jump. Lardo took off. The size of a linebacker, he could run over anyone who got in his way. "Cut right!" Bobby Ray shouted after him. Lardo understood the message and took a left in an alley. Bobby Ray waited for the cops to spot him before leading them on a merry chase. Adrenaline surged through him, heightening his senses.

The sun was coming up when he climbed, unnoticed, through the window of his latest foster parents' apartment.

The next morning, Lardo fell into step with Bobby Ray in the high school corridor. "Where you been all morning?"

"Sleeping in." Chuck, his foster father, had rousted Bobby Ray at ten and told him to get to school. He didn't want social services breathing down his neck again after last week. Chuck spent most of his time sprawled in front of the television, drinking Budweiser. He worked nights at a parking garage. Josey worked days at a grocery store. Bobby Ray could count on his fingers the number of times the three of them had been in the house together. Eight. Always on the day a social worker scheduled a look-see.

Lardo grinned. "You put that red face on the Ellis building? The one making the windows look like eyes?"

"A month ago."

"Someone was taking pictures."

Probably the cops who kept files on gang taggers. Each graffiti artist had his own style. Bobby Ray wanted his work recognized, but he'd have to find ways to work faster or end up in jail.

Lardo started talking about another party

happening. Bobby Ray wasn't interested. He needed to get to American history.

He shoved the door open and slid into a desk at the back. Mr. Newman was lecturing again on the Civil War, but Bobby Ray's thoughts drifted to the Ellis Street building. He'd like to paint it end-to-end with heads, each a different color, all with dark window eyes, doors like gaping mouths screaming, laughing, baring teeth. How many cans of paint would that take? He'd need a crew working with him. He'd have to keep the design simple so others could fill in color. He'd need lookouts and time. Problem was he liked working alone, with one guy on watch.

Someone sitting near him asked a question about Civil War weaponry and brought Bobby Ray out of his dreaming. He tried to concentrate. A girl in the front row took notes. She was one of the quiet ones who kept her head down, studied hard, and dreamed of getting out of the Tenderloin. Bobby Ray opened his notebook and started sketching. He flipped another page and drew a gangsta on the marble steps of city hall, a black briefcase in his hand.

A hand planted itself in the middle of his drawing. Bobby Ray flinched. Mr. Newman turned the notebook and studied the picture. His brows flicked up over his dark-rimmed glasses. "Are you taking art?"

"No."

The teacher took his hand away. "Test on Friday. In case you didn't hear. The chapters are listed on the board." He lowered his voice. "Draw me a Confederate soldier and a Union soldier, and I'll count them toward the term paper you didn't turn in."

Frowning, Bobby Ray shut his notebook and leaned back in his chair as he watched Mr. Newman walk to the front of the class. He itched to get a can of Krylon and break into school so he could put something more interesting than a list of chapters on that sweet black chalkboard. Even if the janitor cleaned it off before the day was over. But he'd get expelled and moved again. He had friends here. He wanted to stick.

He stretched out his legs, thinking. He'd have to do some research at the library if he was going to draw Civil War soldiers.

Lardo met him by the lockers. The two of them were the only ones still attending school; the rest of the gang members had dropped out. They spent most of their days at Reaper's place, playing video games, eating junk food, and smoking pot.

Red Hot, Reaper's older brother, had connected with a cartel. Some hard dudes came by, and Bobby Ray stayed in the shadows when they did. Reaper liked playing the big man when his brother wasn't around. He had two trophy kids under two years of age from different girls. Every time he bragged about them, Bobby Ray thought of his mother. Was that what happened to her? Some guy knocked her up just to prove he was a man, then dumped her and moved on to another?

"Hey, Bird! Wake up!" Lardo punched Bobby Ray in the shoulder. "Are you going to the party tonight or not?"

"Not in the mood." Pot made him slow and dumb, and he'd seen enough of what heroin and meth did to stay away from the stuff. Mr. Newman's offer throbbed behind his eyes like an oncoming headache. He liked going to the library, though he made sure no one knew about his visits. It was a quiet place to chill. He'd rather read than do homework. He'd rather look at pictures of Civil War soldiers than listen to Reaper or Wolf talking about their women. Tonight, at least.

4

Grace met her friends Shanice Tyson, Ashley O'Toole, and Nicole Torres at their favorite Sunday-after-church diner. Shanice looked disappointed. "Where's our little man?"

"He's at home with Selah. He had a fever. I was up and down with him most of the night. He's fine this morning, but sleepy." Grace had given in to Selah's desire to keep Samuel home. She wanted to go to church and have her weekly time out with friends. This lunch gathering had become a lifeline. Talking with her friends helped her work through things. And she needed to talk over her situation with Roman Velasco and get their input.

A kindergarten teacher, Ashley dealt with helicopter parents.

Nicole worked as a paralegal for a law firm and had a hopeless crush on Charles, her work-obsessed boss.

Shanice, the wild one, had graduated from NYU, taken a year off to travel, and landed a studio job where she was on a set design team. She'd met movie stars and said they were no different from anyone else, even though some of them thought they were. Now she was telling the others about her latest job assignment. "The director wants to film in Utah at the salt flats. The place has the right alien-planet look."

"Will you get to go?" Ashley dreamed of traveling anywhere outside Southern California. Hooked on old-fashioned Regency romances, she longed to go to England and stay in a castle, preferably one with an eligible and aristocratic bachelor in residence.

"Not if I can help it." Shanice snorted. "It's hotter than hades in the summer. Mono Lake is closer and more interesting, but they said Utah, and Utah gives tax credits."

"I have a book on Mono Lake." Ashley emptied three packets of Splenda into her coffee.

Nicole sipped hers black. "Pastor Jack was on a roll this morning. He doesn't usually talk for a full hour. I thought he'd never stop."

"Ironic you should complain." Shanice smirked. "Since his sermon was on complaining."

They all laughed with her.

"You're awfully quiet, Grace." Shanice raised her brows. "How's the temp job going? It's been, what, a month now? You thought you might only stay two weeks."

"I'm thinking of putting in my notice with

the agency."

"Why?" Ashley looked surprised. "Roman Velasco is fascinating! And he's gorgeous, and if that isn't enough, he's single!" The others stared at her. "I googled him." She leaned forward, eager to share. "He started doing murals when he was a teenager. Now he works on canvas. Did you know art collectors line up to bid on his work?"

"He still does murals." Grace gave the waitress her order and handed back the menu. She'd overslept this morning and had no time for breakfast. Now she was starving, as well as exhausted. "He's under contract for a project in San Diego."

Ashley's eyes brightened. "What's it going to be?"

"Wildebeests and zebras migrating across the Serengeti." Grace sipped coffee, hoping the caffeine would give her a boost.

Nicole wasn't interested in the mural. "Why do you want to leave? It's the only job you've been able to find."

Shanice gave a derisive laugh. "Gorgeous? Single? And has a reputation as a player?" She shrugged. "Okay. I googled him, too." She gave Grace a sympathetic look. "Too much like Patrick?"

"Actually, he's nothing like Patrick. He works hard, for one thing. And Patrick had charm. Roman Velasco acts like a bear with his foot in a trap. I've never met anyone so discontented, or so quick to lose his temper. You know I almost quit on the first day. He's frustrated with his work, not mine. I don't think he likes what he's doing." She put her coffee cup down. "The man has the most incredible view I've ever seen and never gives it more than a passing glance. He turned the master bedroom into his art studio. I think he practices on the back wall and then covers whatever he's doing with some awful color that looks like a dirty swamp. His language is enough to peel paint."

Shanice looked worried. "Is he verbally abusive to you?"

"No. He's cautiously polite when I'm around, but the house is practically empty. His voice carries."

"You must be attracted to him." Ashley looked dreamy-eyed. "I mean, who wouldn't be?"

"Handsome is as handsome does, my granny used to say." Shanice's phone buzzed. She gave it a cursory glance and put it on mute. "Grace has reason to be careful."

Grace couldn't agree more. "My guard went up the minute I saw him."

"Why?" Nicole studied her.

To avoid the scrutiny, Grace looked down while she smoothed her napkin across her lap. "He's living the American dream and seems to hate his life. It's what I notice whenever I have a conversation with him that lasts longer than two minutes." She let out her breath. "The thing is, I'm exhausted. The commute can take up to two hours each way. I'm lucky to have an hour to play with Samuel. I'll never have the energy to take online classes. And the money isn't very good. I don't know what he pays the temp agency, but I'm barely making ends meet. I need a regular job with better pay so I can be on my own again."

Nicole frowned. "Are the Garcias pushing you out?"

"No, but Selah is taking over completely. I think she's glad I'm away all day." She blinked back tears. "Samuel is becoming very attached to her."

Shanice leaned forward. "You're still his mother, Grace."

"Does he know that?"

"Of course he does, honey."

"Better keep the job until you have another lined up," Nicole suggested.

"I think so, too," Ashley chimed in. Even with tenure, Ashley never took her teaching job for granted. The school district budget could bring layoffs.

"I know, but I still have to try. I have two interviews coming up. I've already put Mr. Velasco's office in order. The next temp will have no problem maintaining the system if he hires a replacement quickly."

"Sounds like he's satisfied with the way

things are."

Grace looked at Shanice. "I'm sure he is, and I'm also sure once the word is out, he'll have women lined up at the door, eager to replace me."

Roman always knew when Grace Moore came into the studio. The air in the room changed. He'd finished another transfer and was taking a break, sketching ideas for a new series of canvases while pretending he didn't know she was standing in the doorway. She cleared her throat softly. He looked over his shoulder. "What's up?"

She tucked a short strand of hair behind her ear. A nervous gesture? "I have to leave early Wednesday and Friday next week. I have two job interviews scheduled."

His pulse shot up. He thought everything had been going so well. "You already have a job. You work for me."

"You pay the temp agency for my services, Mr. Velasco. And I told you — I need to find a better-paying job, closer to home."

"Are you late getting home to fix dinner for your partner?" She wasn't wearing a ring, but that didn't mean she didn't have a significant other in her life.

"Everything is caught up in the office, and I —"

"Where do you live?" Roman faced her, determined to fix whatever needed fixing.

"Burbank."

"It's not that far, less than twenty miles as the crow flies."

"I'm not a crow. I spend hours in my car every day, time I . . ." She hesitated. "Time better spent in other ways."

What other ways? he wanted to ask, but figured she'd tell him it was none of his business. In truth, it wasn't, but he still wanted to know. She wasn't giving him a chance to pry.

"Your office is organized, and I've written a brief procedures manual for your next personal assistant. I'm not leaving immediately, but I thought I should let you know I'll be leaving as soon as I find another position more conducive to my needs." She took a step back, clearly eager to put an end to the conversation.

"Not so fast." The stool scraped across the floor as he stood. "I'm not hiring another temp."

"That's your decision." She shrugged as if she didn't care what he did. "The filing system is straightforward. You could manage it by yourself."

"The last thing I want to be is an office lackey."

She raised her chin. "It's not exactly what I dream of doing for the rest of my life, either. You have the option of hiring someone to do it for you."

Roman muttered a curse under his breath.

"Look. We work well together. What do I have to do to keep you here?"

"We don't work together."

"You do your job so I can do mine. That's the way I like it. You don't like the money. Okay. I'll pay the fee and you can work for me instead of the agency. You don't like the commute. Okay. You can live in my guest cottage. Both problems solved." The expression on her face was downright insulting. "What's the matter with the offer? I'm not asking you to move in with me. You're not my type, and I can guarantee I won't be bothering you." He wasn't sure the blush was due to anger or embarrassment, but he knew he'd said more than enough.

"And what will the neighbors say?"

He couldn't tell if she was serious or joking. "What neighbors? And even if I did have neighbors close enough to see anything, why would they care what we do?"

"I have friends, even if you don't."

She punched low. She wanted out. Because of him? Or were there other reasons? Roman clenched his teeth. What was it with this woman? "We're adults, Ms. Moore. Good friends won't tell you how to live. Your life is your business."

"They keep me accountable."

"To them?"

"God cares what I do, and my friends love me enough to hold up a warning sign if I'm heading the wrong way."

God? How did God get into this conversation? Roman didn't understand what she was talking about. All he knew was he didn't want to lose her. He spoke slowly, reasonably, while thinking fast. "Invite them up. Let them look around." He tried a little charm. "A rent-free cottage in Topanga Canyon? They'll think you've died and gone to heaven."

"Until they meet you."

He could tell she hadn't meant to say that when her cheeks bloomed crimson. "Nice." He gave a low, mirthless laugh. She didn't offer an apology. He tilted his head, giving her a wry look. "I didn't say you could invite them into my house." She couldn't hold his stare. "Just think about it. I'll start you off at what I pay the agency." When he told her how much that was, her eyes widened. "Add free housing to that raise, and you'll be doing pretty well for yourself, won't you?" He could see her making calculations already, but also carrying on an inner debate whether the offer was worth working for him. He'd never had that effect on a woman before. Did it all go back to his bad behavior on the first day? Or was there more to her aversion?

"I'll have to pay you rent."

Was she from another planet? At least she was starting to consider the idea. "As you already know, I don't need the money."

"Nevertheless. I wouldn't be your guest,

Mr. Velasco. I'd be your tenant." She seemed to catch herself and added quickly, "If I agreed to the arrangement, which I haven't."

Yet. He could see her weakening. He'd never had to negotiate with a woman and found it vaguely unsettling. Maybe she sensed he wasn't what he pretended to be. "It'd solve all your problems, wouldn't it?"

"Not all of them." She took another step back. "I'd better get to work."

What other problems did she have? "You said you were all caught up. Why don't we talk?"

"Whatever I decide, I appreciate the offer."

He'd never met anyone less eager to talk about themselves than he was. "Okay, but think it over carefully before you say no."

"I will."

The more Roman thought about it, the better he liked the idea of Grace Moore being his next-door neighbor.

Grace called her friends, and they agreed to talk it over during Sunday lunch. She brought Samuel this time, and they all fussed over him. He loved the attention. She dug into her tote bag for baby food and then gave him a bottle while the others talked about a new praise band member who was teaching the Wednesday evening Bible study. Grace brought up Roman Velasco's offer.

Ashley forgot all about the new guitarist

with a voice like Josh Groban. "What are you waiting for, Grace? He's not asking you to move in with him. You'd have your own place again. Isn't that what you want?"

Nicole wasn't so eager. "You'd better make sure you have a written rental agreement. Without it, he could change the rules anytime he wanted."

"Whoa, girlfriends." Shanice jumped in. "Obviously, Grace is doing a great job or the guy wouldn't make such a generous offer to keep her working for him." She looked at Grace. "What I want to know is what else is going on here." She raised her brows. "Come on, girl. Give."

Grace shook her head. "Nothing is going on."

"Have you prayed about it?"

"Constantly. I'm still praying." Grace looked at the three. "It seems to be a gift from God, or am I just desperate to find any way to be on my own again? It solves one problem, but creates another."

Nicole spoke up. "It would give you a big boost on the financial side."

"And save you all that time on the road," Ashley agreed.

Grace wavered. "What about Samuel?"

Shanice put a hand over Grace's. "Selah and Ruben could keep him weekdays, until you can find childcare nearby. And you'd have him all to yourself on the weekends.

65

Maybe this is the step toward independence you've been looking for."

"You could take online classes," Ashley added. "It's been a while since you've had the time or money to go back to school. Instead of three hours a day on the road, you'd have three hours of study time."

Grace fought tears. She looked at Samuel asleep in her arms. "I don't know what to do. I don't want to make any more mistakes."

Shanice's dark eyes grew moist. "You've had more than your share of heartache, honey, but sometimes what looks like a gift *is* a gift."

"I just want to be sure I'm not setting myself up for more trouble. If you all wouldn't mind, I'd like you to come up and see the place, and meet Roman Velasco. I want your impressions of the man before I give him any kind of answer."

Grace told Roman Monday morning that she'd consulted three friends. "They're free Saturday morning, if that's convenient for you. We won't take up much of your time."

His mouth tipped. "You mean they're checking me out, making sure I'm not some wolf after a lamb." He waited, leaving her with the feeling she should say something. But what? She couldn't pretend she trusted him. She barely knew the man, and her instincts had failed her before. Everyone had seemed to know what sort of man Patrick was. How had she been so blind? She'd been enamored by his looks and popularity in the beginning. Later, she wanted to believe what he said. She'd overlooked warning signs and plunged ahead, convincing herself she loved him. The truth was a cold slap in her face, and he hadn't tried to soften the blow.

"Okay, Ms. Moore." Velasco's expression grew wry. "I guess a girl can't be too careful these days, right? Are you still going on those interviews?"

"Yes."

"Don't expect me to wish you good luck." Annoyed, he entered his studio.

On Wednesday, Grace prayed all the way to the first interview, in a downtown office building. *God, if You're the one bringing all this about, please give me a clear message. I'd be right next door to Roman Velasco. He'd be boss, landlord, and neighbor. He's deep water, Lord, and I'm a lousy swimmer.*

The receptionist gave Grace forms to fill out. She sat in a waiting room with half a dozen other women coated in confidence, several with leather briefcases, wearing designer suits and three-inch heels. When Grace's turn came, the gentleman shook her hand and sat facing her from behind his polished mahogany desk. He'd already perused her application and references. He was polite. The interview lasted six minutes. He thanked her for coming in and wished her well.

As she walked back to her car, her phone alerted her that she'd missed a call. The message said her Friday interview was canceled, the position filled.

Grace brought Samuel with her on Saturday morning. Roman Velasco's driveway was hard to spot, so she stopped and waited just off the road, where Shanice would be sure to see her car. A few minutes before they were due to arrive, Shanice's yellow Volvo roared around the curve. Grace honked. Shanice's brakes squealed as she turned onto the macadam drive. Grace led the way around the giant valley oak and along the curve down to the main house.

Glancing in the rearview mirror, Grace saw her friends gaping at Roman Velasco's modern beige stone house, a fortress tucked against the hillside. Square cement pavers floated in a sea of black pebbles up to heavy, carved wooden double doors, where blue-green, pink, and mauve rosettes of echeveria and spiked agave spilled over two large terracotta pots. Instead of staying on the gravel circle, she took the short drive to the right and pulled in close to the cottage.

Shanice parked behind Grace and got out of her car. "Thanks for watching for us. I would've missed the driveway if Ashley hadn't spotted your car."

"I know. I missed it three times my first day of work." Grace unlatched Samuel's car seat from its base. Still half-asleep, he sucked his thumb as she led the trio along the pathway to the front of the house. A stone wall curved around the paver patio, complete with fire pit. Ashley and Nicole paused to comment on the gorgeous view of the canyon while Shanice took Samuel's carrier so Grace could dig into her pocket for the key Roman had given her.

As soon as Grace walked in, she knew she was in deep trouble. Shanice followed closely behind and gasped.

The living room alone was bigger than the apartment Grace had shared with Patrick. The kitchen was small, but efficient, everything state-of-the-art. Rather than linoleum, the floor was expensive cream-colored travertine. Grace stood rooted in shock. Swooning, Ashley and Nicole pushed past her and went exploring.

"Oh, wow!" Ashley cried out. "Come look at the bedroom!" Numb, Grace followed and stared. A California king-size bedroom set would fit easily, if she had one. Her twin bed and nightstand would be lost in here. One door opened into a walk-in closet bigger than her bedroom at the Garcia home.

"Wait until you see the bathroom!" Ashley laughed in wonder.

Grace admired the yellow-and-white marble floor and counter, two white porcelain sinks with shiny chrome fixtures, a Jacuzzi tub big enough for two.

Nicole stepped into the small hideaway lavatory and flushed the toilet. She squealed with delight. "It's an integrated toilet and bidet!"

Ashley opened a shower door. "There's a rainfall showerhead and jets in the walls!"

"And you're wondering if you should move in?" Nicole laughed. "This place is fantastic!"

"Tone it down, girls." Shanice spoke with less enthusiasm. "We've yet to meet the commander of the fortress."

Roman debated whether to wear his usual jeans and T-shirt or put on more formal slacks and tuck in a button-down shirt, but knew Grace would be immediately suspicious. So, he cranked up his usual style with black jeans and a navy-blue polo, front tucked in behind a brass anchor buckle. He raked his hands through his hair. Maybe he should've shaved, but he didn't want to look like this meeting was the biggest event of his weekend. Even if it was.

Why should this girl's opinion matter to him?

Because she had class, and having her around reminded him how far he had come up in the world. Unlike other women, who just wanted to drag him back down again.

Roman saw the cars arrive from an upper window, but waited another twenty minutes before strolling the paver walkway between the main house and the cottage. If she accepted his offer, she'd be living less than a thousand feet away. He wouldn't be entirely alone out here, not that it had bothered him all that much until now.

The front door stood open, and women's happy, excited voices drifted out. Unfortunately, Grace's wasn't one of them. He knocked on the doorjamb to announce his presence. Grace appeared, her expression enigmatic. "We were just looking around."

"I know."

She stepped aside so Roman could enter and introduced him to her three friends. Strawberry-blonde Ashley O'Toole stared at him with wide blue eyes. Nicole Torres shook his hand firmly. Shanice Tyson looked closer to the kind of girl he understood. Experienced, tough, street-smart, even if she was wearing designer clothes. She held a baby on her hip and gave him a polite, if somewhat cool, nod. He caught the wind of distrust blowing from her direction, the alpha female he'd have to win over.

He extended his hand to Shanice first and looked her straight in the eye. "It's good to know Ms. Moore has friends who look out for her." He included the other two women

71

with a glance. Grace stood by, watchful, noncommittal. She wasn't going to be rushed into any decision, not this girl. Roman told her he was on his way out for the afternoon — a lie, but good for a quick exit. "I'll leave you all to discuss the pros and cons."

Grace walked him out the door. "It's far more than I expected."

"It's just standing here, empty." Would that be enough to silence any further doubts? "It's yours if you want it."

"I still need to think about it."

What had her so worried? "Talk it over with your friends. I want you to feel comfortable with your decision." Comfortable enough to move in, anyway. "I'll see you Monday morning, Ms. Moore."

Roman walked along the path to the main house. He could feel her gaze fixed on him, but didn't look back. He recognized defensive walls when he saw them. He had them, too. He'd give her the same space and courtesy he wanted. For now.

On edge, he decided to turn the lie into truth and went for a long drive. He needed to clear his head. Or put something else in it besides curious thoughts about his personal assistant, where she came from, and what made her tick.

Grace and her friends talked it over.

Ashley giggled. "I can understand the

temptation. How do you concentrate on work around a man like that?" She fanned herself.

"He's in his studio. I'm in the office."

Nicole, more practical, offered advice. "If you have a written agreement, you'll be all right. That way, he can't change the rules. I can have one ready for you by church tomorrow."

Shanice jumped in. "Obviously, Grace has reservations or she wouldn't have invited us up here to see the place and meet Velasco. Now that we've seen him, we know why." She nodded. "He looks like a player."

"Just because he's handsome?" Ashley came to Roman's defense. "Have you seen him in a club?"

"I haven't been to a club for over a year, Ashley, and you know why."

"He seemed polite enough. We shouldn't judge," Nicole remarked.

Shanice gave her a steely-eyed look.

"He didn't give any indication that he's putting the moves on Grace. He called her Ms. Moore." Ashley sounded annoyed.

Shanice raised a brow at Grace. "Any instincts about the guy when you're alone with him? Any vibes?"

"No. He made a point of telling me I'm not his type."

"Okay." Nicole spread her hands. "So, I'll ask the obvious question. What's the problem?"

Grace had to think about it. "Once I'm in, it'll be hard to get out."

Shanice ran her hand over Samuel's head and looked at Grace. "Are you talking about the house or the job?"

"Both." Grace took Samuel. "I don't want to do anything stupid." She glanced around the cottage, and temptation gripped her. She'd never be able to afford a place like this. She'd be lucky to find a one-room flat, and what sort of life would that be for Samuel?

"You like the place, don't you?" Shanice asked.

"Who wouldn't?"

Nicole let out her breath. "Roman Velasco offered you this place for free. Right? You could offer him the same rent you paid on the apartment in Westwood. Paying Velasco rent will keep this a business transaction. You won't be vulnerable. You needn't feel obligated in any way."

Grace kissed Samuel's warm, rosy cheeks. "I wouldn't see my son Monday through Thursday."

"But you'd have him Friday night through Sunday," Ashley reasoned. "*Without* Selah. And once you find childcare, you could have him with you whenever you're not working. I'm sure there are other children up here in the canyon."

"Probably with nannies," Shanice put in. She touched Grace's arm. "Are you worried about Selah and Ruben? The arrangement was always supposed to be temporary."

"She's become very attached."

"So have I." Shanice tickled his chin and got a giggle. "You know I'd take you both in, if I didn't already have a roommate."

"I'd kill for a place like this." Nicole sighed. "And think about the other advantages. The time you'll save commuting. Time you can use for online classes. The more education you have, the better your opportunities. If this job doesn't work out." Her cell phone chimed. She dug it from her purse and checked the text. "It's Charles."

Shanice glanced at her phone. "Time to head back, girls." She blew a raspberry against Samuel's neck. "See you, snookums." She kissed Grace's cheek. "This place looks like a gift from the Lord, honey. I think you can handle Velasco."

Ashley brightened. "I have an idea! Instead of going to the café next Sunday for our get-together, why don't we each bring something up here?" She looked at Grace. "What do you say?"

"Make it two weeks. I have to move in first."

Grace waved as Shanice backed out, picked up speed on the gravel turn, and shot up the driveway. Shaking her head, Grace smiled. Her friend had a lead foot and good reflexes.

Grace changed Samuel's diaper before she settled him into the car seat. He'd be asleep before she reached the road.

With the increase in salary and a nice place to live, she'd be able to make plans. She could afford childcare. She could take online courses toward her degree. Nicole was right. She would have extra hours for study. She had done well enough in high school to earn a scholarship to UCLA. Her goals had gotten derailed when she ran into Patrick Moore.

Glancing toward the main house, she wondered if Roman Velasco was still at home, but decided it would be better to wait until Monday before saying anything.

5

Grace, Age 20

A shock wave coursed through Grace as she caught a glimpse of what might lie ahead. Patrick had been benched from the football team due to an injury. She tried to bolster his spirits, but he was bitter. She'd come home from classes today and found him watching television. When she asked why he wasn't at practice, he said he'd quit the team. He wasn't going to suffer in practice for a team that had no intention of using him.

Grace assumed Patrick would use the extra time he now had to get a part-time job, especially now that he had forfeited his football scholarship. They'd just gotten married and were barely getting by with both their scholarships and her job at McDonald's. When he made no effort to do so, their bills mounted. When she pleaded with him, he called her a nag.

After two months, he went to the campus employment office, but claimed they couldn't find anything that suited him. Library or office jobs were for girls. Fast-food restaurants were for losers. Had he forgotten that's what she was doing to support both of them?

He said he was working hard enough just to keep his head above water with his course load. He had conveniently forgotten that Grace had a heavier load than he did and was also working twenty-five hours a week. When he suggested she add more work hours until he could find a job, she reminded him she had to maintain her GPA to keep her scholarship. He accused her of being selfish, of caring more about school than her husband. Did she have any idea how difficult it was for him to do college-level work? Someday, he'd be the breadwinner. What sort of job could he get if he didn't finish college?

The more Patrick talked, the guiltier Grace felt. School had never been easy for Patrick. She wanted to be supportive and encouraging. Wasn't that what God said a wife should be? And, in truth, between school, work, and Patrick's demands, she was exhausted. She didn't know how long she could keep up with all of her responsibilities.

She tried to pray, but worried instead. Whose education mattered more? His, she decided. With that in mind, she applied for a full-time clerical job at a public relations firm, praying that if God had other plans, the job would go to someone else. When they offered her the position, she saw it as a sign. She withdrew from UCLA, grieving in private, while wearing a smile for Patrick's sake. He was grateful, of course, but it didn't make their lives any easier. He had no intention of taking on any duties around the apartment, considering that women's work.

So Grace would come home after a full day at the company to find Patrick lounging on the couch, watching sports on TV. He'd give her a kiss and tell her about his classes and what assignments he had to do. The apartment was always a mess, his books and papers strewn over the table.

She had to work out a tight schedule so she could get all the shopping, laundry, and cleaning done on one of her days off. She gave up going to church. It had always been a battle between them anyway. Patrick never went with her. He said church was a boring waste of time. Better if she used Sunday to prepare meals for the week ahead, packaging and stacking them in the freezer so all she had to do was warm them up when she came home from work. That left her evenings free to help Patrick with his studies. Often he was more interested in having sex than doing his course work. "We can come back to it." He always fell asleep. Frustrated and worried, she'd get up and finish his work.

Halfway through junior year, Patrick informed Grace he'd changed his major from business administration to physical education. He figured it was a better fit for him. She thought he had a point. When he said he might need postgraduate work to get a really good job, she felt another shock wave of warning. She said that wasn't part of their agreement. He smiled, kissed her, and said they'd talk about it when the time came for a decision.

There was one thing they had to talk about, though. Grace was pregnant. It wasn't part of the plan, but she hoped it would help turn things around for them. There had to be some way to make it work. She'd always assumed they would start a family sooner or later.

"This wasn't supposed to happen!" Patrick raged when she told him. He wanted her to have an abortion. She refused. It was the one time she didn't go along with what he wanted.

She lost the baby in the second trimester. He didn't try to hide his relief. He brought home flowers and a bottle of champagne. "Back to plan A." When he popped the cork, she came close to hating him.

Patrick headed into his senior year, and Grace was promoted to office manager. With her raise, she managed to put away some savings. She would need funds to go back to college. She wouldn't have her scholarship anymore. She'd have to pay for tuition and books. With a little nest egg, she wouldn't feel guilty about the expense, especially if they started a family. Every time she brought up the subject, Patrick said they should wait a couple more years. They were still young. He'd slaved for four years to get through school. He wanted to have some fun before they started talking about kids.

Graduation day came, and Grace felt an overwhelming pride as she sat with Patrick's parents and her aunt Elizabeth. She and Patrick had both worked hard for this day. Patrick looked so handsome in his cap and gown. His parents boasted that he had graduated with honors. Several of his term papers were on file in the university library. Aunt Elizabeth looked pointedly at Grace. The Moores agreed Grace was the best thing that ever happened to their son, and they insisted on a celebration dinner at Lawry's steak house. They also insisted Aunt Elizabeth join them.

The Moores ordered champagne. Aunt Elizabeth declined and drank water. Grace sipped cautiously. Patrick imbibed freely. He told stories about professors and students he'd hung out with at the student union. Grace was surprised to hear that. When his parents asked what he planned to do now that he had his degree, he said he needed a break to consider his options. His mother gave Grace a pained look. Aunt Elizabeth sat in stony silence.

He drained his glass and announced he'd joined a gym, and he'd already talked with someone in management who thought he'd make a great trainer. All he had to do was spend a couple of weeks in a course to get a certificate. Aunt Elizabeth gave a derisive snort and said he could have done that straight out of high school. When Mr. Moore agreed, Patrick poured another glass of champagne and sulked.

Embarrassed, Grace ate in silence. When had Patrick had the time or money to join a gym and get to know the management? He'd never talked about any of this with her. She felt Aunt Elizabeth watching her and tried to keep the smile on her face. She attempted to look as though nothing he said was a surprise and she was happy about the plans he'd made.

On the way out of the restaurant, Aunt Elizabeth gripped her arm and held her back. "You didn't know, did you?"

"Know what?"

"About the student union. About the gym membership." Aunt Elizabeth looked fierce. "Open your eyes. He'll use you until you're a dried-up husk, and then he'll throw you away."

"He's my husband." She couldn't change direction now. She'd made vows.

"I know." Her aunt turned away. "I tried to warn you."

As soon as Grace and Patrick walked into their apartment, she asked him when he'd joined a gym and how he'd been paying for it. Patrick turned evasive. He'd gotten a really good deal. It wouldn't cost her a dime. The way he said it made her feel like a money-grubbing penny-pincher. She dropped the subject.

Two weeks later she came home to an empty apartment and found a note on the table.

Gone skiing with friends.

Needed a break before the certification class starts. I'll be home Sunday night. Enjoy church. Love, Patrick

Enjoy church? Easter Sunday was the last time she'd gone. She'd left halfway through the service because she couldn't hide the tears streaming down her face. And they hadn't been tears of joy. Every time she tried to talk to God, she felt her words bounce back off the ceiling. Why should God listen to her prayers? She hadn't listened to Him. She missed the friend who had come to her when she was a terrified, lonely child. She hadn't heard his voice since the day she gave herself to Patrick.

Skiing was an expensive sport, and Patrick wasn't working. Suspicious, Grace logged onto the savings account. He'd withdrawn five hundred dollars of her hard-earned school savings. She dug her fingers into her hair and wept.

Hurt and angry, Grace confronted Patrick when he came home Sunday night. He dumped his duffel bag and said he knew she would say no, so he hadn't asked. Why should he have to ask? He was an adult, not a child, and they were married. That money was as much his as hers. He could do what he wanted when he wanted.

When she said she wished she had the same privileges, he cursed at her. He'd worked four long, hard years to earn his degree. Some of his friends were going to Europe for the summer. It was bad enough he was stuck in Los Angeles and had nothing to look forward to but a nine-to-five job, without having a nagging wife waiting to harangue him the minute he walked through the door.

His anger frightened her. He kept advancing until he backed her against the sink. Heart pounding, she apologized. He wasn't finished. He said she'd turned into a drudge. All he'd done was go away for three days and have some fun for a change. Maybe he'd go again! Maybe he'd stay away longer next time!

By the time Patrick finished his rant, the seed of fear was firmly planted. He hadn't touched her, but she sensed he'd wanted to hit her. Grace didn't say anything more.

When they went to bed, Patrick turned his back to her. She lay in the darkness, weeping silently, trying not to move a muscle lest she disturb him.

Lord, what have I done? What have I done?

Patrick slept soundly, and Grace knew they'd crossed a line. She was afraid of what lay on the other side. When she finally slept, she dreamed of her mother and father and awakened drenched in cold sweat. Her inner child wanted to drag a blanket and pillow off the bed and hide in the closet.

She survived the next few days, putting in extra hours at work to help her boss, Harvey Bernstein, finish a big project. He commented on her pallor. "Is everything all right, Grace?" She assured him everything was fine. "I don't know what I'd do without you." A bonus would have been nice, but Harvey gave her a half day off on Friday. Maybe she and Patrick could sort everything out over the weekend.

Unlocking the apartment door, Grace walked in and found Patrick on the couch with a shapely blonde, neither wearing much of anything. They sprang apart. The girl grabbed her clothes and fled into the bedroom.

Patrick stood. "What're you doing home?" His face went from red to white. "You're supposed to be at work." He pulled on sweatpants.

Grace looked from him to the bedroom door and back again, speechless.

"You weren't supposed to be here." Patrick sounded annoyed.

Dazed, Grace stammered, "H-Harvey gave me the afternoon off."

The girl came out of the bedroom, her perfect body encased in pink-and-black spandex. Even her socks and aerobics shoes matched. Without looking at Grace, she hurried to the front door, then quickly retraced her steps to grab her pink jacket off the arm of the couch. "I'm sorry." Her voice was a husky whisper. "I'm so sorry you had to find out this way."

Find out what? Grace stood in the middle of her own personal apocalypse.

Opening the front door, the girl slipped out, but not quick enough for Grace to miss the gym logo on the jacket she pulled on or the pleading look she gave Patrick. Grace stared at her husband. "She works at the gym you joined?"

"Her father owns it." He sounded resigned. "Look." He rubbed the back of his neck and let out a heavy breath. "Can we sit down like civilized people and talk this out?"

She knew what he would say even before he started making excuses, but she listened anyway. Patrick said he didn't intend to fall in love with Virginia, but she'd come on strong to him when he joined the gym. At first it was a harmless flirtation, but he and Grace had been having problems by then. "You don't like sex, Grace, and Virginia, well . . ." They had a lot in common.

Grace was always on him about finding a job, so why not work at the gym part-time, even if only to pay for his membership? He got along well with people. He made a lot of friends. Virginia's father noticed. He dropped hints about future possibilities. He said he wanted to retire and hoped his daughter would find a nice, outgoing, ambitious young man who would stand beside her and run the business.

Patrick talked and talked, the words pouring over Grace like hot lava. She understood what he was saying. Patrick had loved her for a while, but she didn't have enough to offer anymore. He'd found someone who did. "I couldn't help myself, Grace. Virginia is my soul mate. Try not to hate me. It's not my fault."

The initial shock and pain turned to numbness. Grace felt nothing.

"Okay. Don't say anything." Patrick grew angry at her silence. "I guess it'd be too much to expect some understanding."

Grace sat at the kitchen table while her husband packed. Part of her wanted to beg him to stay, beg him to love her, beg him for a second chance. Another part kept her silent and frozen in her chair, her eyes fixed on the plates he and Virginia had left on the table, one with a few crumbs and the other with a half-eaten deli sandwich.

She was Patrick's wife. Shouldn't she fight for her marriage? *Say something, Grace. Speak up before it's too late. Don't just sit there and let him walk out the door.*

Another voice gently whispered inside her heart. *Forgive him and let him go.*

6

Roman grabbed the towel he'd draped over the arm of the treadmill and wiped sweat from his face. His T-shirt was soaked. Something was off. He'd only run three miles and felt like he'd run a marathon. Cutting the speed, he walked another mile to cool down before shutting off the machine. Stepping off the tread, he felt light-headed. The moment passed, but left him weak. Maybe he was dehydrated. He uncapped another bottle of water with electrolytes and drank it. He'd skip the weights.

Ah, for the good old days when he did parkour in San Francisco. His graffiti had been in heaven spots, high and dangerous places, where his work stayed longer than the usual few days for other taggers. His initials, BRD, gained him a reputation as the Bird.

The pleasurable memories gave way to thoughts of White Boy. He redirected his thoughts.

The only adrenaline kick he got these days

came from the endorphins he earned working out. Maybe age was the problem. Today was his birthday, not that anyone knew or cared. He was thirty-four. How should he celebrate the passage of another year? Look for a hookup in a club? Sex with a stranger didn't have the appeal it once did.

A cold shower refreshed him, but didn't alter his mood. He raised his face to the spray and thought he heard his cell phone ring. Who would be calling him on a Sunday?

With nothing else to do, Roman went into the studio and dabbed some more paint on the canvases set up near the windows. He wanted to put his fist through one, but tossed the brush into a can of linseed oil instead. He sat at his drafting table and sketched ideas. Crumpled papers littered the floor.

His cell phone rang, and Jasper Hawley's face appeared. His teacher, counselor, and mentor at Masterson Ranch called every month or two, checking up on him. He visited now and then, too, although it had been a while since Roman had seen him.

"Keeping tabs on me, Hawley? Why don't you come on down and do it?"

"Is that a real invitation? I'm in Oxnard. I can stay over at your place tonight. I haven't seen the new house yet."

"Sure, just don't have a bed."

"Still the minimalist. I have a sleeping bag in my trunk."

"What's in Oxnard?"

"Visiting one of my lost boys who just got out of prison. Speaking of lost boys, isn't today your birthday?"

Roman relaxed, pleased. "Have you been poking through my juvie records again?"

"I have all the pertinent facts memorized. See you soon."

Roman went downstairs and sprawled on the couch in the living room, sketching ideas in the black book he kept there.

Awakening to the door chimes, Roman cursed. First thing he'd have Grace do Monday morning was find someone to replace the annoying chimes with a short, functional bell. A straightforward ding-dong would be great. The chimes were still going strong when he opened the door. Jasper stood there laughing.

"Love the chimes. A Viennese waltz? Let me guess. Not your idea."

Roman tried to overcome his shock at Jasper's appearance. His mentor had lost weight, and his hair had gone white. "Man, you got old."

"And you're still the same smart aleck you've always been." Jasper walked in, suitcase in hand. "Quite a place you've got here. Holy Jehoshaphat! Look at that view! Perfect setup for an artist."

"If I painted landscapes."

Jasper glanced back. "Why did you leave

that sweet place in Malibu? Open a sliding-glass door, and there was the beach and all those pretty, bikini-clad girls walking by."

"I needed a change." The condo held one night of memories he couldn't forget and a host of questions he'd never be able to answer about a girl he'd tried to find and knew he'd never see again.

Jasper shook his head. "I keep hoping you'll grow up and settle down."

Roman drove his red Camaro to a seafood diner in Malibu. Nothing much had changed for Jasper. He was still teaching at the Masterson Mountain Ranch and keeping tabs on the boys who would let him. He cared about what happened to every one of them. Most finished the program and moved on. A few stayed in touch. Some called when they were in trouble, like the young man in Oxnard. Jasper had a few extra days. "I figure I ought to live it up."

Troubled, Roman gave in. "What is wrong with you? You've lost about fifty pounds since I last saw you. And don't tell me you're on a diet."

"Nothing wrong with me now. I went through chemo."

Roman lost his appetite. He looked at Jasper and didn't know what to say.

"Don't bury me yet. I went into the hospital with a colon and came out with a semicolon."

Jasper's grin died. "That was supposed to be a joke."

"Ha-ha."

Jasper rubbed his head. "My hair is growing back. That's something."

"All white."

"I think I look distinguished. You're not getting rid of me yet. The tests have been clear, and I'm feeling good." He patted his stomach. "Looking good, too. I'm keeping the weight off and walking a couple of miles a day. Funny thing about cancer. It reminded me I'm mortal. It doesn't make sense to put off the things I want to do."

Jasper talked. Roman tried to listen. Troubled, he thought about death. He'd lost his mother and the only friends he'd ever cared about. It was safer not to care. Less painful.

"Bobby Ray Dean."

The name jarred Roman. "No one has called me that in ages."

"You've come a long way, son, but you still don't know who you are or what you want, do you?"

"More."

Jasper folded his arms on the table. "More of what?"

"Life. Meaning." He wished he knew.

They went back to the Topanga Canyon house. Roman gave Jasper the grand tour. Jasper offered the paintings on easels a cursory look and made no comment. Roman could guess what he thought. Problem was, Roman agreed.

Jasper picked up one of the crumpled papers scattered across the studio floor and opened it. He picked up a few more. Roman knew what they were. Sketches of a gang kid in a leather jacket leaning against a graffiti-covered wall, a young boy looking out a bay window, a naked girl with her back to the viewer, her long hair curling down to her waist. "These are good, Roman. Ever think about doing a show?"

"I'll probably do one this summer."

Jasper glanced at the three unfinished paintings on easels. "You don't have to limit yourself to modern art."

"The pay is good." Roman leaned against his drafting table. "I have no illusions. I took your advice and went to Europe. Remember? I've seen the masters. I even left a calling card at the Louvre."

"Calling card?"

"Never mind." The Bird had left a piece of work glued among the masters — a winking owl perched on a pine branch. He jerked his head toward the easels. "That's the best I can do."

"I doubt that."

"Yeah, well, a lot of people out there like to think they know art. I figured out what sells."

They headed downstairs. Roman opened a

couple of sodas. Jasper looked around the living room with the huge black sectional couch, massive modern table, and big-screen television mounted on the wall. "It's pretty Spartan, even for a bachelor."

"Haven't had time to decorate."

"You need a wife."

Roman gave a derisive laugh. "For what?"

"Companionship. Comfort. Have some children."

"You aren't married. You don't have kids."

"Cheryl and I were married for twenty-four years, the happiest of my life, before she died. We wanted to have children. It just never happened." He smiled. "That's why I'm so attached to you."

"Bull."

"I'd get married again, if I met the right woman. Up to now, no one comes close to the one I had."

Roman thought of Grace Moore.

"Chet and Susan want to know when you're coming home for a visit."

The Mastersons had been the closest thing to family Bobby Ray Dean had ever known. "I'm sure they have a full house, just like they always did."

"Fewer these days, and you were special." When Roman didn't say anything, Jasper changed the subject. "So, you gave up doing murals."

"I've got one more. In San Diego. I found

95

someone to do the fill work. I'll be heading down soon to add in the details. Hector will apply the protective coat. Saves me a lot of time, and I can get on to other things."

"Hector?"

Roman told the story. Dry of ideas and looking for any inspiration, he'd gone to a flea market to sketch vendors. He spotted a man painting ceramic pots. He was skilled, and he was quick. Roman found someone to translate and offered the man a part-time position doing the fill work on a mural project in Beverly Hills. Hector Espinoza agreed, and they shook on it. "He works for me whenever I need him. I don't know what he does in the meantime."

"Nice to know you have friends." Jasper's tone was dry.

Roman laughed it off. He barely talked to Hector. They didn't speak the same language, literally. They still had trouble communicating, but had come up with a system of numbers for colors so Hector knew what to do. Roman didn't know anything about the man and figured he was probably undocumented. He paid him well, and the partnership worked. "Hard to make friends with someone who doesn't speak my language."

"Is that why you hired him? So you wouldn't have to carry on a conversation?"

"Is this a psych session?"

Jasper let it go. They talked of other less

personal things until after midnight. Jasper unrolled his sleeping bag on the leather couch. Both were up early the next morning. Roman made omelets, French toast, and coffee.

"You haven't lost your touch." Jasper raised his cup. Roman didn't tell him he had a personal assistant who could make better. He knew Jasper would start asking questions, and Roman didn't have any answers.

On the way out the front door, Jasper pushed the doorbell and set off the chimes. Roman called him a foul name. Jasper laughed. "I'll be down this way again, sooner than you think."

"The couch will be ready for you." Roman stood outside until Jasper drove out of sight.

At two minutes to nine, the chimes went off again. When Roman opened the door, he knew by the look on her face that Grace Moore had decided to move into the cottage.

"That happy about it, huh?"

"We'll have things to discuss first. After work."

This girl didn't make anything easy.

The hint of triumph on Roman Velasco's face set Grace's nerves on edge. The coffee had already been made. "You must have been up early." She headed toward the office. "I'll check your messages first."

"Not yet." Roman dug into his front pocket

and slapped a key on the counter. "So you can come in without setting off those —" He stopped short of saying something that would offend her. "Make it the first order of business today to find someone who can reprogram that thing before I rip it out of the wall with my bare hands. I'd rather not have it go off like church bells ringing in a New Year."

"I'll take care of that, but you can keep your key." She slid it back to him.

"It's an extra, and it's for convenience, yours and mine."

"I'm not comfortable having your house key."

His mouth tightened. "Take the — darn key, Ms. Moore."

She knew he'd almost said something else. Maybe she was being unreasonable. Harvey Bernstein had given her a key. She took Roman's and attached it to her key chain. "I'll knock before I come in."

"Just to make sure I have my pants on?"

She started toward the office.

"I need your cell number."

Grace faced him. Alarms went off inside her head. "Why?"

"In case I need you."

"I work nine to five. I'm not available before or after that. Or on weekends."

His eyes darkened. "It'll save you steps."

The doorbell sounded again, and this time he forgot to curb his tongue. Her eyes flickered at the words that came automatically. "It's Hector. Another irritating employee. The guy doesn't speak enough English to get what I'm saying. We have to resort to sign language, and I'm not in the mood this morning."

"Maybe I can help you. I took Spanish in high school." She followed him to the front door. Roman opened it and waved her forward to face a wiry Latino with a startled look.

She introduced herself, and he grinned broadly. Hector responded in a stream of rapid-fire Spanish until Grace held up her hands in surrender and said, "Please slow down."

He obliged, and Grace translated for Roman, who stood by watching them with a less-than-pleased expression. "Hector says you called, but he doesn't know why."

"Follow me." Roman headed for the studio.

Hector fell in beside Grace, continuing to talk in his native language. "Who are you, and where did you come from?" She told him she came from a temp agency, and Roman had hired her full-time as his personal assistant. "It's about time. He needs help." He talked faster, and Grace had to concentrate to catch everything. Clearly, the man liked Roman. *El jefe* paid well and was a gifted artist. Hector considered it an honor to work with him. He didn't pause until Roman interrupted their conversation.

"Do you know what he's saying?"

"Most of it. He was just telling me about himself." *And you.*

"Get to know him later. Tell him I still have another transfer to go, but he can get started on the two I have ready. I'll bring the last one down to San Diego when I'm done. Tell him I'll call before I'm on my way. Better yet, I'll have you call. That way, if he needs anything, you can tell me what he says."

Grace relayed everything. Hector had questions. "He needs to know where he's staying while he works down there. He can't keep driving back and forth, and he doesn't like sleeping in his car."

"What the — ?" Roman exploded, but managed to swallow the rest. "The hotel was supposed to put him up. We'll get that straightened out. Pronto. Call the hotel and remind them he was to get a room free of charge so he can stay and work. That was part of the deal. They can now add meals in the restaurant, since he's been running back and forth. And tell him to take time off and go to the zoo, where he can see some real, live animals."

"Is that a suggestion or an order? Zoos are expensive."

Roman dug for his wallet, extracted a hundred-dollar bill, and handed it to Hector, who looked confused until Grace explained. The guy grinned like a happy kid and talked fast.

"He says —"

"Yeah, yeah. I can guess." Roman dismissed the thanks. He picked up two long, numbered cardboard tubes and handed them to Hector. "Tell him to charge whatever supplies he needs at the usual place. I'll see him as soon as I can. I want to get this job finished. Pronto." He held out his hand, and Hector shook it.

Hector grinned at Grace. "I guess that means he's done with me."

She laughed. "I guess so. I'll walk you to the door." She went a few steps ahead before Roman demanded her attention.

"After you show Hector out, I could use a cup of coffee."

"What's in the pot, or fresh?"

"Fresh."

Hector was in no hurry to leave. Grace made coffee while they talked. He said it was going to be a relief having her around. He'd like to get to know the man he worked for. They talked for another ten minutes at the door before Hector said *adiós* and headed for an old Ford pickup.

Grace returned to the studio with a mug of fresh coffee. Roman sat at his drafting table, working on the transfer. There was no place to put his mug. He gave her a strange look.

"You two sure hit it off."

"Hector is very nice. He admires you. He said you do amazing work. I've never seen one of your murals." She came closer, offering the mug while looking at the parade of elephants he'd finished. Even without color, the drawings looked alive and in motion. She spotted something he'd drawn near the bottom and grimaced.

"What's wrong?"

She turned her head and found him staring at her intently. "Isn't this mural going into a hotel lobby?" She pointed to the lion devouring a baby giraffe. "Children might be upset by that."

"It's what happens in real life."

"Not in a hotel, hopefully. If children are upset, you can count on their parents being upset, too."

"I won't be around to worry about it." Roman wore an odd smile. "And most people wouldn't have noticed something hidden in the grass."

"It's right there."

"It's not right there. You just happened to spot the hidden picture people usually miss."

His scrutiny made her uncomfortable. She looked for a place to set his mug, hoping to escape, and noticed he'd done more work on the easel paintings. Talia had been calling every few days asking about his progress.

He certainly had varying tastes in art. "Which style do you enjoy most?" She looked pointedly from the transfer to the paintings.

"Neither." He turned on the stool and

faced her. "And both. What about you?"

Grace couldn't read his expression, and she wasn't about to give her opinion. "I don't know anything about art."

Roman finally took the mug of coffee, his hand brushing hers. "Worried you might hurt my feelings?"

She admired the Serengeti migration. "You have a God-given gift, Mr. Velasco." No wonder he was so successful. He had a wide range of work.

"God-given? I doubt God has anything to do with me. And enough with the Mr. Velasco. You didn't say Señor Espinoza. You said Hector. Time to call me Roman."

"All right. Roman." Something had him upset. He must be stressed about getting the project done. He'd told Hector he wanted it done pronto. Grace took a step back. "I'd better let you get back to work. I'll call the hotel and clear things up for Hector. And the door chimes." She headed for the door.

"Grace. When Talia calls, as we both know she will, tell her the paintings are almost done. She can pick up two on Wednesday, and I'll finish the other before I head for San Diego."

7

Roman, Age 21

Roman shoved his backpack into the overhead compartment of the Boeing 777 and
slid into his seat. He stayed awake long
enough to feel the rush of takeoff, coming to
somewhere over the Atlantic, just in time to
lower his tray as the flight attendant served
dinner. He fell asleep again while the two
middle-aged women to his right went over
their week's itinerary in Rome.

Sergio Panetta had given him directions to
the Cremonesis'. He got lost, but several
nice-looking girls who spoke heavily accented
English guided him to public transportation.
Once in the right neighborhood, he walked
the narrow streets with laundry hanging on
lines outside windows. There were many
more bicycles and motorcycles here than in
San Francisco or Los Angeles, but he knew
how to survive traffic.

Baldo and Olivia Cremonesi didn't speak
English, but they embraced him in welcome

and jabbered rapidly in Italian. Within an hour, their home was packed with relatives eager to meet the American who had painted a fresco for their rich cousin in Hollywood. A dozen Cremonesi aunts, uncles, nephews, and nieces, not to mention Santorini neighbors, crammed into the house. Olivia fretted over Roman not eating enough and kept pushing food at him. The table was laden with dishes he'd never seen before, and all of it smelled good. But a man can only eat so much. Younger members of the clan practiced their English on him, peppering him with questions about America and about Sergio, who had become a family legend with his success as an import-export business owner.

Roman had hoped for quiet lodgings for a day or two until he could learn his way around the city and find a good hostel, but the Cremonesis had the next few weeks of his life all planned out. They'd even appointed a relative to act as guide to the Eternal City. Luigi was young, out of work, and eager to show their American guest around. Grinning at Roman, he raised his wineglass. "We go tomorrow. I teach you everything you need to know." He winked. "We look for girls."

Olivia smacked Luigi on the back of the head and erupted in excited Italian while waving angrily at Baldo, who hollered back. Luigi laughed. Baldo raised his hands in surrender and cried out, *"Olivia!"* Others laughed, too, saying things to Luigi with glances at Roman.

Roman didn't like being the center of attention. He didn't like being in a crowded room among strangers who had no qualms about hugging and kissing him the minute they walked in the room. He didn't want anyone making plans for him for an hour, let alone days. And he didn't want anyone showing him the city. He hadn't come to Rome so people could take over his life. He'd rather sleep on the streets than stay in this house.

The longer the evening wore on, the quieter he got. Olivia noticed and spoke to him in Italian. She put her hands together against her cheek and pretended to sleep. He saw an excuse to separate himself from the throng and nodded.

Olivia called Luigi and waved toward the stairs. Luigi told Roman a bedroom was ready upstairs and down the hall to the left. "I pick you up at noon."

As soon as Roman closed the door, he pulled a sketch pad from his backpack. Leaning against the headboard, he drew rapidly: Olivia in the kitchen with Baldo leaning against the counter, an adoring look on his face. He wrote *Grazie* at the top and signed *Roman Velasco* at the bottom. He stuck the picture in the dresser mirror and looked out the window. It was a straight drop to a cobbled alley. He wouldn't be escaping that way. He'd have to wait for the party to end and the Cremonesis to go to bed.

He pulled out his guidebook on Rome and studied the city map. By the time the house was quiet, he had memorized the city layout. He felt a twinge of guilt leaving in the middle of the night, but not enough to change his mind. He closed the front door quietly behind him. Filling his lungs with the air of freedom, he let it out in relief. He could find his own way. He'd been doing it since he was seven.

It was a couple of miles to the heart of the city, with several places to stay. He walked quickly, putting some distance between him and the Cremonesi house. Mopeds were locked in racks or chained to trees. He remembered what Jasper had said about traveling Europe on a motorcycle. He might buy one if the opportunity presented itself.

It was after midnight, but people were out and about. He figured the rules of survival were the same in any big city. Keep your eyes and ears open. Know what's going on around you. Just as he had in San Francisco and Los Angeles, Roman moved in the shadows, where he felt most at home.

Roman found his way to an inexpensive guesthouse not far from the Pantheon and near a bridge that crossed the Tiber. Vatican

City was only blocks away. He paid for a full week and slept for a few hours before going out to explore the maze of cobbled streets. He wove his way through groups of young and old, hearing Italian, French, English, German. Tourist groups were everywhere. He watched the locals. He ate and drank what they did while he hung out in piazzas sketching buildings, fountains, and girls in short black skirts and high-heeled black boots. The city was a visual feast by day, a hive of activity at night.

He spent a day wandering the Roman Forum and the Colosseum, another sitting on the Spanish Steps and drawing the Trevi Fountain. He bought a ticket to the Vatican and gawked at art-glutted halls, lingering in a corner of the Sistine Chapel, studying Michelangelo's masterpiece until his neck cramped. Rubbing it, he watched groups of tourists with their guides driving them like cattle. He followed along. Every wall, ceiling, and floor was a work of art. Priceless treasures were everywhere: jeweled crowns, gold-covered statues, diamond rings and pendants; masterworks by da Vinci, Raphael, Titian, Caravaggio; tapestries that had taken dozens of artisans decades to weave; mosaic marble floors.

Within minutes of entering the vast complex, his awe transformed into disquiet. By the time he stood in Saint Peter's Basilica before Michelangelo's *Pietà,* encased in bulletproof glass, he wondered whether the vast collections of priceless treasures, the massive acquisition of wealth through the ages, was really for God or merely a show of power. Where had all the money come from to build this monument to religion? From conquest and the conquered? Did the devout fork over offerings?

Hundreds of visitors streamed through, jamming the basilica. Hundreds more walked the halls, and more lined up outside, all eager to pay the hefty admission prices. How much money did it take to get into heaven, anyway? Was there a heaven? Or hell? Did God even exist? Roman had never lived with anyone who thought God was real, let alone necessary. "Live and let live" was religion enough for him.

The crucifix bothered him. Why would anyone worship a man who claimed to be God and yet died on a cross? He thought of a sign in the Tenderloin, right across the street from the flat where he and his mother lived: *Jesus Saves.* Saves from what? Jesus couldn't save Himself. How could He save others?

Two old women in black dresses and shawls stood nearby, tears running down their faces. When they walked away, he followed, curious. They went into an alcove and knelt on a low wooden bench. They held strings of beads and murmured prayers. Roman stood by the wall and sketched them. They stayed for an hour, rose, moved to the aisle, knelt, and touched their forehead, heart, and each shoulder before they rose and quietly left. The tears had dried, and they looked peaceful. He stared up at the statue of Jesus, hands and feet nailed to the cross, body emaciated and twisted, face contorted in agony.

Anger filled Roman. He didn't know where it came from or why. He left the basilica and walked the streets surrounding the Vatican. He saw plenty of graffiti, but none he'd be proud to leave behind. A group of avant-garde youths were hanging around San Lorenzo in Roma Centro. He moved among them, listening and watching until an English girl stopped him and started up a conversation. An Italian girl joined them and said they were all going to Trastevere. Roman spent the evening drinking and asking where he could buy art supplies.

Returning to his lodgings, he sketched a cassocked priest, fingers encrusted with rings, an elaborate crucifix hanging from his neck. He wore pirate boots and had one foot on top of a treasure chest while nearby a skeletal peasant woman cowered with her hand outstretched. He crumpled the drawing and tossed it across the room.

Roman slept fitfully and dreamed about his mother.

Next morning, exhausted and in a foul mood, he found his way to Ditta G. Poggi and bought another sketch pad and more charcoal pencils. He loved the smell of the store and lingered as patrons came and went. A buzz spread when one man entered. He bought tubes of oil paint and expensive brushes, then placed an order for cochineal insects he could grind into powder to produce a specific shade of carmine.

Roman asked for Belton Molotow and Spanish Montana spray paint. The weight of the cans in his pack gave him a sense of purpose. He returned to his rented room and practiced drawing the scene etched in his mind. He simplified it. Fewer lines, more contrasts. He'd have to work fast, and that meant every line and curve had to express something important, something that created an impression. Black, white, red, and gold — four colors, more than enough to make his statement.

Satisfied with the piece, Roman had to practice until he could do it in less than three minutes. When that didn't work, he bought butcher paper, masking tape, and scissors, and made a stencil. When he had everything ready, he walked the streets to find a place to put up his piece. He chose a wall near the Piazza del Risorgimento, and Sunday just before dawn to do it. He put on his black jeans, T-shirt, hoodie, and gloves. He grabbed his gear.

A window slid open with a bang as he taped the stencil to the wall. He kept his head down, his face hidden, as he pulled out the cans of spray paint and went to work. He finished in under three minutes, removed the stencil. He heard someone laughing as he stowed his gear and took off running.

He didn't think his graffiti would last a day, and he felt a rush of satisfaction when it was still there three days later. When a college student at the guesthouse said he'd go back to New York City if he had the money for a return ticket, Roman offered to buy the guy's motorcycle for the price of one seat in economy class. The two storage compartments on the bike were more than enough for what little he'd brought with him.

Roman drove north to Florence. He stayed a month, then moved on to Venice. The summer heat made the air taste like sludge, and crowds of tourists jammed the city. Roman headed for the Swiss Alps.

In every city where he spent more than a day, Roman left a statement behind, a piece of graffiti to speak to the masses. He'd been traveling around Europe for three months when an idea fixed itself in his head, a challenge that would land him in a French jail — or gain notoriety for the Bird. He headed for Paris.

He spent three full days at the Louvre,

haunting the halls, feasting on the art. He watched the guards, checked out the placement of security cameras, timed distances, memorized corridors, floors, and hallways. He bought slacks, a white shirt, a trench coat, and a fedora, then went back to buy a large book on Renaissance art and a canvas bag with the museum logo.

When Roman had his plan and everything he needed to pull it off, he did his first oil painting on an eight-by-ten-inch canvas — an owl on a pine branch, one eye open, the other closed, its beak a smug smile. He signed BRD in small bubble letters in the bottom right corner. He bought a gilded frame and museum wax.

On his last day in Paris, Roman went back to the Louvre. He looked like any one of a hundred other well-dressed visitors perusing the masterpieces in the hallowed halls of the world-famous museum. He wore the fedora pulled forward and down to obscure his face from security cameras. He paused here and there, pretending interest in a painting or plaque, while savoring the adrenaline rush.

Roman knew exactly where he was going and had the timing down to the minute. It took less than that to take his painting from the museum shop bag and press it on the wall space next to an oil of two hunting dogs. Skin prickling, he felt a guard looking his way. Roman shifted the museum shop bag as though the book inside had become heavy. The guard lost interest. Roman stayed for another minute, smirking. He took his time leaving the hall. The guard walked right by his painting without noticing it. Chuckling, Roman left, wondering how long it would take for the staff to realize something didn't belong.

8

Grace barely spoke with Roman over the next few days. He worked as though chained to his drafting table. She'd never seen anyone so obsessed. Did he enjoy the work that much, or did he simply want to put the project behind him so he could move on to the paintings still on the easels, the ones Talia was eager to add to the others Roman had finished for the show she wanted to schedule?

She wondered if he'd eaten anything in the last few days, until she'd seen the frozen dinner boxes and tinfoil trays stuffed in the garbage can under the counter. Grace reminded herself Roman's private life was none of her business, and felt her conscience nagging her. Shouldn't a personal assistant be concerned about the health of her boss? Grace headed down the hall and went upstairs to the studio. She stood in the doorway, but Roman looked immersed in his work. He also looked like he had a blinding headache. "Can I get you anything?"

Frowning, he rubbed his forehead. "More coffee."

"You probably have a headache because you haven't eaten all day. You can't live on caffeine, Roman. I can make you a sandwich."

"Okay. Thanks."

Well, that was easy. "Do you want it delivered or at the counter?" The man didn't have a dining table, unless he counted the one on the patio. It was too cold, and the wind was up, so that wouldn't do.

Roman tossed his ink pen into a tray. "I need a break." Standing, he stretched, the T-shirt pulling taut over his muscled chest. "I'm beginning to see zebra stripes everywhere."

Grace entered the kitchen and checked inside his refrigerator. "What would you like?"

"Whatever you find. Might be some roast beef in there." Roman walked to the windows.

Grace put bread and an unopened package of deli roast beef on the counter. "This is the first time I've seen you enjoy your view." She looked for other things to add to the sandwich. "It would make a beautiful painting."

Hooking his thumbs into his pockets, Roman glanced back at her. "Not my thing."

"Too bad. What do you like on your sandwich? Mustard? Mayo? Nothing?"

"Anything and everything available."

She found lettuce, cheese slices, a tomato, a

red onion, and bread-and-butter pickles. "Hector called. His work is almost finished. He went to the zoo. He loved it." She slathered mayonnaise on a slice of bread. "Talia won't bother you, but she wants to set a date for the show. And you got a call from the mayor of Golden. He's interested in commissioning you to paint a mural for the town."

"Never heard of the place."

"I googled it. It's a new community born out of a ghost town that was once a boomtown during the Gold Rush."

"You can't believe everything you read on the Internet."

"I know." Grace cut the thick sandwich in half and put it on a plate. "Someone named Jasper Hawley left a message." She slid the plate across the counter. "I hope he's a friend because he said he wants a bed to sleep in and a home-cooked meal."

Roman laughed. "Yeah, well, he was my teacher at Masterson Mountain Ranch. It's a group home in the Gold Country, probably not far from the newly invented old town of Golden."

Group home? A dozen questions popped into Grace's head.

Roman sat at the counter. "Not even curious enough to ask?"

She knew she needed boundaries with this man. "Your checkered past is none of my business."

Roman took a big bite out of the sandwich. Raising his brows, he made a sound of male pleasure that brought a tingle she hadn't felt in a long time.

Grace couldn't help but be curious about Roman Velasco, but his surroundings were enough to tell her he valued his privacy. She poured him a tall glass of orange juice.

He looked amused. "Trying to take care of me?"

"I know which side my bread is buttered on." He'd already finished the first half of his sandwich. Was it that good, or did it mean he was starving? He was taller than Patrick, and her ex-husband could put away two sandwiches, an apple, and a bag of chips without effort. Of course, he'd spent most of his time working out. "Shall I make you another sandwich?" He nodded, and she laid out two more slices of bread. "Okay. I'll ask. Why did you end up in a group home?"

"It was that or jail." He picked up the glass of orange juice and washed down the last bite of sandwich.

Jail? "What did you do?"

"Got mad. Tagged a few buildings."

Grace didn't know what he was talking about, and he didn't elaborate.

Roman watched her make the second sandwich. "Hawley still keeps tabs on me. Calls me one of his lost boys. He's making sure I walk the straight and narrow, I guess." He finished the orange juice. "End of story."

She took that to mean the end of the subject, and didn't press. "How long have you been up here?"

"Here? As in Topanga Canyon? Just over a year. I lived on a beach before this."

With his looks, she could easily imagine him on a surfboard in Hawaii. The big kahuna with a bevy of beach bunnies trailing after him. "I can see you in a beach shack."

"One beach is like any other. I got tired of all the people around. I wanted space and quiet."

"Well, you certainly have that." She put the second sandwich on his plate. "It's quiet up here." She closed the packages of roast beef and cheese, wrapped the lettuce, and put everything back in the refrigerator. Dampening a cloth, she cleaned the counter. "Are there any close neighbors?"

"Other than you? No."

She hadn't really thought about the remoteness or that he was the only human being close by.

"Don't get nervous, Ms. Moore. I don't have any ulterior motives for offering you the cottage. It just seemed the best solution for both of us."

She relaxed. "Well, it was certainly the answer to my prayers."

"Prayers." He gave a telling laugh. "I hate to disillusion you, Grace, but prayer isn't what got you the place. You're good at your job. I wanted to keep you around. That's all. There's no one out there listening or intervening on our behalf."

Grace had heard plenty of people dismiss God as though He were a figment of imagination to bring comfort in the dark. She might have come to believe the same thing if she hadn't had a visitation when she was seven years old and hiding in a dark closet, terrified of the night and the monster that came with it. She didn't talk about what had happened when she was a small child. And Patrick hadn't felt any need to believe in anything but himself, or he would have felt bad about what he did.

She had learned a long time ago not to argue theology. She hadn't come to faith because someone gave her all the answers. She came to faith because she met and talked with someone who made her feel enveloped by God's love. Still, she had to say something to this man who looked like he had everything and nothing. "I believe in God. Life can be pretty unbearable without something to believe in." She met Roman Velasco's gaze and didn't look away. She had let herself doubt, and every time she had, disaster swiftly followed.

"Any more orange juice in the fridge?"

She got the message. No more talk about the Lord. She hadn't intended to proselytize.

"There's just a little left. Do you want it in your glass, or would you prefer drinking it straight from the bottle?"

"The bottle is fine." He grinned as she handed it to him.

"You need groceries."

"I guess you'll be making another run to Malibu."

"You're the boss."

Roman pulled out his wallet and extracted a couple hundred-dollar bills. "How about some real food, for a change?"

"I'll need specifics. Can you cook, or is it a matter of adding a new variety and brand of dinners you can microwave?"

"I can cook. I can even do laundry and make my bed. There are just other things I like doing better." He smiled slightly. "That was a great sandwich, by the way. Can you fix anything else?"

Grace knew where he was heading. Her list of duties kept growing. "This and that."

"Anything you cook will be better than what I've been living on. And it takes too much time to drive down to a restaurant."

A restaurant? Was he kidding? "I'm not a chef, Roman."

"Meat and potatoes. Meat and veggies. Meat and salad. Skip the kale and collard greens. I want to stay healthy, but not that healthy. Keep it simple."

He was taking a lot for granted. "Why don't

I make a trip to Walmart and pick up a blender? You can toss in a pound of ground round, some veggies, and press a button. Your dinner would be ready to drink in less than a minute."

He looked at her like she'd grown horns. Grace laughed. "Or I could buy you those protein shakes." She picked up the empty orange juice bottle. "Do you recycle?"

"I don't know. Do I?" Roman got up and then sat on the stool again. He looked ashen.

"I was only kidding." When he didn't say anything, she looked more closely. "Are you all right?"

"Just tired."

"Maybe you should lie down for a while."

"Take a nap, you mean?" He gave her a sardonic look.

"I'm not your mother, but you've taken all of thirty minutes for lunch at three in the afternoon."

"Hector's waiting."

Hector was a lame excuse, but it wasn't her place to quibble. What was pressing Roman so hard? Not money. He had plenty and didn't spend much of it. "Hector works for you. You set the schedule."

"I just want to get the wall done." His color hadn't improved much. Why was he looking at her like that? He tilted his head, studying her. "Are you letting your hair grow out?"

Her hand rose instinctively to touch the hair

that now covered the back of her neck. She'd cut it short in penance. Her friends told her it was time to stop punishing herself. "I guess."

"You'd look good with long hair."

Patrick had said the same thing. "Short is more practical."

He frowned and opened his mouth as though to say something, then changed his mind. "Thanks for the sandwiches." He stood and swayed slightly. "I think I will lie down for a while."

"I'll do the shopping now, if that's all right."

"Sure. Turn off the ringer on the telephone." He paused. "When are you moving in?"

"This weekend."

It was almost six by the time Grace returned to the house. She headed for the studio to ask if she could have comp time rather than extra pay. Coming down the hall, she saw Roman sprawled across his bed. He lay as though he had toppled like a tree and not moved since. She felt a vague alarm.

"Roman?" He didn't answer. He didn't move either. Was he all right? She stepped over the threshold, the urge to remove his shoes and cover him with a blanket almost overwhelming.

Caretaking inclinations had gotten her into a world of trouble and pain once before. She wasn't going down that road again. "Roman?" She spoke louder this time. He made a sound and moved just enough to reassure her.

She retreated to the office, wrote a note, and left it on the kitchen counter, along with the receipt and change. She closed the front door quietly behind her.

Roman awakened sweating, heart pounding. He lay still, fighting the sense of foreboding that hung in the darkness pressing in on him. He felt seven years old again, his mother gone for the night. Dark shadows moved on the wall, and he turned on the lights quickly. Nothing there. No reason for panic. Gradually his pulse slowed, and the fear dissipated. *Get a grip. You're not a kid anymore.*

How long had he been asleep? It had been daylight when Grace suggested he lie down for a while. He didn't even remember what happened after walking into his bedroom. The digital clock glowed 1:36. Hours had passed in what seemed like a minute. Lost time. Wasted time. Sitting on the edge of his bed, he waited for the odd confusion to pass. Flipping switches for more light, he made his way to the kitchen, where he found a note, grocery receipt, and exact change.

Rotisserie chicken and salad in the fridge. See you at 9 a.m. Grace

He might be the artist, but she had better penmanship. Attractive, subtle, classy, with a hint of something he couldn't define. Just like her. She was comfortable in her own skin. *Unlike some of us, who've never been comfortable, no matter what role we play.*

Roman ate half the chicken and all the salad. He needed to work, but he wasn't in the mood for drawing the herd of zebra migrating the African plains. Stretching out on the black leather sofa in the living room, he looked out the windows. Grace was right. He hadn't spent much time admiring the view, now obscured by inky darkness. It must be overcast. The night felt heavy, like tar, moist and cold, threatening. He fought his mood while trying to identify it. A growing emptiness? Hunger? For what?

Grace Moore would be moving into his cottage this weekend. He was already having second thoughts. He didn't want to become too close, and having her right next door might be a temptation. Too late to worry about that now. It was a done deal, unless she changed her mind. She hadn't been wild about the idea in the first place, but her gaggle of friends had helped his cause. Now she saw it as an answer to prayer.

She'd better not start talking religion to him. Though he had to admit that unlike other religious quacks he'd run into, she'd mentioned faith in a natural way.

Why did people believe in a god they couldn't see? The only time he ever heard Jesus' name was in a curse. It went with the territory he'd inhabited until age fourteen. Masterson Ranch didn't push religion. Chet and Susan had rules, but they hadn't posted the Ten Commandments on some wall. Jasper told Bobby Ray the way a man used language made a difference in where he could end up. Gutter talk kept one in the gutter. Roman learned how to blend in, even knowing he'd never belong. He could play whatever role was necessary to get ahead. It had only been lately he'd begun to wonder if it was worth the effort. Roman Velasco's mask kept slipping.

What would Grace Moore think of him if she knew where he'd come from and how he'd survived? A ghetto kid with no father and a whore for a mother. A kid who ran drugs until he talked the head honcho into making him the gang tagger. What would she think of the Bird, who mocked the world that celebrated Roman Velasco but wanted no part of Bobby Ray Dean?

What did Grace do on the weekends? Did she have a steady boyfriend, some nice-looking, button-down guy with a nine-to-five office job? Someone who'd take her to church every Sunday?

And why was he thinking about her so much?

Roman muttered a curse under his breath and sat up. He'd hired her because she wasn't his type. He now had a dependable, trustworthy, nice-looking girl working for him. A *good* girl. All his experience was with the other kind.

He couldn't imagine Grace in a nightclub, let alone looking for a hookup on Friday or Saturday. She wasn't the kind of girl who'd have hot sex with a stranger, call Uber for a ride home at two in the morning, and make it to work the next day.

He'd wasted enough time sleeping. He didn't need to waste any more obsessing about his personal assistant, who had already made it abundantly clear that they weren't going to get personal. He should be happy about that.

Work would get his mind off her. He headed for the studio and drew four more zebras. He tossed his pen in the tray.

What was he doing with his life? Where was he going? What did he want? He felt an aching homesickness. But how would he know that when he'd never had a home?

After his mother disappeared and CPS placed him in foster care, he'd run away from every family who took him in, eventually finding his way back to the Tenderloin to look for her. It wasn't until he was ten that he learned what happened to her. He stopped running away from his foster homes after that, as long as the "parents" gave him freedom to do what he wanted. He did best with those who were only interested in the government money they received to give him room and board. Inside, Bobby Ray kept running.

From what? To what? He didn't know. That's what frustrated him. That's what caused the pressure to build inside him until the Bird had to fly.

The Topanga Canyon house was still and silent. Deserted. He felt like a ghost haunting the place. The property had been in foreclosure, a freak and fortuitous opportunity that dropped into his lap. He couldn't even remember how it happened, but the Realtor said it would make a great investment. So what if the place was far too big for one person and had a guest cottage he'd never use. He wouldn't have to live here long. Market value was climbing. He could sell now and walk away flush with savings. And then what? Go back to Europe? Ride around the country on a Harley? Buy a boat and sail the seven seas?

It had been over a year, and time muddied his recollection. He sometimes wondered if he'd imagined the encounter. He had been high that night, restless, until he saw the blonde. He had only fleeting memories of a long, silent ride to his place, then heart-shaking urgency, starbursts, and tears. She left, like a dream he couldn't fully remember.

He had gone out into the night after her and seen her slip into a car that sped away, tail-light red eyes staring back and mocking him.

That night had been the awakening.

Roman sat at his drafting table again and stared at the migrating wildebeests and zebras. Some were running, some walking, all going somewhere out of instinct. Roman felt like an outcast among his species. He didn't like gathering at the watering hole anymore, or rutting with any attractive, healthy female selected from the herd. He had no plans to procreate. Restless, he wanted to be on the move to his own Serengeti, wherever it was. He feared one more wrong step would take him over the edge into the abyss.

Something wasn't right, but he didn't know what was wrong.

He had already achieved what most Americans wanted: the big house, the fast car, a rising career, money, sex whenever and however he wanted it. He should be happy. He should be satisfied. But he felt hungry for more. How much would it take to fill the void inside him?

Frustrated, he swept the drawing off the table. As it flapped to the floor, Roman grabbed a random can of Krylon spray paint and headed for the back wall of his studio.

9

Bobby Ray, Age 15

Slouched in the front seat of Sam Carter's white Chevy Impala, Bobby Ray watched unfamiliar territory fly by. He'd never been outside San Francisco. Now, here he was in the wilds, more trees than houses, no freeways, just a winding road. They'd stopped once to eat at McDonald's and use the john. The social services caseworker kept close tabs on him. "I know you want to run, Bobby Ray. It's my job to get you to the group home. What you do after that is up to you."

The peaks of the Sierra Nevada grew nearer. The longer Sam Carter drove, the edgier Bobby Ray got. He was used to bustling streets, alleyways, noise. Golden Gate Park had been the closest to what he was seeing out here in nowhere land. Sam glanced at him. "You'll be okay." Bobby Ray clenched his teeth as Sam talked about the Masterson Mountain Ranch. Bobby Ray tried to drown out the man's voice by going over the route in his head. He'd have to remember in order to find his way back. He hadn't seen any buses running on the country road.

"Chet Masterson will understand you, Bobby Ray."

"Yeah. Right. Like you do. How long do I have to stay?"

"Until you turn eighteen."

Two and a half years! Bobby Ray glared out the window. He didn't see himself staying in a group home longer than a couple of days. Not out here in the sticks. A week, tops. He'd find a way out.

And go where? Reaper and Lardo were dead.

He spotted a sign. Copperopolis. It took less than a minute to pass through town. Bobby Ray cursed. "Where are we, anyway?"

"The closest to heaven you'll ever get." Carter smiled. "Getting nervous, Bobby Ray?" He laughed. "Some people have all the luck and are too dumb to know it."

"Do I look like a country boy to you?" Tension coiled in Bobby Ray's belly. How many miles was he from everything familiar? He knew how to survive in the streets. How to get by with less than nothing. "I got a raw deal and you know it, Sam. If I have to be in a group home, why not one in Alameda County?"

"Because it's right across the bay, and you'd run away again."

"San Francisco is my home!"

"Just because it's the only place you've ever been doesn't mean it's the best place for you."

"It should be my choice, shouldn't it?"

"You've been making choices all along, Bobby Ray. Your most recent choice landed you here. When we get to the Mastersons', you're going to have to choose whether you use this time to learn something useful, or see it as time served." Sam gave him a weary look and turned onto another narrow country road. "Don't think I haven't noticed you checking every sign. But I'd better warn you. If you split, you won't get far. People know Chet up here. No one is going to give you a ride anywhere." He gave a nod. "There it is."

A big barn, corrals, a long, single-story ranch house, two pickup trucks parked in a dusty front yard. Bobby Ray's worst nightmare had come true. The court might as well have sent him to Mars.

Sam turned left onto a freshly graveled road. As they pulled into the yard, two large German shepherds barked ominously. Sam chuckled. "Another reason not to run away." He got out as a tall, broad-shouldered man with cropped dark hair came out of the house. He looked half–country hick in boots, jeans, and a plaid shirt and half–action figure. Bobby Ray had seen others with his confidence and aura, most with hard eyes and fists. This man had laugh lines around his mouth and eyes.

A quiet word silenced the two dogs. "Good to see you, Sam!" His voice was deep, rock grinding in an earthquake.

"How's Susan?"

"On the road again." Masterson laughed. "She's in San Antonio, visiting her folks." He took in Bobby Ray with a glance. Bobby Ray pretended not to notice or care. "Long way from your neck of the woods, isn't it, Mr. Dean?" Bobby Ray stiffened, sure he was being mocked. When he met Masterson's gaze, the man grinned. "We're glad to have you."

"I'm not glad to be here."

"Didn't expect you would be. You look like a tough kid. It remains to be seen how tough you really are."

Sam opened the car trunk. He said something low, and Masterson chuckled. "He wouldn't be the first. He can try."

Sam handed over a thick file. "Everything you need to know about him is in there." Bobby Ray knew it held family history, a list of foster homes he had been in and out of over the past eight years, along with his former foster parents' reports, school records, test scores, court records, and whatever else the system had managed to dredge up and commit to paper in an attempt to describe who he was. Nothing worth anything. Nobody knew him.

Masterson held the file flat on his large

hand, as if weighing it. "Impressive." His blue eyes sparkled.

Sam looked edgy, ready to get back on the road. "I promised my son I'd be at his basketball game tonight. If I leave now, I'll just make it."

Bobby Ray felt a twinge of jealousy. Must be nice to have a dad who showed up. Must be nice to have a father, period. Then again, you could always have one like Reaper or Wolf.

Masterson slapped Sam on the back. "I'll call in a couple of weeks and let you know how he's doing."

Bobby Ray didn't plan on sticking around that long. "Where do I go? The barn?"

"You stay where you are until I'm ready to show you in."

Bobby Ray muttered his opinion and turned toward the house. He'd forgotten the two dogs until they stood and bared their teeth. He swore again. Masterson chuckled. "Nice fresh meat, boys. Easy now. Stand still, Mr. Dean. They're about to get to know you." He gave a soft command and the two German shepherds moved around Bobby Ray. The hair rose on the back of his neck when they stuck their noses in private places. "Easy now. If you run, they'll take you down. They're just giving you a good canine hello."

"Don't expect me to reciprocate."

"That's a big word for a street kid."

Masterson gave another soft command and the two dogs sat, tongues lolling in doggy grins. Sam got back in the car and gave Bobby Ray a salute.

"Come," Masterson commanded, and the two dogs walked on either side of him. Grinding his teeth, Bobby Ray followed, making sure his pace let Masterson know he wasn't one of his pets. "A word of warning, Mr. Dean. You go AWOL, and Starsky and Hutch will hunt you down." He grinned at him. "They know your scent now. You can run, but you can't hide."

Bobby Ray felt a chill run down his back. Was this guy for real? "There must be a law against using an attack dog on a kid."

"Did I say I'd command them to attack? All I'd say is 'Go find Bobby Ray.' A city kid can get lost real fast in all those hills and dales. Starsky and Hutch know every tree and bush, every rock and stream. They'll show you the way home." He gave Bobby Ray a measuring look. "I'm hoping I won't have to send them after you."

Bobby Ray didn't say anything more. Better to wait and get a feel for who this man was and what kind of place he was running. It usually didn't take more than a couple of days for Bobby Ray to figure out how things worked.

Five boys lounged in the living room. Two were stretched out on large, brown leather couches reading. Two others were playing a board game. Another was sitting at a table, reading a book and writing in a spiral notebook. They looked up and gave Bobby Ray a once-over when Masterson introduced him as Mr. Bobby Ray Dean. Bobby Ray made eye contact with each one so they'd know he wasn't afraid of any of them, even if several looked older and tough. He wondered which one would be his roommate or if they all slept in a bunkhouse somewhere.

The living room was big and well-furnished. There was money in the leather sofas and the polished oak coffee table. Floor-to-ceiling bookshelves covered one wall opposite a massive stone fireplace. The ranch had an impressive entertainment center with a large-screen television and stereo system. Sliding-glass doors opened to a huge lawn with a soccer net at one end.

The house was bigger than any he'd ever been in, with spacious bedrooms and bathrooms with double sinks, showers, and tubs, a professional kitchen connected to a dining room with a long table and straight-backed chairs. Another corridor had a laundry room and pantry and an office that looked more like a library. Another door led to separate quarters where Chet and his wife, Susan, lived.

"We live a simple life here, Mr. Dean." Masterson summed it up quickly. If you show respect and courtesy, you can expect to receive the same. Check the board daily for your rotation of chores. Everyone living at Masterson Mountain Ranch learned bachelor arts: how to cook, wash dishes, vacuum, wash floors, clean toilets and showers, do laundry and mending. Susan Masterson would start his training as soon as she returned from Texas, which would be tomorrow afternoon. Wake-up call at six, breakfast at six thirty, school from seven thirty, free time when you finished your assignments and chores. A master teacher came daily, and Bobby Ray could set his own pace. If you want to finish high school early, go for it. Any interest in college? No? Well, nothing was set in stone. He might change his mind after a few months of working with Jasper Hawley. Chet would be having one-on-one sessions with Bobby Ray three times a week starting tomorrow. Any questions?

Bobby Ray had been given rules before. He'd never lived by them and didn't intend on starting now.

Chet gave him a slow, knowing smile. "It's a lot to take in. You'll catch on soon enough." He nodded toward the kid at the table. "That's José. Get your gear, Mr. Dean. You'll be sharing a room with him. Second door on the right down that hallway."

José glanced up when they came into the living room. Clearly, he'd already been informed. The look he gave Bobby Ray held a warning. "The bed under the window is mine. You have the left side of the dresser." It sounded like a dismissal. Bobby Ray picked up his duffel bag and went down the hall.

Everything simple and functional: two twin beds; two desks with shelves, one already filled with textbooks; two reading lamps; two bulletin boards, one displaying the Mexican flag and half a dozen family photos; one corkboard with some pushpins. Bobby Ray yanked open the top left dresser drawer and dumped in his few possessions.

He looked around at the clean white walls and itched to have a black marker in his hand. Images came: a party scene at Red Hot's apartment, Reaper high on meth, Lardo dead, screaming faces all around him, a jail mess half-filled with caricatures of homey inmates, the kind that wanted to cut out your heart with a shiv. Bobby Ray sat on the end of the bed and rubbed his face, wishing he could rub away the pictures flashing through his head and the gut-aching sense of loss. He should have remembered it was better not to make friends with anyone. Here today, gone tomorrow.

"What do you say I show you around the place?" José leaned against the doorjamb. He tossed an apple up and caught it.

How long had he been watching? Bobby Ray stood. He was several inches taller than the older boy, but he knew size didn't always win a fight.

Everything about the Masterson Mountain Ranch felt foreign, especially the heavily pine-scented air. The only sounds were the rustle of pines, whinny of horses, birdsong.

They walked around the place for an hour, and Bobby Ray didn't see a single car go by.

"You expecting someone?" José smirked. "You keep looking toward the road."

"How far are we from town?"

"Too far to run, dude." He nodded toward the barn. "Do you like horses?"

Bobby Ray sneered. "I've never met one."

José jerked his head. "Come on, then. I'll introduce you to a few. The Mastersons board horses. One of our jobs is to exercise them. Some of the owners come out to ride every day, but most live in Sacramento and only come on weekends or holidays."

The barn smelled of hay and fresh manure. José opened a stall. "Come on."

Bobby Ray looked at the size of the gelding and stood by the gate. "Is riding part of the bachelor arts program?"

"It's one of the best parts about this place." José ran his hand over the horse's back. The animal nudged him, and he stroked the white patch on its head. José took the apple out of his shirt and fed it to the horse. "Where you from?"

"San Francisco."

"I'm from Stockton. My folks come up once a month. Well, my mom comes. My dad got arrested for grand theft auto. How about you?"

"What about me?"

"Have you got family?"

"What makes you think it's any of your business?"

José's eyes narrowed and darkened. "We have to live together. I'd like to know who's sleeping in the bed three feet from mine."

"Well, rest easy. I'm not gay, and I haven't killed anyone yet." He'd had enough of the barn, horses, and José. "Are we done?"

"With the tour, yes. But we're far from done. We're just getting started."

Bobby Ray headed back to the house. What now? He didn't know any of these guys. He didn't want to know them. Frustration bubbled up inside him. José walked by him and went back to the table where he'd been reading and taking notes. Bobby Ray wandered the room, pausing to peruse the bookshelves: classic novels, biographies, books on carpentry, husbandry, auto mechanics, history, technology, science.

The open archway into the kitchen allowed him to watch Chet Masterson working with one of the boys. Something smelled good enough to make Bobby Ray's stomach ache with hunger. Another boy stacked bowls, napkins, and silverware on the kitchen counter.

"Okay, gentlemen! Come and get it!" Masterson stood in the kitchen archway. "Chili and corn bread tonight."

Bobby Ray hung back until everyone headed for the kitchen. He followed their lead, picking up a bowl, napkin, silverware and serving himself. Tumblers of water sat on the table, full pitchers at each end. Tense, Bobby Ray took his seat. José ignored Bobby Ray while the others gave him quick, assessing glances before digging spoons into their chili. The corn bread was warm enough to melt the butter and honey Bobby Ray spread on it. After the first tentative bite, Bobby Ray dug into the meal. He couldn't remember the last time he'd eaten anything that tasted so good. When others got up for seconds, Bobby Ray did too.

Everyone cleared their own dishes. "Kitchen's open if you get hungry later," Masterson told Bobby Ray. "Clean up after yourself when you're finished." He nodded toward the living room. "We're having our family meeting in fifteen minutes."

Bobby Ray figured he could make it to the road and run a couple miles by that time, but when he stepped out the door, Starsky and Hutch came awake and stood. He went down the stairs cautiously and started across the yard. The two dogs followed. One nudged his hand, and Bobby Ray stopped. Maybe if he made friends, they'd let him go. He stroked the head of one of the dogs, scratched the other behind the ears. He tried maneuvering around them, but a car pulled into the drive.

Straightening, Bobby Ray watched an old, polished red convertible Dodge Dart park next to the brown extended cab F-250 pickup. A middle-aged man got out. He had a short-cropped beard and shaggy salt-and-pepper hair. He snatched a rumpled sports coat from the backseat and shrugged it on over his short-sleeved, open-collared plaid shirt while the dogs bounded around him in greeting. He looked at Bobby Ray. "Jasper Hawley. And you are Mr. . . . ?"

"Bobby Ray Dean." So this was the teacher. He looked a mess, though his grip was firm and his eyes clear.

Jasper Hawley nodded toward the house. "After you."

Bobby Ray found space on the couch. Masterson asked the boys to share a little personal history so Mr. Dean could get to know them. One after another, each talked of gang ties, broken homes, court appearances, and time in and out of juvie. Bobby Ray could have told stories about how many times he'd been moved or places he'd lived, or how he always found a way back to the Tenderloin. In the beginning, he'd run back because he thought his mother was still there somewhere in the streets or in a club or flat. After he learned the truth, he still returned because it was familiar.

"Anything you want to say, Mr. Dean?" Masterson looked at him.

"Just because you tell me your sad stories doesn't mean I'm telling mine. I don't know you." He looked around the room and met the gaze of every boy. "I don't want to know you."

"I know one thing about him." José smirked. "He's afraid of dogs and horses."

Bobby Ray went hot, but before he could retaliate, the others laughed and started telling Starsky and Hutch stories. One boy had refused to step out the front door for the first week. Another had tried to outrun them once. Starsky had snagged his pant leg, and Hutch had planted two paws on his back and taken him down. He thought he was dead meat until they started licking him.

"So they're all bark and no bite?" Bobby Ray looked at José.

"I wouldn't push it." José grinned at Masterson. "I took a swing at the boss once. Bad idea."

Masterson changed the subject. Jasper Hawley dropped a few questions, and the boys talked about everything from sports to politics. They each had strong, sometimes opposing, opinions, but didn't resort to insults or arguments.

After lights out, Bobby Ray lay on his bed, blanket over him. Exhausted and depressed, he wanted to sleep, but the noise outside seemed to intensify in the darkness. "What is that sound?"

"Crickets." José gave a low laugh. "Drove me crazy the first week. Wait until you hear the frogs after some rain." He rolled over. "You'll get used to them."

Bobby Ray accepted defeat, at least until he could find a way to do battle and win. It was get with the program or die of boredom. Hawley gave him a series of exams to find out where he stood academically. He issued textbooks in advanced algebra, biology, and English composition. When Hawley gave him a choice between Spanish and French, Bobby Ray said why not Latin. Hawley laughed and came back the next day with a used, college-level Latin text. "Just happens to be an interest of mine."

"I was kidding."

"Scared you're not smart enough? It used to be standard in public schools. It's the foundation of our language, traditions, systems of thought, politics, science. Studying Latin can teach you how to think analytically."

Bobby Ray was used to teachers just putting in time, not loaded with enthusiasm. Hawley had stories for every subject and taught as though he knew the material inside out, upside down, and backward. He was so excited about what he was teaching, Bobby Ray caught his enthusiasm.

Masterson called Bobby Ray into the office three times a week, and three times a week, Bobby Ray got around the probing questions. Exasperated, Bobby Ray lost his temper. "You've got everything in the file."

"I'm not looking for facts, Mr. Dean. I want to know how you think. I want to know what's going on inside that impressive brain of yours."

"No, you don't." Bobby Ray had no intention of unlocking that door.

"I've been watching you. You do a lot of listening. Talking to someone who cares can help you understand where you've come from and how to get where you want to go."

"I deal with my stuff my own way."

"And how's that working for you?" Masterson shook his head. "The truth is, you don't deal with anything. You're pushing it all down where you think it'll stay buried. It'll eat you alive."

Susan Masterson was harder to deal with than Chet. A blonde, blue-eyed Texan, she wore her long hair in a ponytail and dressed in jeans, Western shirts, and cowboy boots. The boys all had crushes on her. "Stick with me, and you'll know your way around a kitchen. Give me guff, and you'll be mucking out the stables." Bobby Ray balked and found out she was a woman of her word.

Blistered after using a shovel all day, he tried reason. He'd fended for himself for as long as he could remember. He could make sandwiches and ramen noodles, mac and cheese. He could boil hot dogs and scramble eggs. What more did a guy need?

Susan faced Bobby Ray, hands on her hips, and told him that by the time he left the ranch, he'd know how to cook a four-course meal, iron his own shirt despite living in a perma-press world, do his own laundry, and make a bed so tight he could bounce a coin on it. He'd even learn to clean the toilet and remember to put the seat down. "A future wife will appreciate that!" She raised her voice so Chet could hear in his back office.

"Did you say something, darlin'?" Chet called back, laughing.

"Whoa!" She put her hand over Bobby Ray's. "Peel a potato that way, and you'll skin your thumb. I don't want any blood in the mashed potatoes." She demonstrated and handed the peeler back. "Only fifteen more to go."

He balked again when she took him to a cabinet and told him he could pick out something better to wear than what he had. "You're free to take whatever you need. Most of our boys arrive with little more than one set of clothes." She reached in and pulled out

146

a couple of ironed, neatly folded shirts. He said no thanks, he liked T-shirts and hoodies, preferably in black.

"This isn't the end of the road, Bobby Ray. You're going to college or you're going to work. Either way, you have to learn to be comfortable in clothes that will get you a job. You need to look the part for whatever career you choose."

"There's no dress code for dealing dope."

"Don't be a dope. *El que no arriesga, no gana.*"

"Say what?"

"Nothing ventured, nothing gained." She shook her head and hollered. "Hey, Chet. What happened to our boys learning Spanish?"

"Jasper's teaching Mr. Dean Latin."

"Latin!" Susan laughed. "Oh, my. Jasper finally got his wish!" She gave Bobby Ray a malicious grin. "Lucky you."

Like everyone else, Bobby Ray did his time mucking out stables and pitching hay. José spent every minute of his free time with the horses. He rode every day. Bobby Ray tried not to like his roommate, but a relationship grew despite his resolve. He could see a world of hurt coming. Right now, it had to do with José and his love of horses. Bobby Ray wanted to warn him. "They don't belong to you, bro. Blaze Star or Nash might be in a horse trailer tomorrow and out of here. Ever think about that?"

"Sure I think about it. I'm not stupid."

"So why get attached?"

"You see me ever getting a chance like this again? I'll probably end up like my old man, serving time. I'm going to enjoy this until I'm eighteen."

At eighteen, they'd be out of the program, off the ranch, and on their own. That's the way the system worked.

Bobby Ray kept to himself, kept to his studies. He had to remind himself over and over he shouldn't make friends or count on anybody. It always led to heartache. Sometimes when the guys were all talking and laughing together, Bobby Ray would have to go outside to get his head straight. Often, against his better judgment, he'd talk with José after lights-out. One night, José told him a joke and Bobby Ray laughed so hard, he felt tears coming and had to shut himself down before he made a fool of himself.

When José announced during a family meeting that he was planning to join the Marine Corps, Bobby Ray knew it was time to leave the Masterson Mountain Ranch. As soon as lights went out, he stuffed his clothes into his duffel bag and made for the door. José followed, pulling on jeans as he tried to catch up. "Where are you going?"

"Anywhere but here!"

"I turn eighteen next month. We all have to

leave sometime, man. I'm trying to do the smart thing."

"Just shut up and go back to the house." Starsky and Hutch appeared, and Bobby Ray swore.

"Suit yourself." José headed toward the house, calling the dogs. They didn't come.

Starsky sat on one side of Bobby Ray, Hutch on the other. Shifting his duffel bag, Bobby Ray looked down the long driveway to the gate and the dark line of road along the fence. Where would he go? Back to San Francisco? He didn't have any friends there, not anymore. Should he go to Sacramento? He'd have to live on the streets. What were his alternatives? He spit out a four-letter word, then another, louder. After a few more minutes, he returned to the house. He dropped the bag beside his bed.

Chet called Bobby Ray for a counseling session the next morning. Since it was a day early, Bobby Ray figured Chet knew about his attempted escape. He sat, wondering how many days he'd be mucking out stalls this time.

Chet took the seat behind his desk. "Glad you changed your mind last night." He leaned back. "Care to talk about what made you want to run?"

Bobby Ray stared, stone-faced, at nothing.

"Silence is your standard modus operandi,

isn't it, Mr. Dean? Okay. This time we'll just sit here until you start talking."

Minutes passed. Chet Masterson looked as relaxed as he had when they entered the office. Bobby Ray grew edgier. He'd always been the one to use silence as a weapon. Sit long enough and the other person always said something, usually enough for Bobby Ray to use against them. Chet didn't look bothered.

After fifteen minutes of silence, Bobby Ray shifted in his chair. He snarled a couple of words and got up.

"Sit down." Chet Masterson spoke quietly, but with steely calm. "We have an hour."

At least there was an end in sight. Thirty minutes had Bobby Ray's nerves in knots. Maybe he didn't have the guts to run, but he knew how to get kicked out. All he had to do was find a can of spray paint. He let his mind focus on what he'd put on a wall. After the full hour had passed, his blood had cooled to a steady simmer.

Chet looked grim. "Impressive." His smile held sadness, not respect. "You can go, Mr. Dean."

That evening, he spotted a black marker in the dry-erase board tray and felt a rush of adrenaline. Slipping it surreptitiously into his pocket while the others lounged and watched a baseball game, he headed for his bedroom. He could hear the guys cheering over a hit.

"Hey! Why don't you join us?" José stopped

just inside the door. He uttered a four-letter word and stood staring. He went out again, closing the door behind him.

Bobby Ray felt like he'd been kicked in the stomach; then the rush returned, dimming the pain, focusing the anger. Tense, he kept working.

He heard the murmur of voices from the living room as the nightly meeting started without him. No one would miss him when he was gone. After a while, he heard the television again. The door stayed closed.

The marker ran out of ink before he finished, but he figured he'd done enough. He tossed the empty marker into the wastebasket and sat on the floor at the end of his bed. He wished he had a couple more pens so he could finish what he'd started, but it didn't matter. He had done enough to get kicked off the ranch.

Someone rapped on the door and opened it. Bobby Ray saw Chet Masterson's scuffed brown boots. *Here it comes. Time to go.* It's what he wanted, wasn't it?

The fear came up from deep inside him, gripping him by the throat. *Where do I go now? Where am I going to end up this time?*

"You're finally talking, Bobby Ray." Chet Masterson stood calmly studying the wall. "Looks like you have a lot to say."

Jasper Hawley looked at what Bobby Ray had

drawn. The next day, he came back with a box of books and dropped it on the table in front of Bobby Ray. "We're adding art to your curriculum."

"You expect me to read all these?" After glancing at the first, Bobby Ray itched to see what else was in the box.

"You've got time." He took books out one by one: art history, the works of Leonardo da Vinci, Francisco Goya, Paul Cézanne, Vincent van Gogh, Hieronymus Bosch, Emil Nolde. Intrigued, Bobby Ray opened the last one. Hawley took it back. "Not now. First things first. Math, Latin, and social studies." He spread his hands flat on the pile of art books. "These are incentive to buckle down. As soon as you finish your assignments, they're all yours."

Bobby Ray finished his class work in a couple of hours. He had to be reminded to do chores, but did them quickly. He spent hours looking at John Singer Sargent's watercolors of Venice and paintings by John William Waterhouse, transported to other places and times. He loved the sharp, bright colors of Van Gogh, the mask faces of Nolde, the starkness of Picasso.

When Hawley gave him pens and sketchbooks, Bobby Ray filled them. Hawley brought a book on twentieth-century muralists. Bobby Ray did more drawings.

Susan peered over his shoulder one afternoon. "Can I take a look?" She grabbed his sketchbook before he had time to answer. She turned the pages. "Ohhh, I like this one." She put the sketchbook in front of him. "Do you want to paint a wall?"

Was she kidding? She looked serious, even excited.

"I'll give you the one in the kitchen if you'll do something like this. I've always wanted to see Italy. Paint something Roman. Or places Vasco da Gama might have seen on his voyage around the Cape of Good Hope."

"Rome and Velasco." Bobby Ray grimaced.

"Vasco." She gave a laugh. "But wait. Roman Velasco. That would be a great name for an artist!" She put her hands up as though framing the wall. "Roman Velasco lived here."

"Pseudonyms are for writers." Chet laughed.

"Tell that to Bruce Wayne and Clark Kent. If pseudonyms are good enough for superheroes, why can't an artist have one?"

Susan was kidding, but she planted a seed nonetheless. Bobby Ray Dean was the boy with the thick social services file, the castoff, the nobody who belonged nowhere. Roman Velasco had class. With a name like that, life could be a whole lot different.

10

Grace loved the feel of Samuel snuggled against her body, warm and relaxed in sleep. She should put him in the crib, but every minute with him was precious. She didn't want to miss even one. Selah and Ruben sat with her in the living room, quiet, pensive. They'd opened their home when Grace was most vulnerable and made her part of their family. Circumstances were changing rapidly, and Grace knew Selah wanted to keep things as they were. No. That wasn't true. Selah wanted more. She wanted to adopt Samuel, might even feel entitled to him after giving so much.

Ashamed of her unplanned, crisis pregnancy, Grace had kept it secret until she started to show. Her boss of four years, Harvey Bernstein, had recently retired and sold the business, putting her out of work. Her unemployment would run out before the baby was due, and she wouldn't be able to get another job until after the birth. Patrick had emptied her savings account on the way out of their marriage. She didn't know where to turn.

Finally, swallowing her pride, she told her friends after church during their weekly lunch. Shanice looked physically ill. "Oh, Grace, I'm so sorry."

Ashley took Grace's hand. "What are you going to do?"

"She could have an abortion," Nicole said in a matter-of-fact tone, as though that were the most logical way to get out of trouble.

Shanice glared at Nicole. "Sometimes I don't know you, Nicole. What are you thinking?"

Nicole's face reddened. "Fine. Since you have all the answers all the time, what's she going to do?"

"She can go to a pregnancy counseling center and get help. She can have the baby and give it up for adoption." She looked at Grace, tears filling her eyes. "I'll go with you. You're not alone in this, girl."

Grace had known that Shanice would relate to what she was facing more than their other friends would. She said more than once that she wished she could take Grace in and offer a home to both her and the child. But the condo she shared with another woman was just too small for a third roommate.

A nurse at the crisis pregnancy center listened to Grace's circumstances with compassion, not judgment. It took a few weeks, but the lady connected Grace with Selah and Ruben Garcia, candidates for an open adoption. Grace found herself living with a family who loved her and gave her hope for a future. She knew her child would have a loving home with Selah and Ruben and their two teens, a much better life than she could offer. They had all the papers drawn up to be signed as soon as the baby was born.

She had been confident that adoption was the best plan until the day Samuel was born and she held him in her arms. She bonded with him immediately. She didn't know how she was going to make a life for the two of them, but she knew she couldn't give her son to someone else to raise.

Grace was honest with the Garcias about her change of heart. They all knew nothing was final until Grace signed the papers, and she told them she had decided she couldn't do it. Selah understood in the beginning, but it had become clear over the last few months that her attachment to Grace's son had grown stronger.

"Are you sure about this move?" Selah sounded more like a grieving mother than a supportive friend.

"I can't live here forever, Selah. I need to be on my own. I can't stay dependent on you and Ruben."

"You're part of our family. We're not asking

you to go."

Grace held Samuel closer. "As soon as I'm settled, I'll start looking for childcare."

Selah looked crushed. "Why would you give him to a stranger when you have me?" Ruben put his hand on his wife's knee. Selah ignored him. "I've been a mother since Javier and Alicia were born. I've been . . ." She hesitated. "You know Samuel will be happier with me than some stranger. You know that. You can leave him with me during the week and have him on weekends. You can pick him up on Saturday and bring him back on Sunday. He will be safe with us. You want him safe, don't you? You know how much we love him. He's like a baby brother to Javier and Alicia. Please, Grace. Don't give him to someone you barely know."

Grace felt torn.

Ruben looked as worried as Selah, but she wasn't sure it was for the same reason. He'd accepted Grace's decision to keep Samuel, and though Selah said she had, they both knew she still hoped Grace would change her mind again.

Selah had been in the delivery room with Grace, holding her hand and encouraging her through a difficult birth. Selah had been the first one to hold Samuel after he was born. Even after Grace changed her mind about the adoption, Selah wanted her to stay. She insisted Grace stay home and nurse Samuel for the first three months before trying to find a new job.

Seeing Selah's distress, Grace felt ungrateful and selfish. Selah had been as much a mother to Samuel as she had, and more so in the last few weeks since she'd started working for Roman Velasco. She was gone up to twelve hours a day and barely had any time with her son. Last Saturday, he'd cried in her arms and reached out for Selah.

"Samuel thrives here, Grace. He has family. You wanted us to be his family."

Grace felt a sharp pang at Selah's reminder.

Ruben gripped Selah's hand firmly this time. "Selah." His tone was full of disapproval.

Selah's eyes filled with tears.

"We will not hold Grace back. Samuel is her son, not ours. Would you have given up Javier?" Selah started to speak again, but Ruben pressed on. "This is part of a healthy transition, *mi amor.*"

The sooner Grace left, the better. "I have most of what I need in storage to set up the cottage. I've called my church. Volunteers are helping me move on Saturday."

Selah gasped. "Saturday! You don't have a crib." Her eyes glistened. "Where will Sammy sleep? On the floor?"

"I bought a crib yesterday." She had gone back to the thrift store where she'd purchased the gently used car seat as well as a high chair, crib bedding, and toys. "I have what I need."

Selah looked hurt and angry. "You still need time to find childcare."

"I know."

"You need to check references carefully."

"I know." Grace fought tears.

Selah's tone softened. "Please, don't take him like this. Let me take care of him for you."

Ruben looked ready to cry at his wife's anguished appeal. He gave Grace a pleading look. "Perhaps a little more time would help, *chiquita.* You could leave Samuel with Selah while you move in. I can help, too. I'm free on Saturday."

Grace knew she couldn't help with a baby in her arms, and Selah seemed to understand everything was going to change. Maybe a little more time would be good. She didn't want to make a hasty decision about childcare. Selah was right. One couldn't be too careful these days. She'd have to talk to people, check references. Meanwhile Samuel would be safe and happy with people he knew.

Samuel stirred in her arms. Heart aching with indecision, Grace kissed the top of his head. He should be asleep in his crib, but she'd wanted to hold him so she'd be strong when she talked with Selah and Ruben. It hurt to accept the logic of Selah's arguments.

Selah would give him better and more loving care than he would receive in a day care center, even if she found a good one. He would be one among a dozen other children, while here, he would have Selah's complete attention.

That's what worried Grace most. Was she being selfish? Was jealousy driving her? Would leaving Samuel in Selah's care a while longer help her adjust or make things worse? She didn't know, but she couldn't allow her insecurities to overrule good sense. "I'm not trying to hurt you, Selah. This would be temporary." She searched Selah's face, wanting her to understand. "I'll leave Samuel with you during the week. And I'll pay you for childcare."

"I don't want money! I do it for love."

"I know, but it's part of me being independent again. Please. Try to understand. I love you, Selah. You've been like my sister. I appreciate everything you've done for me and for Samuel, but I want my son with me full-time and as soon as possible."

Selah let out a shuddering breath. "Yes. *Yo comprendo.*" She nodded, calm now. "It will all work out as it should."

Grace prayed she was doing the right thing. "I'll pick up Samuel Friday afternoon after work and bring him home Sunday afternoon." She hadn't meant to say *home*. She felt quick tears threaten and blinked them back.

"Yes. Good." Selah spoke gently now. "Taking care of Samuel has always been my pleasure. He is our little angel." Selah held out her arms, ready to take him.

Grace stood. *You can't have him,* she wanted to cry out. *Stop trying to take him from me!* But to say such things was unthinkable after all Selah and Ruben had done for her. "I'm grateful to you both. Truly, I am."

"We know." Ruben understood, even if Selah didn't.

"It's late, and Samuel and I should both be in bed." She put her hand on Selah's shoulder. "Thank you."

Selah looked up at her. She lifted her hand and cupped Samuel's foot.

Grace didn't put Samuel in his crib that night. She kept him snuggled in bed beside her.

Roman watched four men move furniture and boxes into his cottage. Grace had taken a large, wrapped item in earlier and made two more trips with boxes. She carried in a vacuum cleaner and didn't come out again. He imagined her inside, issuing orders like a general. *Put the couch over there, the swivel rocker over here, the coffee table just so.* Everything would have to be in its proper place. She didn't have much, so the process didn't take long. Three of the men left, and the fourth stayed. Mexican, Roman guessed.

When Roman looked again later, Grace and the man were sitting on the low wall overlooking the canyon, talking. He didn't seem in any hurry to leave. Roman thought about how well she'd gotten along with Hector. Maybe Grace had a thing for Hispanics. Roman had been mistaken for one a few times. Then again, he'd been mistaken for a lot of things, especially when he traveled and went through security. His mother had been white. It was anyone's guess what the sperm donor was. Jasper said a DNA test could tell his ancestry. Roman Velasco didn't want to know, but Bobby Ray Dean sometimes thought about it.

Roman concentrated on the transfer sheet. Last one and almost finished. In a few days, a week at the most, he'd be heading south to San Diego. He'd stay whatever time it took to finish the project. Two weeks, maybe less if he pushed himself hard. He'd start where Hector began and work his way across the wall. Hector would do the final protective coat.

Tossing the pen into the tray, Roman flexed his cramping fingers. He'd worked on giraffes dining on thorn trees for hours, struggling with the irony of drawing beasts free in the Serengeti for a hotel housing tourists eager to see captured animals living in enclosures.

He paced, daydreaming. What would it be like to go on a photo safari and take up-close-and-personal shots of lions and wildebeests? He had the money to spend time in Africa. Unfortunately, he couldn't leave this project unfinished.

Maybe he needed another trip somewhere closer.

He went to the bank of windows overlooking Topanga Canyon. Grace and the guy were still talking. For a woman who barely said twenty words a day to him, she sure had plenty to say to that guy. They stood and hugged. The man kissed her cheek. Good friends, then. They headed for the front drive and disappeared. Roman's pulse kicked up a notch when Grace came back alone and entered the cottage.

Maybe he should go over and say hello. It would be the polite thing to do.

Bad idea. They'd already established boundaries: boss and employee, now landlord and tenant.

He scrounged through cabinets and the fridge for something to entice his appetite. He wasn't hungry enough to fix anything. Turning on the sixty-inch wall-mounted television, he channel surfed. Nothing but sports and news, reruns of canceled TV shows and old movies. He turned the set off and stood at the living room windows, thinking about how much Grace liked the view.

He'd seen far better during his travels. Bored and tired, he stretched out on the couch and let his mind drift. Images formed in his imagination. Pulling the black book and pencils from under the couch, he sketched quickly. A woman looked back at him with wide, dark eyes, her lips curved in a Mona Lisa smile. Muttering a curse, he ripped the page out and crumpled it in his hand.

Roman pressed the heels of his hands against his forehead. He was getting another headache. A drive with the windows down would help. He'd kill time walking the beach at Malibu, have a hamburger before he came back. Maybe he'd meet a hot, willing girl. He'd been celibate far too long.

Two hours later, Roman sat on the beach, watching the crash of waves. All he'd done was change scenery, not his mind. He could almost hear Jasper Hawley's voice. *Where are you going this time, Bobby Ray? What are you looking for?*

Roots? Wings? He didn't know. He just needed to get out of the house and away from his next-door neighbor.

It was after two in the morning when he got home from dinner at a seafood restaurant and a long drive up the coast and back. He slid the glass door open. Outside, the stars shone brightly, but he ended up looking over at the cottage instead. The lamps were on inside. Grace must still be organizing the place.

Or maybe she was afraid. No city lights out here.

It had taken time for him to get used to the darkness, too.

11

Bobby Ray, Age 15

The library had halls of books and quiet alcoves. Bobby Ray pulled books and turned pages, making quick sketches of Civil War uniforms and gear. He got so immersed in pictures of Gettysburg, he didn't think about the time until his stomach cramped with hunger. He hadn't had breakfast or lunch. Books still open on the table, Bobby Ray left the library and headed for a hot dog wagon. He bought two hot dogs and ate on the steps of the Civic Auditorium, imagining what he'd paint on the pristine white surfaces of government buildings.

He returned to the library to finish the drawings, then headed for Reaper's party. It would still be going strong.

An ambulance and two police cars with lights flashing were parked in front of Reaper's apartment building. Probably another domestic disturbance. Reaper laughed the other day about a guy getting knifed by his old lady when she caught him coming out of another woman's apartment. Bobby Ray headed for the side of the building, figuring he could go up the fire escape and use the door on the roof to get into the building. As he moved among the curious bystanders, he overheard a man talking. ". . . couple of boys got shot at a party on the third floor . . ."

Bobby Ray stopped. "What'd you say?"

The man looked at him and frowned. "You live in there? I've seen you around."

"I have friends in the building."

"Good thing you weren't with them."

Bobby Ray got a bad feeling in the pit of his stomach. Parties went on all the time in this place. It didn't mean anyone he knew got shot or did the shooting.

Two paramedics brought out a stretcher. Bobby Ray exhaled a curse when he recognized Reaper. He was ashen, unconscious, an IV attached to his arm. Bobby Ray tried to push through, but a cop blocked his way and held up a hand in warning. "Stay back."

"He's a friend of mine!"

"Then you'll want him to get to the hospital."

Reaper didn't look good.

As the ambulance left, sirens blaring, a coroner's van pulled into the vacant space. Bobby Ray waited, feeling sick. When the men finally came out with the gurney, Bobby Ray knew by the size and shape of the body bag that Lardo was inside it. He struggled not to shed the hot tears burning his eyes.

Bobby Ray spent the rest of the night spraying wrath on the walls of the Tenderloin. He emptied his marker and every spray can in his backpack. A cop car rounded the corner and screeched to a halt. Bobby Ray ran. Tires screamed as the squad car backed up and spun. Bobby Ray bolted down the nearest alley and over a wall. Stripping off his gloves, he tossed them into a pile of trash. He heard the siren's *whoop-whoop* and saw flashes of light as he heaved his backpack behind a Dumpster. Not slowing, he cut across the street. Another squad car pulled right in front of him. Bobby Ray's momentum took him over the hood. He hit the pavement hard and lay stunned, gasping for breath.

A cop stood over him. "You okay, kid? Anything broken?"

Bobby Ray managed a laugh. Okay? Broken? He felt betraying tears spill. Humiliated, he pressed the heels of his hands against his eyes. He never cried! The officer told him to stay still; they'd call an ambulance. Groaning, Bobby Ray sat up. Shoving helpful hands away, he stood on wobbly legs. He didn't want an ambulance. *Why were you running, kid? I'm late, and my mama will be worried. Is that so? We'll give you a ride home. Where does your mama live? Have I done anything wrong, Officer? That's what I'm wondering, kid. You want to try a different story? Why were you running?*

Another squad car arrived and parked behind them. An older cop got out, shifted his thick leather belt, and pulled out a heavy Maglite. A younger cop followed. The older man aimed a beam of light straight into Bobby Ray's face. "Gotcha! This boy's been busy tonight."

Bobby Ray winced, but didn't look away. "I don't know what you're talking about."

"Hold out your hands."

Bobby Ray did what he was told, knowing the cop was looking for paint stains on his fingers and clothing. Some taggers didn't have the brains to wear gloves. "I'm clean. You wanna check behind my ears?"

"No need." He asked the other officers which direction Bobby Ray had been running. Their answer pleased him.

Surprised, Bobby Ray found his wrists bound with zip-tie cuffs and himself shoved into the rear of a squad car. He leaned his head back against the seat and swore. The older officer drove while the younger radioed the station. The older officer looked at Bobby Ray in the mirror. "You got messy tonight, Bobby Ray."

Pulse rocketing, Bobby Ray played dumb. "Who's Bobby Ray?"

"Bobby Ray Dean, I've had my eye on you

for a while. I know where you live. I know who your friends are." He looked at the road ahead. "You're lucky you weren't at that party tonight."

"Is that what you think? I'm lucky?"

"And too stupid to know it."

If the officer knew about the party, maybe he knew what happened. "Who did the shooting?"

He didn't get an answer.

Bobby Ray spent the next few days at the juvenile detention center, going through the drill. His caseworker, Ellison Whitcomb, had retired and moved to Florida. The new one, Sam Carter, eventually showed up with Bobby Ray's file. Carter didn't have Whitcomb's cynicism, but he was a realist.

"They're not going to be lenient this time, Bobby Ray."

"You're assuming I'm guilty."

Sam Carter gave him a wry smile. "You want to sit there and tell me you're not?"

Furious, Bobby Ray shoved the chair back and paced. "They haven't got any evidence!"

"They have all they need. This might be a good thing, Bobby Ray."

"A good thing? Tell me how."

"It'll get you out of the Tenderloin."

"What if I don't want to go?"

"I doubt you know what you want. Now the court decides."

Bobby Ray found himself living in temporary lockup with kids older and tougher. He knew how to cover his fear while living in a dormitory with fourteen other roommates. He kept his eyes open and his back to the wall. He barely slept because every sound jarred him awake. He kept his distance, recognizing predators.

A guard brought Bobby Ray to a room furnished with a metal table and two chairs. He expected to see Sam Carter, but a tall, broad-shouldered stranger in a gray suit, blue shirt, and tie stood waiting. He smiled as he extended his hand. "I'm Willard Rush. I'm handling your case." He had a firm grip. Willard Rush glanced at the guard, and the man went out, closing the door quietly behind him. "Sit down, Bobby Ray. We have some serious talking to do."

Clasping his hands on the table, Bobby Ray gave Rush what he hoped was a cool look. He figured the judge had reviewed whatever evidence the cops had and decided it wasn't enough.

"You have a court hearing Thursday next week."

His stomach turned over. A week? "They didn't have anything on me." Rush's expression changed enough to make Bobby Ray forget his fear and get mad. "You think I'm lying?"

"You had paint on your sleeve that matched

the graffiti on eight walls."

"So what? A little paint doesn't prove anything. Maybe I accidentally brushed up against something and got it on me." He leaned forward. "They need more hard evidence than that."

"They'd need more in the adult world, but you're a juvenile. The DA's office took that little bit of paint and ran with it. They're doing what they think best."

Sam Carter had said something similar. Bobby Ray's heart pounded a war beat. "They should be jailing the ones who shot my friends!"

"They'd have to catch them first, and since no one is talking, that will take time." He tilted his head, studying Bobby Ray. "If I had to guess, I'd say the shooter was after Edoardo Gerena, and your friends just happened to be in the right place at the wrong time."

"Who's Edoardo Gerena?"

"The party was in his apartment. You probably know him by his street name, Red Hot. From what I gather, he was in jail. One boy died at the scene." All the time Rush talked, Bobby Ray felt the man studying him closely. Like a germ under a microscope. "Gerena's brother died on the way to the hospital."

The small world Bobby Ray had carved out over the last few months imploded. He tried to sit still and calm, but inside, he roiled in fury and pain.

"I'm just curious, Bobby Ray. Why weren't you at the party?"

Maybe he should have been there. Maybe he could have done something to save his friends. Maybe he could have gotten shot, too. What difference would it have made? "I had other things to do."

"Where were you that day?"

"School."

"After school."

Bobby Ray pushed his fingers through his hair and held his head. He should have gone to the party. He should have been with his friends. "The library."

"That's not what I expected to hear."

Bobby Ray's face went hot. He wished he hadn't answered.

Rush pressed. "What were you doing at the library?"

He just looked at Rush. Let the man think whatever he wanted. He was done talking. Rush asked a few more questions. Bobby Ray didn't say a word. Rush sighed, stacked papers, and put them in his briefcase. He stood and tapped the door. The guard opened it. "He's all yours." Rush walked out, leaving Bobby Ray alone with the guard.

That night, Bobby Ray dreamed of his mother again. He begged her not to leave, but she pushed his hands away and said she'd be back. *I always come back, don't I? Don't hold on to me, baby. I gotta go to work.*

12

Grace overslept Sunday morning, and awakened to her cell phone buzzing on the nightstand. Fumbling for it, she saw Shanice's face on the screen and answered. "What time is it?"

"Where are you? We're at the café. Are you okay?"

"Fine. I'm still in bed. I was up until three."

"I didn't know you had that much stuff to put away."

"I don't. I just couldn't sleep."

"Grace, honey, we have something to tell you. We wanted to tell you in person. Unfortunately, you didn't show up."

She wasn't sure she could survive another of Shanice's ideas.

"What is it?"

"You have a date this coming Wednesday, at seven."

"Are we going to a movie or a Bible study?"

"You and Brian Henley are going to dinner at Lawry's. Nice, huh?"

Groggy, Grace yawned. "I don't know any Brian Henley."

"Well, you will. We signed you onto a Christian mingle site, and when this incredible guy popped up, we responded."

Grace's eyes opened. "What? You'd better be kidding."

"Just listen. He's a widower, a youth pastor with a master's, handsome as all get-out, loves kids. He's perfect for you —"

Wide-awake now, Grace sat up. "I don't need or want a man, Shanice."

"It's too late. The date is made."

"Then you keep it."

"He saw your picture. He'll expect you to show up. He looks like a great guy. It'd be rude to stand him up."

"Tell me how to contact him and I'll —"

"Please, Grace. Do it for me."

Grace knew what was bothering Shanice. "Why are you still feeling guilty? What happened wasn't your fault. It was mine. I've never blamed you, ever."

"I know, honey, but maybe I'll feel better if you go on this date."

"That's blackmail!"

"Not if it turns out the way we're all hoping."

"And if it doesn't, will you promise never to do this to me again?" She waited, but Shanice wasn't one to make a promise lightly. "Shanice?"

"You might be interested to know how many gentlemen responded to your profile."

Grace groaned. "Not really."

"Okay. Okay. You're not fully awake. I caught you at a bad time. But you'll thank us later, I'm sure."

Grace could hear Ashley in the background talking about how cute Brian Henley was. If he was a Brit, Grace wouldn't have to worry. She could send Ashley in her place.

The warm waterfall shower felt so good, she lingered. *Wash all my sins away, Lord. Cleanse my heart and mind from those memories that taunt me. Wash me whiter than snow.* She could have let the water run forever. Grace combed her wet hair and shook it so the soft, natural curls loosened. She still had to make this cottage a home for her and Samuel.

Thankfully, Ruben had put the crib together. She had planned on doing that herself, but he insisted he had the necessary tools and experience. The sheets had tiny red, blue, and yellow airplanes. She set up the Baby Einstein Sea Dreams, hung the Fisher-Price Rainforest mobile, and put the plush lamb that played "Jesus Loves Me" in the corner. Samuel liked blankets with silky edges, and she had bought two, one with blue elephants and the other with yellow-and-orange giraffes. She couldn't wait to have Samuel all to herself for a few days, no Selah eager to snatch the baby away or tend to his needs.

Oh, Lord, I know I'm being selfish, but Samuel is mine. I want more time with my son, not less. I want to be a good mother, even if I can't be with him full-time.

The grocery store in Malibu had what she needed, but the prices were outrageous. She'd shop at Walmart or take Ashley's suggestion to share-shop at Costco. They could split the supplies and the bill and both save money. With all her purchases put away, she opened the door to let in fresh air. Her mind kept buzzing with ideas. She'd need shelving for textbooks. She'd kept every one of them from the classes she had completed, as well as the ones from classes she dropped so she could work full-time to support Patrick. He'd promised she could go back after he graduated.

No point in thinking about all that now. She'd worked hard at ripping out the root of bitterness so she could forgive Patrick.

Forgiving herself was another matter.

Restless, Roman drove down to Malibu again and picked up lunch at the grocery deli. On impulse, he bought an orchid, figuring it would be a nice welcome gesture for his new tenant. He'd given her a full day and a half to settle in. What harm could it be to check on her?

Her front door stood wide-open. Roman

took that as an invitation. He stopped short of stepping over her threshold. Grace didn't even notice him as she sat at a small table, hand holding a thick book open as she wrote in a spiral notebook. He stood watching her for a moment. "Settled in already?"

Startled, she dropped her pen. Recovering quickly, she pushed back her chair and stood. "Sorry. I didn't notice you standing there, Mr. Velasco."

Were her eyes narrowing because of the sunlight or because he was crossing a line? Roman could almost read her mind. *What is he doing here?* It wasn't the usual expression he saw on a woman's face. "You were pretty deep in concentration." He came inside, curious to see what she was doing to his cottage. He did own the place, after all. "Just making sure you aren't repainting the walls."

"I'd ask first."

Of course she would. She looked tense. "Catching the afternoon breeze?"

"I didn't want to run the air-conditioning. I forgot to ask about utilities."

Utilities? Was she that hard up financially? "They're included in the rent."

"Which reminds me." She moved papers aside and picked up a check. "First and last month's rent." She held it out.

"Already planning to move?" He took the check and stuffed it into his front pant pocket.

"It's usually how things work. And a security deposit in case I do repaint the walls." She smiled.

Roman smiled back. "Everything by the book, Ms. Moore." He set the orchid on the table in front of her. "A housewarming present."

She blinked. "Thank you. It's beautiful."

Then why was she staring at it like he'd put a snake on her table? Roman decided not to ask. He wanted a look at her living room. She liked blue, green, pink, and yellow. Everything was cheap chic, warm and cozy. Three pieces of art hung on her wall: *"Be still and know I am God"* in colorful hand lettering, and two prints of men in Arabic dress, one a bearded shepherd carrying a lamb over his shoulders and the other with head bowed, hands clasped in prayer. "Do you have a thing for Middle Eastern men?"

"I have a thing for Jesus."

She said it so simply, without the least hesitation, it caught him off guard. Her brown eyes shone clear until she caught his mood, then became perplexed. Something about the way she tilted her head made his heart give an odd double beat. The feeling passed as quickly as it came. "Your lights were on when I came home last night. It was after two. Everything all right?"

"Just restless. Couldn't sleep. It's very quiet out here. No traffic sounds. Would you like some coffee? It's not fresh."

Was she hoping he'd say no? "Yes. Thanks." She opened a cabinet, displaying a neat row of unmatched mugs. "You've already put all your stuff away." His gaze drifted over her. She looked good in skinny jeans. She was barefoot, her toenails painted pink. Her shirt rode up enough to reveal pale skin. No tats. None that he could see, anyway.

He glanced at her textbook. *Contemporary Clinical Psychology.* Surprised, he gave a slight laugh. "Doing some light reading?"

"It's from a class I had to drop at UCLA." She handed him a mug of steaming coffee.

College girl. "UCLA? That wasn't on your résumé."

"I didn't graduate."

"Didn't like school?"

"Loved it."

"Flunked out?"

"I had to go to work full-time."

Roman lifted the mug and read *Trust in the Lord with all your heart.* He sipped, looking at her over the rim. "Hard-core, aren't you?"

"I have a Dodgers mug, if that would make the coffee taste better. Or the Raiders."

Was she teasing him? He gave her a roguish grin. "I'm more a raider than a dodger." Even her old coffee tasted good. She looked like a teenager with her hair tucked behind her ears. He liked the shape and fullness of her mouth. In truth, he liked everything about her, what

180

little he knew. Neither spoke. Grace sucked in a soft breath. She came around the table, walked out the door, and didn't stop until she reached the wall. She ran her hand along it.

Turning, she looked at him calmly. "It's a beautiful day, isn't it?"

Roman wasn't fooled. She wanted him out of the cottage. Okay. He could take a hint. He sat in the same place her friend had occupied during their long conversation. She didn't seem to have anything to say now.

"Is something worrying you, Grace?" Did she think he was coming on to her? He told himself he was just checking in, like a good landlord. "Everything working? The fridge? The stove? The washer and dryer?" He jerked his chin. "It's only the second time I've been in the place. I didn't even bother to check things out before you moved in."

"My friends did. Everything works perfectly. The fridge and stove anyway. I haven't done any wash yet."

Ms. Moore was rambling, nervous. He felt on firmer ground. "Good."

Clearing her throat, she looked at him. "How is the last transfer coming along?"

He shrugged. "Everyone is always in a hurry." Especially him. He couldn't wait to be done with it. The sooner he got back to work, the sooner he'd be done. He finished the coffee and held out the mug. "You make good coffee." Maybe she'd offer him a second cup. Maybe they could both relax enough to have a real conversation, something unrelated to business.

"You're just hooked on caffeine. Too much isn't good for you."

She didn't want him to linger. "Okay, Mama." Roman stood. "We're all hooked on something." What was her addiction?

"Thank you for the orchid, Roman. That was very thoughtful of you."

He'd never been accused of that before.

Grace backed away. "I'll see you tomorrow morning."

Obviously clinical psychology held more allure than he did. "Turn on your air-conditioning whenever you need it, Grace. It's not wise to leave your door open out here. You're in wild country. You don't want any wily coyotes wandering in."

She laughed. "No. I definitely do not want that." Now over the threshold, she closed the door.

Despite traffic, Grace arrived at Lawry's on time. She recognized Brian Henley from the picture Shanice had forwarded — handsome with sandy-blond hair and blue eyes. He saw her come in and stood, recognizing her from whatever photo her friends had posted. He was a head taller than her and had an athletic frame. Smiling, he extended his hand. "Grace

Moore? I'm Brian Henley. It's a pleasure to meet you." He didn't try to hide his relief. The hostess showed them to a booth. Brian seemed as uncomfortable as she, and she felt odd trying to put a man she hadn't wanted to meet at ease.

"I was told you're a youth pastor."

"Told? Are you saying this wasn't your idea?"

Grace blushed. "Well . . ." Why not be honest? "You seem like a very nice person, Brian, but meeting someone through a website hasn't been on my list of things to do. My friends created my profile and set up this date without me knowing. And they wouldn't give me your contact information so I could call and set the record straight."

Brian grinned. "My youth group did the same thing to me."

"Seriously?"

He nodded. They both laughed.

Brian leaned back. "Well, we could call it an evening right now . . . or see what happens."

She liked his attitude. "We're here. I'll pay my share." She could afford a dinner salad. A pity her friends had suggested such an expensive restaurant.

"The youth group gave me a gift certificate generous enough to pay for two very nice dinners, dessert, and wine."

"I don't drink."

"That makes two of us."

They talked easily. Brian had met his future wife, Charlene, at the Urbana student missions conference when they were still in high school. They discovered they were both headed for Bible college in Wheaton, Illinois. Both worked and went to school, and they married after their sophomore year. While working on his master's, Brian took a position at a megachurch on the outskirts of Chicago. Charlene worked in an after-school day care program. One winter night, less than a mile from home, she hit black ice, spun off the road into a tree.

Brian had tears in his eyes. "It's been four years. I needed to get away from all the familiar places. I put out applications across the country and ended up here in LA. Still a big city, but much smaller church. A challenge. Room to grow."

"How long were you and Charlene married?"

"Six years."

"That's not very long when you love someone as much as you clearly loved your wife."

"No. Not nearly long enough. How about you? Any serious relationships?"

Grace sighed inwardly. *Just tell the truth.* "I'm sorry. I guess my friends left out a few pertinent facts in the profile they created. I'm divorced, and I have a child." When Brian didn't say anything, she figured this one date would be the end of what might have been a promising relationship.

"I'm listening."

She looked up in surprise. How much do you tell someone on a first date? Her story was bleak and embarrassing, enough to expose her stupidity and stubborn foolishness.

"Patrick was a high school football star struggling with algebra, and his coach said I'd make a good tutor. Patrick received better than a passing grade and asked me to the prom. I think that was his way of paying me." She winced. "That sounds terrible."

"Is it true?"

"I don't know. I'd rather believe he liked me as much as I liked him, but my aunt didn't think so." And Aunt Elizabeth was always right about everything. Why hadn't Grace seen the warning signs?

"What about your parents?"

Grace felt Brian studying her. She had to say something. "My parents died when I was seven." She didn't want to talk about the circumstances. "My aunt raised me." Another topic she didn't want to discuss. Aunt Elizabeth had taken Grace into her home out of familial duty, not love. Grace had never met her mother's sister before that. Grace was taken into child protective services the night her parents died and had been placed in foster care until Aunt Elizabeth turned up. In truth, as Grace learned later, her aunt had taken the job at the IRS in order to be as far away from Grace's mother and father as possible. "My friends called me a brainiac, and Patrick was all about sports. And he loved adventure." And other women.

"So how did you two end up together?"

"We both went to UCLA. He had a partial football scholarship."

"And you?"

She didn't want to brag. "Enough to get me through, but Patrick needed to finish school first." She smoothed the napkin on her lap, avoiding Brian's perusal. "We got married partway through freshman year. When he lost his scholarship, it made sense for me to work, so he could concentrate on school." She gave him a bleak smile. "We were going to take turns." She lifted one shoulder. "A few months after he graduated, I came home early and found Patrick in bed with another girl. He said he loved her, packed up, and left."

Brian winced. "Painful."

Not as painful as it should have been. She'd been hurt, angry, and most telling, relieved. Their last year together had been difficult. She'd seen the truth. "I hated myself more than Patrick. I saw plenty of warning signs, but chose to ignore them. I tried to make it work. What is the old saying about fools rushing in?"

"And you have a child."

Grace hesitated, understanding the assumption Brian was making. She wasn't ready to confess more sins. "Yes. A son. Samuel. He's five months old and the love of my life." Had he noticed her blush? Brian seemed to sense something, but didn't press.

"Charlene and I wanted children. That's how I ended up in youth ministry. I love kids." A good sign, Grace thought, then admonished herself. Brian talked about the program he'd started and ways he was trying to get the older and younger generations together. He joked about how too many people thought teenagers were out of control, beyond redemption, and to be avoided at all cost. He laughed. "Nothing's changed. Plato bemoaned the younger generation." He admitted teens could be perplexing and frustrating, especially the girls.

Grace didn't have to wonder why. "I can imagine how many develop crushes on you." A handsome, charismatic, young widower? "You'd better be careful, Pastor Brian."

"Believe me, I am careful. I make sure I'm never alone with a girl, and I have plenty of adult supervision at our youth functions. A pastor can't be too careful these days. It doesn't take much to destroy a man's reputation."

Or a woman's.

They talked over prime rib dinners. Grace

ordered crème brûlée. Brian had warm chocolate fantasy cake. They lingered over coffee. Grace couldn't remember ever having felt so comfortable with a man. Brian slipped the gift certificate and a twenty-dollar bill into the leather folder for the waiter.

Grace noticed another couple leaving. "I think they came in after we did." She glanced at her phone to check the time. "Oh, my." She and Brian had been talking for over two hours.

They left the booth and went outside. Brian held her sweater for her. They walked to her car, and he opened her door. "How far do you have to drive?"

"I'll be home by eleven. It's been a real pleasure meeting you, Brian. Thank you for a wonderful evening." His hand was warm and firm.

"The kids will want to know how it went tonight. I'll be telling them the evening far exceeded my expectations."

"My friends will be asking the same questions, and I'll tell them the same thing."

Brian grinned. "In that case, would you like to join me and twenty-odd teenagers for a beach party Saturday after next?"

"Were you setting me up?" Grace laughed. "Sounds like fun, but only if I can bring Samuel."

"Absolutely. Can't wait to meet him."

On the drive home, Grace heard her phone

signal an incoming text. She read it after she had parked. Shanice, of course. Call me when you get in. I want to know details.

Shanice, a night owl, answered on the second ring. "Good time?"

"It turned out to be a very nice evening." Grace kept her tone bland.

"Oh." Shanice sounded disappointed, then brightened. "Nice enough to see him again?"

"Yes."

"Fantastic! Tell me everything."

"You'll have to wait until Sunday." Grace said good night and ended the call.

Roman used a paint roller on the back wall of his studio before Grace showed up Monday morning. He didn't want to see the look on her face if she discovered where his real passion in art lay. When she came in with his mug of coffee, the scent of fresh paint still hung heavily in the air. She looked at the back wall. "You painted the wall again." She grimaced. "What do you call that color? Mud?"

"Good description. It's a little of this and that all poured into the same can, and that's what you get." He hesitated, then added, "Cities use it to buff graffiti."

"I hope that's not your idea of redecorating."

He dabbed more red on the one remaining painting. Talia had picked up the other two.

"I finished the transfer. I leave for San Diego this afternoon. I'll be gone a week, at least. Maybe two." Less if he worked long hours. If he ran short of any supplies, he could order what he needed and have it delivered. "I'll finish this painting before I go. Talia can come and get it in a couple days."

"Is there anything in particular you want me to do here while you're gone?"

Her gaze kept drifting to that blasted wall still marred by faint outlines of the darker colors and shapes beneath. Was she trying to figure out what he'd painted? He made a downward stroke of red, lifted the brush away, and set his palette aside. "Why don't you shop for furniture? Jasper Hawley said he wanted a bed to sleep in the next time he comes to visit."

She kept looking at the wall, tilting her head slightly. "I need to know your taste."

"Anything but shabby chic or French country."

She laughed. "I'll have you know I paid good money for my furnishings. Only the best of what the Salvation Army had to offer."

"You won't need to be that frugal on my dime."

"What about bedding?"

"That, too. Pillows to sleep on."

"How about decorative pillows?"

"Like the five you have on your couch?"

She looked surprised. "You counted them?"

"I remember what I see. You also have one on your swivel rocker, and I'm guessing a dozen more on your bed." He wiped his hands on an oily cloth and decided he'd better change the subject. "Buy something that never goes out of style."

He'd been striving for quality since his beginning in the Tenderloin, where it was scarce as money.

"How much are you willing to spend?"

"My bedroom set cost forty grand."

"What?" Grace gasped. "Where do you find furniture that expensive?"

"I hired an interior decorator."

"Oh. Why don't I call her? She'll know what suits you better than I do."

"What makes you think it was a she? And maybe I want something different this time." Grace was about as different as a girl could be from those he'd known up to now. "Something a little more . . . I don't know. Classy. Use your instincts."

"You might be sorry."

"It's only furniture, Grace."

She looked at the wall one last time. "If you leave the ladder in here, I can repaint that wall a nice eggshell white."

"It'd take more than one coat, and what's the point?"

"It'd be a nice clean canvas so you can start fresh."

Start fresh. If only he could.

13

With Roman in San Diego, the big house felt empty, the polished gray French oak floors echoing Grace's every footstep. She spent the first day painting the studio wall, and then called Selah. "I'll pick Samuel up after work. He can stay with me this week."

Selah said he would be too much for her on the job. Grace should leave him with her and keep to the plan for weekends only. Grace insisted she could manage. Selah asked if she had permission. Grace lied and said of course. She hadn't asked, but why would Roman care, as long as the work got done? When he returned, she might ask if he minded a child in the house.

Selah didn't think it was a good idea. "Samuel has an appointment with the pediatrician on Thursday. You would have to take time off for that, and you know how fussy he is after a shot. He always runs a fever. It'll be much better for him to stay here with me."

Grace bristled. Why did it have to be a tug-of-war? "I want more time with my son, Selah."

"I know you do, *chiquita,* but you must think of what's best for him. Samuel will be bouncing back and forth enough as it is, staying with you on weekends. He needs continuity. You don't want him to feel like a yo-yo, do you?"

Grace wanted to insist, but she felt selfish for pressing. Selah was probably right. Samuel might not be content entertaining himself in a playpen in her office. She wouldn't be able to put duty aside to play with him whenever he or she wanted. Selah would be able to see to his every need. "I suppose you're right."

"Everything in good time, *chiquí.* He's doing so well. Everything will work out just as it should." Selah's mantra — and true enough.

Grace went shopping for guest room furniture and bedding and didn't spend anything close to forty thousand dollars. By the time Roman returned, all would be in place, including the few touches she had added to make the room more welcoming. Back at the house, she checked the office voice mail and found a message from Roman. "Where are you? Call me." He sounded irritated and repeated his cell phone number twice. "Call me!" She added it to her contacts, but called him back on the office line. He didn't even give her a chance to say hi.

"Why didn't you answer the phone?"

"I've been shopping for bedroom furniture."

"Oh."

"I just got back. Your guest room will be furnished by the end of the week. Stickley Whitehall." Hopefully that information made it clear she hadn't been sunning herself on a beach in Malibu.

"Whatever that is." He sounded calmer. "Am I going to like it?"

"I don't know, but your guests will be very comfortable."

"Guest. Singular. Jasper. What about sheets, blankets — ?"

"Purchased. Jasper will have two pillows from which to choose. I'll make the bed as soon as everything arrives." She told him how much, and hoped he was a man of his word and wouldn't yell at her. "It's the kind of furniture that will grow in value."

"I'm sure it's perfect."

He sounded distracted. Did he have something else on his mind? "I have some messages for you." One from his financial adviser, another from a Realtor who had a buyer if he was interested in selling. Roman told her to tell the financial adviser he'd be in touch after the art show, and he wasn't ready to sell.

Grace gave a soft laugh. "I'm glad to hear that. I just moved in."

"Oh?" He laughed low. "Are you sleeping

in my bed?"

"I meant the cottage, of course." At least he was in a better mood. "Do you have anything else you want me to do around here other than the usual? Anything that doesn't involve entering your bedroom or studio? I did repaint your wall, by the way. You didn't say I couldn't." When he was silent, she wondered if she'd overstepped. "I hope that's all right."

"Just thinking. You could deliver the last painting instead of having Talia pick it up."

"I've heard Laguna Beach is a lovely town."

"You've never been there?"

"Nope. All I've ever seen is what's between Fresno and Los Angeles. Now I can add Topanga Canyon, Burbank, and the supermarket at Malibu." She hadn't had the money or time to travel. "Someday I'll make it to Disneyland." With Samuel.

"You've lived a sheltered life, haven't you? Well, here's your big opportunity if you want to hand-deliver the piece. Which reminds me. I need your cell phone number."

Grace dispensed it without hesitation.

"When I call, pick up."

"Yes, boss." As soon as Roman hung up, she downloaded a suitable ringtone, then called Talia to set a time to meet at the gallery the next day.

Talia Reisner didn't look anything like the

hard-edged businesswoman Grace expected. Dressed in a tiered, multicolored skirt and peasant blouse with a chunky turquoise-and-red coral necklace, her mass of curling red-and-gray hair pulled up in a loose chignon and held by Japanese hairpins, she looked like an aging love child from Haight-Ashbury.

"Grace Moore! It's nice to finally meet you in person." Talia ignored the extended hand and hugged Grace. "Did you know there was a movie star by the same name? Grace Moore was around long before you were born and could sing like a nightingale. Where's the painting?"

Grace opened the trunk of her car. Talia reached in and carefully extracted Roman's most recent painting. "Oh, look what the boy has done this time."

The boy again. Grace couldn't help but laugh. She closed the empty trunk and followed Talia inside.

The gallery had several showrooms with a variety of paintings, not walls laden with modern art as Grace had imagined. She paused to admire an oil of an elegant Renaissance vase filled with purple lilacs that looked so real she could almost breathe in the scent. She liked another of blue herons among reeds. A display pedestal showed off a bronze whale and calf; another, a pod of six dolphins. A large pottery platter looked like a star-studded night sky. Grace leaned in and read the price. "Oh, my!"

"We go for the gusto."

"Everything in here costs more than I'll ever make in a year."

Talia carefully placed Roman's painting against a wall. "So? What do you think of it?"

"I'm hardly one to ask."

"Because you know what you like, and it's not modern art." She gave Grace a sly smile. "I'll tell you a secret. I wasn't wild about Roman's work in the beginning either." Talia stood back and studied the painting as she talked. "He came in here with a chip on his shoulder the size of a boulder. He'd been up and down the row, and no one would even look at what he had in his car." She laughed. "He was ticked off. Do you know what he said to me? 'Just take a look. If it's no good, I'm out the door.' In much more colorful language, of course." Talia tilted her head. "I know exactly what kind of frame this one needs." She picked up the painting and moved it into her office.

Grace followed. "What changed your mind?"

"Nothing ventured, nothing gained, as they say. And it was a very slow day. I told him to bring in his best. He lined up a couple of paintings and wandered off while I studied them. I was going to say sorry, but then a customer came in. I can tell a serious buyer when I see one. He went through the gallery on a mission and stopped at Roman's paintings. He wanted to buy one on the spot. I told him I hadn't put a price on it yet. When he handed me his card, I knew I had something special. Roman had caught the attention of a curator from one of the finest modern art museums in the country. He was in Laguna Beach on holiday, just for the day. Talk about coincidence. He bought Roman's first piece. For his private collection. An investment, he called it."

Grace looked at the painting again. "Clearly, I don't appreciate art."

"It's a matter of taste, but some people have an eye for new trends. Roman knows what he's doing."

Roman's mural impressed Grace far more than the modern art he set up on easels like an assembly line. The transfers anyway. She might never see the actual mural in San Diego. "This piece is so different from his other work."

"His murals, you mean." Talia looked mischievous. "He did one for a friend of mine. An Italian Riviera scene — columns, bougainvillea, urns, and nymphs pouring water from pitchers. Roman has a wicked sense of humor. It took Leo six months to discover the phallic symbol. Several guests noticed before he did and had wagers on how long it would take him to spot it."

"What happened when he did?"

"Leo's a good sport. He laughed. He told me recently he gets a kick out of watching people's expressions when they spot the hidden picture. It's very cleverly done, I must say. He never figured out that Roman was calling him a nasty name, of course. Men like Leo never do." She shook her head. "Roman has more gifts than he knows what to do with, but he hasn't found himself yet. All he cared about when he came into my gallery was getting the paintings on a wall and seeing if they'd sell. I told him a real artist doesn't care what people think. He said if Michelangelo could prostitute himself, so could he. I told him he either believed in what he was doing or he didn't. He said he didn't believe in anything."

That saddened Grace. She had noticed the restlessness in her employer, as though even the best of what he did brought no sense of accomplishment or satisfaction. He worked hard but never looked content.

"There was something about him," Talia went on, "aside from how good-looking he is." Her mouth tipped in a worldly smile. "Of course, I put his picture on every brochure. His face brings in the women, ones with money or with husbands who have money. The name Roman Velasco has a nice ring to it, too, don't you think? Oh, so foreign and mysterious."

Grace caught her meaning. "You don't

think that's his real name?"

"Do you? Whatever mix he is, I don't think he has a drop of Italian blood. Indian, perhaps; Arab, possibly. Black. Not that it matters. He's not just beautiful. He's interesting. Wouldn't you say?"

"I keep my distance."

"Probably wise."

Why would Roman make up a name? Did he have something to hide? She pushed curiosity away. Whatever his reasons, it wasn't her business.

Grace accepted Talia's invitation to lunch. The waves glistened in the sunlight, seagulls rising and dipping on the wind. Talia talked about art, customers, travels. Roman's ringtone came on: Elvis Presley singing "Big Boss Man."

"Roman." Talia laughed as Grace dug for her phone. "Yes, boss?" She grinned at Talia.

"Are you going to Laguna Beach today?"

"I'm in Laguna Beach right now. The painting has been safely delivered. Talia and I are just finishing lunch. I'll be heading back soon."

"You're halfway to San Diego. Why don't you come down?"

Grace froze. He must be joking! Talia's laughter stopped, and she watched Grace. Embarrassed, Grace looked out at the sea. "It's after two. It'd take me hours to get back."

"Spend the night."

"What?" Her pulse shot up. "No!"

His tone dropped. "I'm not asking you to spend it in my room, Grace." He sounded amused. She felt the blush fill her cheeks. Talia noticed, too, and then he made it worse. "I can arrange for you to have a nice mini suite."

Annoyed, she dumped caution. "No, thank you."

"Don't you want to see the mural?"

"Another time."

"I won't be here after it's done."

"I know."

"Wow. That was cold." He didn't sound particularly upset.

"You asked for it." Her own emotions were another matter. "Did you have an errand you wanted me to run?" She tried to keep her tone neutral, so he wouldn't guess what his teasing had managed to do.

"No." He ended the call.

Grace gave a soft gasp at the abruptness and stared at her phone. Shaking her head, she tucked the phone away.

"The boy can be exasperating, can't he?" Talia had a speculative gleam in her eyes.

More than Grace wanted to admit.

Roman didn't call Grace again. He caught himself watching the clock every afternoon around three, usually minutes before she called him. She went over his messages and whatever mail had come in. She asked how the work was going, but he couldn't tell if she was really interested or just being polite.

Roman eliminated the lion eating the baby giraffe before Hector arrived to start the final protective coat. People stood around, watching them finish the work. The wall looked impressive. It was the best work he'd done.

Clearing supplies and tarps, he wondered why he felt vaguely disappointed, as though he'd failed to include something essential.

"You don't look happy, *señor.*" Hector spoke in accented English. He'd been improving greatly over the last few weeks, and Roman felt a twinge of jealousy.

"Is Grace tutoring you in English?"

Hector grinned and raised his brows. "No. I met a girl. On the beach. *Muy bonita.* She teach me English. I teach her Spanish."

Roman could tell by Hector's expression that the two had jumped over more than language barriers. "Sounds like a nice arrangement."

Hector pulled out his phone and showed off a selfie. The girl, a plump, sunburned redhead, looked smitten with her Latino Romeo. Hector looked victorious with his arm around her.

He pocketed the phone. "Is Grace coming down?"

"Isn't one girl enough?"

Hector laughed. "To see the mural, *jefe.*"

"I don't know." Roman wasn't about to admit he'd invited her and she'd said no. He caught Hector looking at him and stared back. "What?"

Hector nodded toward the reception desk, where a man was pointing him out to a middle-aged couple.

Roman faced Hector. "Let's go have dinner. I don't feel like playing nice with strangers."

They got a booth in a nice restaurant down the street. Hector spent most of the time texting with his girlfriend. Conversation had never been easy with Hector, but even a stilted conversation would have been nice. Whatever she said made Hector decide to head back to Los Angeles rather than spend the night at the five-star hotel in San Diego. Roman waved him off and sat alone and had a brandy.

It was a little after eight when he got back to his hotel suite. He stood at the windows, feeling adrift. Grace hadn't called today. Good excuse to call her. He took out his phone and tapped her number.

It took five rings before her voice mail kicked in. She didn't offer the usual pleasantries or give her name, just instructions to leave a message. She didn't even say she'd get back to whoever called. Roman didn't leave a message. It was a Friday night and well past five o'clock. Why should she answer?

The heaviness increased in his chest. Too much steak, too much alcohol. His jaw ached. A dentist said he must grind his teeth in his sleep and recommended a custom mouth guard. That and less stress in his life. He felt a little off, and not just because he'd had a few drinks.

Why should he be stressed? He had everything everyone else wanted.

Stretching out on his bed, he tried to sleep. He was edgy, in need of something. He could go back to his old habits. Go to a club, hook up with a girl. But the emptiness always came back later. The inner tension never went away.

He turned on the television and rented a movie violent enough to distract him. His arm ached from reaching up and doing the fine work every day for the last several days. He rubbed the muscles. Another drink might help. He opened the minibar and took out three shot bottles of Scotch.

Roman relaxed after the third drink. Only the heaviness remained. He called Grace again. She answered on the second ring. "What?" She sounded groggy and annoyed.

"Are you in bed?

She let out her breath sharply. "No. I'm singing in a karaoke bar. What do you think?"

"Man, you're grumpy." Roman craned his neck to look at the clock on the nightstand. "What time is it?"

"Please tell me you didn't call to ask for the time. It's after midnight. Are you in a movie theater?"

"I'm in my room watching a movie. I doubt it's one you'd like." He shut it off.

"What do you want, Roman?"

You. The thought caught him by surprise. Thankfully, he hadn't said it aloud. Oh, he could tell her what he wanted, but she was too far away to do anything about it, and she wouldn't anyway.

"Are you all right?"

When had the sound of her voice started doing things to his body? "I think I had too much to drink tonight."

"I can tell."

"How?"

"You don't sound like yourself."

That sobered him. How did he sound? Vulnerable? Clearing his throat, he sat up and rubbed his face. "You didn't call me with an update."

"I told you I wouldn't bother you unless it was necessary. It was a quiet day. There was no reason to call."

What if he wanted to be bothered? "The mural is done." He spoke carefully, not wanting to sound as drunk as he now realized he was. "Hector finished the protective coat tonight. He went home. He's got a girlfriend."

"I know."

"You met her?" How often did she and

Hector talk, and why should that annoy him?

"Not yet. He showed me her picture. She looks nice."

Roman could hear Grace moving around and hoped she was making herself comfortable. He didn't want to end the conversation yet.

"Congratulations on finishing the mural. I guess that's why you've been celebrating."

Celebrating? Was that what she thought? The longer she worked for him, the more he wanted to know about her. There was something about Grace Moore that had caught his attention right from day one. "Actually, I just felt like getting drunk in my room." He realized how pathetic he sounded. What a loser! *Just shut up, Roman, before you say something even more stupid.*

"I'm sorry, Roman."

"Sorry about what?"

"I don't know. That you're alone after you've finished something people are going to enjoy for years to come. You have every reason in the world to be happy and proud of what you've accomplished, and you're not." She didn't say anything for a few seconds. "I've never known anyone who needed the Lord more than you do."

"The Lord?"

"Jesus."

Roman felt the energy seeping out of him, like air from a punctured tire. He thought of

206

the sign in the Tenderloin, right across the street from the flat where he and his mother lived. "Jesus saves," Roman said sardonically. "I used to sit in a window at night and ask Him to save my mother. He didn't do squat."

"Do you want to talk, Roman?"

He figured he'd already said too much. He knew he'd said more than he ever intended. Tapping End Call, he tossed the phone onto the nightstand.

14

Grace, Age 15

Grace started working at McDonald's as soon as she was old enough to get a permit. She worked while friends came and went. They'd say hi, order hamburgers, fries, and sodas, and say bye. Or they'd sit at a table together, talking and laughing while she was busy behind the counter.

Salim Hadad, her supervisor, tried to schedule her for Sunday shifts. "I can't, Mr. Hadad. I go to church with my aunt." He said it was good a teenager took religion seriously, even if she was a Christian.

Mr. Hadad said she was his best worker. If she were older, he'd make her a manager. She never stood around idle, even at quiet times when no cars were in the drive-through, no customers at the counter. She washed tables, swept floors, cleaned grills, scoured the women's bathroom, and restocked toilet paper and towels without being asked. She cleaned milk shake, soda, and coffee machines, refilled napkin and straw dispensers, anything to keep busy during her shift. Salim told her she could study, but she said her conscience wouldn't allow it. "You're not paying me to do my homework."

Today Salim was rushing around, grumbling about a worker who hadn't shown up. He grew more frustrated when two others couldn't seem to do anything without bumping into each other. Grace remembered how overwhelmed she had felt the first few days until she caught on to the routine. She delivered a tray of Happy Meals to a lady with half a dozen girls in soccer uniforms. Filling drinks, she had the uncanny feeling of being watched.

When the woman and girls left, Grace stood ready to take the next order.

Patrick Moore stepped forward. Her stomach fluttered, and her heart picked up speed. He'd moved from Colorado at the beginning of the year and made the varsity football team. It wasn't long before he became the star quarterback. Every girl in school had a crush on the blond, blue-eyed hunk with the ski-slope tan. Even the guys liked him. "Hi." Patrick's smile made her blush as he looked at her name tag. "Grace . . ." Stammering, she asked for his order. His smile broadened into a teasing grin, flushing her face hotter.

"Two Big Macs, two large fries, and a large soda. For here."

Grace punched in the order. He gave her a twenty, and she made change. She put the food on a tray. Maybe he had a girl with him. She resisted the urge to see who it was. Lindsay? She was head cheerleader, and they'd been a couple for a while. Grace set the tray on the counter. Patrick seemed in no hurry to take it. "Nice to see you, Grace."

She didn't know what to say. He picked up the tray and took a step before turning around. "When do you get off?"

Her mind went blank for a moment. "Six."

"I'll give you a ride home."

"I have a bike."

"I have a bike rack."

Patrick took a booth where he had a straight-shot view of her at the counter. Grace didn't even notice an older gentleman standing in front of her until he spoke. "Ah, Cupid does his dirty work again." He chuckled. "I'll have a Whopper."

She smiled. "You'll have to go down the street to Burger King."

Patrick Moore read a graphic novel while he waited. When Grace was ready to go, he took her backpack and carried it. She felt small walking beside him. He snapped her bike into a rack on his sea-mist Buick Regal. "Nice car." Did he think her shallow for noticing?

"I'd rather have a Jeep Cherokee with a ski rack on top. This baby is three years old and

210

has eighty thousand miles on it. My dad did a lot of traveling in his last job." He opened the door for her. She slipped in and strapped on her seat belt. When he got into the driver's seat, he looked at her. "My dad signed it over to me on my sixteenth birthday."

"Nice present."

"It's got some kick."

Patrick didn't clench the steering wheel like Aunt Elizabeth. His hands were relaxed. He drove six blocks and gave her a sideways smile. "You'll have to tell me where you live."

If her face got any hotter, she'd set the car on fire. "I guess it is hard to read minds." She gave directions rather than the address. She asked about Colorado. He shared his life story: born in Fort Collins, grew up in the Springs, loved to ski and snowboard; Fresno took getting used to after the Rocky Mountains. Fortunately, it was only a few hours' drive to the coast. He wanted to learn how to surf. "What about you?"

What could she say that wouldn't bore him? "Not much to tell. My parents died when I was seven. My aunt took me in. I go to school. I study. I work at McDonald's. I go to church every Sunday. That's my life." She was far more interested in his. "Are you playing baseball this year?" She didn't want to say she knew he'd played football and basketball, too.

"Yeah." He laughed. "I love sports. Playing

them and watching them."

"Live games or TV?"

"Both." He gave her a quick, smiling glance. "How about you?"

"I played soccer in grade school. I wasn't very good at it." She'd never had time to watch much television, and the last thing Aunt Elizabeth would be interested in was a sports program. "Turn right at the next intersection."

Patrick pulled up in front of the house just as Aunt Elizabeth turned in to the driveway.

"Would you like to meet my aunt?" It wasn't until the words escaped that she realized introducing a boy to her aunt might sound more serious to him than giving her a ride home and dropping her off.

"Sure. Sit tight." He got out, retrieved her backpack from the backseat, and came around to open her door. She held the pack while he unlocked her bike and set it on the sidewalk.

Aunt Elizabeth stood just outside the garage, watching and waiting.

Grace made introductions. "Patrick is a student at Fresno High, Aunt Elizabeth. He moved here from Colorado. He gave me a ride home from work." Grace couldn't seem to stop herself.

"I gathered he gave you a ride home."

Embarrassed, Grace took hold of her bike. Aunt Elizabeth smiled tightly as she shook hands with Patrick. "It's nice to meet you, Patrick." She drew back, a faint frown forming. "Moore. Colorado. Are you any relation to Byron Moore?"

"Yeah. He's my father. You know him?"

"We work in the same building."

"Small world."

"Indeed." An arctic wind had blown in. "Well, thank you for bringing Grace home safely." She gave Grace a pointed look. "You have things to do."

What had just happened? Grace thanked Patrick for the ride and watched him drive away. She wheeled her bicycle into the garage as her aunt took a bag of groceries from the backseat of her car. Her face was rigid. "What's wrong?" What had she done now to annoy her aunt?

"Nothing." Aunt Elizabeth hit the button to close the garage door as she went through the door to the kitchen. She set the bag of groceries on the counter. The chicken she'd put in the Crock-Pot smelled ready to eat. "I'm going to change my clothes." She walked past Grace. "Set the table."

When they sat down to dinner, Aunt Elizabeth said grace and snapped her napkin. Grace knew something was on her mind. "Did I do something wrong?"

"Patrick looks like his father." She raised her head, her mouth tight. "Concentrate on school."

■ ■ ■ ■

Grace opened her locker, switched out her textbooks. When she closed it, she turned and bumped into Patrick Moore. Startled, she took a step back, blushing as he grinned at her. "I'll walk you to class." Everyone looked at them as they went down the hallway. Grace could imagine what they were thinking. *What's Patrick Moore doing with her?* When she entered class, she made her way to her desk and sat dazed.

Word spread fast. Crystal caught up with her at lunch and wanted to know how long Grace had been going out with Patrick. Grace said she wasn't. "Yeah, right. Come on! Tell me everything!" Grace insisted there was nothing to tell. Crystal snorted. "I heard he dropped you off after your shift at Mickey D's."

Gasping, Grace felt her face go hot. "Who told you that?"

"Someone who saw you."

High school gossip moved faster than a mudslide, and Grace was mortified to find herself in the middle of it. She refused to answer Crystal's question, but the girl was a bulldog. "If there's nothing to tell, why are you blushing? Have you had sex with him yet?"

Yet? "He gave me a ride home. That's all.

He was being nice. It's not like anything happened." She headed for civics. Crystal fell into step beside her and gave her the scoop on Patrick Moore, whether Grace wanted to hear it or not. He took Lindsay to homecoming. Remember? Well, they went all the way. Then he dropped her like a hot rock and went out with Kimberly. He wasn't a make-out artist or a kiss-and-tell guy, but girls talk. Grace had better be careful. Frustrated, Grace finally stopped. "Why are you telling me all this?"

"Because he was asking about you in the boys' locker room!"

"How would you know that?"

"Nathan told me."

Grace didn't want to grab on to false hope regarding Patrick Moore. And she did very well telling herself that, until he showed up at McDonald's again on Saturday. He brought his homework with him this time. "I hear you're good at algebra." She helped him on her breaks. He gave her another ride home. He talked about his dreams for a scholarship. She asked where he wanted to go to college. UC Santa Cruz, but his dad said it was a party school. Patrick laughed. His dad wanted him to go to UC Berkeley, but Patrick shook his head. "I'm not that smart." Grace gobbled up every word he said all the way to the front door of her aunt's house, and then he surprised her again. "Can I call you?"

215

"Sure."

He handed her a fancy phone. "Here. Give me your number."

She tapped in her aunt's phone number and handed it back to him. He smiled as he tucked it into his pocket, just over his heart.

He called a couple nights later, but Aunt Elizabeth answered the phone before Grace could reach it. She gave Grace an annoyed look. "I'm sorry, Patrick, but Grace can't talk right now. She's doing homework." Grace held out her hand with a pleading look, and her aunt turned her back. "You can see her tomorrow at school." She hung up.

Grace wanted to cry. "Why did you do that?"

"Because I thought it best. You're fifteen, and —"

"He just wanted to talk!"

"How do you know what that boy wants?" She looked exasperated.

"Every girl in school would die to have Patrick Moore call!"

"Is that all you care about? How popular he is?"

"No! He's nice! I like him! He's smart, too."

"Oh, I'm sure he's smart. It remains to be seen how he employs his intelligence." Her eyes darkened. "Don't look at me like that. I'm not trying to ruin your life. I'm trying to teach you some common sense. Don't base decisions on teenage hormones. Your mother did, and look what happened to her."

Grace felt like she'd been punched in the stomach. "Nothing I do will ever be good enough for you." Fighting tears, she pushed back the kitchen chair, gathered her books, and fled to her bedroom. She sat against the headboard and pressed the heels of her hands against her eyes. It didn't stop the tears, but she could think again.

Mrs. Spenser, her Sunday school teacher, always said to pray when things got bad. Wiping her face, Grace poured her heart out. *Is she ever going to forgive me for what happened to my mother?*

The answer came like an arm around her shoulders and a gentle whisper. What troubled Aunt Elizabeth wasn't Grace's fault. *Be still, and wait. I love you and I am here. I am always here.* Wiping away the tears, she picked up her civics textbook and focused on what she had to get done.

Patrick Moore showed up at her locker the next morning. Later that afternoon, he appeared at McDonald's. "Take a look." He grinned as he handed over his algebra worksheet. He'd gotten 100 percent and a note from Mr. Edersheim: *Good job!* Patrick laughed, triumphant. "You're a better teacher than he is." He had another assignment. Was she willing to help him again?

A tiny warning bell went off inside Grace's

head. Was algebra Patrick's only reason for seeking her out? Or was algebra an excuse because he really liked her?

Once Patrick fixed his attention on Grace, everyone at school considered them a couple. He walked her to class and sat with her at lunch. They were often seen together in the library, bent over textbooks and talking in low whispers. Grace had always had the reputation of nice-girl-with-a-brain, but as Patrick's grades went up, he was seen as more than a handsome jock. Girls still pursued him, but he didn't do anything about it. Nothing that Grace ever heard, anyway.

When Grace invited Patrick to church, he always had something else going on. He made it to Good Friday services and held her hand in the dim candlelight until Aunt Elizabeth gave them a fierce look. He squeezed her hand and let go. When Patrick asked her to junior prom, she didn't think Aunt Elizabeth would let her go. But her aunt surprised them both: "You can take her if you have her home by eleven." He seemed about to argue about the curfew, but one look at Grace silenced him. Aunt Elizabeth told Grace later she'd have to pay for her own dress, and it couldn't come out of her college savings account. Grace found a green gown for ten dollars at the Salvation Army thrift store and added a pair of rhinestone earrings she'd bought for two dollars.

Patrick looked like a model in his tuxedo, and he knew how to dance. He held her close and made it easy for her to follow his lead. She felt little tremors every time their bodies brushed against each other.

He'd never kissed her, but that night in the car he did. "I like it that you've never been kissed by anyone but me." Blushing, she asked him how he knew. "The way you keep your lips pressed tight together." He leaned in. "Let me teach you a few things." Grace put her hand against his chest. A shiver of alarm went through her when she felt how hard his heart was pounding and how warm he was. He drew back, studying her. "Okay." He started the Regal. "You're right. We don't want to go down the road everyone else is on."

She didn't know if he was disappointed or relieved.

When summer break came, Patrick flew to Colorado Springs. He called her twice the first week. He was staying with friends and having a great time. He didn't know when he'd be back. She didn't hear from him again. In mid-July, he walked into McDonald's looking tan and happy. Sorry he hadn't called, but he'd been on a camping trip in the Rocky Mountains. No cell reception up there. "We had a blast! I'll tell you all about it when you get off work." He took it for granted she'd been waiting for him all these weeks. Of course she had.

Compared to Patrick's, her life was dull routine. She loved hearing about his close encounter with a bear and how many fish he caught in a mountain stream and how they tasted after being cooked over an open fire. She drank in his stories of how he had to help rescue one of his buddies by rappelling down a mountainside. The only things she had to talk about were James Agee's *A Death in the Family*, Willa Cather's *My Ántonia*, Joseph Heller's *Catch-22*, and four or five other books she'd read from the college-prep list. She could tell the moment Patrick lost interest and asked him more questions. He could have talked for hours about the wilds of Colorado.

Senior year brought changes in their relationship. They spent more time studying than going out. They both needed scholarships. Patrick put his energy into football and dropped basketball. "I'm not tall enough to make it on a college team." Grace maintained a 4.0 GPA, but her aunt insisted Grace needed more outside activities and community service for university applications. Grace wondered if her aunt was intent on filling every waking hour so she would have no time to be with Patrick. Grace dropped ten hours at McDonald's to make sure that didn't happen, and then volunteered at the local library literacy program. She took on the third-grade Sunday school class and spent Sunday afternoons at a local convalescent hospital running errands for the nurses, which usually meant sitting and paying attention to agitated dementia patients who never received any visitors.

By graduation, plans had fallen into place. Patrick would receive a partial scholarship to play football at UCLA. His parents had set aside savings, but he would still have to work part-time off-season. Grace qualified for several scholarships and received acceptance letters from Berkeley and UCLA. If she maintained her grades and worked part-time and summers, she could make it through debt-free. She decided on UCLA.

Aunt Elizabeth got out the shovel and went to work in the backyard. Grace stood inside watching her aunt through the sliding-glass door. Aunt Elizabeth attacked the ground with fury, turning soil. She didn't have to ask what had angered her aunt this time. "Only a fool turns down Berkeley for UCLA." Aunt Elizabeth was so angry she had tears in her eyes. "No matter what I say or do, it always turns out the same."

"I'll work hard, Aunt Elizabeth."

"Oh, I know that." She had a look of anguish Grace didn't understand.

She and Patrick didn't see much of each other that last summer. He didn't show up at

McDonald's. She wondered if he'd gotten a job. Hurt, Grace tried to put him out of her mind. Aunt Elizabeth didn't ask or say anything about him.

Grace moved into the university dorm and started working ten hours a week at a coffee shop on campus. She thrived in her classes. She ran into Patrick once. He'd scorned the dorm and rented a small apartment, even knowing he'd blow through all his parents' savings by the end of the year. He'd been in a hurry, and they hadn't talked long. A couple months passed, and then he called. He was struggling with grades. She listened. He told her how lonely he was. She was lonely, too. He told her how much he missed being with her. She said they could meet at the library, study together the way they used to in high school. He said they'd get more done if she came to his apartment. She knew that wasn't a good idea, but he sounded so depressed, she agreed.

They only kissed once that first day. The second time, they managed to study a few hours before they ended up on the couch. The next time, Patrick didn't want to stop. "I love you so much. I've loved you since I walked into McDonald's and saw you behind the counter. I need you, Grace. Don't say no."

Grace thought she loved him, too, but she knew what they were doing was wrong. She could hear a whisper in the back of her mind. *This isn't what I want for you, beloved. Leave this place.*

When she tried to get up, Patrick groaned. "You can't stop now." He pulled her down beside him. "You can't turn a guy on like this and not go all the way." She felt guilty for letting it go so far. How could she say no now? Before she could make up her mind, it was too late. She gasped in pain. Patrick said he was sorry, but didn't stop. When it was over, he held her. "Let's get married. We're old enough. Grace, I can't make it without you." Sitting up, he lifted her with him. Drawing her into his lap, he dug his fingers into her hair and kissed her. "Don't tell your aunt."

Grace didn't want to think about what they'd done. She didn't want to analyze what she was feeling now. A bubble of panic? The feeling she was at a crossroads and about to take another wrong turn?

Grace closed her mind to the convicting voice. *I don't care. He loves me. He said so. And it's too late anyway.* She just wanted to be loved. Was that so wrong? She wrapped her arms around Patrick and kissed him back. "Yes. Let's get married." Maybe then everything would be all right.

Patrick's family was pleased when Patrick called with the news that they'd gone to Las Vegas rather than have a wedding in Fresno. Byron Moore couldn't have been more supportive. "Elizabeth will say you're too young, but you saved her a bundle of money." He laughed. "And I think my son knows his own mind." The Moores suggested a reception over spring break. Patrick agreed. He hoped they would receive gifts and money.

Grace had to gather courage to call Aunt Elizabeth to share the news of her marriage to Patrick. She held her breath, wondering if her aunt would say something affirming.

Aunt Elizabeth gave a defeated sigh and said, "Why am I not surprised?" before hanging up.

15

Grace met Brian at the church on Saturday morning. Half a dozen other adults showed up to chaperone the teen outing at Zuma Beach. Charlie, one of the church deacons, drove the bus while Brian talked with the kids. He'd loaded his iPhone with Christian rock music. The teenage girls sitting behind Grace thought Samuel was adorable. Grace turned sideways on the bus seat so she could hold him while talking with them. One asked if she was the lady who went to Lawry's with Pastor Brian. Grace admitted she was.

A pretty girl with a pierced eyebrow and a butterfly tattoo on her neck leaned forward. "He's so cool. Anyone would want to be his girlfriend."

She wanted to quell any gossip. "Pastor Brian is very nice, and we're friends. That's why I came along to help today."

The two teenage girls shared a smiling look and changed the subject.

As soon as the bus driver turned in to the

beach parking area, Brian assigned teens to help unload supplies and claim an area for the barbecue. "No shirkers! Help each other." He worked harder than anyone. It was early, breezy and cold, but beach enthusiasts were already arriving. The chill would soon be gone, the sun out, and the beach packed. Girls complained of being cold. Brian drafted help to put up a volleyball net and got a game going. Within minutes, sweatshirts were tossed.

Several girls descended on Grace and asked if they could hold the baby. Seeing that Samuel was more than happy with them, Grace joined the game.

By noon, the sun was high and hot and everyone glistened with sunblock. Brian and the teens bodysurfed or took turns riding boogie boards. Most of the adults didn't want to get their feet wet. Grace went in knee-deep, holding Samuel in front of her so he could feel the frothy salt water tickle his toes. Squealing in delight, he kicked his legs. Laughing, Grace felt lighthearted and happy for the first time in months.

Brian joined her. "He wants to swim already."

A day in the sun made the teens mellow and ready to talk on the drive back. Grace admired the way Brian connected with his kids. He joked with them and easily turned light conversation into the more serious discussion of faith and what it meant to walk with God. When asked pointed questions, he shared some of his own struggles and mistakes. Surprised, Grace listened to him talk about sex and the challenge of staying chaste until marriage. Several teased him at first, but a few exchanged glances telling Grace they might have already gone too far.

"All our friends are having sex, Pastor."

"It can seem that way." Brian rested his arm on the back of the seat. "Everyone was saying it was okay in my day, too." Several said sex was no big thing anymore. As long as the two parties consented, it was no one else's business. "It's God's business," Brian said firmly. "Don't kid yourself. Sex has always been a big thing. Let me tell you what I've learned." He had their complete attention. "Girls play at sex to get love, and guys play at love to get sex. Charlene and I wanted to do everything God's way. That meant staying virgins until we got married."

"How'd you manage that?" a boy asked from the back, and another gave a crude answer. A girl told him to shut up.

Brian held up his hand. "Brady asked a question. How did we manage to stay virgins? We pushed up the wedding date." The kids all laughed at that. "We got married while we were still in college. We had six great years together before I lost her in a car accident." Anyone looking at his face would know he still loved and missed her. "What I'm trying to tell you is sex is powerful. In the right context, it's a beautiful gift from God. Used in the wrong way, it can wound and break hearts. It can ruin lives."

Grace could attest to that.

The conversation moved to drugs and partying, music and parents. Brian walked forward and talked to the deacon driving the bus. Then he faced the group. "Who's hungry?" Hands shot up. Brian grinned. "That's good, because we're stopping for pizza." The kids whooped and cheered.

The bus pulled into a Round Table, and everyone piled out and headed inside. Grace sat with two girls while Brian went from booth to booth, talking with the kids. A boy who was not part of their group sat in a booth nearby. Brian paused to talk to him, too. After a couple of minutes, he slid into the seat facing him. Grace thought of Roman. He was a loner, too, though he wasn't as unapproachable as he'd seemed at first.

The kids were quiet on the ride back to the church. Some slept. Others talked in low voices. Samuel slept on Grace's lap, his head against her chest. Brian looked at him and smiled at her. "Nothing like the sleep of the innocent." His mouth tipped. "We'd just gotten the word we were expecting when Charlene was in the accident. Our baby would have been almost four years old now."

"I'm so sorry for your loss, Brian." Grace didn't know what else to say.

"You can't take anything for granted in life." His expression softened. "I'm glad you came along today. The kids took to you."

"They took to Samuel."

"He's a charmer." He got up and moved again, checking on people one by one.

As soon as the bus pulled into the church parking lot, the students gathered their beach towels and bags and met parents in the parking lot, or headed for their own cars. Brian was busy, talking to the adults, making sure everyone had a ride home. Grace secured Samuel in his car seat. When she straightened, Brian joined her. "I hope you had a good time."

She smiled at him. "The best in quite a while."

"Glad to hear it. We didn't have as much time together as I hoped. Sorry about that."

They hadn't had more than five minutes at a time all day, but she'd spent most of the day observing Brian Henley, and learned a lot about how he viewed and treated people. Even strangers like the boy sitting alone in a booth at the pizza parlor. "You have great rapport with your group, Brian. They listen to you and respect you." Clearly, he had earned both. "Samuel had fun, too." She laughed. "All those pretty teenage girls gushing over him."

"Every boy's dream."

"I had ten babysitters begging for work."

"And all of them hoping to someday have a cute little baby just like him."

"Hopefully not under the same circumstances." She spoke without thinking and blushed. When Brian looked at her, she lifted her shoulders. "Not all of us were as wise as you and Charlene."

"Is it something you want to talk about?"

Was he putting on his counselor's hat? "Not today." Maybe never. So much depended on how well she and Brian got along.

Brian didn't press. "I'd like to see you again. Outside church activities."

"I'd like that, too." Grace opened the driver's side door and slid into the seat. She put the key in the ignition and lowered the window. Hooking on her seat belt, she looked up at Brian. "Thank you for inviting me along today."

Brian put his hands on the door and leaned down. "Glad you could make it. How about dinner Monday night? It's my day off. I'll pick you up at your place? All I need is the address." Pleased, she gave him the information. She hadn't expected him to ask her out so soon, if he did at all. Especially after her precipitous remark. He pushed himself back from her car. "Drive carefully. I'll see you day after tomorrow."

Even on such short acquaintance, Grace

felt certain Brian had all the qualities she dreamed of for a future husband and father for her son: a man of God, honest, dependable, intelligent, and attractive. Someone truly nice, someone who loved children, someone who worked for a living. She wasn't sexually attracted to Brian, but that could be a good thing. She didn't want emotion clouding her judgment.

Lord, Brian Henley is the kind of man I want to marry someday, if I ever marry again. He's a good, solid, dependable, nice guy who could love someone despite glaring faults and failures. Someone like Brian could love Samuel like a son. So, I'm asking. If this is your plan, Lord, please make it clear. You know how stupid I can be, how blind to who people really are. Please, Lord. Protect me. I don't want to pick the wrong guy again.

Roman awakened late Saturday morning, head pounding, and thirsty. Now that he was awake, he wanted to get back to Topanga Canyon. He shaved in the shower and called the valet to have his car brought around. Tossing clothing and toiletries into his duffel bag, he zipped it shut and slung it over his shoulder. He picked up a five-dollar coffee from the lobby vendor and headed out of the hotel. Grace made better. Saturday and Sunday were her days off. He'd have to wait for a good cup of java until Monday morning.

It was midafternoon before Roman pulled into his garage. His mail was on the kitchen counter, opened and neatly stacked in chronological order, sticky notes on the more important items that needed his personal attention. She'd balanced his accounts and left a computer report of his income and expenses, everything neatly logged in categories. His tax accountant was going to love her.

On his way to his bedroom, he saw the guest room. He took a step back. Grace had chosen a mahogany sleigh bed, nightstands with lamps, and a high dresser. She hadn't stopped with bedroom furniture, but added a comfortable chair, reading lamp, and Persian-style rug. Roman dumped his duffel bag in the hall and went in to look around. Blues, greens, touches of red and yellow, but no pastels. The room was masculine without being macho. She'd hung two sets of blue towels in the bathroom. On the counter were three clear glass canisters, one filled with seashells, another with colorful river rocks, and the smallest with wrapped soaps.

He'd left his own bedroom in all its glory: bed unmade, towels and clothes on the floor, closet doors open. Embarrassed at the contrast with the immaculate guest room, Roman stripped his bed. He gathered the dirty towels and headed for the laundry room. Maybe it was a good time to go over to the cottage, tell her he was back and she'd done a good job on the guest room. He knocked on her front door. No answer. He tried again, listening. No footsteps. No radio playing. She didn't own a television.

She'd gone out. Why should that surprise him?

He went back to the big house and killed time watching a basketball game and making sketches in the black book he kept under the couch. He went over again as the sun was going down. Still no answer.

It's Saturday, stupid. It's her day off. Why shouldn't she be off someplace having fun? She probably has a boyfriend.

That thought unsettled him. He didn't want to think about why.

He put the sheets and towels in the dryer and went into the kitchen to make himself a sandwich. Later, while making his bed, he thought about Masterson Ranch and the bachelor arts Susan had taught him. Oddly enough, he'd liked the routine, the order, set meals at set times, the rules for how to treat one another.

When and why had he turned into a slob?

The TV blared as one of the teams won — he didn't know which and didn't care. He picked up the remote and shut it off. He went up to his studio and noticed the cottage lights were on. Grace was home.

The solar lights had come on along the path

between the big house and cottage. He knocked rather than ringing the bell. Was that a baby crying? The door opened, and Grace's expression was anything but welcoming. She held a red-faced, crying baby in her arms. Roman grimaced. "He doesn't look happy." Neither did she.

"He's had a big day. Sometimes when he's overstimulated, he gets fussy."

Roman guessed she'd babysat enough times to know.

When Grace left the door open as she walked away, he took it as an invitation to enter. "I came over to tell you the guest room looks great." He closed the door behind him.

She smiled at him. "Thank you." The baby seemed calmer, leaning his head on her chest and peering at him as Grace swayed her body, rocking him gently. He had thick, dark hair, café au lait skin, and dark-brown eyes.

Her place felt like an oasis. A Bible lay open on the kitchen table, along with a journal. Curious, Roman wanted to pick it up and read what she'd written. Not a good idea. "You have him again." Shanice probably stuck Grace with her kid as often as possible so she could go off somewhere and party.

Grace rubbed the baby's back. "I have him every chance I get."

"I don't think he wants a nap."

"Unfortunately, he already had a long nap on the way home from the beach."

Grace laid the baby in the middle of a plush, ribbon-edged blanket on the carpeted floor. "All right, little man." She handed Samuel a rattle. He shook it several times and hurled it. Grace stretched to retrieve it, exposing smooth white skin at the waistband of her jeans. Samuel rolled over and pushed himself up.

Roman chuckled. "Looks like he'd rather do push-ups."

Still on her knees, she looked up at Roman. "I'm glad you like the guest room."

She wasn't rushing him out the door. He smiled slightly. "The canisters of seashells and rocks were a bit much."

"I have the receipts. I can return them."

"I was kidding. I might let you redo my bedroom."

"Oh, no. Nice try, but I'm not cleaning up your mess."

He gave her a wry smile. "I stripped my bed and washed the sheets. I've been doing laundry since I got back."

Baby Samuel let out a distinct noise, drawing their attention. When the baby's face turned dark red, Roman laughed. "I think you're going to be doing laundry, too."

Grace sighed. "It's the formula. Thankfully, he's wearing disposable diapers."

"I thought you were a recycling activist."

"Within reason." Grace got up and went into the bedroom. Roman watched Samuel

235

push his knees under his chest. The baby rocked back and forth and toppled face-first. Pushing himself up again, he let out a ferocious scream. Grace appeared, hands full of diaper-changing supplies.

Roman raised his hands. "I didn't do anything."

"Then don't look so guilty." Kneeling, she turned Samuel over. "He can sit up. Now he wants to crawl." In less than two minutes, she had the soiled diaper removed, the baby's bottom clean and fitted with a new one. Leaning down, she blew on his belly. Samuel grabbed her hair and let out a baby giggle. Turning him over again, Grace patted Samuel's freshly diapered bottom. He pushed himself up again and looked at Roman. Grace smiled. "He wonders who the strange man is."

Roman sat in the swivel rocker and leaned forward. "I'm her boss, kid."

"He's not a goat. He's a child, and his name is Samuel."

"Hey, Sammy . . ."

"I'd rather you called him Samuel."

Her tone offered no compromise, and the look on her face made him wonder why such a little thing mattered. "What does Shanice call him?"

Grace looked confused. "She calls him 'little man.' That's his nickname, not Sammy." Her phone rang, distracting her. She rose quickly and went to the kitchen table. Roman could tell by her tone it wasn't one of her girlfriends. "He's tired, but fine. I had him slathered with sunblock." Her tone had noticeably warmed. Why should that annoy him?

When Grace glanced at him, Roman stood. Time to go. Leaning down, he patted Samuel's behind. "Have fun, buddy." She asked the caller to wait a moment, no doubt wanting more privacy than she had right now. Roman didn't give her a chance to say anything. "I'll see you Monday morning."

Back at the main house, Roman decided to toss his self-imposed celibacy to the wind and spend the rest of the evening at a club.

16

Grace didn't know what was bothering Roman. He'd been different since his short trip to San Diego. He should be excited about the gallery show in Laguna Beach. Instead, he'd become quiet and introspective. He stayed in his studio sketching, but wasn't making headway. She heard him swearing more than once, and the last time she'd entered his domain, wads of paper had lain helter-skelter around him. When she started picking them up, he told her to leave them.

The doorbell rang, a simple ding-dong rather than the melodious chimes that had irritated Roman. Grace hurried from the office, but slowed when she heard heavy metal music coming from Roman's exercise room. He was running on his treadmill again. She expected to find Talia at the front door, eager to go over last-minute details for Roman's show at the Laguna Beach gallery that evening. The poor woman had been as nervous as a backpacker facing a grizzly the last time she talked with Roman. The invitations had gone out, and responses flooded in. Talia would be serving champagne and canapés. Roman said he didn't care if she handed out beer and pretzels. Talia had asked Grace what was eating him, but Grace had to admit she had no idea.

It wasn't Talia ringing the bell, but a tall man with short white hair and intelligent hazel eyes. He had a suitcase in his hand and a look of surprise. "Well, hello." He extended his hand. "I'm Jasper Hawley, and you are . . . ?"

"Grace Moore, Roman's personal assistant." The older gentleman had a firm handshake and an easy smile. "Come in. Please." She stepped back. This must be the man who wanted a bed in the guest room.

"By the look on your face, Roman forgot to tell you I was coming for a visit." He laughed low. "He also forgot to tell me about you."

"He has a lot on his mind."

"I'm sure that's not the reason." Jasper stopped in the living room. "Do I have a bed this time, or shall I get my sleeping bag and pillow out of my car?" She showed him down the hall to the guest room. "Holy cow! Look at this place! This is better than a suite in a high-class hotel." He put his suitcase on the end of the king-size bed. "I think I'll move in."

"Don't bet on it." Roman stood in the

doorway, toweling perspiration from his face. He looked like a professional athlete in his running shorts and wet T-shirt. Grace wished he had more clothes on — preferably, a sweatsuit that covered him completely. Roman's gaze shifted to her. Her heart did an alarming flip.

Jasper looked around. "Bare walls? I thought you'd have every square inch painted by now."

Grace found that a curious statement.

"I do enough painting on canvas these days, Hawley."

Jasper ignored him and looked at Grace. "I'll bet he's never told you about his graffiti work."

Grace looked at Roman. "Oh. Is that what you meant about tagging?"

Jasper raised his brows slightly and started to say something, but Roman gave him a quelling look. "Are you here to make trouble?"

Grace turned to go. She wanted to leave them alone to sort out whatever problem seemed to have reared its ugly head.

Roman put his hand on the doorframe, effectively blocking Grace's exit. "Have you heard from Talia?" He was close enough for her to breathe in the scent of healthy male sweat.

"Not yet, but she said she'd probably come by this morning."

He said a word she hadn't heard since the first day she came to work for him. "I wish I'd never gotten myself into this thing." He lowered his arm to let her pass.

Grace overheard Jasper as she headed down the hall. "How is it you never mentioned Grace?"

"She's my personal assistant."

His dismissive tone hurt. What did it matter? She'd known what sort of guy he was the minute she saw him. She was putting on a pot of fresh coffee when Jasper came out of the guest room and joined her in the kitchen.

"Roman will be out in a few minutes." He sat on a barstool as she filled the carafe. "How long have you been working for him?"

"Four and a half months." She gave him a wry smile. "Sometimes it feels longer."

He chuckled. "I don't doubt that. He's a hard nut to crack." She wanted to ask why that was, but doubted Jasper Hawley had any answers. And if he did, why would he share them with her? He studied her. "You're not going to ask any questions about him, are you?"

"No. I'm not."

"He must like you if you've been here almost five months. So, tell me about yourself, Grace."

"Not much to tell. Roman hired me from a temp agency, then made it full-time. I answer correspondence, field phone calls, pay bills,

241

run errands." She shrugged. "I'm here to make Roman's life easier."

She looked toward the wall of glass. "It's a beautiful day. Would you like to sit on the patio, Mr. Hawley?" Roman might object, but Jasper Hawley was the guest, and what he wanted took precedence.

"Call me Jasper, please, and the patio would be perfect." When they were both settled with fresh coffee, he studied her over the mug of steaming brew. "It's quite a view, isn't it?" He nodded toward the canyon. "Makes you wonder why he never paints it."

"I've wondered the same thing."

"The boy is complex."

The boy. Like Talia, Jasper said it with tolerance and affection. She gave a soft laugh. "I wouldn't call him a boy."

"Depends on your definition. And he's been called a lot of names by a lot of people."

Having fielded calls over the last few months, Grace knew that only too well. The most recent woman had a few choice things to say about him, none Grace wanted to hear. "You're the only guest Roman has had here since I started working for him. Other than Talia Reisner, who only drops by."

"She would be the gallery owner where the party is being held tonight."

"Yes. She's very nice. And interesting. She thinks Roman has great potential."

"And you?"

242

She didn't know what was behind his question. Thankfully, the sliding-glass door opened and interrupted their conversation. Roman came out, wearing jeans and a red T-shirt, hair still wet from the shower. He took a seat and looked between the two of them.

Jasper's smile was half-teasing. "You appear to be in tip-top shape, Roman."

"Just trying not to get old and flabby like you."

"Still running? Or can I hope you're training for the real marathon?"

Grace sensed undercurrents in the conversation. She started to get up. "I'd better get back to work."

Roman gave her a quick glance. "Sit." It wasn't an invitation, and she didn't care for being addressed like a dog on a leash.

"Grace was just telling me you met her through a temp agency."

"What did you think? I picked her up in a club?"

Grace's face filled with heat.

Jasper looked surprised, then annoyed.

Wanting to escape, Grace rose again, determined this time. Roman didn't say anything as she headed for the house. She sat, elbows on her desk, face in her hands. It was a few minutes before her cheeks felt cool again. Was it the show that had him so tense? Was he worried people wouldn't like his art?

She busied herself with Roman's correspondence and answered several telephone calls. The doorbell rang at one. Talia swept in, her mass of curly hair tied up with a colorful scarf.

"Where is he? Most artists drive me crazy wanting to know every detail of what's being done for their show, and Roman couldn't care less!" She waved her hands in the air and spotted him on the patio. She marched through the sliding-glass doors and went outside to join the two men.

Safely back in the office, Grace breathed more easily. She finished her work and called Selah to check on Samuel. "He's playing on the rug. He's crawling."

Grace had known the milestone was coming and hoped she'd be the one to witness it.

"He wanted his bunny. He learns quickly. He was so pleased with himself." Selah would have gone on, but Grace said she needed to work and ended the call. The hurt sank deep. Would Selah be the one to hear Samuel's first word and see his first steps? If she had a choice, would she rather Selah be the one to see these things or a day care worker?

Talia peered in. "Everything all right?"

Startled, Grace glanced up. "Yes. Fine."

"You looked so serious."

"How was he?"

"Grim. The show isn't the only thing on his mind. Well, I'm off and running. See you this evening." She ducked out and then came back in again. "What do you know about the divine Jasper Hawley?"

"Not much."

"I'd like to know that gentleman better." She waggled her brows. Grace laughed and wished her luck.

The two men came inside and talked in the living room. Grace thought she'd go out and clear the patio table, but the tray with coffee mugs was on the kitchen counter. Jasper looked happy to see her. "Roman said you went to UCLA."

"I didn't graduate."

"But you were studying clinical psychology? Do you have plans to finish your degree?"

"I'm chipping away at it. One online class at a time."

Roman wore an odd expression. "I don't know why you bother. I pay you more than you'll ever make as a social worker, which is all you'll be qualified to do with a bachelor's in clinical psychology." He gave Jasper a glance. "She'd need a PhD for anything better, wouldn't she?" He raised his brows at her. "How old would you be by that time, Grace?"

She was tired of being on the receiving end of his bad mood. "About your age — and a lot happier."

Jasper laughed.

Mortified, she waited for Roman to say something nasty. His mouth tipped slightly. Had he been baiting her? She ignored him and addressed Jasper. "Right now, the main thing I'm studying is my Bible."

"A worthy endeavor." Jasper smiled. "I've been known to read the Good Book myself."

Roman looked preoccupied. "Grace, I need you ready at five. Talia wants us there early."

"Brian is picking me up at four. I told Talia I'd —"

"Brian?" His eyes narrowed. "Who's Brian?"

"A friend. He's interested in your work."

"What's he do for a living?"

"He's a youth pastor."

"He couldn't afford it, and you'll be working."

She let both the insult and the reminder go. Jasper was watching the exchange with far too much interest.

Roman stared at her. "Why don't you take the rest of the afternoon off? You'll need time to get ready."

Her lips parted. Did he just imply it would take hours for her to make herself presentable? "I'll try not to embarrass you." She wished he'd do the same. Roman started to say something and pressed his lips together. She looked at him and waited. Maybe he wanted to ask her what she was wearing. When he didn't say anything more, she gave

Jasper an apologetic smile. "I'll see you later."

"Yes. You will."

Roman would need a handler.

Grace returned to the cottage. It was going to be a long, tense evening, if this morning had been any indication. At least she wouldn't have to worry about what to wear. Shanice had taken her shopping last week. "You've been out to coffee and dinners with Brian, but this is your chance to shine, girl! You need to dress up!" She knew of a classy boutique in North Hollywood that sold gently used designer clothing at great prices. They found the perfect little black dress with a ballet neckline, fitted waist, and straight skirt. "Grace, you're a stunner in that dress!"

"No one will be looking at me, Shanice. This is Roman's night."

"You're there with Brian. We want him looking at you. Leave your hair down. If I had hair like yours, I'd let it grow to my waist."

She'd kept it short for a year or so, but it was getting longer now. Patrick liked long hair, so she let it grow while they were together. He also liked blondes, so she bleached her hair. She was glad to be past that nonsense.

With a few extra hours on her hands, Grace checked to see if she had any new responses to her post for a babysitter. Three applicants had answered Grace's questions and left references. Grace made a few calls and eliminated two. The third had already taken a position as a full-time nanny.

Grace took her time getting ready. When Brian arrived, Grace didn't have to wonder if she looked good. His gaze took her in from her legs to her hair. "Wow!" His response pleased her. She said he looked very handsome in his black suit. He admitted it was a gift from a lady parishioner, a widow whose husband had been active in a Masonic lodge. Brian had needed a good suit to perform weddings. He grinned and said he figured it was appropriate for a gallery gala.

Grace wondered if Roman had a suit and felt a shiver of alarm that she hadn't thought to ask.

She and Brian talked all the way to Laguna Beach about upcoming youth events, the latest local, state, and international news, and his plans for a summer mission trip to Mexico. His kids had held a couple of fundraisers. Brian had enough adults already signed up to help mentor and monitor the students.

Talia knew how to be a show as well as run one. She looked like a colorful work of art in a Bohemian caftan. She shook hands with Brian and hugged Grace. "You're stunning! This evening is going to be fantastic! I feel it in my bones!" She beamed with excitement. "I'll bet we sell every one of Roman's paintings before nine." She leaned in closer. "Even with the ridiculous prices I've put on them."

It didn't surprise Grace when Roman came in wearing black jeans and a white V-neck T-shirt under a black leather bomber jacket. What did surprise her was the way her heart quickened. Dismayed, she looked away and met Jasper Hawley's gaze. He spread his hands as though helpless to do anything about Roman.

Talia groaned. "I should have known he'd rather be dead than caught in a suit."

Grace knew Talia wouldn't have cared if Roman showed up shirtless and in jogging shorts, as long as he came to the party.

Roman hated crowds. He hated being the focus of attention. He hated even more when people talked as though they understood his art and knew something about the way his mind worked based on what he painted. At least he had the satisfaction of watching them pay through the nose for pieces that didn't mean anything, let alone reveal hidden secrets about his psyche. Someday, someone would figure out he was a fraud with no pedigree, education, or real talent.

Someone touched his arm — a voluptuous blonde in a designer gown that screamed money. She talked about her search for new talent and how she loved to collect pieces from little-known artists. Her smile left him without doubt what kind of collection she was talking about. A few months ago, he would have taken her up on the invitation. Right now, he was trying to be polite and civilized. He looked at Jasper, thankful when he stepped closer and joined the one-sided conversation. Roman glanced around the room and spotted Grace.

The black dress fit perfectly. She smiled at Prince Charming, who stood right beside her, dressed in a suit. The guy had his hand at the small of Grace's back as they talked with an older couple, the touch of ownership. Brian whatever-his-name-was looked like the kind of man who'd fit in anywhere. That guy was a minister? Had he and Grace had sex yet? Did youth ministers even have sex? Why should he care if they had sex or not?

Roman emptied his glass of champagne and plunked it on a display pedestal with a bronze eagle in flight. A server quickly picked it up.

"Could you try to smile?" Talia offered Roman a canapé. "Maybe another glass of champagne will help." She plucked one from a tray and offered it to him.

"I think I've had enough." He wasn't talking about champagne.

Jasper was watching him, too, and had an oddly speculative gleam in his eyes.

Roman glared at him. "What?"

"You tell me." Jasper lifted his glass of bubbly. "I never thought I'd see the day."

Roman wanted to put his fist through one of his own paintings, even if it cost him fifty grand. He said a word under his breath that would have rocked Grace, if she'd been near enough to hear. She stood across the room, as far away from him as she could get. He said the word again. He wanted to be anywhere but here. This would be a good night to have a backpack loaded with cans of Krylon. He'd start on the side of his own cottage.

Grace turned, as though feeling his attention. Their eyes met, and he felt things he knew were going to bring trouble. Someone said something to him, and he pretended to care. The place was buzzing, and he was the center of attention. He should be eating it up. He should be enjoying himself.

Some man prattled on and on about Roman's work. Losing patience, Roman excused himself and almost pushed his way through the guests as he headed for the rear of the gallery. Was there a back door out of this place?

Talia caught up with him before he could get away. "Are you all right?"

"We shouldn't have done this."

"Of course we should. Do you have any idea who some of these people are?"

"I don't give a — !"

"What is the matter with you tonight?"

"Just tell everyone I'm a temperamental artist."

"They can see that already. You should be happy, Roman. You've already made a hundred thousand dollars, and the party isn't even in full swing."

Happy. Yeah, right. He felt hot all over. His heart hammered.

Roman went into the bathroom and locked the door. Raking his hands through his hair, he tried to relax. He forced himself to breathe slowly. The familiar wave of weakness came. He closed his eyes and swore softly. Squatting, he put his head between his knees, hoping he wouldn't pass out. Not now. Not here. Was it the champagne? He'd only had two glasses.

The weakness passed. He gave himself another minute before he stood, and another before he opened the door.

Grace stood in the dimly lit hallway. "Are you all right, Roman?" Her brown eyes were so full of concern.

"Why wouldn't I be?"

"Are you perspiring?" She reached up.

Roman pulled his head back as though her touch would burn him. She closed her hand and lowered it. The lighting was too dim to see her blush, but he knew he'd embarrassed her. Again. He'd been taking potshots at her all day.

They stood close, staring at each other. He

was having a hard time breathing normally. He wanted to step closer. Was she trembling?

She inhaled a soft breath. "I didn't mean to treat you like a mother hen. Do you need anything?"

You.

Movement caught his attention. Prince Charming stood at the doorway to the main room. What would the guy do if Roman pulled Grace into his arms right now and kissed her? Roman looked at her again. What would she do? Her expression altered just enough to let him know she sensed something dangerous going on inside his head. She took a step back, and Roman knew what she'd do. She'd slap his face, quit her job, move out of the cottage, and he'd never see her again.

It might be worth it. She'd be gone, and he'd be safe.

"Roman." Jasper Hawley appeared out of nowhere, and Roman let out his breath. Until that second, he hadn't known he was holding it. Grace touched his arm before she turned away. Reassurance? She walked down the hall. Brian Henley slipped his hand around her waist and guided her away.

Jasper tilted his head, studying Roman. "This is something new for you."

"I'm not sure I'll agree to any more of Talia's ideas." Roman rubbed the back of his neck. His head was beginning to pound.

"I wasn't talking about the show."

"What then?" He wasn't in the mood for Jasper's cryptic remarks.

"You can't keep your eyes off Grace."

"She's supposed to be working!"

"Are you looking for an excuse to fire her?" Roman glared at him. "You said you liked her."

"I like her a lot, but it doesn't matter what I feel. She's gotten under your skin. You're not comfortable with the working relationship, are you? Maybe you ought to play it safe and get rid of her."

Roman knew what Jasper was doing, but he was in no mood to play the game. "Leave it alone."

Jasper stepped in front of him. "What are you afraid of, Bobby Ray?"

"Don't call me that."

"There's nothing wrong with who you are."

"And who is that?"

"You have a real opportunity here, son. A chance for friendship, affection, maybe love. What're you going to do with it?"

Roman went hot. "You've misread the situation."

"Anger. Your favorite hiding place."

"Are you done yet?"

Jasper shook his head, his expression filled with compassion. "Do me a favor. Try not to stamp Grace into the ground so you can put out the fire." He sighed. "Let it burn, Bobby Ray. Get closer. Get to know her. See what happens."

"She doesn't know what I am."

Jasper looked perplexed. "What are you?"

"You know better than anyone else where I come from. What do I have in common with a girl like her?"

Jasper let out his breath. "Lord, have mercy. We're finally getting somewhere." He stepped closer. "You don't know Grace any better than she knows you. Take it easy. Listen. Learn. See what happens."

Roman wondered if it would be worth the risk.

Grace sat silent as Brian drove her home after the Laguna art show. It had been a long evening, at times fraught with drama. While she and Brian mingled, she stayed aware of Roman. He'd reminded her that afternoon she would be working during the show, but he avoided her most of the evening. If he needed anything, he didn't ask her. She'd checked in with Talia, but everything was so well organized she wasn't needed.

When Roman headed for the back hall, Grace worried something was wrong. She waited a few minutes before whispering to Brian that she was going to check on her boss. Roman was ashen when he came out of the men's room. When he'd looked at her, she'd felt the jolt. Even now, sitting in the car with Brian, she felt stirred by Roman's intensity. What had he been thinking? What would he have said — or done — if Jasper and Brian hadn't been close?

After that tense moment in the hall, Roman settled down, talked with people, even smiled a few times. At ten, he was out the door like Cinderella at midnight. Jasper followed. Talia had been exasperated. "I thought you'd keep him here."

As if Grace had any control over the man.

Brian glanced at her. "You're very quiet."

"It was a strange evening."

"Is your boss always like that?"

Like what? Moody, impossible to understand? "Pretty much."

"Was the show a success?"

"I have no doubt. I was a little distracted."

Brian gave her a rueful look. "I noticed. What happened between you and Roman in the hall?"

"Nothing. I thought he might be ill. He said he was fine." She shook her head. "I think the show mattered more to him than he wanted to admit."

Brian made a turn. "The evening was a resounding success from where I was standing. He has quite a few fans."

"Especially women," Grace muttered under her breath. Roman hadn't been in the gallery five minutes when a blonde in a dress that must have been spray-painted on her approached him. Even from across the room,

Grace knew the woman was more interested in the artist than art.

"Are you worried about him?"

She lifted her shoulders. "No reason I should be." She didn't want to spend any more of the evening thinking about Roman Velasco. "Did you enjoy the show?"

"Plenty of interesting people there." He talked about several he'd met. "A couple of lawyers who collect modern art, an airline pilot, an LAPD officer and his wife. I talked with Talia for a few minutes while you were checking on Roman. She's an interesting lady."

Grace grinned. "Guess what she studied in college."

"Art history."

"That's what I thought." She laughed. "Talia majored in economics and marketing." Grace had learned more about Talia's personal history over one lunch than she knew about Roman's after months of working for him. "She went to Cal in the seventies, as a registered Republican. Her boyfriend was in ROTC. They married right out of college so she could get pregnant before he ended up in Vietnam. He made it home, but died of cancer in his forties. She blames Agent Orange, some chemical they sprayed along the rivers to defoliate the jungle. They had a daughter who is now a successful estate planner in Florida. She's happily married with two boys. Talia flies there once a year to visit."

"Not what I expected. How did she end up with the art gallery?"

"She married the owner. She was his tax consultant. He taught her about art; she taught him about business. They had eleven happy years together before he passed away."

Brian turned in to the driveway. Lights were on in the main house. As she and Brian walked along the pathway to her front door, he took her hand. Surprised, she smiled at him, and noticed the lights on in the upstairs studio. What was Roman doing? And why was she thinking about him again?

She realized Brian hadn't said anything since he parked the car and helped her out. "Thank you for coming to the gallery with me tonight, Brian." She slipped her hand from his, took her keys from her purse, and unlocked the door.

"Can we talk for a few minutes before I go, Grace?"

She hesitated, wondering if tonight might be a turning point in their relationship. "Do you want to come inside? I can make coffee."

Brian glanced at the main house and shook his head. "It's nice out here." He'd seen the light on, too. A pastor had to care about appearances. He took her hand again as they sat on the wall together. "I like you, Grace. I like you very much. I think you know that."

This was what she'd hoped for, wasn't it?

Why didn't she feel the least bit excited? "I like you, too, Brian." She tensed when he raised his hand and tucked her hair over her shoulder.

"May I kiss you?"

She'd only kissed two men in her life, and neither had asked permission. Covering her surprise, she said yes. Curious what she would feel, she leaned forward and met him halfway.

Brian's kiss was tender and unhurried, pleasant. She didn't feel the faint stirrings she had with Patrick, the promise of something that never happened. She hadn't felt much more with Samuel's father.

Someday her son would grow up and ask who his father was. What could she say? *I met him at a club. When he asked if I wanted to go to his place, I said yes. You were the result.* If she surrendered Samuel to Selah and Ruben, she wouldn't have to confess. Selah could tell him honestly that she'd planned for and chosen him to be her son.

And why was her mind wandering hither and yon when Brian Henley was kissing her?

Brian drew back, his expression enigmatic.

"What's wrong, Grace?"

"I'm not good enough for you."

"We're all sinners, and friendship is a good place to start a lasting relationship. It's how Charlene and I started." He took her hands and stood, drawing her up with him.

Grace was again relieved not to feel any particular physical attraction. She had been enamored by Patrick, and that relationship had been a disaster. The second, worse. She'd allowed anger and hurt to excuse a night of following the crowd of irresponsible young adults who thought casual sex was perfectly all right between consenting adults. She'd been lonely and miserable, desperate to feel something, anything. She barely remembered the evening, but she remembered waking up in the middle of the night in a stranger's bed. Throwing on her clothes, she'd fled. She ran down the beach, crying, and up onto the road, where she'd had enough sense to arrange for an Uber.

She liked Brian. He was kind and caring. He was handsome. They could talk about anything and everything. They had faith in common. She wanted to live a life pleasing to God, and Brian's clear calling was to serve the Lord. She felt safe with Brian, no hint of temptation. Surely, that was a good sign.

"Are you up for a hike on Solstice Canyon Trail next Saturday? I'll get a pack so I can carry Samuel."

"Sounds wonderful."

"I'll call you tomorrow." He leaned in and kissed her softly on the mouth. Grace wished she felt a spark.

She tossed her purse on the table. If hiking was Brian's favorite form of entertainment, she'd better invest in something more than tennis shoes. She'd need hiking boots. Maybe Roman would allow her to use the exercise room so she could build enough muscle to shoulder a pack. She let out a mirthless laugh.

She changed into pajamas, washed her face, and brushed her teeth. She heard Elvis Presley singing "Big Boss Man." Heart racing, she went into the kitchen and pulled her phone from her purse. Glancing at the microwave clock, she answered. "It's after midnight, Roman."

"You're still up."

"Not for long."

"I'm in my studio. If you'd invited Prince Charming in for the night, I wouldn't be calling."

Grace gasped, cheeks on fire. "Were you watching us?"

"I was curious what two Christians do at the end of a date." He laughed low. "That kiss earned a G rating."

Grace ended the call. She'd turn the phone off completely if it wasn't her only lifeline to Samuel in case of emergency. She put it on her nightstand and slipped into bed. Elvis sang again. She put a pillow over her head.

17

Bobby Ray, Age 7

Bobby Ray Dean awakened to the whoop of a police car siren and red lights flashing across the ceiling. He pulled the smelly blanket higher over his shoulders. Drowsy, he stared at the orange, red, and gold neon *Jesus Saves* across the street. Still cold, he cocooned into the worn cushions of the old sofa.

Voices drifted from behind the bedroom door: a man, irritated; Mama cajoling. Bobby Ray knew that whenever a man came home from work with her, he had to leave the bed and sleep on the couch.

Bobby Ray's stomach growled. He'd found cereal in the cabinet to eat for supper, but no milk in the refrigerator. Other than the bottles Mama kept around for her guests, the cupboards were empty. He hoped Mama's new friend would leave enough money to buy a few cans of Dinty Moore stew and Spam, maybe even some eggs and bread and milk.

Most of what she earned went for the white powder that helped her forget everything and feel good until she had to get up and remember again.

He could get something to fill his belly at the Salvation Army café, and he would get lunch at school for free. But that was hours away, and the only way to ease the pain now was to go back to sleep. It was hard with the lights flashing. He kept thinking about the grocery store. He'd managed to steal an apple once, but the next time he reached for a banana, the grocer grabbed his wrist and said unless Bobby Ray could show him a dollar, he'd better put the banana down. Bobby Ray kicked him and ran, the green banana still clutched in his hand. The grocer chased him two blocks before Bobby Ray managed to escape. He didn't go by that store anymore.

Mama stopped talking in the bedroom, and other sounds made Bobby Ray pull the foul-smelling blanket over his head and plug his ears. He might only be seven, but he knew what Mama let men do to her so she could pay the rent. At least this man had looked nice. The last one had knocked Bobby Ray across the room. Mama jumped on his back, and he hit her, too, and kicked her before he left.

Sobbing, Mama had crawled to Bobby Ray and gathered him in her arms. "I'm sorry, baby. I'm so sorry. How bad did he hurt you?" When she tipped his chin up, she cried harder. She told him to tell his teacher he'd fallen down the stairs by accident. "I don't want CPS coming to take you away from me. We'd never see each other again." The thought of being taken away from his mother had scared Bobby Ray more than the man who'd hurt him and Mama.

Bobby Ray heard angry voices in the street below. Mama had told him never to look out because you never knew when people might start shooting. "Stay down and safe, baby." Two men shouted. Glass shattered.

Mama's friend started talking in the bedroom. Mama laughed. "It's no big deal. Lie down, honey. We were having such a good time. . . ." The man said he had to go. People might wonder where he was. More conversation, quieter now. The bedroom door opened, and the man came out, half-dressed. Mama followed in her pink robe. "Well, if you gotta go, you gotta go." She flipped a switch, flooding the room with light.

Mama's friend had black shiny shoes and nice dark slacks, a glossy leather belt. He fumbled at the buttons on his white shirt. Catching Bobby Ray looking at him, he blushed deep red. "Sorry, kid." The apology made Bobby Ray feel the hard punch of wrongness in everything about Mama's life.

Mama held the jacket for the man to slip on. When he had trouble with his tie, Mama brushed his hands away. "Let me do it for you." She pouted prettily. "Fifty bucks doesn't go very far these days. I barely make rent, and I have a growing boy to feed." The man's eyes narrowed, his lips pressing tight. Mama sighed as she dusted his lapels. She stepped back. "What'd you have for dinner tonight, Bobby Ray?"

"Cheerios."

"And you drank the last of the milk two days ago, didn't you, baby? I'm sorry. Mama's doing the best she can."

"Don't you get welfare?"

"Rent's higher in the Tenderloin than in Wichita. But you'd know that, considering the hotel you're staying in for your conference."

The man gave Bobby Ray an embarrassed look and pulled out his wallet. Bobby Ray noticed the gold ring on his finger as he chose some bills and thrust them into Mama's outstretched palm. She kept her hand out, and he added one more before folding his wallet and tucking it away. He didn't look happy. Mama smiled. "You have a good heart." She sounded sincere. She went to the door, removed the chain, turned the two dead bolts, and opened it. "Be careful out there. You're not in Kansas anymore." She gave a soft laugh, as though she'd told a joke.

The man looked unsettled. "I left my rental car near the club. I was a little drunk. How do I get back?"

"Turn left, go two blocks, turn right. You'll see the light." Mama closed the door in his face. She turned both dead bolts and put the chain on again. Her smile died along with any hint of pleasure as she picked up the shoulder bag she'd tossed on the old orange recliner. She shoved the money into it and dropped it again. Yawning widely, she rubbed her back. "I need a long, hot shower. And then I'm going to sleep until noon." She leaned down and kissed Bobby Ray. "You get yourself up and ready for school, sweetie." She went into the bathroom.

Bobby Ray did what he had to do. He stole a twenty-dollar bill from Mama's purse.

As soon as school let out, Bobby Ray headed for CVS and pushed a cart bigger than him up and down the aisles. Everything cost so much! He decided on a jar of Smucker's Goober peanut butter and grape jelly stripes, a loaf of Wonder Bread, a box of twelve crayons, a package of four Ticonderoga pencils with a small sharpener, and a lined notebook on sale for a dollar. Maybe Mama had gone shopping with the rest of the money the man had given her last night. Maybe there'd be milk in the refrigerator and cereal in the cabinet.

Mama was up and dressed for bear, as she put it. She was happy, too, which meant she had another supply of white powder. "So what did you buy with the twenty bucks you took, baby?" She took the plastic bag from him and emptied it on the table while Bobby Ray looked in the refrigerator. No milk. "Sorry, honey. I haven't had time to go shopping. I had to make myself presentable. Tell you what! I'll find some nice man to take me to dinner at a fancy restaurant and bring you a doggie bag." She laughed. "Alioto's! How's that sound? Or the Franciscan! I'll order lobster!"

"You want a sandwich, Mama?" Bobby Ray didn't want her to leave. "I'll make it for you." When she was happy like this, she stayed out all night.

"No, baby. That's all for you." She looped her large bag over her shoulder and headed out. "Lock the door after I leave."

Bobby Ray hated it when his mother left high and happy. The last time she did, when she came back, she'd cried all the next day and had to put on lots of makeup to cover bruises before going to work at the club. "Don't go. Please?" His lip quivered, and he let the tears come, hoping they'd make a difference.

Mama came back, anguished. "Oh, honey, you know I've gotta go. Mama does so much better when she's had something to help. You know? I'm doing the best I can. Sometimes I . . ." She shook her head, her hand on his shoulder. "Don't look at me like that, Bobby Ray." She leaned down and cupped his face. "You know I love you more than anything in this whole world. I'm gonna take good care of you, baby. You wait and see."

"Mama . . ." He hugged her tightly. She was soft and smelled of sweet perfume. He clung to her like ivy on a brick wall.

"Let go." Mama pried his arms loose and held him firmly at arm's length. "Stop it right now! You know I'm gonna come back. Don't I always? Now be good. Stay inside. Lock the door. You can watch TV as late as you want." She left without looking back again.

Bobby Ray went to the window and tried to open it. He fought the latch, but it wouldn't budge. Mama appeared on the street below. He knocked on the glass, but she didn't look up. She walked like she knew exactly where she was going. He wished he knew where that was.

He opened the box of pristine crayons and drew on a page of newsprint. He ate a peanut-butter-and-jelly sandwich. When the sun went down, he watched TV. Worried, he dragged a kitchen chair to the window and sat watching for Mama to come home. The neon sign came on across the street. He wondered who Jesus was. Mama said her daddy had been religious and tried to beat hell out of her. Bobby Ray made a pillow of his arms and focused on the beauty of those intense, rich colors.

Boyish laughter awakened him. A teenager dressed in black was spray-painting the wall across the street. Another was standing guard at the corner. Bobby Ray listened and watched as the painter opened a backpack and pulled out another can, yellow this time, green the next. The lookout motioned him to hurry up. The painter worked fast, making large bubble letters. Bobby Ray was enthralled. The teen at the corner whistled. The painter stashed his spray paint, shouldered his bag, and disappeared around the corner just as a police car came to the intersection. The squad car paused, a beam of light searching and finding the newly painted wall. The police car turned in the direction the boys had run, the beam of light waving from one side of the street to the other.

Giving up his vigil, Bobby Ray climbed into the bed he shared with Mama. He curled into a ball on Mama's side. She'd wake him up when she got home. Maybe she'd bring another man home with her, a nice one like the last, one willing to hand over an extra twenty. He slept fitfully.

Mama still wasn't home the next morning. Bobby Ray didn't know whether to go to school or wait. Scared and angry, he grabbed his books and headed down the stairs.

Mr. Salvaggio came out of his apartment looking like a pumpkin in his Giants sweatshirt. "Hey! Where's that mother of yours? She owes me rent!" Bobby Ray darted around him. "Hey! I'm talking to you, kid!" Mr. Salvaggio made a swipe for him, but Bobby Ray ran quick as a rat for the front door.

"Sheila!" Mr. Salvaggio shouted up the stairs. "You better pay up or my cousin Guido and I are gonna put you out on the street for good. You hear me?"

Frightened and wondering what would happen if Mama didn't have any money when she got home, Bobby Ray went to the nightclub where Mama worked. He slipped in a side door while a delivery was being unloaded. It was dimly lit inside. The place smelled bad. A man in shirtsleeves and a loosened tie signed paperwork on a clipboard and handed it to the uniformed truck driver. Opening a box, he pulled out a bottle and then spotted Bobby Ray. "What're you doing in here?" He jerked his chin. "Get out of here, kid! You trying to get me shut down?"

Bobby Ray stood his ground as the man came toward him. "I'm looking for my mother." His voice quavered.

"How would I know who your mother is?" The man grabbed him by the shoulder and thrust him toward the door. "Get outta here and stay out!"

Fighting tears, Bobby Ray stayed inside. "Her name's Sheila Dean. She works here."

The man spit out a foul word. "I didn't

know Sheila had a kid. I'd like to know where she is, too. She was supposed to dance last night and didn't bother showing up."

Bobby Ray didn't know where else to look and didn't want to go back to the apartment house and risk getting grabbed by Mr. Salvaggio. So he went to school. Class had already started, so he had to sneak into the room when Mr. Talbot wasn't looking and slip into his seat, hoping no one would say anything. No one did, but Mr. Talbot looked from Bobby Ray to the wall clock and then went back to explaining an arithmetic problem he'd written on the chalkboard. At least Mr. Talbot didn't send him to the office for a tardy slip. He would have had to make up a lie for the school secretary.

The classroom was warmer than the apartment, and Bobby Ray fought to keep his eyes open. He tried to make sense of the arithmetic problems on the paper Mr. Talbot handed out. His stomach hurt. He put his head in his arms.

The bell startled him awake. He hadn't finished the assignment. Kids headed out to recess. Mr. Talbot stood beside his desk. "Everything all right, Bobby Ray?"

Bobby Ray said everything was fine. At lunch, he ate only half of his sandwich, keeping the rest, worried he might not have anything to eat later.

When school let out, Bobby Ray ran all the

way home. The apartment was unlocked. Heart leaping with hope, Bobby Ray ran to the bedroom, expecting to see Mama asleep. She wasn't there. When he came out, he saw the empty space where the television had been. Had burglars come in or had Mr. Salvaggio taken the only thing of any value in the apartment? Bobby Ray was afraid to go downstairs and ask. Instead, he went out again and searched the neighborhood for Mama.

The liquor store owner said he hadn't seen Sheila Dean in three days. Bobby Ray walked until Turk Street ran into Market, then followed Market to Grant. He came up to Geary and walked around Union Square, then on down past the Curran Theater until he came to Leavenworth and headed down to Turk again. It was dark by the time he got home. The apartment lights were off and didn't come on when he flipped the switch. Mama still wasn't home.

Exhausted, hungry, and afraid, Bobby Ray sat on the old sofa. What should he do now? Where should he look? Mama always came home by morning. Why hadn't she returned?

Bobby Ray stretched the Smucker's Goober PB and J and the Wonder Bread for three days. He still had a couple of dollars in his pocket, but he was afraid to spend it.

Mr. Talbot asked him again if everything was all right, and Bobby Ray said yes again, throwing a little attitude to make it sound true. "Why wouldn't I be okay?"

"Because you've been wearing the same shirt for three days."

"Mama hasn't gotten around to doing the laundry. Okay?"

"All right, but where is your homework? You always do your homework, and you haven't turned anything in for two days. And you're not finishing what I'm giving you in class. That's not like you, Bobby Ray. What's going on?"

"I just forgot. That's all. I'll do it. I'll give it to you tomorrow."

He had to fight hard not to cry when Mr. Talbot put a hand on his shoulder and squeezed gently. "You'd tell me if you needed help, wouldn't you?"

Bobby Ray bought a banana and a Snickers bar on the way home. He worked on homework at the kitchen table. Someone knocked on the door, and Bobby Ray's heart picked up speed. He tiptoed over and peered through the peephole. Mr. Talbot stood outside the door. He rapped again. "Mrs. Dean? Bobby Ray?" His teacher knocked again, louder this time. A man's voice rumbled from below. Mr. Talbot said he was checking on a student. He left the doorway, and Bobby Ray couldn't see him anymore. What was Mr. Salvaggio saying to him?

Bobby Ray worried about that visit. He

tried to concentrate on his homework and finish everything he was supposed to. He took a shower, washed his hair, and brushed his teeth, hoping Mama would open the bathroom door and tell him he was taking too long.

He wore different clothes the next morning. Mr. Talbot looked him over and didn't say anything. Bobby Ray's stomach growled so loud the students around him laughed. Face hot, he kept his head down while Mr. Talbot called them all to order and went on with the lesson.

When Bobby Ray got home from school, Mr. Salvaggio was in the entry hall near the mailboxes with a man Bobby Ray didn't recognize. Mr. Salvaggio nodded at Bobby Ray. "He's the one. Nobody'll miss him." The man slipped a wad of folded bills into Mr. Salvaggio's fat fingers as Bobby Ray ran up the stairs.

The door was open this time. "Mama!" Relief surged until he saw the empty living room. All the furniture was gone. "Mama!" He ran for the bedroom. Not finding her there, he came out again, confused. The apartment was empty, except for a couple of boxes of Mama's clothes in the middle of the room.

The man who'd been with Mr. Salvaggio came into the apartment. "You're coming with me, kid."

Bobby Ray backed away. "My mother's coming home."

"When was the last time you saw your mother? Four days ago, from what I hear. She's gone. I'm gonna take care of you." When Bobby Ray tried to dart past him to the door, the man caught him by the arm. When Bobby Ray fought and screamed, the man clapped a hard hand over his mouth. Bobby Ray bit him. The man backhanded him so hard, Bobby Ray saw yellow and black spots before being tossed over the man's shoulder and carried out of the apartment, his legs trapped against the man's rock-hard chest.

"What do you think you're doing?" Bobby Ray heard his teacher's voice coming from the landing below. Pounding the stranger's back, Bobby Ray screamed for help. "Put that boy down!" Another man was asking for ID. Bobby Ray felt himself dumped. He bounced down half a dozen steps before someone caught hold of him. "I've got you."

Mr. Talbot held him while a police officer went up the stairs, talking fast into a small radio mounted on a shoulder harness. "Six foot, 190, white, dark hair cropped short, brown bomber jacket, Levi's, and black boots . . ."

Mr. Talbot asked Bobby Ray if he was hurt. He hurt everywhere. Mr. Talbot lifted him onto his lap and held him close. "It's okay,

275

Bobby Ray. We're here to help." Sobbing, Bobby Ray pressed into his teacher's arms, his heart still pounding in fear. "Who was that man? Anyone you know?" Bobby Ray had never seen him before. "Where's your mother?"

"I don't know." He hiccuped. "She promised she'd come back. She always comes back." When asked how long ago she'd left, Bobby Ray scrubbed at his eyes and tried to think. He didn't want to say five days. "I did my homework."

Mr. Talbot's eyes moistened. "Don't worry about that now. Don't worry about anything. Okay? We're going to get you help." The police officer came back down the stairs. The man had gotten away. Mr. Talbot sat in the backseat of the squad car with Bobby Ray and said everything was going to be okay. The police officer talked into his radio.

Bobby Ray didn't want to leave. How would his mother find him if he left the apartment? He cried and screamed curses, kicking the back of the police officer's seat.

When they got to the police station, Mr. Talbot sat with him until a lady with sad eyes came. Mr. Talbot ran his hand over Bobby Ray's head. "Take care of yourself." Bobby Ray knew then he'd never see his teacher again.

"I want my mother."

The lady nodded. "We're going to try to

find her. In the meantime, we have a safe place for you to stay."

Bobby Ray ended up across town with strangers. How was his mother going to find him? He didn't argue or say anything. He ate what was set in front of him. He took the bath the foster mother said he should, put on the pajamas, and went to bed without a word. As soon as the house was silent, he put his clothes back on and climbed out the window.

The police picked him up in the Tenderloin the next day, near the apartment house where he and Mama had lived. Authorities sent him to another foster family farther away. The people kept a closer eye on him, but he still made his escape in less than a week.

18

Roman made coffee and fixed breakfast for Jasper early Monday morning. He folded the omelet and slid it onto Jasper's plate. Dumping the pan into the sink, he suggested they sit outside.

"Not eating?"

"Maybe later."

Jasper slid the glass door open. "It's a bit fresh out there."

The morning mist hadn't burned off yet, and wouldn't for hours. "I can loan you a jacket."

"I'm fine." Jasper finished the omelet and leaned back. "What's on your mind, Bobby Ray?" He lifted his mug of coffee.

"I'm not sure what I'm going to do next."

"Are you talking about art or Grace Moore?"

"How did she get into this conversation?"

"Is that what we're having? A conversation?"

Roman got up and went to the wall. Half-sitting, he looked back at Jasper. He shouldn't have called Grace that night. He shouldn't have laughed at her. "I think I've painted myself into a corner."

"How do you mean?"

"I paint what sells. That doesn't mean I like it."

"The work or the money?"

Roman stood, angry. "Can we have one conversation when you're not asking me a bunch of questions?"

"It's the only way I can get you to talk. I'm not here to tell you what to do."

Roman gave a hard laugh. "You've been sticking your nose in since the day I met you."

"You were a ward of the court and a royal pain when you arrived at the ranch, but we knew you were something special. Your art was a cry for help."

"I was hoping to get kicked out."

"Sit down, son. You're making me nervous." Jasper waited until he did. "You had something to say back then. You just stopped talking."

"Graffiti doesn't pay very well."

"True. And it could land you in jail." Jasper drank half of his coffee. "But that isn't stopping you. The supplies in your studio, that back wall with a coat of fresh paint tell me that." Jasper set the mug down. "You went out again last night."

"I didn't do anything." Roman had dealt

with his emotions the way he always did. He filled a pack and headed for the city. He drove around for an hour before returning to the house, where he blasted the back wall of his studio.

"Graffiti was always your go-to medium when you were stressed. What's bugging you these days?"

Roman didn't duck and parry with Jasper this time. "I like the adrenaline rush. It beats putting a fist through a wall."

"You weren't angry, Bobby Ray. You were burning up with jealousy. You didn't like seeing Grace with another man."

Roman wanted to deny it. "It's none of my business who she's with. She works for me. That's it."

"Why don't you try getting to know Grace Moore as a person and not just an employee? I barely know the girl, and I like her."

"She has more walls than I do."

"All the more reason to find out what's behind them. Just don't bust through or try to climb over. Look for a gate. When you find it, knock; don't pound." He smiled slightly. "And wait."

"I've never had to wait before."

"If sex is the only thing you want, leave her alone. Grace isn't the kind of girl who hooks up with a guy and won't care when he walks away."

The door of the guest cottage opened, and

Grace came outside and walked over. "Good morning." She smiled at Jasper. "I was hoping I wouldn't miss you before you headed home."

"I wouldn't have left without saying goodbye." He rose.

Roman stayed seated while Jasper gave Grace a fatherly hug. Since when had they gotten so chummy?

"It was nice meeting you, Jasper. I hope I'll see you again."

"You will." He grinned over his shoulder at Roman. "Unless our friend moves again and leaves no forwarding address."

They talked for a few minutes, and then Grace turned to go into the house. "I'd better get to work or the boss will fire me."

Jasper looked at Roman with a raised brow. "And I'd better hit the road, or he won't lay out the welcome mat next time."

Roman followed them inside. Jasper headed for the guest room to collect his suitcase. Roman stood at the breakfast bar, watching Grace rinse the plates and put them in the dishwasher. "You're still mad at me."

"I was furious, but I'm over it." She closed the dishwasher firmly and straightened. "Now that I know I live next door to a Peeping Tom, I'll be more careful."

"I wasn't looking in your windows. You were standing right out in the open."

"An apology would be nice."

He'd never apologized to anyone in his life and wasn't about to start now. "Let's call it an error in judgment."

She rolled her eyes and headed for the office.

After Jasper left, Roman had nothing to do. He didn't feel like sketching or painting. When the phone rang, he made it an excuse to check in with Grace. She didn't look at him standing in the doorway. She was still on the phone. Prince Charming? She glanced at him, wrote a quick note, and held it out. *Talia. Do you want the numbers?* He shrugged. "He's right here." She handed him the phone.

All his gallery paintings had sold. He'd have enough in savings to take a year off. Maybe that'd give him time to figure out what he wanted to do. "Thanks, Talia."

Talia laughed. "Say that again. I'm not sure I heard right."

"You heard me." Roman ended the call and handed the phone back to Grace. "We had a good night."

"Talia told me." She had turned her chair and sat facing him. The phone rang again. Roman started to leave as she answered it, but she held up one finger. "That is odd. Here, you can ask him." She held out the phone.

"What?"

"Talia says a police officer came to the show."

Roman took the phone. "What did he want?"

"I'm not sure," Talia answered. "He asked a lot of questions."

"About what?"

"You. He wasn't asking anything that others haven't asked before, but it felt more like an interrogation."

He leaned against the doorjamb, pretending the conversation wasn't anything important. "Probably habit. Did he buy anything?"

"He was interested in your painting of the blackbirds. He asked if I knew anything about the bird. I told him I wasn't an ornithologist."

Roman's pulse kept climbing. He could feel the sweat breaking out. "When was this?"

"When you disappeared into the men's room. I was going to introduce you, but he got a phone call. I didn't see him after that. Is there something I should know?"

"About what?"

"You tell me."

Roman forced a laugh. "I don't have any outstanding warrants that I know about. Maybe he likes blackbirds. Did he make an offer for the painting?"

"Are you kidding? On a cop's pay?" She'd sold it to a movie producer known for sci-fi films. The police officer was forgotten as she talked about several other important people she'd met.

Roman told her he had work to do and handed the phone back to Grace. "I'll be in my studio."

Still sweating from the conversation, he wished he'd never allowed Talia to take that painting out of the house. He'd been in a dark mood when he painted the flock of blackbirds attacking a grotesque man crouched and twisted in self-defense. He hadn't intended to show the piece to anyone, let alone put it in the gallery for sale. Talia had seen it on his easel. She called it the most evocative work he'd done. Her assessment lifted the darkness and fanned his pride. He'd been poking the bear when he let her show it.

A prickle of fear went up his spine. He'd wanted to be caught during those dark days. He'd wanted the Bird caged. Now, he had too much to lose.

Maybe it was time to get out of town for a few days. After the San Diego mural and then finishing all the paintings needed for the show, he felt burned out. If a police officer was nosing around about the Bird, this would be a good time for a trip.

Any chance Grace would come along with him? Doubtful. Not unless he came up with a good reason to have her along. But the idea of leaving her behind didn't hold any appeal. Get to know her, Jasper said. He might find it easier if they were away from the office.

Every time they started to have any kind of personal conversation, she used work as an excuse to retreat.

He mulled over ideas until she came upstairs with messages. She glanced at his drafting table. "I don't think I've seen a blank piece of paper there since I started working for you."

"I'm short on inspiration right now."

"There's always the view out your window."

"Landscapes aren't my thing." But she'd given him the opening he needed. "Didn't you have an inquiry about me doing a mural for some town in the Gold Country?"

"I'll get you the file." She came back a few minutes later and handed it to him. "Golden. There's not much information on the place."

He flipped the papers and handed it back. "I want to see the town."

"The gentleman who called will be very happy to hear that. I can contact him and let him know you want to make the trip. When did you have in mind?"

"We can leave tomorrow morning."

She froze. "We?"

"Yes, we. I figure it will only take a couple of days."

"A couple of days?"

Clearly, she wasn't as eager to be alone with him as he was with her. He figured Prince Charming was the reason. "You don't have to repeat everything I say. And don't call the guy and tell them we're coming. The last thing I want is propaganda. This trip is about seeing whether I want to have anything to do with —" he glanced at the file again — "Golden."

"I can't go with you."

"You're my personal assistant. You'd be along to take notes and give your opinion."

"You've never asked for my opinion before."

"In this case, I'll want it."

"Okay. Everything there is to know about Golden is in the file. It doesn't look worth your time."

"I still want to go, and I want you along. You might see something I miss."

"You're the artist! You'll see whatever you want to see." She looked shaken. "I'm not going on a trip with you."

He'd never seen her so agitated. Maybe she wasn't as indifferent as he thought. He wasn't going to jeopardize their current relationship unless . . . unless what? "I can see you're uncomfortable with the idea, but I don't see a problem. People take business trips together all the time. Didn't you travel with your previous boss?" He could only hope.

"Harvey was sixty-six years old and happily married." As soon as the words were out of her mouth, color flooded her cheeks.

"So you object because I'm thirty-four and single."

"I can't go, Roman. I have responsibilities."

"Such as?"

"I have Samuel Friday night through Sunday evening."

"Let Shanice take care of her own kid for a change."

Grace's mouth fell open. "I thought you knew. Samuel is *my* son, not Shanice's."

"Yours?" Roman tried to take in this startling revelation. Grace was a mother? "No. I didn't know. You didn't tell me." Grace must have joint custody with her ex-husband if she only had her son on weekends.

She clenched a hand against her stomach. "Mrs. Sandoval knew. It's never been a secret. Samuel is the reason I didn't want to work so far away from Burbank."

"I thought money changed your mind."

"I have to make a decent living."

"What about alimony?"

"I put my husband through college. He left a few months after he graduated. Thankfully, he didn't ask for any."

Roman thought she was joking, but she looked dead serious. What sort of guy had she married? At least the guy cared enough about his kid to want to have him during the week. Another thought came. Maybe Grace was dating Prince Charming in hopes of finding a better father figure for Samuel. She wouldn't be the first woman to see marriage as the answer to all her problems. His mother always thought some guy would come along

287

and take care of her, but all they did was pay for her services. She sold herself cheap to keep a roof over their heads and food on the table. Some left bruises. One of them left her pregnant with him.

Grace stood silent. She looked so ashen, he wondered what sort of expression he'd been wearing. He forced a slight smile. How many other surprises might he find out about Grace Moore on a road trip?

"We'll be back by Friday. Be ready to go early. I want to be on the road by seven."

"Where will we be staying?"

"In a hotel. Where do you think?"

"I meant, what town? Golden doesn't have a hotel."

"Don't worry, Grace. We'll find a place to stay." He held up his hands to halt the flow of objections he could see coming. "You'll have a nice private room and bath, nowhere near mine."

"Can we discuss this, please?"

He didn't want to argue with her. "I have to get out of here." He headed for the door. Maybe he'd go to the Getty. He hadn't been there in a while. "Seven in the morning, Grace. If you're not up and ready, I'll come over and get you."

Strictly business, Roman said. Why did she have the feeling this trip was about anything but business? *Lord, am I overreacting?* Harvey

288

had taken her to conferences. Patrick had thought it a great opportunity for her. Looking back, she knew why he'd been so eager for her to spend time away.

What excuse could she offer Roman for not going? She wouldn't have Samuel until the weekend. Just because she'd realized her attraction didn't mean he had any ulterior motives. Though sometimes he looked at her in a way that made her wonder. Maybe she should talk with someone she trusted.

Shanice understood immediately. "The fact that you're asking what I think tells me you're nervous about going anywhere with him. Has he given cause for distrust?"

"He's never made a pass, if that's what you mean. He said he wants to see Golden."

"Okay. What are you really worried about?"

Sighing, Grace rubbed her forehead. "I'm not good at reading men."

"Well, I am."

Grace understood her friend was making sad reference to her pre-Christian, club-hopping days. Even after becoming a believer, Shanice had seen nothing wrong with having a good time with friends at a club. All that had changed in one night.

"You thought he was a player, Shanice."

"I shouldn't have judged. I only met the man once. Just because a man is good-looking doesn't mean he's a jerk like Patrick. You've been working for Roman Velasco for five months. You should have some idea what kind of guy he is by now."

"He's a workaholic, and right now he doesn't have a project." He hadn't even set up a fresh canvas on an easel.

"Sounds like he's looking for something to inspire him."

"That's what he said." Grace felt somewhat reassured. "I've never been to northern California."

"It's beautiful up there."

"I've never been farther north than Fresno."

"Oh, honey, then go. If anyone deserves some R & R, it's you." Shanice let out a breath. "Forget I said that."

Grace knew why Shanice retracted her words so quickly. "I'm just nervous about spending all day with him."

"You spend all day with him every day."

"He's in his studio. I'm in the office. We talk about what's on the schedule in the morning. I go over messages midday and before I leave."

"Oh. Well. It doesn't sound like you need to worry."

Everything did seem strictly business with Roman, but Grace had felt undercurrents lately. Especially at the show in Laguna. Maybe she was imagining something that wasn't there.

"Listen, Grace. If you find yourself in over your head again, call me. And I don't think it would hurt to get a man's opinion about this trip. Why don't you call Brian and talk to him about it?"

"I think I'll do that." If Brian really cared about her, he wouldn't want her going off on a trip with another man. It might also be a way to find out how deep his feelings ran.

Brian asked the same question Shanice had. After a brief and somewhat-disappointing conversation, he left it up to her.

Grace called Selah to ask her advice. "Oh, that's wonderful. It's always good to get away and see new things. This is a great opportunity for you, *chiquita.* Enjoy yourself. If Mr. Velasco decides to extend the trip, just let me know. Don't worry about anything. Sammy is fine."

Grace wondered if Selah meant to imply Samuel wouldn't miss his own mother. What hurt even more was knowing it might be true.

19

The next morning, Roman threw a duffel bag into the trunk of his car. He checked his watch — 6:57. Grace came around the corner, wearing jeans and a lightweight pink sweater, not her usual business attire. She looked ready to travel with her small suitcase, backpack, pink tote bag, and purse. He stowed the suitcase and tote bag. Taking the backpack, he grimaced. "What do you have in this thing? Bricks?"

"My laptop and a couple of textbooks."

Roman arranged the suitcase and duffel bag to protect her backpack. Grace was in the passenger seat before he could play gentleman and open the door for her. Sliding into the driver's seat, he looked at her. "We don't need a map." He put his finger on the ignition and the engine roared to life. "The car has GPS."

"I like maps. I know it's a little old-fashioned." She lifted her shoulders.

"A little?" He grinned.

"I just want to see the big picture and know where we're going and how we're going to get there."

"Have your life all planned out, you mean."

"I haven't had much luck with that."

When she looked away, he got the message. *Don't ask.* "Okay. We'll do it your way. I'll drive. You navigate."

She looked surprised. "You're sure?"

"If you get us lost, GPS will find us." He didn't tell her he already knew how he wanted to get where they were going. The long way.

"If you want to get to Golden by this afternoon, we should take the freeway."

"I hate freeways."

She looked at the map and suggested the coast highway rather than head inland to the city and then north. She'd been nervous about this trip yesterday, but seemed relaxed, even eager, this morning. "What changed your mind?"

"About what?" She refolded the map as he drove toward Malibu.

"Coming on this road trip with me."

She looked at him. "You didn't call it a road trip. You said it was strictly business."

"Take it easy. I'm not kidnapping you."

"Are we going to Golden or not?"

"We'll get there." He nodded to the map in her hand. "Find Ojai."

Frowning slightly, she refocused on the

map.

Roman glanced at Grace. She was looking out the car window. She'd hardly spoken on the drive to Ojai. Was he getting the silent treatment? Roman wondered what she was thinking, but didn't dare ask. He had tricked her. She didn't know the full extent yet. "Have you been to Ojai?"

Her smile was relaxed. "I'd never driven through Ventura until today."

Surprised, he gave her a quick look before he pulled into a parking space on Ojai Avenue. "We'll check out a few galleries after breakfast. Might be good to see what other people are selling." He was also curious what would catch her eye. He knew she didn't care for his work.

He found a café on a side street near the Arcade. The hostess seated them by the window. Grace thanked her. Tucking her purse under her chair, she looked across at him. "Is something wrong?"

"Not at all. I'm just beginning to realize how little I know about you."

"I could say the same."

"Where were you born?"

She leaned back, studying him. For a moment, he didn't think she'd tell him. "Memphis, Tennessee. What about you?"

"San Francisco. Do you have family in Memphis?"

Her expression clouded. "I was young when my parents died. My aunt brought me to Fresno when I was seven. Are your parents in San Francisco?"

She didn't want to talk about her parents, which made him curious how they'd died. Better to answer her question before asking another. "You and I have something in common. I was seven the last time I saw my mother. She went out one night and never came back. CPS took over after she disappeared. I moved around a lot." A slight understatement. He couldn't even remember all the foster homes he'd run away from.

Roman had just told her more about his past than he'd ever told a woman. Thankfully, she didn't look at him with pity. He couldn't tell what she was thinking. He gave in to curiosity. "How'd your parents die?"

She let out her breath softly and avoided his perusal. He knew she wasn't going to tell him when the waitress arrived with their coffee and asked if they were ready to order. Roman said they needed a few more minutes. Grace avoided further conversation by hiding behind the menu. The waitress returned and took their orders. Grace faced him again, expression enigmatic. "When did you decide to become an artist?"

She didn't want to talk about her parents. Okay. "I didn't decide. It just happened. A teacher caught me doodling in class and said he'd accept drawings in lieu of incomplete homework assignments."

"You told me you tagged buildings. Were you in a gang?"

He smiled slightly. "Quid pro quo." He'd answered her questions. She shook her head.

Breakfast was a quiet affair.

On the way out of the restaurant, Roman paused at a display of tourist brochures. "Let's take a walk." Grace fell into step beside him. He found the first gallery around the corner from the Arcade. Roman wandered, taking note of where Grace lingered. She liked seascapes, landscapes, watercolors. No wonder she didn't like his work. But then, neither did he.

She must have felt him looking at her because she turned. "Time to go?" They headed for the car.

Roman felt edgy when she stayed silent as he drove. He'd never had a problem getting a conversation started with a woman. He stopped at a coffee shop in Ventucopa. "I need a caffeine break. How about you?" Grace asked for a latte. She talked with a woman at the bakery counter. He had to wait for the coffees, and saw there was no lull in Grace's conversation. She glanced over when he collected their order. The women exchanged a few more words, and Grace touched her arm before joining him.

He handed her the latte. "You don't have

any trouble making friends, do you?" He wished she'd be that open and friendly with him.

"Veronica says the wildflowers are still in bloom on the Carrizo Plain."

Veronica. Grace probably knew the woman's entire family history.

Back on the road, she talked more. Her aunt had been a career woman and didn't enjoy travel. "We had to take several connecting flights from Memphis to Fresno. It's the only time I've ever been in an airplane."

Roman told her about flying to Rome and traveling around Europe on a motorcycle. The more he talked, the more relaxed she looked.

"You've visited places I'll only see on the Travel Channel."

He looked at her. "You never know."

"Did you study art in Europe?"

"I never studied anywhere. Formally, anyway." He eased off the gas as he went around a curve. "I never did well in an environment where someone was telling me what to do or how to think."

"Talia said you don't follow rules. Maybe that's why people like your work so much."

"But not you."

"I don't matter." She looked away and gasped. *"Stop!"*

Roman slammed on the brakes, sure he was about to hit something. The car fishtailed.

He corrected and pulled onto the side of the road. He uttered a foul word. "What'd I hit?"

"Nothing. I'm sorry I startled you." She opened the car door.

"Where are you going?"

"Roman, look around you!" She laughed, her face radiant.

The hillsides were covered in purple, yellow, and orange wildflowers. He gave them a cursory glance, and watched her picking her way into the field. She looked around in wonder and then back at him. "Veronica was right. Have you driven this way before?"

"Once." He hadn't chosen this route to see the color-splashed hillsides. "It'll be over in a few weeks."

"Then it's perfect timing we're here now." She spread her arms. "Look what God can do with weeds."

God again.

She kept walking farther into the field. She bent to pick something up and tucked it in her pocket. He took out his phone and snapped a picture of her standing among the lupines and poppies. Leaning against his car, he took several more. He pocketed the phone when she headed back.

She looked at him. "I guess you want to get going again."

"We're in no hurry." She was showing him a world he'd never noticed. "Why don't we stop in Fresno for the night? I can meet your aunt."

The joy left her face. "Aunt Elizabeth doesn't like surprises."

"I take it you don't get along."

"We get along. I call her twice a month and visit whenever I can."

Roman hadn't noticed any older women showing up at the cottage, and Grace hadn't mentioned going on any trips, short or long. "Give her a call. We can swing by on the way back." He wanted to meet the woman. The aunt might also be more forthcoming with information.

Grace didn't take her phone out of her purse.

After a couple more hours on the road, they stopped for a late lunch in Lemoore. The time passed pleasantly enough, even if Grace was less than open with personal details about her past. When they returned to the car, Roman sensed Grace's tension. She barely talked as they approached Fresno. He had a dozen questions he wanted to ask, but knew better. He merged onto 99, heading north out of Fresno. Her body relaxed. She took a breath and let it out slowly. He glanced over, but she avoided eye contact.

Roman touched the car computer screen and did a search of Merced hotels with pools. After a day in the car, it'd be nice to swim some laps. "Did you bring a swimming suit?" The look she gave him was answer enough. Roman used the voice activation system to ask for directions to a sporting goods store. "I'll buy you a suit." When Grace protested, he cut her off. "You can pick it out or I will, and I'm paying for it. I'm hot, I'm tired, and I want to swim."

"I'm your personal assistant, Roman, not your lifeguard."

"You need to cool off as much as I do." He pulled into a shopping mall and parked. "Come on."

When they got into the store, Grace meandered until he looked pointedly at a neon-pink two-piece on a mannequin and grinned. She quickly found a functional black one-piece suit. He couldn't resist needling. "Chicken."

He paid for the suit before he realized she'd opened her purse and pulled out her wallet. She didn't thank him or even look at him on the way to the car. Roman glanced at her when he got in and saw the hot blush that had climbed up her neck and filled her face. Why was she so embarrassed? "It's not lingerie, Grace."

Roman told the hotel clerk they needed two rooms, on separate floors. As soon as the clerk handed Grace a key card, she shouldered her backpack, lifted her suitcase and tote bag, and headed for the elevator. He stopped the door just before it closed. "I'll see you at the pool in twenty minutes."

"Yes, sir." She glared at him. "Are you getting in?"

"I think I'd better wait." He let go of the door and stepped back as she punched the button. What had he done wrong?

He thought he'd be alone with Grace in the pool and they could talk. Kids were everywhere! Muttering a curse under his breath, Roman opened the gate. He could forget about swimming laps. Three women sat on the pool steps. Grace wasn't one of them. Pulling off his T-shirt, Roman tossed it with his towel on a vacant chaise lounge. The three women looked at him. The freestyle tribal tattoo he designed to be wrapped around his rib cage and chest usually drew attention. He'd suffered hours of pain and paid thousands of dollars to get inked. He wouldn't be wasting time and money again.

Roman spotted Grace in the deep end, batting a beach ball back to a child in the shallow end. He found free space and dove in. Staying under, he headed for her. It was worth the chlorine burn to see Grace underwater. She had legs like a ballet dancer and more curves than he'd imagined. When he came up right in front of her, she pulled back, startled. Her dark hair was wet and slicked against her head; her pale shoulders glistened.

Raking his hair back, Roman grinned at

her. "The water feels good, doesn't it?"

"Yes." She put a little more distance between them. "You were right." She gave him an impish smile. "But you're going to have a hard time doing laps."

"I gave up on that idea when I came out the door." He moved closer again. "How about a game of Marco Polo?"

"It's against the rules."

"Rules are made to be broken, Grace."

Her eyes flickered. "Not by me, and certainly not with my boss." She swam away.

He shouldn't have flirted with her. She was going to be even more uptight with him now. She walked up the steps and sat near a woman holding a toddler on her lap. They fell into easy conversation. Children swarmed the deep end. One tossed a ball at him. He caught it in one hand and tossed it back. "Let the man do his laps," the woman sitting with Grace called out to them. When they kept getting in the way, she called them to the shallows, gathered her brood, and headed for the gate.

Grace was back in the pool, but keeping her distance. When she lifted herself onto the side, he swam over. Crossing his arms on the edge of the pool, he smiled up at her. "You look cooled off."

"I'm sorry I got mad."

"I didn't intend to embarrass you. It was my idea to swim, and right that I paid for the suit. It's no big deal, Grace. I wasn't expecting anything in return." *Shut up, you idiot.* He raised himself and sat beside her. Unlike other women he'd met, she didn't look at his body. She looked away, then straight ahead. "We're going to Yosemite tomorrow." That brought her head around.

"What about Golden?"

"It's not going anywhere. Have you ever been to Yosemite?"

"No, but —"

"If you think wildflowers are something, wait until you see Half Dome." He curved his hand over the edge of the pool, as close to hers as he could get without touching her. She moved her hand away. She looked uncomfortable. He stood and held out his hand. "Let's get dressed and find a place to eat." She hesitated before accepting his help. Her hand was cold, and she shivered. Roman grabbed his towel from the chaise lounge and swung it around her. "What time do you want to go out to dinner?" He took another towel from the pile by the gate.

"Whenever you want."

He looked at her. "I'm starving right now." *And not just for food.* "How soon can you be ready?"

Half an hour later, Roman sat in the lobby, waiting. Grace came out of the elevator, back in uniform: black slacks, loose button-up white blouse, a single strand of pearls, and low black heels. Classic, professional. Was she trying to remind him this trip was supposed to be strictly business?

The hotel clerk had given him directions to a nice steak house. Roman gave the host a twenty to seat them in a quiet booth. When they were offered drinks, Grace asked for water. If he wasn't the one driving, he'd have ordered a Scotch, maybe two. He was beginning to feel as tense as she looked. When he picked up the wine list, she turned her glass over.

"Okay." He dropped it on the table and studied her. "What's wrong?"

"How long are we going to be gone, Roman?"

Was that all that was worrying her, or was there more? "We'll be back by Friday. We can swing by and pick up your son on the way home. It'll save you the trip back to wherever he is when he's not with you." Her expression altered, like a veil dropping over her face. "Is that a problem?"

"It's not on the way."

He'd wait. Maybe she'd trust him enough to talk about what was going on in her life. Then again, how much of his own was he willing to share? He didn't want to talk about his past. Maybe he should. Maybe that would open her up as well. Aside from the growing attraction, something else was happening here. He didn't want to back away this time.

Why not take Jasper's advice for a change and see what happened?

She looked ready to take the bus home.

"Try not to worry, Grace. This is more about me than you." A lie. "I needed to get out of the studio for a while, to think." True. "And since you told me you haven't seen much, I thought why not see something on the way." He'd been to Yosemite Valley and Half Dome, but he'd never gone over Tioga Pass or down to Mono Lake. "Have you ever been to Bodie?"

"Bodie?" She shook her head. "I've never been anywhere."

She'd told him that. He just wanted her to remember. He'd read a few brochures in the hotel tourist information rack while waiting for her to come downstairs. "It's a ghost town ten miles off the highway." He spent the next few minutes telling her everything he remembered from the brochure. He was beginning to sound like a travel agent trying to sell a tour.

Grace didn't look like she wanted him as guide. "That's a lot of miles to cover in a couple of days."

"We have time. Let's enjoy the ride."

She put her hand on the table as though bracing herself. "Why are we really on this trip, Roman?"

He let out his breath slowly and leaned back, surveying her. "I don't know. I want more, I guess." He smiled slightly, trying to ease the worry flickering in her eyes. "More life. I want whatever it is you have that makes you see what I miss."

She didn't say anything, but her face softened as she searched his. "When I started working for you, I had the distinct impression you wanted convenience without complications."

"And you think getting to know one another would complicate our relationship?"

"I hope not."

He hadn't expected to feel hurt. Was she worried about what Prince Charming might think? Why was he working so hard to get close to this woman? Roman signaled the waiter.

"Ready to order, sir?"

Roman looked to Grace for an answer. Without opening the menu, she ordered a salad. Annoyed, Roman asked the waiter to give them another minute. He leaned forward. "I didn't bring you to a steak house so you could have a dinner salad."

She gasped. "You're impossible." She leaned forward, too. "It's a waste of money to buy a steak I can't eat."

"Oh. You're a vegetarian."

"No, but I'm not a glutton either."

At least he'd gotten a rise out of her. "Eat what you can." He signaled the waiter again. The man approached cautiously.

Roman didn't know where to pick up the conversation after that tirade.

She was looking at him again, but her anger had already dissipated. "You're impossible to read. Do you know that?"

He gave a bleak laugh. "You're telling *me* that?" There was something new in her expression. "What?"

She bowed her head, smoothing the napkin on her lap. "I'm not sure what you want from me."

Neither was he, but she'd unlocked the gate. He could hear Jasper's voice in his head. *Don't push. Wait to be invited in.* He'd had only three friends growing up, all dead before they turned eighteen. The responsibility for one could be laid at his feet. Maybe that was the reason he'd never gotten close to anyone since. And never a woman. Jasper Hawley had his theories about Bobby Ray Dean's reasons. Roman didn't want to know.

"I'd like to find out if we can be friends."

Grace sat at the desk in her hotel room, responding to Shanice's text asking how the road trip was going.

He wants to find out if we can be friends.

And you said?

I didn't say no. He's been different since we left Topanga Canyon.

Different how?

I don't know exactly. We've been talking more.

307

Talking about what?

Places he's seen. He had a motorcycle and rode all over Europe. He has a tattoo wrapped around his rib cage and up onto his chest.

And you know this how?!?

We went swimming at the hotel. Lots of moms and kids. Don't worry. My room is on a different floor. He's been a gentleman. Most of the time. He can still be aggravating and rude.

Should I be worried about you? Don't forget Brian.

Grace had forgotten all about Brian. That wasn't a good sign. She thumbed a response. Nothing has changed in that regard. I'd better get back to studying.

OK. I'll check in with you again. Be careful.

Tonight, over dinner, Grace had caught a glimpse of Roman she hadn't seen before. Vulnerability. It surprised her because he'd always come across as a man who knew exactly who he was and how to get what he wanted. Was he playing with her? She didn't need Shanice to tell her to be careful. It had become her natural inclination.

Whatever Roman's real intent, she should get to know him. Maybe there was more to the man than what she already knew. Until this evening, she thought he was a cynical, discontented loner driven to succeed. He worked hard, made a truckload of money from his art and investments, and used some to buy himself a fortress.

Roman Velasco was certainly no knight in shining armor. Oh, he had armor, all right, and cannons aimed at anyone who dared intrude. He went out occasionally to dally with a peasant girl. She'd learned about a man's physical needs from Patrick. Roman would have as little trouble as Patrick finding a willing girl.

She had learned from her marriage to Patrick that she didn't know what went on in men's minds. Sometimes she'd feel a hint something was off, that their relationship had less to do with love than with his goals. He hadn't forced her to give up anything, but he'd known how to make her feel guilty enough to surrender all her dreams so he could attain his.

Friends she trusted had picked Brian. They knew men better than she did. And she liked Brian. She'd be able to think straight with a man like that. He wouldn't be like Patrick: needy one moment, demanding the next. Brian felt safe.

Roman wasn't safe. Sometimes she felt like she was in deep water with him, monsters circling and coming up from below. *Lord, I don't know if I should be friends with this man. He has only two friends — Talia Reisner and Jasper Hawley. Why is that? If this is a bad idea, let me know in a way I'll understand. Please, Lord.*

She slept fitfully, dreaming of her mother looking out the kitchen window, her face pale with tension. And then it happened again, and all the fear came rushing back. With a cry, Grace sat up in bed. Trembling, body damp with cold sweat, she listened intently, half-expecting her father to come through the door.

I'm in a hotel. It was a nightmare. Everything is all right now.

She lay back down. Pulling the blanket up, she curled on her side. She'd had the nightmare before, many times, but that was years ago, when her aunt first brought her to Fresno. What had roused it tonight? The evening with Roman? *Lord, please, don't let it start up again where it left off. Please, God.*

20

Grace, Age 7

Gracie sat at the kitchen table with her Little Mermaid coloring book open to a page with Ariel, Flounder, and Sebastian exploring sea rocks. Perplexed, she pointed at shapes on the page. "Mommy, what are these things?" Her mother went on peeling potatoes in the sink, her glance lifting to look out the window. Daddy would be home soon. Gracie needed to finish her picture quickly. If she did a good job, Daddy might smile. "Mommy?"

"Oh, Gracie. What did you say?" Her mother rinsed her hands and dried them with a small towel. She glanced out the window again before looking over Gracie's shoulder. "Those are sea anemones." She tapped the picture. "That's a spiny sea urchin. This is coral, and that's seaweed." She looked out the window again. Mommy's expression made Gracie's stomach tighten. Would Daddy come home mad again?

"What color should they be?"

"I don't know, sweetie." Mommy bit her lip and looked away again, distracted. "Can't you remember what they looked like in the movie?" A car door slammed out front, and Mommy's body gave a slight jerk. She stepped to the sink and looked out the window. Her breath came out. "Time to play hide-and-seek, Gracie."

"But I haven't finished —"

"Now!" Grabbing her arm, Mommy yanked Gracie off the chair and hauled her quickly to the front hall. "Daddy's not feeling well again." Leaning down, she spoke in a hushed voice, her eyes wild and darting to the front door. "Find your best hiding place and stay still and quiet as a little mouse until Mommy comes and finds you. Go on now." The look on her mother's face frightened Gracie so much she started to cry. Mommy hushed her. "Go! Hurry!"

Gracie fled down the hall just as Daddy opened the front door. Daddy's voice rumbled like a gathering storm. "Where were you this afternoon?"

Gracie looked frantically for a place to hide.

"I was here." Mommy's voice was high, frightened.

"Liar!" Gracie heard another noise and Mommy's sharp cry of pain. Daddy's voice darkened. "I called, Leanne. Twice! You didn't answer. Who were you with?"

Gracie slid open the mirrored door of

Mommy's closet and ducked inside. She closed the door quietly, climbed over some pairs of shoes, and crouched in the back corner. She hugged her knees against her chest and made herself as small as she could.

Daddy kept shouting and Mommy talked fast, pleading for him to listen. "I went grocery shopping, Brad. I worked in the back garden. I picked up Gracie at school. I was on the phone with —"

Daddy shouted, "Shut up!" Glass shattered. Mommy cried out. Gracie heard a loud thump and covered her ears.

After a moment, she lowered her hands, panting softly, heart pounding. Daddy was talking now, storm over, his voice so different from anything Gracie had heard before. Was he crying? He said something low and broken. "Leanne, honey, I'm sorry. Leanne . . . What have I done?"

Gracie could hear Daddy moving around, pacing, sobbing. "What am I going to do? What am I going to do?" When he started down the hall, Gracie froze in terror. She could barely breathe. He came into the bedroom where he and Mommy slept together. She heard dresser drawers opening, banging. Daddy made a moaning sound. "Where did you hide it, Leanne? Where is it?" Gracie pressed back hard against the closet wall.

The mirrored door banged open. Daddy's

black office shoes and gray slacks appeared. He took a box from the shelf and tossed it over his shoulder, then another. He let out a relieved breath and took something from a shiny wooden box. Metal slid against metal with a sharp snap, and her bladder emptied. She felt the warmth spread in her panties and onto the rug beneath her. A frightened whimper escaped, and Daddy froze. Gracie pressed back so hard, her bones hurt. Her father reached up and slid hangers along the pole until they were crushed together above Gracie's head, revealing her hiding place.

His face twisted, his cheeks pale and wet. Daddy didn't look like Daddy. He stared at her, his mouth moving as though he wanted to say something but couldn't. He closed his eyes tightly and stepped back; then he dragged the hangers of clothes back into place so she was hidden again. When he lowered his arm, Gracie saw the gun in his hand. He was shaking. She heard the closet door close again. She waited, listening to his footsteps go down the hall toward the living room.

Gracie jumped at a loud bang from the living room.

The doorbell rang, and she opened her eyes, staring into the darkness. It rang a second, then a third time. Someone knocked hard on the front door and called out, "Memphis Police. Open the door."

More voices outside, moving away from the house. Shouted orders.

Shivering, Gracie listened, but didn't move. She waited for Mommy to come and find her. Why was she taking so long? Would she be upset because Gracie had wet her pants? Scrubbing away tears, Gracie covered her head.

Sirens sounded in the distance and came closer. She heard tires squeal. More shouts outside, silence inside. Something big hit the front door, and there was a crash. Footsteps entered quickly. Men talked in low voices. "Woman's body in the kitchen. Man dead in the living room — .357 on the floor; looks like a suicide. Neighbor said there's a little girl — Grace."

Stay still and quiet as a little mouse, Mommy had said, and so Gracie did.

The closet door slid open, and a big man in black lace-up boots, baggy black pants with pockets, a thick vest with white letters, and a helmet pushed clothes aside. "Found her!" Flinching, Gracie pressed back again. Hunkering, the man smiled sadly. "It's okay, Grace. You can come out now." When she didn't move, the man held out his hands, palms up. "Come to me. I won't hurt you."

The officer had a deep voice like Daddy's.

When Gracie didn't come, the man in black leaned in, slipped his big hands beneath her arms, and lifted her out. She opened her

315

mouth, but no sound came out. She felt engulfed by his strength. "You're safe, Grace. No one is going to hurt you." He held her easily, his voice gentle. "I have a little girl about your age. Her name is Ellie."

Another black-garbed officer stood behind him, but turned away, speaking into a radio mounted on his shoulder. Gracie's body shook like the last leaf of autumn clinging to a broken branch.

"We're taking you out of here, Grace. I want you to put your head on my shoulder and close your eyes tight."

Gracie twisted in his arms. "I want Mommy. Where's Mommy?"

The officer's arm tightened beneath her, and she felt his hand cup the back of her head. "Close your eyes, honey. Just for a minute. Can you do that for me, Grace?"

"I want Mommy." Her voice quavered and tears came.

The other officer took a pink parka with a hood from the closet. "Use this."

"Good idea." The officer set her down and put the jacket on her. The officer zipped the jacket all the way to the top and pulled the hood up over her head. When she tried to push it back so she could see, he brushed her hands away. "Leave it." He lifted her again.

Carried down the hall in strong arms, Gracie felt the air change from warm to cold. When the police officer stepped down, Gracie knew she was outside the house. She peeked out from beneath the hood and saw police cars parked out front, red lights flashing. Two men pulled something on wheels out of a big white van. Mrs. Channing, the next-door neighbor, stood on the lawn, crying and hugging herself as she talked with another police officer.

Gracie struggled. "Mommy!" She couldn't see her anywhere. Where was she? "Mommy!"

The officer lowered her to the ground. Hunkering in front of her, he held her by the arms. "You're going to be okay."

"I want my mommy."

His eyes grew moist. "I know you do, honey. Your mommy and daddy wouldn't want you to see them like this."

What did that mean? Tears poured down her cheeks. Men came and went from the house. Why were all these people here? Why wouldn't the policeman let her back inside? Why didn't Mommy come when she called? Why did Daddy have a gun? Why was Mrs. Channing crying and all bent over? Gracie tried to pull away, but the officer wouldn't let go of her arms. She screamed for Mommy. Mommy was in the kitchen. She knew she was. The light was still on. Two men were standing in there. She could see them through the window. "Mommy!"

Another van pulled up with big letters on the side. The side door slid open, and a woman got out quickly with a microphone and a man with a camera. The officer holding Gracie captive said a short, sharp word Daddy said when he was mad. He looked around. "Can someone give me a little help here?"

Mrs. Channing hurried over. "I can take her to my house." She took Gracie by the hand. "Come on, honey-child. I'll make you some hot cocoa and read you a story. They'll come get you in a little while." Gracie thought she meant Mommy and Daddy would come, and left with Mrs. Channing willingly. When they went inside the house next door, Mrs. Channing asked if Gracie was hungry. Did she want some dinner? Some cookies? Did she want to watch TV? "Oh, honey, you're wet." Mrs. Channing looked ready to cry again. "I still have some of my daughter's clothes. Come on, now. Let's get you a nice warm bath."

It wasn't Mommy and Daddy who came to get Gracie. It was a woman with dark hair, a stranger Gracie had never seen before. Mrs. Channing didn't know her either, but took the business card from her hand and invited her inside. Before Gracie could understand what was happening, she found herself buckled in the backseat of the woman's car. She tried to open the door, but it was locked. She twisted around in the seat, trying to claw her way to the back window as she screamed for

Mommy. The woman talked in a calm voice as she drove, and Gracie's house disappeared behind her.

The night darkened as Gracie moved from a car to an office where another stranger, a gray-haired lady this time, told Gracie to sleep on the sofa. The woman covered her with a soft blanket and gently brushed the hair back from her face. "Just close your eyes and try to sleep." The two women shuffled papers and talked in low voices. One made several phone calls.

Gracie didn't want to go to sleep, but awakened confused when the gray-haired lady put a hand on her shoulder. "We have a place for you." She said a nice foster couple was waiting to meet her. What was a foster couple?

"I want my mommy," Gracie cried.

The gray-haired lady sat on the sofa with her and put an arm around her shoulders. "I know you want your mommy, but she's gone, honey. So is your daddy."

Gone? Gone where? "They're at home."

"Mr. and Mrs. Arnold are very nice people. They're going to take good care of you for a few days. There are things for us to sort out. They love children. You'll be safe."

Gracie yearned for Mommy, but every time she asked, Mrs. Arnold said Mommy had gone to heaven. She didn't say where Daddy had gone. Gracie had bad dreams every night. She'd hear Daddy shouting and Mommy crying. Then other sounds and strangers everywhere. She hid in the closet and screamed for Mommy. Mrs. Arnold would slide the closet door open and lift her out and hold her and rock her. "You're safe with us, honey. You don't need to hide or be afraid anymore." She'd tuck Gracie back into bed with the brand-new teddy bear the Arnolds had given her. "He'll make you feel better."

One morning, Mrs. Arnold told her, "Your aunt Elizabeth will be here tomorrow, Grace. She's your mother's sister. She's coming all the way from Fresno, California. Isn't that wonderful? She's going to take care of you."

Aunt Elizabeth didn't look anything like Mommy. She was pretty, but she didn't look happy. Or friendly. Mrs. Arnold and Aunt Elizabeth talked while Grace sat on the sofa, the stuffed bear in her arms. Scared, she kept her head down, but heard every word.

"I don't see the need for more talk." Aunt Elizabeth spoke firmly.

"But she's been through a terrible ordeal, Miss Walker." Mrs. Arnold sounded distressed.

"Yes, and delaying will only make matters worse." Aunt Elizabeth stood and shouldered her purse. She looked down at Gracie with

320

bleak eyes. She faced Mrs. Arnold and extended her hand. "Thank you for looking after my niece until I could get here. I do appreciate it."

"She's a perfect little angel."

"Come, Grace." Aunt Elizabeth headed for the door. Opening it, she looked back. Her mouth tightened. "Time to go home."

Grace's heart leaped. The bear clutched close with one arm, she ran to her aunt. Aunt Elizabeth didn't take her hand, but walked ahead to a white car parked at the curb. She opened the back door, tossed Gracie's small suitcase to the far side of the backseat, and gestured to Gracie. "Get in."

Gracie knew how to strap herself in. Aunt Elizabeth watched until the buckle clicked, then slammed the door. Mrs. Arnold said something, and Aunt Elizabeth faced her again. Finally, Aunt Elizabeth went around the front of the car and got into the driver's seat. Without a word or backward glance at Gracie, she started the engine and drove down the street.

Gracie banged her heels against the backseat in her excitement.

"Stop that right now!" Aunt Elizabeth scowled into the rearview mirror.

Gracie froze. She waited and waited. "Are we there yet?"

"I'm still driving, aren't I?"

"How long — ?"

"As long as it takes! Don't ask again." Staring straight ahead, Aunt Elizabeth drove fast, both hands gripping the steering wheel. Gracie's stomach knotted so tight it hurt. She looked at Aunt Elizabeth's face in the mirror and saw her anger. Aunt Elizabeth met her look. "Stop staring at me! It's rude!" Gracie looked down and crushed the bear against her chest.

After a while, Gracie spotted the post office where Mommy bought stamps and mailed letters. She saw the library where Mommy took her to hear the story lady read. She saw the church where Mommy took her to Sunday school while Daddy slept in. She recognized houses. Aunt Elizabeth passed the park near the school. Mommy always sat on a bench under the magnolia tree while Gracie played with other children.

Aunt Elizabeth turned onto the street where Gracie lived and pulled into the driveway. Before the car had fully stopped, Gracie unbuckled herself and had swung the car door open. Aunt Elizabeth slammed on the brakes, and Gracie rocked hard against the front seat. Spilling out of the car, she ran. She fell and skinned her knee, but jumped up again. "Mommy!" She tried to open the front door, but it was locked. "Mommy, I'm home!"

Grasped by the shoulders and spun around, Gracie faced a livid Aunt Elizabeth. "Stop it!

Do you want the entire neighborhood to hear you?" Gracie fought free and pounded on the door. "God, help me." Aunt Elizabeth's voice broke. Unlocking the door, she pushed it open. "Go ahead and look."

Gracie ran in, crying out for Mommy. She ran from the kitchen to the living room to the master bedroom. She looked in the bathroom and living room. She went outside. "Mommy! Where are you? Mommy!" Confused, raw, terrified, she raced back inside, where Aunt Elizabeth stood like a statue. "Mommy!" Gracie screamed, sobbing now. Why didn't Mommy answer? Why didn't she come?

Aunt Elizabeth took her firmly by the hand and brought her back into the living room. Gracie noticed Daddy's chair wasn't there anymore. A big square of carpet had been cut out where it had sat. Aunt Elizabeth sat on the sofa and held Gracie by the arms. "Look at me, Grace. Your mother is dead. So is your father. Do you understand what that means? They're not here." She pressed her lips together and looked away. Blinking back tears, she swallowed and looked at Gracie again. "We're only staying for as long as it takes me to clear out the house and put it on the market. I have to get back to work. So you're coming with me to Fresno. That's in California, in case you didn't know."

"I don't want to go."

"That's too bad, because what you want doesn't matter. You get what life has handed you, thanks to your son of —" She stopped and shook her head. "I know it's not what you want. It's not what I want either. But we're stuck with each other. Your mother wrote it in a will." She looked angry. "That tells you something about her situation, doesn't it?" Her hands clenched and un-clenched at her sides. She looked out the window and gave a heavy sigh. When she looked at Gracie again, her eyes were cold, but not angry anymore. "From now on, you'll do as I say. I'm not your mother, but she made me your guardian. I'll do the best I can for you. Now, go to your room and take a nap while I get some work done."

Gracie finally saw Mommy again. Aunt Eliz-abeth took her to a big building that had a small room with pretty colored-glass win-dows. Mommy was lying asleep in a wooden box with shiny white satin. Her hands were folded around a bouquet of pink roses. She looked different. "Mommy?"

"Go ahead." Aunt Elizabeth stood beside her. "Touch her. Maybe that's the only way you'll understand."

Gracie patted Mommy's hand lightly. Her skin was cold and felt strange. "Wake up." Gracie looked from Mommy to Aunt Eliza-beth and back to Mommy. "Mommy doesn't wear makeup. Daddy doesn't like it."

"She's not there, Grace. Her soul has gone to heaven."

"Is Daddy in heaven, too?"

Aunt Elizabeth gave a snort. "I had him cremated." She spoke through tight lips in a low voice. "It seemed a fitting end for him."

The pastor introduced himself to Aunt Elizabeth. A few others from church had come to pay their respects. Mommy had only just begun attending church and taking Gracie to Sunday school. Not many people knew her. The pastor seemed sorry about that. "She seemed such a tender soul."

A big black car took Mommy's box to a park with a high arch entry and open iron gates. Aunt Elizabeth parked her car and sat silent in the front seat. Eyes closed, she gripped the steering wheel with white hands. When she got out of the car, she came around for Gracie. Taking her by the hand, she led her across the grass to a big hole in the ground, Mommy's box above. The pastor talked about dust and ashes. Her aunt's hand trembled and tightened until Gracie cried. She let go abruptly, and crossed her arms. The pastor prayed, and Mommy's box lowered into the ground. Aunt Elizabeth leaned down, took a handful of dirt, and sprinkled it on Mommy's box. "Your trials are over, Leelee. Rest in peace." She looked down at Gracie. "Say good-bye to your mother."

■ ■ ■ ■

That night, Aunt Elizabeth packed Gracie's things in a suitcase. She snatched Grace's stuffed bear from her arms. "You're too old for this!" Aunt Elizabeth took it outside and threw it in the trash can.

The next morning, they drove to a big airport. Aunt Elizabeth lifted her suitcase and Gracie's from the trunk. Gracie heard a loud roar and looked up at an airplane overhead. It rose like a giant bird into the sky. Her aunt told her to stay close and keep up. Gracie had never been around so many people and stayed on Aunt Elizabeth's heels. They waited in a long line where everyone had suitcases. When they reached the counter, Aunt Elizabeth talked to the clerk. A man tagged their luggage and placed it on a moving belt.

Gracie had so many questions, but Aunt Elizabeth looked tense and agitated. She walked fast, and Gracie had to struggle to keep up. They sat in a waiting area until it was time to stand in another line and get on an airplane. Inside, people shoved small suitcases and tote bags and packages into the overhead compartments before sliding into their seats. Aunt Elizabeth led Gracie all the way to the back of the plane and told her to sit by the window. She gave a weary sigh when she took the seat beside Gracie. "Try to sleep. That's what I plan to do. We have two more flights after this one. It's going to be a very long day. Don't wake me up unless you have to go potty." She jerked her head toward the back. "The lavatory is right behind us."

Gracie forgot about everything when the plane roared down the runway. At first, she felt the sluggish pull of earth; then the plane rose, heavy and then growing lighter the higher it went. She looked down and wondered at how cars and houses got smaller, and then the plane went into the clouds. It kept going up and up. Gracie prayed they would go to heaven to see Mommy and Jesus.

21

Yosemite held an awe-inspiring beauty with its hanging valleys, waterfalls, giant granite domes, and moraines, but Roman couldn't keep his eyes off Grace. She was clearly enjoying herself, and it shone in her face.

"If I had your talent, Roman, I'd be painting this." She spread her arms, encompassing the valley in front of them.

"And get nowhere. It's been done a thousand times." He pocketed his phone and joined her.

She looked at him. "What were you doing? Texting a girlfriend?"

"I don't have a girlfriend." He smiled slightly. "Not the kind you mean, anyway."

"Then why do you always have that thing in your hand? You're missing everything!"

He'd seen it before, but saw it differently this time. "Half Dome is pretty spectacular. I wouldn't mind climbing that rock someday."

"You'd need a lot of mountain-climbing experience."

"I used to climb tall buildings."

"Okay, Superman."

He liked her smile. "They weren't that tall. Five or six stories." He looked up at Half Dome. "I wanted to do heaven spots. The higher, the better." He glanced at her. "Earn street cred." She didn't understand a word he said, and he wasn't ready to explain. "Never mind. Why don't we get back on the road and cover some more ground before we call it a day?"

She gazed at Half Dome. "What a pity."

"You're the one who has to be back by Friday."

"Yes. I do. Can you wait one minute?" She walked over to the stream and picked out a small stone.

"What're you going to do with that?"

"Remember Yosemite."

They were well on their way when Grace asked him to pull over. She just wanted a few minutes to see a cirque lake. Roman followed her to the edge. Grace stood looking up at the mountain and the mirror image on the surface of the water. "It's like an oval mirror. It doubles the beauty."

It was a magnificent scene. "I'd never attempt to paint this. I couldn't come close to what we're seeing."

She faced him. "No one could."

"Some come close."

"Isn't art all about interpretation?"

"Partly." He sat on a boulder.

She looked back at the lake. "I should've bought postcards." She took out her phone and took a few pictures, then came over and sat beside him. "Tell me about your paintings. I don't understand them, you know. The mural, yes. The great migration, and it's beautiful. Your other work baffles me."

Leaning forward, he rested his forearms on his knees. "They're people I've known, exposed, but disguised so no one can recognize them." He gave a rueful laugh. "By the time I'm done painting, I don't even know who they are."

"Who were they when you started?"

His mother, the landlord of the Tenderloin apartment house, foster family members, CPS workers, the girl who introduced him to sex, gang friends, and a wannabe tagger who didn't know how to stay alive. "Some I want to remember; others I wish I could forget."

Scooping up a rock, he stood and sent it skipping across the water. Concentric circles spread, ruining the mirror image. He picked up a white stone and tossed it to her. "For your collection. We'd better go."

They reached the top of Tioga Pass, and Roman grinned at her. "Hang on. It's going to be a scary ride down."

"You can see for miles!"

"That's Mono Lake down there." The car hugged the curves on the steep grade. She looked more excited than afraid. "I'll bet you like roller-coaster rides."

"I've never been on one."

The tires squealed as Roman took another curve. He heard Grace's intake of breath and slowed on the next one. "No trips to amusement parks or county fairs?"

"No trips anywhere. My aunt didn't take a lot of time off, and I found a job as soon as I was old enough for a work permit."

"And when you were married?"

"I worked."

So much for the idyllic lifestyle he'd imagined. She pulled her map from the door pocket and opened it. "There's a visitor center down there."

"And you want to stop."

"You're the boss."

"Okay." He accessed the computer and asked about Lee Vining hotels. Switching to the phone system, he made the call and booked two rooms. Grace put the folded map back in the door pocket. He couldn't tell if she was upset or had run out of things to say. "I thought we should book something so we'd have time to look around and not feel rushed."

She gave a soft laugh and shook her head. "You don't need a personal assistant on this trip. Your car can do everything for you. I'll bet it can even take notes and carry on a conversation."

"Probably, with prompts." He grinned at her. "You're not jealous, are you?"

"Oh, what I wouldn't give to have half its brain."

They spent over an hour in the visitor center, reading through the information, before going out to the Mono Lake Tufa reserve. Everything fascinated Grace. "This is the strangest place I've ever seen."

"Well, you haven't seen much."

She pointed. "That looks like an ancient city over there. It could be Sodom and Gomorrah after God rained down fire and brimstone." She wondered aloud if Mono Lake looked anything like the Dead Sea in Israel. Another place she'd love to visit, even with terrorism on the rise. The sky looked more blue against the white formations. She pointed out shapes; he saw shadows. She asked how he would paint this place. He'd use bright colors, sharp, jagged lines, white and black. She listened intently, as though trying to hear more than what he was saying.

He bought sandwiches at a deli, and they sat at a picnic table. Grace enjoyed the view of Mono Lake. She was attentive to everything around her, drinking it in, savoring it. A breeze came up, and she closed her eyes. He could see the relaxed pleasure in her face. She was beginning to loosen up with him. Or was it the other way around?

What exactly was he looking for on this

journey? The not knowing made him nervous. He'd never thought Grace beautiful, but she stirred him deeply. He'd always gotten his adrenaline rush painting graffiti and outrunning cops. She looked at him, and he felt his pulse kick up.

He'd been attracted to women before, but not the same way he was with Grace. She scared him. He could put a stop right now to whatever was starting to happen between them. Jasper said that was his pattern. The old voice spoke in his head. *Don't get too close, Bobby Ray. You know how much love hurts. Walk away before you feel anything more than you already do. She's going to rip your heart out.*

Jasper said it had to do with his mother. Bobby Ray couldn't trust women because the one he needed most had abandoned him. Was that why he kept his relationships with women shallow and physical? Was anything ever that simple?

Why go over old stories, unlock doors, or find what was under the lid of a garbage can? His mother hadn't kept her word. She hadn't come back. How could she? She was dead. Jasper tried to get him to deal with it, find closure. Bobby Ray had survived. Why go back? Roman wanted to keep moving on.

If he did have abandonment issues, so what? His mother had been less to blame than the man who'd fathered him. Maybe he never knew. Maybe he did and turned his back on Sheila Dean. Roman had always been careful, even the first time. He didn't want a child of his growing up fatherless with a mother who had to turn tricks for a living.

Grace crumpled the paper that had held her deli sandwich and stuffed it into her empty soda cup. She smiled at him. "Thank you for dinner." She gathered his debris and headed for the trash can.

Roman watched her walk away. He loved the way she moved. His body warmed. He'd better not think about going down that road with this girl.

Not this soon, anyway.

She came back and sat so she could watch the sunset. He came around the table and sat beside her. She smiled at him. "It's beautiful, isn't it?"

He'd rather look at her than the sunset, but he knew better. "For a little while, and then it's gone."

"Pessimist. It'll happen again tomorrow. Every sunset is different."

"The colors have to do with pollutants in the air."

She gave him a pitying look. "Colors come from a phenomenon called scattering. The wavelengths of light and the sizes of the particles determine the colors. I learned that in a college science class."

He'd never taken a college course, but he'd read a lot. "By particles, they meant pollutants."

"You see it as you wish, Roman, but I see sunrise as God's good morning, and sunset as God's good night." She pulled out her phone and checked the time. "We'd better get to the hotel, don't you think?"

"I take it you want to get to your homework." He didn't want to spend the evening alone, but he remembered her heavy backpack. Could he talk her out of it? Maybe, but what sort of guy made a girl give up something that mattered to her? "Let's go."

Roman checked them in. When he took their luggage from the trunk, she gathered hers. He offered to help, but she said she could manage. He'd already noticed. "A pity I didn't bring something to read." He intended to sound pitiful.

"Check your nightstand. I'll bet you find a Gideon Bible."

He laughed. "Thanks a lot. Sounds like a real page-turner."

Grinning, she opened her hotel room door. "It's been on bestseller lists for years." She went inside and closed the door behind her.

Bored, Roman grabbed the remote and turned on the television. News. Sports. Stupid sitcoms. More news. He flicked through the channels, one after another, and found nothing to interest him. He turned the set off and lay on his back. His mind circled around Grace. Swearing under his breath, he got up and took a cold shower. Cooled down, he cranked up the temperature, but then the room felt stuffy. He turned on the air conditioner. Giving in to impulse, he picked up the phone and called Grace's room. Stretching out on the bed, he put his arm behind his head. "What're you doing?"

"You know what I'm doing."

He scrambled for something to delay the end of the conversation. "Tell me about Sodom and Gomorrah."

"You can read about them yourself." He heard her open and close a drawer. "There's a Bible in my room. I'm sure there's one in yours. Read Genesis."

"Which is where?"

"In the beginning. The story is somewhere in the first half. Wait a minute." She put the phone down. He could hear pages riffling. She picked up the phone again. "Start with chapter 18 on page 16 and keep reading. See you in the morning."

It wasn't the first time Grace had hung up on him. She was still his employee, and office hours were over. At least he hadn't waited until after midnight to call. At least he wasn't calling to needle her about a placid kiss from Prince Charming. At least she wasn't mad this time.

Roman turned on the television again. After

fifteen minutes, he gave up, shut it off, and yanked open the nightstand drawer. If the Bible was as boring as it looked, he'd be asleep in five minutes.

Grace wondered if Roman was upset with her the next morning. He hadn't said much over breakfast, and now that they were on the road, heading north toward Bodie and Bridgeport, she couldn't stand the silence any longer. "Didn't you sleep well last night?"

"No, I didn't. Thanks to you."

"Me?"

"I read until two in the morning. Genesis. Exodus. Gave up on Leviticus, whoever he was. Do you believe all that stuff?" He sounded ready for an argument.

She wasn't the kind of girl eager to pull on boxing gloves, but she still wanted to know. "Which stuff do you mean?"

"God created everything in seven days. The serpent in the garden, Adam and Eve being kicked out, the angel keeping them from going back in, the plagues of Egypt. All of it."

She decided not to hedge. "Yes, I do."

Roman glanced at her with a sardonic smile. "Seriously?"

He wasn't the first to dismiss what she believed. Patrick had complained when she went to church on Sundays. He wanted her home with him. He nagged so much, she gave up church. She realized soon enough all he wanted was a cook to make touchdown taco dip for his chips while he watched sports on TV, or a quick, rough roll in bed so he could sleep through to Monday morning. Giving up church hadn't changed the inevitable outcome of their relationship. She'd gone back to the Lord wounded and floundering. Work then became her way of coping, until a caring friend talked her into a night out.

Grace swore she'd never stray again. *Hold me close, Lord. Never let me go.* Alone, she knew she'd drown and wash up on a sandy shore.

Roman looked at her again. "Why?"

The single word implied she was stupid. "Because it's true."

"Give me a break!"

"You needn't be insulting. I'm as serious about my faith as you are about yours."

"I don't believe in God."

"You believe in yourself. You believe you have control over your life and can live accordingly. That's your religion."

He didn't say anything for the next five miles. Grace wished she'd kept quiet. So much for being friends. "I didn't mean to offend you, Roman."

"Who brainwashed you? Your aunt?"

"It doesn't matter." He'd never believe an angel came to her any more than Aunt Elizabeth had. The visitation had opened her heart to the Lord. How do you explain that kind of experience to an atheist? Or was he an agnostic? Did it matter?

"I'd like to hear."

He looked serious, and she couldn't see a way out. "There's order everywhere: the stars, the seasons, the currents of the ocean, the air that moves over the planet, down to the cells that make up everything. I don't believe that's by chance or a series of accidents. It takes intelligence to create all that, intelligence beyond anything human beings can understand. That's part of why I believe in God."

"There was a serpent in the garden."

Was he mocking her, or did he seriously want her to talk about what she believed? "Satan."

"You believe in a devil."

Just when she was beginning to enjoy his company! Was the rest of the trip going to be like this? "Yes, and I believe in hell, too. Everyone these days likes to think they'll go to heaven or a better place somewhere. The truth is, the price for sin is death and hell. That's why Jesus came. That's why God sent His Son. Only Jesus could live a sin-free life and be the perfect sacrifice to ransom us. All He asks is that we believe. And I believe."

"I must have pushed a button and gotten the recording."

"You asked." Hot tears threatened, and she looked out the window. *Lord, You deal with him.* "My ex-husband didn't believe either."

"If faith matters that much to you, why did you marry him?"

She gave a bleak laugh. "You have no idea how many times I asked myself that same question. He needed me. I thought I loved him. I was warned." By her aunt as well as the quiet voice within her. "I just didn't want to listen." She had been so desperate for someone to love her she swallowed a lie.

She didn't like feeling exposed. Let Roman do the talking. "Why don't you tell me what you believe?"

"We're born. We survive as best we can. We die. End of story."

She glanced at his profile. He looked grim, as though hope didn't exist. "No wonder you're so miserable." She turned her face away. "Why don't you read Ecclesiastes tonight? You have a lot in common with King Solomon." *Including his taste for women.*

Roman gave her an irritated glance and made the turn to Bodie.

She sighed. "Do you want to hear some history?"

"Something other than the brochure I read and practically recited to you?"

Grace breathed in and out slowly as she did a search on her phone. She read about the gold- and silver-mining boomtown that had boasted ten thousand inhabitants in its heyday — sixty-five saloons, gamblers, prosti-

340

tutes, and a reputation for violence and lawlessness. A little girl, on hearing where her daddy planned to move the family, said, "Good-bye, God. We're going to Bodie."

Roman parked and got out of the car.

They walked among the dilapidated buildings. Grace paused to peer through windows, while he stood waiting, hands in his jacket pockets. A church, a saloon, a store. She looked through the window of a small house where a prostitute had once conducted business. "What a miserable life that must have been."

"She picked it."

Annoyed, she started to walk on, then decided not to let his comment go unchallenged. "Do you really think a woman wants to be a prostitute? I can't imagine anything worse than having to sell my body to any guy who wanted to use me. I think women do that kind of work as a last resort."

He looked angry now. "They aren't forced into it."

She was sick of being the brunt of his ill temper. "That depends on what constitutes *force* in your dictionary, Mr. Velasco."

"Spoken like a college girl, Ms. Moore."

"What if a woman lost her husband on the way out West? They didn't have the same rights and opportunities men did. Or the physical strength. What if it was a girl on a wagon train and her family died of cholera or typhus? Can a woman plow a field and build a cabin on her own?" The only way she could stop herself from saying more was to walk away from him. He fell into step beside her. She quickened her pace.

"She could get married again."

"What if all the men were like you?" Grace blushed, but she couldn't bring herself to apologize. "If the girl had an education, she might find a job as a teacher, but most women weren't allowed the privilege of education back then." She made a sweeping gesture encompassing Bodie. "How many schoolhouses do you see out here?"

"What about now?"

"Now?" She didn't know what he was talking about.

"What excuse does a woman have now?"

How could he be so insensitive? "Sometimes people make mistakes they can't undo. Sometimes people are so beaten down they don't know how to get back up. And there will always be people who want to keep them in their place."

"And you know this how? From some text-book?"

Trembling with anger, Grace faced him. "What happens to a fourteen-year-old girl who gets pregnant and her parents kick her out? What if her boyfriend was just using her and doesn't care what she does? How does she make a living? The people she thought loved her don't. Where does she go? How does she earn money to buy food or keep a roof over her head? So she sells herself once, just so she can eat. Then she feels so dirty nothing matters after that. People look at her like she's trash anyway. Now she believes she is. She can't see any way out."

All the anger went out of him. "Any of that ever happen to you?"

"No, but it doesn't mean I can't have empathy." Clearly, he didn't. Feeling sick, Grace walked away.

Roman didn't follow her, but she felt him watching her. She went to the next corner of the town grid before she looked back. He stood where she'd left him, hands shoved in the pockets of his black leather bomber jacket, looking at the ramshackle house where the prostitute once lived.

They met at the car, both calm. "I'm sorry, Roman. I didn't mean to get on a soapbox."

He pushed the ignition button. "I can see why you like psychology. You can make a career of rescuing people for the rest of your life."

Like Patrick. "No, thanks. Been there, done that, and it ended badly. I'm having enough trouble sorting out my own life to be of any use to others."

"Sounds like we may have something else in common."

22

Bobby Ray, Age 10

Bobby Ray reckoned he had been in more than fifteen foster homes by now. He ran away from eight. If he couldn't get out, he got thrown out. He set fire to one garage. He threw a foster brother's bicycle into traffic. He kicked dents in the side of a brand-new foster family van. He chucked a bag of dog feces into another foster family's hot tub. Some foster couples collected monthly checks and let him run wild, until the police found him back on Turk Street.

He was smart. He was shrewd. Every textbook parenting technique was tried on him. None worked. He didn't get along with other children. He didn't trust adults. Several families said the boy needed stability and a forever home and tried to adopt him. He said no, hating them for what they were trying to do. Sheila Dean was his mother, and no one was taking her place. Not ever. She was out there in the city someplace, and he was going to find her.

Miss Bushnell, the sad-eyed, weary social worker, had handed his case over to her supervisor, Ellison Whitcomb, a man who had put in twenty-five years in social services. Whatever feelings of hope and purpose he'd had when he started his chosen career had long since died in the heavy caseload of heartache and human tragedy. Bobby Ray was just another rootless, troubled kid with a thick file. Whitcomb talked with another caseworker in the corridor while Bobby Ray sat waiting and listening.

"At least he hasn't killed anyone."

Whitcomb gave a bleak laugh. "Give him time."

Whitcomb took a seat behind the desk. He looked worn-out. He opened a package of Tums and popped a couple into his mouth. A poster of a white, sandy beach with *Florida* in blazing letters hung on his wall. He asked Bobby Ray how many times he planned to run away.

"As many as it takes."

"To do what?"

"Find my mother."

Whitcomb didn't say a word after that. He didn't push or pry or even try to make Bobby Ray talk. He just leaned back, folded his hands, and studied him. Bobby Ray stared back, angry. He knew the game and didn't break eye contact.

"You're not doing yourself any favors, kid."

Bobby Ray told him what Whitcomb could do to himself. Whitcomb tapped the file on his desk. "I'm going to be gone for five minutes; then I'll be back." Bobby Ray got the message. As soon as Whitcomb left the office, he grabbed the file.

Bobby Ray Dean. Father: unknown. Mother: Sheila Dean.

Bobby Ray read quickly.

. . . arrested four times for prostitution . . . released on her own recognizance . . . overdosed on heroin in Starlight Motel, listed as a Jane Doe until identified by fingerprints.

Bobby Ray's heart stopped. He reread the last part, hoping he had gotten it wrong. His stomach dropped, and cold seeped through him. *Mama's dead.* How could that be? Wouldn't he have felt something? Known somehow, someway?

Whitcomb returned, took the file from the desk, and tucked it away in the tall metal filing cabinet. "So now you know, Bobby Ray."

Mama still spoke to him in his dreams sometimes. *I'm doing the best I can, baby. You know I'm gonna come back. Don't I always?*

23

Back on the mountain road, they passed high meadows, icy lakes, and towering pines. Grace was silent so long, Roman glanced over to see if she was asleep. She was wide-awake, faintly pensive. "What's on your mind?"

"I'd like Samuel to see this. You can't look at all this beauty and not believe. It's harder in a city. There's too much going on, too many distractions."

"And temptations?" Roman gave her a teasing glance. "Not to mention, all those angry people on the freeways. Always in a hurry to get somewhere." Like him, they probably didn't know where they really wanted to go or how to get there.

"Can we stop?" She looked apologetic. "Just for a few minutes."

Roman pulled off the road at the next wide spot. Grace thanked him and got out of the car. He came around the car and leaned against it, watching her. The air smelled heavily of pine. Grace picked her way among some boulders and climbed up onto a granite ledge overlooking a narrow, plunging valley. A breeze came up, and she spread her arms as though she might take a few steps and ride the wind. Roman lifted his phone. She took another step forward, and his heart lurched.

"Grace, stop!" Pocketing his phone, he went after her. He couldn't see her for a few seconds and almost panicked. "Grace!"

"I'm right here." There was another ledge just below the one she'd been on. "I could walk another ten feet and still be safe." She took a few more steps.

He caught up to her, and gripped her arm. "Close enough." When she looked at him in surprise, he let go of her.

"You were the one talking about climbing Half Dome."

"Enough wandering around. Let's go."

Roman went ahead of her and lifted her down from the stone table. She gave a soft, tense laugh. "You're as sure-footed as a mountain goat."

"Comes from practicing parkour." She picked up a pinecone on the way to the car. "You're keeping that?"

"It's the perfect souvenir, don't you think?" She held it to her nose and inhaled. "A gift from the Lord that smells like the forest."

He was getting used to the natural way Grace talked about God. He opened the car door for her. She slid in and tucked the pinecone into the tote bag, along with the rocks she'd collected along the way.

"Your bag must weigh a ton by now."

"The Israelites picked up great stones when they crossed the Jordan River. When they reached the Promised Land, they made a memorial so they'd never forget what God had done."

He'd read the Exodus story the night before, but he didn't want to get into another God conversation. Maybe there was a God, but Roman doubted He cared. He pulled onto the road again. "We're only two hours away from Golden."

"Think you'll accept the job?"

"Doubtful." Before she asked why they were on this trip if he'd already made up his mind, he told her to call Jasper. "See if he can meet us at Masterson Ranch." He could have made the call himself with one press of his thumb on the steering wheel, but he wanted to change the subject.

Phone to her ear, she looked at him. "Are we staying there tonight?"

"No. We're just stopping in to say hello." The Mastersons probably had a full house. Roman wondered what kind of reception he'd get after so many years of avoiding this visit. He'd only seen Jasper because the man insisted on showing up periodically, invited or not. He hadn't seen Chet and Susan since he aged out of the program at eighteen. They sent a Christmas card every December with a handwritten note inviting him to visit anytime. *The door is always open.* Roman figured it was merely a polite gesture. Why would they want to see him again?

Maybe stopping by was a bad idea.

"Anything wrong, Roman?"

How long had she been looking at him? "Everything's fine."

The old barn came into view as he rounded the curve of the narrow country road. Surprised, he saw the second mural he'd ever done still there, faded after so many years. The gates were open, Jasper's blue Chevy parked in front of the house. On the porch, two German shepherds stood and barked. Roman remembered his first meeting with Starsky and Hutch nearly twenty years ago.

Starsky and Hutch must be long dead, but these two shepherds could be related.

Chet came outside and called out, "Be polite, boys." The dogs' demeanor changed to one of cautious greeting. A few sniffs at Roman, and they moved quickly to Grace. She held out her hand, and one licked her. The two dogs moved around her with wagging tails. Smiling, she stroked one, until the other nosed in for his turn.

Susan and Jasper joined Chet on the porch. Roman pushed down the rising tide of emotions. Of all the places he could have taken

Grace, why had he brought her here? He should have kept driving, rather than risk what could — would — turn into something humiliating. Chet came down the steps. He still had a full head of hair, though now white. He walked slower, shoulders slightly stooped, body thinner. Susan, wearing jeans and a button-up plaid shirt, still had a blonde ponytail. She'd put on some weight, but they both looked good for sixty-plus years of age.

Roman held out his hand, but Chet pulled him into a bear hug. "It's about time you came home!" Roman couldn't speak past the lump in his throat. Why hadn't he come back? What excuse did he have to offer?

Chet let him go and slapped him on the back. "Look at you! You're not a skinny kid anymore."

Susan put her hands on her hips. "I should be mad at you for staying away so long." Laughing, joyous, she threw her arms around Roman. When she drew back, she looked at Grace. "And who is this pretty lady? Your wife?"

Roman quickly dispelled that misconception. Smiling and relaxed, Grace shook hands with Chet and Susan. Jasper gave her a hug and kissed her cheek like they were longtime friends. The dogs stayed close to Grace. She scratched one behind the ears. If he'd been a cat, he would have purred.

"That one is DiNozzo." Chet chuckled.

"And I think he has a crush on you. The other is Gibbs." He clicked his tongue, and the two dogs followed him to the house.

"Come on inside." Susan waved everyone toward the house. "We have coffee, tea, lemonade."

Roman looked around. The place was quiet, but there were horses in the corral. "You still keeping boys in line, Chet?"

"Off and on. Trying to ease ourselves into retirement. Sold off fifty acres and kept enough to give us plenty of open space. We still stable horses. Remember José?"

"The gang kid from Stockton? Yeah, I remember. He went into the military, didn't he?"

"Served six years in the Marines, and came out a sergeant. He and his wife, Abbie, take care of the place now. He's a good worker, a natural with the horses. Frees Susan and me up to travel when we don't have any resident boys. We're heading out again the end of the month. Spend some time in Yellowstone and then Glacier. How about you?"

Roman felt like they were picking up where they'd left off all those years ago, no time in between. He told Chet about traveling around Europe on Jasper's advice. Grace walked a few feet ahead of him, in conversation with Jasper and Susan.

The living room had been redone with pale-beige carpeting. Wheat-colored couches replaced the brown leather, but they hadn't buffed the wall he painted when he was seventeen.

"Yep. It's still there." Chet grinned. "That and the one on the barn are our claims to fame. 'Roman Velasco' lived here."

Roman struggled with his emotions. "I thought you'd have developed better taste by now."

After he'd painted the scenes Susan had asked for in the kitchen, Chet had offered the barn for his next project. Chet had set down a few rules: Whatever Roman painted had to be recognizable and reflect positively on Masterson Mountain Ranch. "When I approve the drawings, we'll negotiate the price. I'll buy whatever supplies you need. Take into consideration what you might have to pay a crew, if you need one. We're going to draw up a contract, teach you how to do some business."

The edgy simplicity of Roman's stylized horses and cows grazing in a neon-green pasture had people stopping by to ask who did the mural. "A kid did that?" One rancher offered to hire Roman to paint his barn up the road. Jasper Hawley started teaching him how to put together business proposals. They studied costs and hours of labor and profit margins. Jasper took him to Wells Fargo to set up checking and savings accounts, taught him how to do his state and federal taxes. "If you're going into business, you'd better get it right from the beginning."

By the time Bobby Ray Dean earned his GED, Roman Velasco had five thousand dollars in savings and several more jobs lined up. All thanks to Chet and Susan and Jasper and their investment in a kid nobody else had time for.

"Come on into the kitchen." Susan led the way, laughing over her shoulder. "We always end up in here anyway."

Grace lingered, studying the living room mural. Roman put his hand against the small of her back, wanting to steer her away. "You don't like my work, remember?"

"Who's Sheila?"

Roman froze. "What?"

"Sheila. It's right there. And Reaper." She tilted her head. "White Boy." She looked at him, perplexed. "And there's a bird in flight in the corner. Or are those letters, too? BRD."

"Bobby Ray Dean." His heart pounded. "We'll talk about it later."

Jasper spoke from the archway leading to the kitchen. "Is there a problem?"

"No problem." Roman glanced over his shoulder. "We'll be with you in a minute." He blocked Grace and lowered his voice. "Don't say anything about the wall." The mural had been there for years, but Roman doubted that Chet and Susan had ever seen what he'd painted in it. How was it Grace

354

saw what he'd been so careful to hide?

Her eyes flickered in surprise, but she nodded.

The kitchen had been remodeled, too, the scenes of Italy he'd painted long gone and replaced by pale-yellow walls and white crown molding. Susan slid a prime rib into the top oven and announced dinner would be ready by six thirty.

"We're only staying an hour or two."

She gave him a look he remembered from his time living in this house. "You're staying for dinner, and you're spending the night."

Roman could be stubborn, too. "We have a lot of road to cover."

"Chet, go let the air out of his tires or kill the computer in that fancy car of his."

"Or you could let him go." Grace shrugged. "But if it's all right with you, I'd like to stay." She pulled out a chair and took a seat at the table.

The Mastersons laughed. Jasper grinned at Roman. "I think you're outnumbered."

Roman relaxed. "Okay, but don't listen to these people. They don't know me as well as they think they do."

Susan and Chet launched into what a pain he'd been when he first came to the ranch. "Couldn't get more than a growl out of him."

"He still growls." Grace smiled at him, obviously enjoying his discomfort.

Chet poured himself a cup of coffee. "We

355

didn't know how to reach him until he got his hands on some paint." He winked at her. "Now we put the tough cases in his old room." He lifted his mug to Roman. "They understand that piece. It's started a lot of conversations."

"What room?" Grace looked at Roman. "What piece?"

Roman didn't answer. Chet nodded toward the door. "Go on through the living room down the hall, second door on the right. You can have that room tonight, if you want."

When she pushed her chair back, Roman spoke up quickly. "Don't bother."

"Why not?"

"It'll give you nightmares." When she turned to go, he caught her wrist. "You won't like it, Grace." He let go of her quickly, aware that he had everyone's attention.

"Don't be so worried. My opinion shouldn't matter anyway."

He muttered a foul word under his breath when she left the kitchen. He stood, not sure whether to follow or wait. Panic rose. It was a second or two before he realized Chet, Susan, and Jasper were watching him. "She doesn't like my work." He felt light-headed.

"Neither do you." Jasper pulled back the closest chair. "Sit down. You don't look well."

Roman sat heavily and wondered what was wrong with him.

Jasper gripped Roman's shoulders. "Put

your head down." He squeezed. "Have you had a checkup lately?"

"I'm fine."

"I don't think that wall is going to scare Grace away, son."

Roman heard Jasper's voice through a tunnel. The weakness passed, and Roman felt better. Jasper let go and took a seat, studying him. Chet and Susan started talking again, telling him how they'd followed his career. They brought up some of the other boys who had been on the ranch the same time he was — all doing well, most married with kids.

Why was Grace taking so long? Jasper leaned forward. "You should see a doctor."

Roman gave a mocking laugh. "I'm thirty-four, in the peak of health."

"You had a couple of these episodes when you were here. Have you been having them all these years?"

Roman shrugged. "Not enough sleep." He smiled wryly at Chet. "Wake-up call at five, as I recall."

"Whiner." Chet frowned. "You fell off the barn roof once. Remember?"

"Someone dared him to walk the ridge."

"Good thing you landed in a pile of hay." Susan shook her head. She smiled when Grace returned. "What do you think of that piece?"

"It's very different from what Roman's doing now." Grace looked at him. "More revealing."

Roman felt exposed. "I pilfered a marker and drew a hole in the wall."

"He was trying to get kicked out." Jasper winked at Grace.

"It's where he was going I find interesting."

Chet shoved his chair back. "How about a walk around the old homestead? Stretch our legs a bit before dinner."

Roman stood and nodded for Grace to come along. Susan spoke up. "Grace, why don't you stick with me and let the men talk."

"Sounds like a good idea."

Roman hesitated. Susan grinned at him. "Don't look so worried. I'm sure she already knows you're no angel."

Grace couldn't understand why Roman was so uneasy. The Mastersons clearly loved him. They welcomed him like a prodigal son. "How long has it been since Roman visited?"

"He hasn't come back since he aged out of the program. Once the boys reach eighteen, they're on their own. He could've stayed, but . . ." Susan lifted a shoulder. "An opportunity knocked, and he answered."

If Grace had a family as loving as this in her life, she'd find a job close to home. She'd visit every chance she had. She offered to help with dinner preparations, but Susan said she'd have everything done in a few minutes.

"Comes with cooking for a houseful of boys."
She washed potatoes, poked holes in them,
and put them in the oven. "How do you like
working for him?"

"He spends most of his time in his studio.
I'm in the office." She knew it didn't answer
the question.

They sat together at the kitchen table. "He
could have a wide circle of friends in the art
world, if he wanted." Susan smiled impishly.
"Jasper keeps us up on what's happening with
our boy. He says Roman has a beautiful place
at the top of a mountain overlooking a canyon."

"With a magnificent view all the way to the
coast." *And he doesn't even enjoy it.*

"And you're his closest neighbor."

Grace blushed. What might Susan Masterson make of that proximity? "I couldn't afford the commute. Roman offered to rent
—"

"I know. Jasper told us. I'm not suggesting
anything is going on. Roman never lets
people get too close." Her smile was apologetic. "I knew you two weren't married. I just
wanted to see Roman's reaction when I said
it."

He'd been quick to set the record straight.
"I'm his employee. Nothing more."

"That doesn't mean you two can't become
good friends."

Grace wasn't sure that was possible anymore. Her feelings were changing, heading in an unwelcome direction. "He's not an easy person to understand."

"I don't imagine you are either." Susan put her hand flat on the table. "He was the smartest boy we've ever had here at the ranch. Brilliant, in fact. Quick learner, photographic memory. He could have gone through college, but didn't want anyone telling him what to do. We've kept up with him on the Internet, and Jasper is a pit bull. He fights for his boys and never lets go, especially the ones with the deepest wounds. One look at that bedroom wall, and Jasper knew how to get closer. Books on art. Roman devoured them. Jasper kept fanning that flame. We found places for Roman to experiment. He filled every sketchbook we gave him. I still have them."

"I'd love to see them."

"I thought you might. Sit tight." Susan went down the back hall off the kitchen. She returned carrying a short stack of notebooks.

Grace took one and turned the pages slowly: a boy currying a horse, the black oak in front of the house, Chet smoking a pipe on the front porch, Susan working in the garden. Jasper standing at a chalkboard. Each book showed steady improvement and gave her insights into Roman. Her throat felt tight.

"We didn't sit for him." Susan looked teary. "He drew them from memory. After lights out, with a flashlight." She shook her head. "He never did like rules."

"These are so good."

"The rawness is still in his work now, but he doesn't draw or paint people anymore, does he?" Susan shook her head. "He has bonding issues, understandable after what he went through."

Grace put the last sketchbook down. "Can you tell me?"

Susan studied Grace. "His mother disappeared when he was quite young. He was passed from one foster home to another. He was a runner and always ended up back in the Tenderloin, where he and his mother had lived. Not a new story. We've had a lot of boys from dysfunctional families — or no family at all. They don't attach to people. It takes time to build trust, and some of them do their best to sabotage any relationship, especially if they start feeling something. That was Roman from the get-go." Her eyes glistened. "He left the sketchbooks behind so he could forget us."

Leafing through the last sketchbook, Grace shook her head. "I think he left them behind so you'd know how much he loved you."

Susan wiped tears away. "I'd like to believe that." She got up and checked the oven. When she sat down again, her eyes were clear. "I will believe that."

Grace studied one picture of a young, pale-skinned girl with dark hair and eyes. "A girl-friend?"

"His mother. He was seven when she disappeared. He was in and out of thirty foster homes between the ages of seven and fifteen. There's a lot of deep-seated anger in a child who's been abandoned. Some turn to violence. Roman used paint to fight back."

"Some hide or become people pleasers." Grace realized she'd spoken aloud. She shrugged. "I was seven when I lost my parents. My aunt raised me." She looked at Roman's mother, trying to see any resemblance between mother and son. He must take after his father. Had he been a constant reminder to his mother of someone she had loved? Or someone who'd used and abandoned her? She remembered what Roman said about prostitutes in Bodie. "Roman talks about his travels, but not his past."

"Don't talk. Don't trust. Don't feel." Susan nodded. "The mantra of kids who suffered at the hands of their parents."

Grace never spoke of her past either. She'd always felt vaguely responsible for what happened in Memphis, though she didn't know why. Her aunt couldn't bear to look at her because she looked so much like her father, and Aunt Elizabeth had hated him. She had said as much to Miranda Spenser. It didn't matter that she'd been quickly shushed and corrected. Grace had heard, and the seed was planted. She grew up doing whatever people wanted her to do. Aunt Elizabeth above all others, until Patrick came along and usurped her. Grace constantly tried to make up for whatever she'd done wrong.

How do you make amends for something you don't understand?

Men's voices came from outside. Footsteps on the porch announced their return. Susan closed the sketchbook she'd been looking at. "These are good, but not even close to what he's capable of doing. Chet and I went down to San Diego last week and spent a few days. We wanted to see Roman's mural." She picked up the sketchbooks. "He keeps getting better and better, but he hasn't come close to his real potential. If he can't let go of the past, he never will."

Grace knew the same truth applied to her.

The Mastersons invited José and Abbie over with their two tweens. Dinner was lively with conversation. José had been a tough gang kid when Roman shared a room with him. Now he was quick to laugh, fit and content. His wife, Abbie, an ordinary-looking girl with brown hair and hazel eyes, made Carlos and Tina mind their manners. Abbie brought two homemade cherry pies for dessert. Carlos and Tina, far from shy, talked about school and friends and what they were doing this summer. They teased their father about lazing around the ranch on horseback while they had to muck out the stables. José said he'd had his day; now it was their turn. Roman reminded him of the hours they'd both spent shoveling horse manure into wheelbarrows and spreading it over an acre garden.

When Susan rose to clear dishes, everyone helped. The men talked sports and local politics. Chet invited them all to make themselves comfortable in the living room. Abbie sat next to José. José put his hand on his wife's thigh, and she smiled at him. Clearly, twelve years of marriage hadn't put the fire out. Grace stood by the bookshelves, talking with Jasper.

When Roman started to get up, Susan reclaimed his attention. "Tell us about the Laguna Beach show."

They must have heard about the event from Jasper. "The paintings sold."

"Roman always was good with words." Chet grinned at him. "Where are you and Grace heading tomorrow?"

"South." He wasn't ready to go home, but he'd promised Grace they'd be back by tomorrow so she'd have her son over the weekend.

Grace came to sit on the couch across from him. "Golden wants to commission Roman to paint a town mural."

"Golden?" José laughed. "You'll have to invent some history."

Roman looked at Grace with fixed attention. No doubt, she had been getting an earful about his private life. He intended to learn more about hers. "We're skipping Golden and going to Fresno." She didn't look happy with that announcement. He gave her a steely smile. "Grace hasn't seen her aunt in a while. Seems an opportune time."

Hands clenched, Grace sat on one of the twin beds and stared at the wall. She'd like to step through the hole Roman had painted and get away. Why was Roman so set on stopping in Fresno? Even if Grace called first thing in the morning, Aunt Elizabeth would see the short notice as a gross breach of etiquette. She stood when Roman came into the bedroom with her suitcase.

"I left your backpack in the car. I didn't think you'd be up to studying this late at night."

"You won't get the same warm welcome in Fresno that we've received here."

He put the suitcase on the dresser. "Why is that?"

"Just take my word for it." She didn't want to talk about Aunt Elizabeth. "You said you'd tell me about Sheila, Reaper, White Boy, and BRD."

"BRD. Bobby Ray Dean. That's the name on my birth certificate — that and my mother's, Sheila Dean. No father named. Susan came up with the name Roman Velasco. Writers have pseudonyms. Why not painters? She was kidding." He looked at the wall, a muscle jerking in his jaw. "I thought Roman Velasco would have a lot more class than Bobby Ray Dean ever could."

"So Sheila is your mother."

"Yes."

"And Reaper and White Boy?"

"Boys I knew in the hood. One was shot dead at a party where I should've been. One died in a fall."

Three names to honor the dead? Or did he see himself as dead, too? Did he feel guilty because he was alive and they weren't? Grace felt close to tears. She understood the feeling.

"Why don't you want to go to Fresno?"

He didn't know he was opening old wounds. "My aunt took me in when my parents died. She did it to fulfill my mother's wishes, not because she wanted me. You were welcomed into the Mastersons' life. I wasn't welcome in hers."

"This was a business, and I was sent here by court order."

"To start, but they love you like a son."

"Your aunt is a blood relative."

"Blood doesn't always matter. I've had to make a family. Shanice, Nicole, Ashley, the Garcias."

"Who are the Garcias?"

People she thought she could trust . . . and now wondered how hard she'd have to fight to reclaim her son. She felt the burn of tears and shook her head, looking away. She swallowed hard. "You shouldn't stay in here."

"I'll leave when you tell me what you think about this piece." He nodded toward the wall he'd painted.

"It looks like a prison break. What I'd like to know is why you'd want to run from love and go back where you had no hope."

"I knew who and what I was in the streets." His jaw tensed. "Tomorrow, I'm going to find out what you're hiding."

24

Roman stowed the bags in the trunk of his car, then observed the affectionate good-byes. Susan hugged Grace and whispered something that brought a smile to Grace's face. Chet and Jasper had their turns. Roman had never been comfortable with physical affection, but this time he didn't resist. Chet stood with him. "If you don't stay in touch, we might just show up on your doorstep unannounced."

"The door is always open." Roman meant it.

Jasper looked smug, but didn't gloat. "I'll be down in a couple of weeks to see how things are going." He looked at Grace.

Roman got the message. "You don't have all the answers, old man."

"None of us ever do." Jasper embraced him briefly and slapped his back. "At least you're showing yourself brave enough to drive forward instead of staring in the rearview mirror."

Before getting in the car, Roman saw something on the ground. Bending down, he scooped up two acorns on a twig. He gave them to Grace after she fastened her seat belt. "For your collection." Punching the starter, he put his hand on the back of her seat as he backed out.

Chet, Susan, and Jasper stayed outside, waving as Roman turned onto the main road. Grace waved back and then closed her window. Roman glanced over. "They sure took to you fast."

"I like them."

"I think they're hoping you'll end up more than my personal assistant." He saw the pink rise into her cheeks. "I told them you're dating a youth pastor." She didn't say anything to correct him. He concentrated on the road. "Did you get ahold of your aunt?"

"She's busy this morning, but said she'd be home after one. It's okay if you'd rather keep going. She won't mind."

He knew what she hoped he would say. "We have plenty of time."

"We should have lunch before we go."

He got the message. *Don't expect my aunt to give you so much as bread and water.* "We can pick up sandwiches and have a picnic somewhere."

They didn't speak for a while. Roman could tell she was distracted by more than the scenery out her window. "What's your aunt like?"

"She's a good person. She made sure I had everything I needed. She never asked me to do anything more than she did herself." Grace folded her hands. He'd noticed she did that when she was tense. "She told me to do the best I could at anything I did. She's very hardworking and dedicated to her job."

"Doing what?"

"She was an executive at the IRS." She smiled slightly. "No need to worry about that. She now has her own business as a forensic tax consultant."

He gave a slight laugh. "I'll try not to get on her bad side."

"It might be safer if we skipped the visit altogether."

"Nice try, Grace. Tell me more about her. Is she a Bible-thumper, too?" He hadn't meant to say that.

"Aunt Elizabeth took me to church every Sunday, but no, she doesn't thump a Bible. Nor did my Sunday school teacher. Miranda Spenser might come over while we're there."

Roman sensed there was more she could tell him, but figured he'd find out what he wanted to know soon enough. They stopped and bought sandwiches, water, and a pink-and-blue hydrangea as a gift for the aunt. Grace gave him directions to Woodward Park, where they found a bench beneath an oak, near a pathway along the lakeshore.

"Did your aunt bring you here for picnics?" Roman took a bite out of his po'boy.

"No, but I came with Patrick. My ex-husband." Grace folded the paper carefully around her turkey croissant. She seemed to have lost her appetite. She looked away. "I wish we had time to go to the Shinzen Japanese Friendship Garden. It's really lovely."

Another place she'd been with her ex? He uncapped his bottle of water. "I can imagine you on a cross-country trip. You'd want to stop at every weird tourist trap: tepees in Arizona, space alien museums in Roswell, New Mexico, a roadhouse with a bucking bull in Texas."

"And you'd just want to keep moving." She gave him a sad smile. "You're right. I would want to make a lot of stops. Did you know there are over twenty national parks and monuments in Arizona alone, and another eighteen in New Mexico? I have maps."

He grinned. "I'm sure you do, and the routes all neatly marked in red."

"Everyone has a dream."

"I don't."

"That's depressing."

Roman finished his water. "Tell me about it."

Grace took the plastic water bottle from him, gathered everything, and threw it in a trash can. "My aunt hates it when people are late."

Roman looked around as Grace gave him directions. She'd grown up in a nice, middle-class neighborhood. The tract houses looked the same except for the front yards, all well tended. Grace pointed out the house, which turned out to be the nicest one on the block. It had enough curb appeal to be a Realtor's dream. The red front door could be a welcome or a warning.

Grace didn't produce a key from her purse. She rang the bell and took a step back like an unwelcome solicitor preparing to have the door slammed in her face. Roman wanted to put his hand at the small of her back, but thought better of it.

She gave him an apologetic look. "If she doesn't answer, don't take it personally."

"Why would I? She's never met me."

The door opened. Roman expected a grim-faced older woman in polyester pants and a flowered tunic. Elizabeth Walker looked ready to take office. She was attractive and fit for a woman in her forties, her makeup perfect, dark hair smooth. She stood a little over five feet tall, in black pumps, black slacks, a white silk blouse, and a single strand of pearls. Roman now knew where Grace had learned to dress as a professional.

"Hello, Aunt Elizabeth." Grace offered the potted hydrangea. Roman bristled when the

372

woman took it like a queen accepting a gift from a peasant too far beneath her to rate a thank-you. Then it occurred to him that he'd often treated Grace the same way.

Elizabeth Walker made room for them to enter. Her cool, hazel eyes fixed on him as he stepped over the threshold. Grace made formal introductions. Elizabeth had a firm grip. Plenty of women had looked him over before, but none the way this one did. He had the feeling she'd like to cut his heart out and put it on a scale.

"Why don't we sit in the garden?" Elizabeth led the way through an immaculate and well-designed living room. She liked the same colors Grace did, but darker, more intense tones. He followed the two women out through the sliding-glass door, where he was invited to sit beneath a white pergola surrounded by a natural wonderland. The lawn could have served as a putting green. The waterfall in the back corner flowed into a pond with lily pads in bloom. Birds flittered and twittered around feeders; bees hummed. Roman didn't have to wonder where the serpent was in this pseudo Garden of Eden. Elizabeth sat in a white wicker cushioned chair that looked like a throne.

Grace looked awestruck. "It's beautiful, Aunt Elizabeth."

Clearly, Grace hadn't been home recently.

"It should be, considering the time and

money I've spent on it." She speared him with those cool eyes. "Grace told me you're an artist, Mr. Velasco. What sort of art do you do?"

"A little of this and that." He'd bet the cost of one of his paintings she'd already googled him or called one of her minions to pull his tax files. "Grace said you worked for the IRS." She could get the full picture of what kind of art he did. Commercial.

"Once upon a time. You must be successful if you need a personal assistant. What exactly does Grace do for you?"

Grace spoke quickly. "I field calls, answer correspondence, pay bills, shop for groceries —"

Roman interrupted the flow. "Grace takes on whatever needs to be done so I'm free to paint."

"Then your art isn't all about waiting for inspiration."

He stared back at her. "I paint what the market wants." He waited for a snide remark, but she gave a simple nod and then told Grace to serve the refreshments. "There is a Bundt cake on the kitchen table and lemonade in the refrigerator. Make a pot of coffee, too. Miranda will be by shortly. I'll have tea with lemon."

Heat surged through Roman's veins. He glanced at Grace, and saw she didn't look the least bit upset that her aunt treated her like a servant. She stood and disappeared inside. Elizabeth leaned back and crossed her legs. Her hands rested on the arms of her throne. "So why are you here, Mr. Velasco? I know the spontaneous visit wasn't Grace's idea."

"Why not?"

"She knows me well enough to give me a week's notice."

He leaned back, too. "I was curious."

"Idle curiosity? Or is there a purpose behind it?"

"Why do I have the feeling you don't like me?"

"I don't have feelings about you one way or the other." She tilted her head and raised one brow. "Yet."

"I was curious what kind of family made Grace the way she is."

Her eyes narrowed. "And what way is that?"

"She works hard and does well. I trust her with my finances." That ought to tell this accountant something. "She's a *good* girl." That should tell her the rest.

"Is that your way of saying you two aren't sharing a bed on this business trip of yours?"

"Your niece has the morals of a nun, Mother Walker."

She looked amused, not insulted. "Good for her."

Roman figured he wasn't going to learn anything if he didn't cool off. "Grace said you took her in after her parents died."

"Yes." She paused, assessing him. "I was the only family left, and she was only seven. I had to fly back to Memphis and sort things out. Hardly an easy thing to do, considering the circumstances. And then I brought her back here to Fresno to live with me."

"Circumstances?"

She raised that brow again. "Are you on a fishing expedition, Mr. Velasco? You'll have to ask Grace for details. She may not remember everything, in which case, you'll have to do some research. It's all in the public record."

The doorbell rang. Elizabeth stood, ending the conversation. Excusing herself, she went inside, leaving the glass door open. Roman could hear Grace, Elizabeth, and another woman talking indistinctly. An older woman in a black-and-white polka-dot dress followed Elizabeth outside. Her gray hair was cut short, her blue eyes warm and openly curious. She didn't wait for formal introductions, but came toward him with a hand outstretched. "I'm Miranda Spenser, and you are the famous Roman Velasco! It's such a pleasure to meet you." She glanced at Elizabeth's rigid face, and wasn't cowed into silence. "We've been curious since Grace mentioned her new job. I don't have to ask how she's doing. She always gives her best to anything she does."

Grace came outside with a tray and set it

on the table. She served coffee to Miranda first and poured a cup of tea and added a slice of lemon for her aunt. She handed him a frosty glass of lemonade before cutting slices of Bundt cake. He noticed Grace took nothing for herself. Miranda settled in another wicker chair, less royal than Elizabeth's. "Tell us about yourself, Roman. I've never met an artist, and the Internet didn't tell us much about you, just about your work, which is very interesting, by the way. You don't seem to settle on any one particular style."

Roman had come to learn about Grace, not to talk about himself.

Grace gave him a sympathetic look. "Have some cake, Miranda." Grace handed her a thick slice.

Anything to stop the questions. "There's not much else to say."

"Are you a believer?" Miranda held his gaze.

He didn't understand. "A believer of what?"

"Take that as a no." Elizabeth's faint smirk told him she was enjoying his discomfort.

Miranda didn't seem put off, but spared him an interrogation as she attempted to catch up on Grace's life. Was she still taking night classes? How was Samuel? How was she managing? Grace answered in generalities and turned the focus back on him. She talked about his work and then the gallery show in Laguna Beach. "All of Roman's

paintings sold before the end of the evening."
She told them about Golden and the request
for a mural representing the history of the
area, but didn't admit they hadn't even
bothered driving through the place. She was
rambling, nervous, and the women knew it.

"How many days have you been on the
road?"

"We left Tuesday morning."

When they exchanged a look, Roman decided to rescue her from further questions. "I
took her to the Masterson Ranch, where I
was incarcerated for three years. The propri-
etors are close friends of mine." That made
the two women forget all about Grace and
any possible sins she might have been
tempted to commit along the road.

"Incarcerated?" Miranda repeated, eyes
wide.

Google wouldn't have that information.
"For painting graffiti."

Elizabeth studied him over her cup of tea.
"From illegitimate art to legitimate."

"Some people believe art should be free."

She put her teacup on her saucer. "And yet
you've allowed yourself to become a capital-
ist."

Pale and tense, Grace stood and collected
dessert plates. He wanted to take them from
her and dump everything in Elizabeth
Walker's lap. Elizabeth smiled slightly. "Sit,
Grace." She spoke gently this time. She stood

and took the tray. "Everything is fine." When Grace sat, Roman saw bewilderment, then tears glisten, before she regained control.

Grace watched Roman grow edgier as Miranda talked about church and faith and how much it had always meant to Grace when she was growing up. "She memorized more Scriptures than any student in my class."

"I think he can handle Miranda," Aunt Elizabeth said softly. "Come with me. I want to show you some of the changes I've made in the garden since you were last here."

Grace steeled herself for the inevitable questions about Samuel and what she was going to do about the future. They walked together in tense silence.

Her aunt sighed. "Do you like working for this man?"

"Yes. More as time goes on."

Aunt Elizabeth looked back at the two sitting beneath the pergola. "Well, thankfully, he's not like Patrick. I saw through *him* the first time I met him. This man isn't so easy to read. He doesn't like to talk about himself, and what he did say wasn't something to make himself look good."

"I don't think Roman cares what people think."

"It was his idea to stop by, wasn't it?"

"I didn't think you'd want to see me. You

told me what you thought about my situation."

"I've had time to think more clearly. Not that I've changed my mind about certain things."

Grace looked away. "I understand. Believe me, I do." Sometimes the shame was almost overwhelming, until she held her son. She was surprised to feel her aunt's light touch on her arm.

"I had no right to condemn you or say the things I did, Grace."

Grace's eyes filled with quick tears. It was the closest to an apology she had ever received from her aunt.

"How are you doing?" Aunt Elizabeth sounded concerned.

"I haven't made a decision. I know what I want, but I don't know if it's best." She shook her head, unable to say more.

"You and I need to talk about our family, Grace." Aunt Elizabeth sounded burdened by the past, and Grace knew why. She didn't want to hear what she had overheard already.

She decided to change the subject. "The garden is beautiful."

"He's been watching us, you know."

Grace glanced at Roman. "He probably wants to go."

Aunt Elizabeth pinched off a few dead blossoms. "I've been cautious my entire life, Grace. Maybe too cautious." She tossed the dead petals into the garden.

"You were right about Patrick. You tried to warn me. I didn't want to listen."

"Yes, I was right, but that doesn't mean you can never trust your heart again." She nodded toward Roman. "He wants to know more about you. You're on firmer ground now. You know how deceptive the heart can be." She headed back toward the patio. "Don't hide away and punish yourself for the rest of your life. It's no way to live."

Roman watched Grace while listening to Miranda. The woman talked about "the Lord" as though God was a friend and was sitting in the garden with them right now. This must be the source of Grace's brainwashing. Grace seemed more relaxed when she joined him beneath the pergola. Whatever her aunt had said seemed to have stripped away the tension. He knew he wasn't going to learn anything hanging around this house, and Miranda Spenser made him uncomfortable with her Jesus talk. When he stood, the three women understood he and Grace were leaving.

Elizabeth Walker escorted him through the house, while Miranda and Grace took their time following. "I'm glad you stopped by, Roman."

"Are you?" He didn't believe that for a second.

"I was as curious about you as you are about me."

He hadn't learned much about anything. "If I had to guess, I'd say I don't meet with your approval."

"You weren't looking for it, were you? You're here to audit my niece's life."

Roman didn't feel like sparring with her. "You did a great job raising her."

"I didn't have much choice, and I won't take credit. Grace takes after her mother." Grace and Miranda hugged in the entry hall. Elizabeth lowered her voice. "If you hurt my niece, I swear I'll hunt you down like a dog and carve out your heart with a dull spoon."

He gave a soft laugh. "You know something, Ms. Walker? I like you a whole lot better for saying that. I was beginning to wonder if you cared."

"She's been hurt enough by cavalier treatment."

"Not by me."

"Not yet, anyway."

25

Grace took off her sweater, folded it, and tucked it neatly behind her seat. "You and my aunt seemed to get along."

"She's not exactly warm and fuzzy, is she?" He accelerated onto the freeway, wove through cars, and settled into the fast lane. "Although Ms. Spenser was overboard."

"She was like a second mother to me. It's just her way to love people. If I needed mothering, Aunt Elizabeth called her. My aunt couldn't abide teen angst or hormonal drama."

"Teen angst?" Roman gave her a droll look. "How did that look on you?"

"Subterranean. I didn't have time for emotions. I had to keep my grades up to earn a scholarship, and hold down a job so I could save for living expenses."

"She didn't give you any help? Looked like she was pretty well off."

"I never asked." She knew the answer would be no. "She gave me a home. That was more than she really wanted to do."

"What about love? Is she capable?"

"Maybe you should examine your own life before you judge my aunt." What right did he have to be critical? He'd cut off Chet and Susan for years. Jasper was his only true friend, and only because Jasper made all the effort. "You don't know her."

He didn't say anything for so long she felt ashamed. She didn't want him to judge, and here she was doing it. "I'm sorry."

"What for?" His tone was bland. "You're right."

"Her life wasn't easy. She left Memphis to get away, and then got dragged back in when —" She caught herself. She couldn't say more without bringing up what she didn't want to remember.

She wished she'd had time to finish her psychology class, maybe take more of them. The courses that fascinated her all had to do with human behavior. She longed for answers. What had made her father snap? Why had her mother stayed in an abusive relationship? Was she her mother's daughter, as Aunt Elizabeth believed, prone to make the same mistakes? Did she have to repeat the same patterns? Why had it been easy for Aunt Elizabeth to read Patrick's character and impossible for her to see? And if Aunt Elizabeth could see the truth about people, what terrible thing had she seen in Grace that she could never love her, not even as a niece?

So many questions. A decade of searching for answers and trying to make good decisions.

"When what?" Roman looked annoyed. "Finish what you were going to say."

Her heart pounded.

Roman's expression softened. "Whatever you tell me stays with me. Who am I going to tell?"

"You might broadcast it on social media." She hoped making light of it would end the conversation.

"I want to know more about you, Grace. I want to know what makes you tick. We're trying to become friends. Remember?"

If she wanted to know him on a deeper level, she was going to have to take risks. Did she have the courage to open the door into the old darkness, that awful place of nightmares?

Tell him, came the soft whisper.

She released her breath. She recognized that still, small voice. She might not understand why He wanted her to speak, but she obeyed.

"Aunt Elizabeth hated my father. She didn't tell me that, of course, but shortly after I came to live in her house, I overheard a conversation between her and Miranda. My mother was Aunt Elizabeth's only sister, younger by six years. They were apparently very close until my mother started dating my father. Aunt Elizabeth warned my mother not to get involved with him. She said he was just like *their* father. But my mother wouldn't listen. She got pregnant. With me. They eloped. Aunt Elizabeth told Miranda she knew what would happen, and couldn't bear to watch. She left Memphis before I was born. I never met my aunt until the day she came for me. She called once. My father told my mother she loved her sister more than him. It was the first time I saw him hit her."

Roman's hands shifted on the steering wheel. "Did he ever hit you?"

"He broke my arm once. He cried and said he was sorry. My mother took me to the doctor. She told me on the way he didn't mean to hurt me. He didn't know his own strength." The doctor had wrapped her arm in a cast and asked what happened. Her mother had told her to say she fell out of a tree. It explained the other bruises, too.

"He killed her, didn't he?"

Hearing him say it aloud made the old anguish come up. "My aunt thinks so. I overheard her tell Miranda the coroner's report said it was an accidental death. My mother fell against the kitchen counter and broke her neck. I don't know any more than that."

"Where were you when it happened?"

She clenched her hands to keep them from

shaking. "My mother always watched out the front window for my father. If he came home looking angry, she'd tell me we were playing hide-and-seek again. I'd hide until she came to find me. I was hiding in the back of their bedroom closet. I didn't hear what he said, but my mother was talking so fast. She was crying and saying, 'Please listen; please listen . . .'

"I covered my ears. It got quiet for a few minutes, and I listened, hoping my mother would come. But my father was talking. His voice was different. He kept saying, 'Leanne, Leanne . . .' He sounded scared. And then he started opening doors and closets. I thought he was hunting for me. And then he slid the closet door open. He threw boxes off the top shelf and found a gun. I must have made a sound because he pushed the clothes aside and saw me in the back corner."

Roman drove with eyes straight ahead. "Did he say anything?"

She wiped tears away with a trembling hand. "No. He just stood there staring at me." Her voice broke, and she looked away for a moment. Closing her eyes, she could almost see her father's face. "After a minute, he pushed the clothes along the rod so I couldn't see him anymore. I heard him leave the room. I was afraid he'd come back, but a few minutes later, I heard the shot."

Grace wondered what Roman was thinking. She gave a bleak laugh. "I'll bet you're sorry you asked."

"No. I'm not. But it's not the life I imagined you'd had."

"Others have been through worse." *Bobby Ray Dean, for one.*

A wry smile curved his mouth. "I assumed you grew up in a nice family in some middle-class neighborhood, had lots of friends, went to church every Sunday . . ." He grimaced and uttered a curse. "Were you the one who found him? Your father?"

"No. A police officer found me. He put my mother's parka on me and covered my head before taking me out. A neighbor kept me until CPS came. I was placed in foster care until my aunt arrived." She wanted Roman to understand. "It was hard on Aunt Elizabeth. She'd just lost her sister. Unfortunately, every time she looked at me —"

"It wasn't your fault, Grace."

"In a way it was. My mother wouldn't have married my father if she hadn't gotten pregnant with me. When I married Patrick, Aunt Elizabeth said I was just like her." She hadn't meant to say that.

"You were pregnant, and he was abusive?"

"No." She felt the heat surging into her cheeks. "We never did anything but kiss in high school. Then we ran into each other at UCLA, started studying together. And he, well . . . we . . ." Embarrassed, she looked away.

"You had sex."

What a blunt way of putting it. "I wanted to make things right. Patrick wanted to make things easy."

"And Samuel?"

"My son came later."

"How long were you married?"

"Long enough to get Patrick through UCLA." She shrugged. "A few months later, I came home early from work and found him in bed with someone else. The girl's father owned the gym where he worked out."

Roman winced. "That must have hurt."

"Not as much as it should have. I think I knew why he married me right from the beginning. I just didn't want to face the truth. Patrick needed me to get where he wanted to go. He never loved me. I was pretty pathetic when I think about it." She didn't want to talk about her life anymore. She didn't want to be cornered with any other questions that might arise. Especially about Samuel. "Your turn to talk."

"As you pointed out a while ago, I had the Mastersons and Jasper. They loved me."

"They still love you."

"I have no idea why. I haven't made it easy."

He didn't make anything easy. "God was taking care of you." God had taken care of her, too, even when she hadn't realized it.

"There it is again." Roman gave her a half smile. "The God thing. Miranda talked about Jesus the same way you do. Like He's a close friend."

Grace could let it pass, but it mattered what Roman thought, more now than ever. "He *is* her closest friend. He's mine, too. I just haven't been a very good disciple." She had certainly missed shining any light for Roman or Bobby Ray Dean or whoever he was. If he knew her whole story, what would he think about her then?

"When did you start believing? In Sunday school?" His smile was condescending. "Not going to say anything? And here I thought Christians were always eager to proselytize."

"How many do you know?"

"I've met a few. In clubs." He sounded cynical.

She turned toward the window.

"Talk to me, Grace."

His moods changed quickly. "I came to faith when I was seven, after my aunt moved me to Fresno."

"That's about what I figured."

His tone implied he knew everything, but he knew nothing at all. She gritted her teeth. She hated that mocking tone. They had been talking about things that mattered. Who had started this conversation, and why? "My aunt didn't proselytize, as you put it, and I'd only been to Sunday school a few times. I was still

390

hiding every night when —" *Just be quiet. Let him think whatever he wants.*

"When what?"

Tell him, beloved. Now, while there's time.

Time? She didn't understand. She and Roman had plenty of time, didn't they? She worked for him. But something impelled her to heed the command. "I believed." It was the truth. Part of it anyway. She wouldn't say more unless he asked.

"Just like that, you believed. How? Why? To please your aunt?"

"It didn't please my aunt!" She lifted her hands. "Let's talk about something else."

Beloved, obey Me. Trust Me.

Roman glanced at her. "I want to know."

"You'll laugh."

Roman pressed. "I'm not laughing now, am I? Your aunt took you to church, but didn't want you to become a Christian. What am I missing?"

Lord, please make him believe. "Wherever I was, I slept in a closet. At home, when I was in foster care, in my aunt's house. It was the only place I felt safe." He didn't say anything. "I was afraid of my aunt, afraid of the nightmares that always came. I wanted my mother. Aunt Elizabeth was angry all the time, not like my father had been, but I felt it, even when she tried to hide it. I was afraid of her." She closed her eyes tightly. "I was afraid of everything."

She took a deep breath, gathering courage to tell him the rest. "One night, I saw light under the closet door. It was different. I can't explain it, but I was curious, not afraid. I came out and saw a man standing beside my bed. He didn't look like anyone I'd ever seen before. He was bigger than my father, and light was all around him. All the fear I'd been feeling went away. I climbed onto my bed and sat there and talked to him. I told him everything that happened. He told me I didn't have to be afraid anymore, and I believed him." She let out a shuddering sigh. "I never slept in the closet again."

"You're saying an angel came to you."

Grace didn't have to wonder if he was dubious. It was written all over his face. *Okay, Lord, I did what You told me. He's all Yours.*

"What did your aunt say when you told her?"

"I didn't tell her. I didn't tell anyone about him until Christmas, when Miranda talked about angels in my Sunday school class. She showed pictures, and I said angels weren't girls and didn't have wings and mine was big and strong and glowed. The other children laughed at me, of course. Just like you're laughing."

"I'm not laughing." He sounded angry, but then so was she.

"My aunt heard about it later. She was furious. She told me to stop telling lies to get attention. I never mentioned him again."

"Until now." His expression gentled. He drove for a few minutes, pensive. "Considering what you went through, it's no surprise you had an imaginary friend."

See, Lord? "He wasn't imaginary, Roman. I don't expect you to believe it, but I know he was real and everything he said was true."

"What did he say?"

"He said God loved me. I believed him. I still believe. He told me I'd never be alone, and I believed that, too. I never stopped believing in God, even when I listened to people who didn't." Patrick for one. She'd never told him about the angel. Perhaps she should have remembered that before pouring out her most precious memory on Roman Velasco—Bobby Ray Dean. What was she hoping would happen? Had he ever shown the least interest in spiritual matters?

"Does he still come to you?"

Grace studied Roman's profile before she answered. "No. Sometimes I wish he would."

"Why do you think he left you?"

"I've wondered about that a lot. I think it's because I didn't need him anymore. When I accepted Jesus, the Holy Spirit came to live in me. That's what the angel meant when he said I'd never be alone. I sense when God speaks to me. I don't have to see an angel. Unfortunately, I haven't always listened." She'd dreamed about her angel several times

393

over the last few years. After Patrick left. When she was expecting Samuel. In the dream, her friend simply came and sat beside her and didn't say anything, his presence comfort enough. It was when daylight came that the worry returned, the fear she'd make another mistake, a bigger mistake.

Was she making one now, telling her secrets to this man, allowing him to see inside her? Was she hoping he'd reciprocate?

Roman looked so troubled, she felt sure she'd failed. "You haven't the faintest idea what I'm talking about, do you?"

He shrugged. "I've been in the Vatican and a few of the famous cathedrals in Europe. I've seen people who believe. I wasn't looking for God. I was there for the art."

They didn't talk for a long while. She wondered what he was thinking, but didn't ask.

"You needed to believe someone cared."

He was trying to explain the inexplicable. "Someone does care, Roman."

His hands moved restlessly on the steering wheel. "My mother went out one night and never came back. CPS put me in foster care. Let's just say I didn't stick with the program. I kept looking for her until someone finally got around to telling me she'd died." He gave her a cynical smile. "She was a prostitute like the ones you defended in Bodie. She died of an overdose at twenty-three. I was seven when she disappeared. You can do the math."

Pregnant at fifteen, a baby in her arms by sixteen.

Roman looked pale, almost ashen. He spit out a word he hadn't said since the first day she worked for him. "I don't know why I told you all that."

She could hope it was for the same reasons she had shared her secrets.

He moved into the fast lane again. "Where was God in everything you and I have been through, Grace? Tell me that. Where was God when your father was beating your mother to death and then blowing his brains out? Where was God when my mother was selling her body to keep a roof over our heads? She used drugs to feel better. Maybe she wanted to forget how she made a living. Maybe she wanted to forget she had a kid. Where was God in all that?"

She gripped the edge of her seat. Did he realize how fast he was driving? "I don't have answers. I have faith."

"I don't believe in God." His glance held a challenge. "If He exists, He's a sadist. He's a puppet master who tires of people and throws them in the trash. He's a —" He used words that would have made Grace cover her ears if she hadn't heard the pain behind them.

"If there's a hell, it's right here on earth. And the only heaven we get is what you can make for yourself. This life is all we have, like it or not."

They both heard the siren at the same time. Roman glanced in the rearview mirror and swore again. The police car came up close, right behind them, lights flashing. Slowing, Roman moved right until he reached the shoulder. He put his head back against the seat and closed his eyes. "Just what I need to cap the day." He dug for his wallet.

The officer tapped on the window. Roman lowered it and handed over his registration and driver's license. The officer leaned down. "Do you know how fast you were going?" One hundred and ten. The officer took the documents back to the patrol car.

Roman gripped the wheel with both hands, knuckles white. Grace saw the pulse throbbing in his neck.

The officer returned and tore off the ticket. "Keep it under seventy, Mr. Velasco." The patrol car stayed behind them as Roman pulled onto the freeway again.

Roman didn't speak for five miles. He turned on the radio. Less than a minute passed before he switched it off.

"Okay. Let's finish this conversation and be done with the God talk." He gave her a grim look, as though he was about to dispense bad news. "I read a chunk of that Gideon Bible you recommended. Sure, it's got some great stories, better than what was on TV that night. But that's all it is, Grace — a collection of stories and some history mixed in. Same for all the rest of the religions in this world. There is no God. There is no Satan. No heaven or hell. We're born. We do the best we can. We die. Game over."

Grace's eyes filled with tears. Roman sounded like he wanted life to be fast and short.

26

Grace, Age 7

Grasped by the arm and hauled out of sleep, Gracie awakened screaming. "Hush!" Aunt Elizabeth pulled her up roughly. "Stop that noise right this minute!" She stood Gracie in front of her. Leaning down, she stared into her face. "You have a perfectly good bed, and I find you in the closet." She looked exasperated, her hair disheveled, her face clean of makeup.

"I'm sorry." Gracie hung her head and stared at Aunt Elizabeth's red toenail polish and pink satin pajama legs.

"You're not sorry or you wouldn't have done it again." Aunt Elizabeth sighed. "Look at me!" She crossed her arms as though warding off the chill of night. "Why on earth were you in there?" Her arms loosened, and her voice quieted. "Stop crying, Grace. I'm not going to hurt you. Just get back into bed." She tucked the sheets and blankets beneath the mattress so tightly Gracie could hardly move. "Close your eyes and go to sleep." She flicked off the light as she left the room, shutting the door behind her.

Gracie lay wide-awake until she heard Aunt Elizabeth's door close, then wiggled out of bed, grabbed her pillow, and went back into the closet, quietly closing the door behind her. She could breathe again. She felt safe tucked in the back corner, hidden in the darkness. She wished she had the bear Mrs. Arnold had given her.

Aunt Elizabeth took Gracie to Sunday school. Mrs. Spenser used a felt board and talked about Jesus loving children. She put a little girl next to Jesus. Gracie kept looking at that felt figure. Daddy used to hold her on his lap sometimes and ask her questions.

"What did you and Mommy do today? Did Mommy talk to anyone? Tell me the truth, honey." When Daddy finished asking questions, he'd say, "Good girl," kiss her cheek, and tell her to go play.

Would Jesus hold her on his lap and ask questions, too? Would he want to know everything Aunt Elizabeth did? Gracie had no idea what her aunt did all day.

"Grace?"

Startled, Gracie focused on Mrs. Spenser. "Yes, ma'am?" Her heart pounded. She was supposed to pay attention to her Sunday school teacher. Aunt Elizabeth would ask

Mrs. Spenser if she had. And now she didn't even know what Mrs. Spenser had said.

Mrs. Spenser's expression softened with a smile. "Do you know Jesus loves you, Grace? Just like that little girl standing beside him on the felt board." She put up another figure. "He loves little boys, too." She winked. "Even rascals like Tyler."

Gracie's heartbeat slowed. She listened intently to every word Mrs. Spenser said after that. When people started singing upstairs, Mrs. Spenser put away the felt figures and told the children to gather their sweaters and coats. Big church was over, and their parents would come soon.

The other children had all gone by the time Aunt Elizabeth came. She apologized to Mrs. Spenser, calling her Miranda. "Everyone wanted to know what happened back in Tennessee, as if it's any of their business." Aunt Elizabeth glanced at Gracie sitting alone at the table. "How did she do this morning?"

"She was a perfect angel."

Aunt Elizabeth's mouth curved into a sad smile. "Maybe there's more of my sister in her than that —" Mrs. Spenser put a hand on her arm, and she stopped. Aunt Elizabeth shook her head. "Come along, Grace. Time to go."

On the drive home, Aunt Elizabeth asked what Grace had learned.

Gracie thought about the figures on the felt

board. "Jesus loves boys and girls."

"I'm sure you already learned that much in the church your mother attended. What story did Mrs. Spenser tell you this morning?" She looked in the rearview mirror and scowled. "You didn't listen, did you? Mrs. Spenser works very hard to put together lessons. You're not there to play. You're there to learn about God. Next time, pay attention. I'll be asking Mrs. Spenser how you're doing, and I want to hear good reports. Do you understand?"

"Yes, ma'am."

"Don't call me ma'am. Call me Aunt Elizabeth." When Gracie didn't respond, Aunt Elizabeth glared at her in the mirror. "Did you hear me?"

"Yes, m— Aunt Elizabeth."

"All right. We understand each other." She came to a stoplight. Her hands relaxed on the steering wheel. "I'm not trying to be mean, Grace." She turned a corner. "I know you're not happy." She flicked a glance in the mirror before refocusing on the road. "Well, neither am I." She fell silent as she drove on. "I'm going to do my best, and I expect you to cooperate."

Gracie didn't know what *cooperate* meant.

Aunt Elizabeth seemed able to read her mind. "*Cooperate* means you do what I tell you when I tell you. No dawdling. No daydreaming. No arguments. Do you understand?"

"Yes, Aunt Elizabeth."

Gracie learned to make her bed with hospital corners. She learned to use the vacuum. She folded the bathroom towels exactly the way her aunt taught her. She cleared dishes, but wasn't allowed to wash them because Aunt Elizabeth didn't want any of her Villeroy & Boch broken. The only thing Gracie could not get right was her hair. She brushed it, but couldn't get it into a proper ponytail. Every morning, Aunt Elizabeth had to take it down, rebrush it, and put it back up again.

One morning, Aunt Elizabeth lost her temper. "That's it." She took scissors out of a drawer, yanked the ponytail up, and cut it off right under the tangled rubber band.

Gracie uttered a gasp of pain and burst into tears, knowing Mommy would be very upset. She always said she loved Gracie's curly dark hair. *It's wavy, just like Daddy's.*

Aunt Elizabeth stood with the severed ponytail in her hand and stared at Gracie. Sinking onto a kitchen chair, she dropped the scissors and ponytail, covered her face, and wept. "I can't do this!" She sobbed harder than Gracie. "I can't! God, why did You do this to me?"

After a few minutes, Aunt Elizabeth stopped crying, wiped her face, gathered up the ponytail, and pitched it into the trash can under the sink. She tossed the scissors back in the drawer. "No use crying about it. It's done. We can't undo it. Let's have breakfast, shall we?"

Aunt Elizabeth didn't say another word until she stopped the car in front of the school. She didn't look in the rearview mirror either. "Remember who you belong to, Grace. Go on, now, or you'll be late."

Gracie fingered her hair as everyone stared at her. Miss Taylor grimaced. At recess, the girls laughed. "What did you do to your hair? You look awful!" A couple of boys came over and said she looked like a short-haired mutt. Miss Taylor blew her whistle, and the boys scattered.

When school ended, Aunt Elizabeth stood outside the door. They went to a beauty parlor, where Aunt Elizabeth introduced Gracie to Christina Alvarez, who was going to fix her hair.

"I can make this good." Christina sat Gracie in a big black leather chair and pumped a pedal to raise it. "Do you want it shorter, or shall I work with it at this length?" She was looking at Gracie, but Aunt Elizabeth answered.

"Short and easy."

Christina met Gracie's eyes in the mirror and leaned down, whispering, "What about you, Grace? Do you want it shorter?" Gracie shook her head slowly. Christina's cheeks dimpled when she smiled. "All right, then. We'll work with what we've got." She turned the chair and lowered it, washing Gracie's hair in a sink hung on the wall. Towel-drying it, Christina fluffed Gracie's hair again. "People pay a lot of money to have curls like you do." She talked as she combed, snipped, styled, and snipped some more.

"There!" She put her hands on Gracie's shoulders and they both faced the mirror. "What do you think?"

Aunt Elizabeth tossed the magazine back on the stack and stood beside them. She looked more relieved than pleased. "Much better."

"Wash-and-wear hair." Christina winked at Gracie. "Just shampoo, rinse, and towel-dry. Use a pick to get rid of any snarls —" she handed Gracie a white plastic comb with wide teeth — "and then fluff it up with your fingers. Easy breezy. A couple of minutes, and you're ready to roll."

Life settled into a routine. Sunday, church. Monday through Friday, school, after-school care, homework. Chores every day of the week. On Saturday, Aunt Elizabeth put on jeans, a T-shirt, and plastic clogs and went outside to work in her garden. She expected Gracie to help. Sunshine was good for the soul, she said, and the vegetables and fruit good for the body. Aunt Elizabeth grew squash, cucumbers, tomatoes, carrots, and bell peppers. She also had fruit trees: apricot, nectarine, cherry, and apple. Gracie liked being in the yard. Sometimes her aunt would sit back on her heels, dab perspiration from her forehead with the back of her hand, and look happy. Aunt Elizabeth was pretty when she smiled, her face smooth and peaceful.

Mrs. Spenser came to visit. Gracie could tell the two women liked each other. They hugged at the door and kissed each other's cheeks. Aunt Elizabeth offered Mrs. Spenser tea and cookies, and Mrs. Spenser said yes. "Is Grace any trouble?"

Mrs. Spenser laughed. "Never. She's good as gold. You shouldn't worry so much." She saw Gracie standing in the entryway and beckoned her. She ran a gentle hand over Gracie's hair. "I just wanted to stop by to see how you two are doing."

Aunt Elizabeth told Gracie to go play in her room, then invited Mrs. Spenser into the kitchen.

Had Aunt Elizabeth forgotten all of Gracie's toys and dolls had been left in Tennessee? Everything had been put in boxes and put on the same truck that took Mommy and Daddy's furniture. She could find things to do outside. As she came down the hallway again, Gracie could hear the two women talking. Aunt Elizabeth sounded angry again. Gracie ducked around the corner into the living room. If she opened the glass door, her aunt would hear her. So she sat on the sofa.

"Leanne wouldn't listen. I knew the first time I met Brad he was trouble. You know how you can sense that sometimes." Mrs. Spenser said yes, she did. "Well, she went out with him anyway, and it wasn't long before he got her pregnant. I told her not to add another mistake to the one she'd already made. He'd already cut her off from friends, and he didn't like me. Of course, he said it was because I didn't like him, which was true. Why wouldn't she listen to me?"

"People in love seldom do."

"If you can call that love." Aunt Elizabeth spoke in a sneering tone. "She said he needed her. He'd been waiting for her all his life. He knew just what she wanted to hear. He was like our father, handsome and charming. A devil! He made my mother's life a living hell and ours right along with her. I reminded Leanne how we grew up, but she couldn't see the similarities. She said Brad wasn't anything like our father."

"Do you think he killed her? Is that what you're thinking?"

"The coroner ruled her death an accident. But how do you fall that hard unless someone shoves you? At least he felt guilty enough to blow his brains out."

"Beth!"

Gracie heard a teacup set heavily in a saucer. "I know. I know!" Aunt Elizabeth gave a sob. "God says to forgive, but I hope Brad is burning in hell. Forgive? I just . . . can't."

"Not in our own strength."

"I left Tennessee when they got married. Did I tell you that? I didn't want to stay around and watch what I knew would happen." Aunt Elizabeth sounded as though she was crying. "But I should have stayed! Maybe she would have left him if she'd had some place to go. Now, it's too late. Leanne is dead, and I have the child that made my sister give in to that son of a —"

"You can't blame the child."

"I know that in my head, but every time I look at her, I see him."

"Isn't there any of your sister in her?"

"She cries a lot." Aunt Elizabeth's voice was despairing. "And she hides."

"Hides?"

"In her closet. Every night."

Gracie bowed her head.

Before Mrs. Spenser left, she went down the hall to Gracie's bedroom, then came out again and into the living room. "There you are." She studied Gracie with a troubled expression. She gave Gracie a firm hug. Her eyes were moist when she straightened. She and Aunt Elizabeth spoke softly at the front door, and Mrs. Spenser hugged and kissed her, too. As soon as the front door closed,

Aunt Elizabeth came into the living room. "Were you listening the whole time?" Gracie didn't answer. Aunt Elizabeth's shoulders drooped slightly. "So now you know everything, don't you?"

Yes. Gracie knew. Aunt Elizabeth was glad Daddy was dead, and she didn't like Gracie because she looked like her father.

When Aunt Elizabeth tucked her into bed that night, she ran her hand gently over Gracie's head. She searched Gracie's face, her eyes shiny with moisture. "Try to stay in bed tonight." Gracie turned away before the door closed. She stared through the curtains at the streetlight. She waited for a long time, then took her pillow and went into the closet. Tears rolled down her cheeks as she sat with her knees pulled up against her chest. She put her head down, wanting to wail and scream for Mommy, but didn't dare make a sound. Her breath came in little hitches of pain.

Light shone under the closet door. She hadn't heard Aunt Elizabeth come into the bedroom or click on the light. She waited, holding her breath in fear, but Aunt Elizabeth didn't open the doors and tell her to get back in bed right this minute. Nothing happened. The light stayed on — a soft, warm glow, not the bright white of the one on the ceiling or the lamp on the nightstand.

Tentative, curious, Gracie carefully opened the sliding door a crack and peered out.

Someone sat on the side of her bed. He smiled at her, but didn't say anything. She felt him telling her she could come out. He wouldn't hurt her. The fear went away, and she came out. The man didn't look like anyone she'd ever seen before. He glowed. She stared at him, wide-eyed. He rose, towering over her like a giant, but she wasn't afraid of him at all. Instead, she felt loved. He sat in the chair by the window, and she climbed back onto her bed, sitting in the middle. He talked to her gently, words of comfort in a language she'd never heard before, but somehow understood. She didn't know who or what he was, other than he was her friend and she didn't have to fear him. He told her she could go to sleep now without worrying about tomorrow. Tomorrow would take care of itself, and he would be watching over her. When she lay down and pulled the covers up, he sang over her.

Aunt Elizabeth awakened her in the morning. "You slept in your bed. Good. Time to get up for school."

Gracie's friend came back again that night. This time she came right out of the closet and climbed up on the bed. He didn't say as much, but she felt he didn't mind when she whispered to him about school and missing Mommy and Daddy and what Aunt Elizabeth had said to Mrs. Spenser. He didn't hush her or tell her to go to sleep. He listened, his soft, cozy glow making her warm inside.

The next night, Gracie didn't go into the closet, and he just appeared, as though he'd been in the room all the time and she hadn't been able to see him until that moment.

When Aunt Elizabeth found out about Gracie's angel, she was angry. "Don't start making up stories to get attention."

"I didn't."

"Don't argue with me. And don't you dare lie. Miranda — I mean, Mrs. Spenser — said you announced to the whole class that an angel comes to your room every night."

"He does."

"Oh, for heaven's sake, am I going to have to take you to a psychologist?"

That evening, Aunt Elizabeth tucked Gracie into bed. An hour later, she threw open the door and came in. She stood at the end of Gracie's bed, hands on her hips, and looked pointedly around the room. "So? Seeing is believing. Where is he? This angel friend of yours."

Gracie didn't know what to say.

"No more talk of angels ever again." Aunt Elizabeth spoke in a hard voice. "It makes you sound crazy." She went out, closing the door firmly behind her.

Gracie looked at her friend. "Why couldn't she see you?"

"Believing is seeing."

27

Roman regretted venting his frustration. Grace sat silent, making no effort to argue with him. She didn't seem angry, but then what did he know? Had he been hoping she'd debate, prove him wrong? He doubted anything he said would kill her faith. Was that what he'd been trying to do? Or was he testing her to see how deep it ran?

An angel. No wings. A man. Grace based her faith on what she thought she saw as a scared kid who'd just lost both parents and then been moved across the country by an embittered aunt who didn't want to look at her, let alone take care of her. And she thought God loved her? She was convinced He did? How does that happen? Roman had been afraid, many times, but never so deeply he'd imagined some celestial being coming to the rescue or offering words of comfort. He'd waded through his fear, crushing it with anger.

All his assumptions about Grace Moore

had been wrong. He hadn't expected to share common roots: devastating loss, fear, pain, no love. He'd run away and put up walls. Grace had hidden and then come out, been repeatedly wounded, and still poured all her hope into an unseen God.

Even with similar backgrounds, he felt the difference. He had a house, fancy cars, money in the bank. She struggled to stand on her own. He didn't have anyone depending on him. She had a child, a son who needed her. He had a few friends and kept them at a distance. She carved out time with hers. He no longer had goals. She still pursued hers. He lived from one day to the next, doing whatever seemed right in his own eyes, and felt rootless and adrift. She lived to please an imaginary friend and seemed grounded — secure in her faith, if nothing else.

The highway rose and snaked through the Tehachapis. Grace looked out at the mountains. He looked at her. He couldn't bear her silence, but he'd never apologized to anyone. Especially when he believed what he'd said. "Everything okay?"

She smiled at him. "I've driven this road a dozen times and every single time I see something new. I stopped once at Fort Tejon when the park was hosting a Civil War re-enactment. Cannons firing, men shooting rifles, some screaming and falling to the ground as though they'd been shot. It was pretty terrifying."

Roman relaxed. She wasn't mad at him. "A Renaissance faire might be more fun. There's one in Irwindale. Maybe we should go."

"I can't imagine you at a Renaissance faire." Her smile lingered, her expression warm. "I've seen places over the last few days I've only dreamed of seeing, Roman. Thank you for insisting I come along. Even if it's obvious you didn't need me on this trip."

I need you more than you know.

"Glad you enjoyed yourself. It's been good for me, too." He didn't want the journey to end, but knew better than to try to prolong it. Grace wanted to spend the weekend with her baby boy. She'd probably invite that clean-cut pastor over for barbecue and maybe share another kiss, just to see if the second round turned out better than the first. What if it did?

Get a grip, Roman. Grace Moore deserves the right kind of guy. Even if the wrong kind wants her.

He'd put out a feeler with the idea of taking her to the Renaissance faire. Her answer came through loud and clear. *Thanks, boss. See you Monday morning. I work for you, remember?* Roman wanted to respect her boundaries. And he should be satisfied. He'd set out on this road trip for one purpose: getting to know Grace. The problem was the more he knew, the more he wanted to know; the closer he got, the closer he wanted to be. He had told her more about himself than he'd ever told anyone. He'd kept only one secret back, one he knew could ruin everything he had tried to make of his life.

She broke the silence this time. "Did you see anything over the last few days that inspired you?"

Oh, yeah. Plenty. "I took a few pictures."

"Carrizo Plain, Yosemite, Mono Lake, the Dardanelles. Enough to inspire a lifetime of painting."

Roman glanced at her. Every mile he drove put them closer to the end of whatever was happening in this car. "We should stop for supper."

"Oh, good. I'm starving."

He laughed. "Why didn't you say something?"

"You seemed in a hurry to get back." She grinned at him. "One hundred and ten miles an hour. I've never gone that fast before."

He'd forgotten the ticket in the door pocket. "Want to do it again?"

"Don't even think about it."

They passed a sign. "Santa Clarita is coming up. There should be a nice restaurant near Magic Mountain." Roman took the exit, wishing he could see how she'd handle a roller-coaster ride. "Are you in the mood for seafood or Mexican?"

"I love anything I haven't cooked."

Pulling into a space beneath a shade tree, Roman told her to sit tight. He came around the car and opened her door. When he held out his hand, she hesitated briefly before accepting his assistance. Her hand trembled in his. Nice to see she wasn't completely indifferent. He'd been on a roller-coaster ride this entire trip — highs and lows, that sudden drop in his stomach and the rush of his pulse when their eyes met. The feeling he was having right now. Off-balance.

He stumbled slightly. His mind blanked. He felt suddenly weak.

"Roman?" Grace gripped his arm. "Are you all right?"

He thought he'd be fine once they got inside the air-conditioned restaurant, but he barely made it to the sidewalk before his legs turned to jelly. Grace cried out, trying to break his fall, and he took her down with him. He wanted to ask if she was okay. He wanted to say he was sorry if he hurt her. She was screaming for help and rolling him onto his back. He didn't feel anything but a heavy pulling sensation.

He barely heard Grace cry out. "Roman. Oh, God . . . Jesus, help him. Help us!"

Her voice faded as he sank into a sea of darkness.

■ ■ ■ ■

Roman didn't feel any pain. No need to breathe. The hot cement gave way beneath him and then flung him up, light and free. He saw a crowd around a body and Grace on her knees, doing CPR. A man appeared, gripped her shoulder, and knelt beside her. He took over. Others had their phones out, most taking pictures and texting, one or two talking. Roman looked at the dead man lying on the sidewalk. What the — ? That was him! Was he hallucinating?

Looking away from the scene on the sidewalk, he noticed two men standing on either side of him. Instinctively repelled, he shrank back. They looked ordinary, nondescript, but something about them scared him. One showed jagged teeth. "Time to go, Bobby Ray."

"Get away from me!" Roman stepped back.

"You can't run now." Hollow black eyes stared at him as they advanced.

"Who in hell are you?" Taking another step back, he raised his fists.

They laughed. "You know what we are." They moved fast, each grabbing hold of him with claw hands.

Crying out in fear as much as in pain, Roman tried to break free. Why was he so weak, and they so strong? Terrified now, he thrashed. "Let go of me!" Rivers of fire spread through his body, and he screamed.

The air shimmered like a mirage in a desert as he passed through a veil into another world. A dark tunnel opened ahead, and the demons dragged him in. The curved walls and ceiling were alive with creatures, their faces twisted and grotesque. They crawled above and around him, spewing foul names, writhing, grabbing at him, their mouths snapping like great white sharks hungry for flesh.

Cringing, ducking, dodging, Roman tried to go back. Dragged forward by his captors, he saw darkness ahead and felt rising heat. He heard human shrieks and groans of agony.

Pain exploded inside Roman's chest. He arched, body stiffened, eyes opening to light and voices all around him.

"Stop! Stop! He's back!" Grace cried out.

A stranger lifted his hands away and Roman tried to draw breath. He felt the darkness encroaching again. Terrified, he rasped, "Don't stop. Don't . . . stop."

Sucked back into the darkness, Roman kicked at his captors, struggled against their grasp. The demons laughed louder, still gripping him, dragging him further, deeper inside the pulsing mouth of hell. The morbid, decaying fiends in the walls and ceiling licked their lips and taunted him with vile names and horrific descriptions of what they intended to do to him. They reached out putrid fingers, the stench of rotting flesh pressing in like a suffocating fog. Roman could taste it.

"No! Oh, God, no!" Roman tried to dig in his heels. He tried to yank free. He saw that he wasn't alone. Thousands were in the tunnel, all screaming and fighting as they moved, as though on a huge, terrifying conveyor belt, toward the abyss. A cliff lay ahead, an endless black pit beyond. Humans spilled over, howling as they disappeared. Roman screamed. He looked for something, anything, to grab on to, but there was nothing but the lost souls with him and the loathsome creatures relishing their misery.

Weightless and weak, Roman felt the cold wind blow at his back and the fiery heat of hell ahead. He screamed out the last thing he remembered. *"Jesus!"*

Shrieks rippled through the cavernous tunnel.

Roman cried out again. "Oh, God! Christ, help me!"

Blinding light filled the darkness. Someone clasped his wrist, lifting him, and in the midst of hell's cacophony, whispered, "I am."

Claws grabbed him from beneath, and a dark, hate-filled voice echoed. "He's mine! Give him to me!" Roman screamed as the hand tightened and talons dug into his calf, sending shards of pain up his leg. He had no strength to kick loose.

"Release him." A quiet voice spoke from

above, and the being from the pit fell away into darkness.

Roman arched again. Fire riddled his body as the shock of electricity spread through his nervous system. He opened his eyes and saw two men bending over him. "We've got him!" An EMT leaned in closer. "Hang on, buddy. We're almost to the hospital."

Wild with fear, Roman looked around. He tried to move, but he was strapped down.

"Easy now. Lie still."

White cabinets, yellow tubing, and green monitors surrounded him. A siren screamed overhead. The speed told him he was in an ambulance. His chest and ribs hurt so much he could hardly breathe, let alone talk. His body started to shake.

"Grace . . ." The EMT didn't hear him. He tried again. "I need Grace."

"Good thing your girlfriend knew CPR, buddy. Hang in there. We're almost there." The vehicle slowed and turned. It stopped. The doors opened.

Two EMTs slid the gurney down a track, lowered the wheels, and locked them in place. Roman got a glimpse of blue sky and then white ceiling. An IV drip was attached to his right arm. He was wheeled into a corridor and heard voices. Thrashing, he tried to get free. "Oh, God." He moaned, crying now. "Oh, Jesus, don't let go of me." The veil had been wisp-thin between life and death. All his strength hadn't been enough to break free, but one soft word from Christ, and he was alive again.

Grace tried to stay calm as she drove Roman's car to the hospital. Thankfully, she'd remembered the fob before the ambulance left. One of the EMTs fished it out of Roman's pocket. He gave her quick directions. Too shaken to take them in or to figure out the car's computer system, she used the GPS on her phone. The calm, computerized voice helped steady her. She parked and ran into the emergency room. When she asked about Roman Velasco, the nurse wanted to know if she was his wife.

"He's my boss. We were on a business trip."

Consigned to a waiting area, Grace perched on the edge of the seat, praying, watching every movement of the medical personnel, listening for any slip of information. Others sat with her, upset and waiting for news of their loved ones. Apparently, Friday afternoons could be busy. Close to tears, she covered her face and prayed some more. She wanted to be doing something. Pulling out her phone, she texted Shanice. I'm in ER in Santa Clarita. Roman had a heart attack. Please pray.

"Anyone here named Grace?"

"Yes!" She surged to her feet. "I'm Grace." Tucking her phone into her purse, she fell into step with the nurse.

"He keeps asking for you. Try to calm him down. We want to prep him for surgery, but he's convinced if he goes under anesthesia, he'll end up in hell. He said the leg injury came from some demon —"

"What leg injury?"

The nurse frowned as he pushed the door open. "The doctor is on his way."

Roman's skin was ashen. Hooked to machines, an IV in his arm, an oxygen mask covering his nose and mouth, he looked terrified as he jerked at the restraints. Fighting tears, Grace came closer. She had to stay calm for his sake. "Roman." She put her hand on his arm. He looked at her, eyes wild, and said something she couldn't understand. He yanked at the belts that held him. She leaned down. "These people know how to help you." He didn't take his eyes off her. "I'm here. Focus on me right now." The nurse put medication into the IV. She squeezed Roman's hand. "I'll be in the waiting room, praying for you. I'm not leaving. I promise."

His eyes filled with tears as he tried to speak.

"You're going to be fine." *Please, God, make it so.*

The nurse touched her shoulder. "We're good to go."

Grace called Selah and told her what had

happened. "I promised him I'd stay here."

"As you should, *chiquita*. How is he doing?"

"I don't know yet."

"Sammy is fine. Don't worry about him. Stay with your boss, and keep us posted. We'll be praying, too."

Grace phoned Brian to ask him to pray for Roman. She told him the situation and then said she needed to make another call.

Shanice answered immediately. "Hey, girlfriend, what happened? Is Roman okay?"

Grace started to cry. She'd held herself together as long as she could. Wrapping an arm around her middle, she rocked.

"Grace, honey? Talk to me."

The words came, choked at first and then in a flood. "He went into cardiac arrest. He's in surgery right now. Henry Mayo Newhall Hospital. Please get everyone praying. One minute he was standing, and the next he was dead. I couldn't find a pulse and started CPR. A man took over, and Roman came back. I wanted to thank the man, but he was gone. And Roman — oh, Shanice, I've never seen anyone so scared. He looked like he'd seen hell." She wiped tears away.

Others in the waiting room stared at her. She got up and went into the hallway. "He might die. And he doesn't believe in Jesus. I'm so scared for him."

"Don't go down that road, honey. He's alive. He's in surgery. He has a chance. I'll call Ashley. She'll activate the church prayer chain and let Nicole know what's happened. I've got my keys in hand right now. I'll be there as soon as I can. Just stay cool, Grace. God's in charge. Remember that."

An hour passed. The waiting room emptied until she was the last person waiting for news. She wasn't family, but who else did Roman have? Jasper! The Mastersons! Why hadn't she thought to call them? Should she? They should know. She decided to wait until she had more definite news before calling Jasper. He would know how to reach Chet and Susan.

Another hour passed. Grace paced. Would hospital staff allow her in recovery or ICU? What if Roman didn't make it? What if he'd died and no one bothered to tell her? Maybe the shift had changed and those at the desk didn't know she was still waiting. She was afraid to ask. No news was better than bad news.

"Grace?"

Gasping, Grace lifted her head. "Oh, Brian." Bursting into tears, she flew into his arms.

He held her closer, chin resting on top of her head. "I got here as soon as I could. How is he?"

"I don't know." She drew back. When he pulled out a handkerchief, she took it. "I haven't heard anything."

"Sit. I'll go check and be right back."

Grace couldn't read his expression when he returned. He sat beside her and took her hand. "He'll be out of surgery soon. You won't be able to see him for a while." He squeezed her hand gently. "How long since you've eaten?"

"I don't remember. We were stopping for supper. I don't want to leave. The doctor might come. Someone has to come sometime, don't they?"

"You need to eat something. I'll be back." He left the waiting room.

Shanice arrived a few minutes later, looking harried. "Sorry it took so long. There was an accident. I thought I'd never get here. Oh, honey." She hugged Grace. They sat on the sofa together. "The whole church is praying. You're shaking. Try to breathe."

Brian came back with a vending machine sandwich and a bottle of orange juice. He stopped in the doorway. "Hello." He stared at Shanice.

"Hi, Brian. I know you from your picture. I set up the first date."

"Oh. A thank-you would be in order. And you are . . . ?"

Grace remembered her manners. "This is Shanice. She's my best friend. And you can give her the sandwich. I'm not very hungry."

Shanice held out her hand. "She'll eat it if I

have to stuff it down her throat. Ask the powers that be what's happening, would you?"

"He already did." Grace glanced toward the door, wishing someone would come.

Shanice looked at Brian. "No harm in checking again."

He left, and Shanice patted Grace's knee. "Sometimes a pastor can get more information than a regular citizen." She gave Grace an encouraging smile. "Eat up, honey. You won't do Velasco any good if you go in looking like death warmed over."

Brian returned. "We should hear something soon."

A doctor came in half an hour later. "Grace?" She followed him into the hall. The surgery had gone well. Roman now had an ICD, an implantable cardioverter defibrillator, a small computer that would regulate and monitor his heart. "He's lucky to be alive. He's probably had a few episodes and didn't know what they were. Has he ever blacked out before today?"

"I don't know." She remembered finding him sprawled across the bed once. She'd assumed he was sleeping.

Before going into ICU, she cleaned her hands with antibacterial gel and put on a mask. The doctor opened the door for her and spoke softly. "We'll keep him here for twenty-four hours and then move him into a room, barring complications. Good thing he's in peak physical condition. Is he an athlete?"

"An artist."

He looked relieved. "His heart was an easy fix. We have another doctor handling his leg."

"What's wrong with his leg?"

"Can't say."

He couldn't say, or he didn't know? When could Roman have injured his leg?

Though he was still clearly in pain, Roman's color had improved. He was tethered to monitors beeping heart rate, oxygen levels, blood pressure. An IV drip stood beside the bed, the needle inserted in the top of his hand. A thin tube connected to a bag measuring urine. His eyes were open, wide-open. "Grace." He breathed out her name, his body relaxing.

Grace moved to the side of his bed and took his hand. "I told you I'd stay." She managed to smile. "You're doing better than the last time I saw you."

His hand tightened on hers.

Her emotions tumbled one over another. She didn't want to think about how much she cared about him, and what kind of complications that would bring to their working relationship — not now. "A lot of people are praying for you, Roman. I hope you don't mind that I spread the word."

"No."

"Brian and Shanice are in the waiting room."

"He got me out."

Grace didn't understand. "You don't have to talk right now. Try to rest."

He squeezed her hand again. "I was in hell."

Grace felt goose bumps rise all over her body. Leaning down, she put her free hand on his forehead. "What are you saying?"

"Jesus," Roman rasped. "He got me out. They were hanging on to me. Ripping at my leg."

A nurse checked one of the machines. "He's under medication." He came around the bed and injected something into a small port attached to Roman's IV. He gave Grace an understanding smile. "Another minute, and you should go. He needs to rest."

Roman's body tensed. "She stays." When he looked up at the IV drip, his expression changed. The heart monitor beeped faster. "What'd you put in it?"

"Just something to help you relax."

Roman's eyes fixed on Grace. "Don't let them put me under. Oh, Jesus, don't let me die again."

The nurse frowned. "I guess you can stay with him a while longer." He made an entry on the computer terminal. "I'll check back in a few minutes." He left the room.

Roman's grip loosened, but he didn't let go of her hand. He groaned. "That nurse put something in the IV." His eyes drooped. He widened them, fighting sleep. "Jesus, I don't want to die. I'm not ready to die."

Grace couldn't bear it. She cupped his face. "Listen to me, Roman. Jesus would not rescue you from hell and then throw you back."

"It grabbed me. It ripped me . . ."

"Roman." She spoke quietly, calmly. "Jesus saved you."

He looked broken and confused. "Why?"

What could she say to that? "He'll tell you later."

He was losing the battle against whatever medication had been added to the IV. "Don't go."

"They may not let me stay, but I promise I'll come back."

He couldn't keep his eyes open. "My mother used to say that."

The nurse returned and checked vitals. "He'll sleep now. You look like you could use some rest, too."

"Do you know where I can stay, a hotel with a kitchen? Somewhere I can wash clothes?"

He suggested an Extended Stay America only minutes away.

She returned to the waiting room, expecting to find it empty or filled with strangers, but Shanice and Brian were still there, sitting on the sofa together, deep in conversation. They didn't even notice her come into the room. Grace watched them a minute before she cleared her throat. They both glanced up sharply and stood. Brian met Grace halfway. "How is he?"

"He's asleep. He said Jesus got him out."

"Wow." Shanice joined them. "Nothing like a near-death experience to get a man's attention. I'll drive you home. You can get a good night's sleep and —"

Grace shook her head, decision made. "I'm going to stick around."

"Oh, girl, are you sure?" Shanice sounded worried. She glanced at Brian.

"He wants me to stay."

Shanice stepped closer. "Honey, you look exhausted already. I know this whole thing has put you through the emotional wringer, but Roman doesn't need you. He has good doctors and nurses."

Grace understood Shanice's concern. Some time and distance would help her think more clearly. But right now, she wanted to stay as close as possible. "I gave my word."

"What about Samuel?"

"I've already talked with Selah. She encouraged me to stay."

Shanice rolled her eyes. "Of course. She would."

Her son was happy and safe with Selah. For now, Roman was the one who needed her.

28

Panting, heart pounding, Roman awakened from the nightmare. He'd been back inside the tunnel, surrounded by shadows and monsters. Disoriented, he gasped when he found someone standing beside the bed, a hand on his shoulder.

"Sorry I awakened you, Mr. Velasco, but you were having another nightmare." A different nurse, this one a middle-aged woman with a kind face.

"Oh." His breathing slowed. "Thanks." He could still feel the visceral impact of the echoing screams, moans of anguish, the gnashing of teeth of those he'd seen in hell. The heart monitor showed his rate slowing to normal. "Where's Grace?"

"She'll be back soon." The nurse readjusted the blanket, asked if he needed anything, and left the room.

It was quieter now that he was out of ICU, but people passed by in the outer corridor: nurses, a doctor, visitors. Roman watched the

430

door for Grace. He lay still, attuned to the sounds around him: low voices, squeaky shoes on a polished floor, beeps. His roommate turned on the TV. A news report and talk of the weather. Roman listened, wanted to forget the memory of demonic monsters and a fiery pit.

Hell existed. He'd been there. Every time Roman tried to talk himself out of what he'd experienced, he felt the pain in his leg. He'd seen it when the nurse changed the dressings, and he remembered the doctor asking about the injury. Emotionally raw, Roman said a demon had dug talons into his leg and tried to pull him back down to hell. Jesus told the creature to let go, and it did. The physician stood silent, looking at him the same way Roman must have looked at Grace when she told him about the angel who came to her when she was a child.

"I'm sure there's a rational explanation, Mr. Velasco."

"Great. Tell me. Please. I'd like to hear one."

The doctor thought for a moment, then shook his head. "I don't know."

Roman had felt the demon's claws. He remembered the weight pulling at him. Jesus Christ whispered a word and Roman was set free. Had he been a soul outside his body, or had he been flesh and blood? He tried to wrap his mind around what happened and couldn't.

The doctor had asked about family. The condition was often hereditary. Maybe his father had passed down the heart problem. There was no way for Roman to know, no way to find out. Was his father still alive? Maybe he was in that seething pit of fire and darkness. Was White Boy in the outer darkness, too, gnashing his teeth in agony?

The curtain slid back. "Good morning, Roman." Dr. Ng had a chart in his hand. "Still having nightmares, I hear. Do you want to speak with a psychologist?"

Roman pressed a button, raising the head of his bed. "No." He told the truth once and wasn't believed. Better not to mention it to anyone again.

Where was Grace? What was taking her so long?

Dr. Ng checked the site of the defibrillator. "Looks good. Working perfectly. Swelling is gone. No sign of infection. Helps that you're so healthy."

Dr. Ng tapped something into the computer terminal. "We'll get going on the paperwork and have you out of here tomorrow. The nurse will make an appointment for a three-month checkup."

When Grace entered the room shortly after the doctor left, Roman's pulse kicked up. Thankfully, the heart monitor had been removed, along with IVs and all the other tethers that had kept him tied down. How was it possible for a woman to soothe and stir him at the same time? Their relationship had changed subtly over the last few days. He saw something new in her eyes and welcomed it.

Grace had stuck by him through the entire ordeal. She even read to him when he couldn't sleep. He'd awakened once and seen her asleep in the chair, one of her textbooks open on her lap. When he woke later, she was gone, but she'd left her Bible on his tray table. Paging through, he found passages she'd underlined in different colors, notes she'd written in the margins, names beside certain passages. Was his written somewhere?

Relieved she was back now, he smiled. "We can leave tomorrow."

"Isn't it too soon? You've only been here three days." Her eyes were the color of dark honey.

"My heart is working just fine." *Pounding like a jackhammer right now.*

Grace dug into her backpack and handed him a leather-bound Bible. "I wanted to have it engraved, but wasn't sure what name you'd want on it — Bobby Ray Dean or Roman Velasco."

Her phone jingled in her purse. She took it out and read the text. Thumbing a quick answer, she dropped it back in her purse. "Samuel has an earache."

His situation had probably made things more difficult for her. "You missed your weekend with your son. You can have time off when we get back."

"I'll take you up on that."

Jasper appeared around the curtain. "Here you are, hiding out with Grace." He shook his head. "You're always causing trouble, aren't you?" Jasper greeted Grace before grasping Roman's hand. "Has the boy been cooperating?"

"He hasn't had much choice." Grace got another call. Talia, this time. She handed the phone to Roman. Talia was relieved Roman sounded so good. She'd been worried she'd be attending his funeral. Why hadn't he told her he had a heart problem? She wouldn't have pushed him so hard. What did he mean he didn't know? How could he not know? Maybe he needed a vacation. He should go to Europe. Or lie on a beach in Tahiti. Roman let her talk until she noticed his silence.

"Are you still there, Roman?"

"I'm breathing, but my ears are getting sore with all this motherly concern."

"I don't know why I put up with you!"

"The 50 percent commission."

"Yes, there is that." She chuckled. "When are you going home?"

"Tomorrow, but don't expect any paintings anytime soon."

"Whenever you're ready, you know where

to find me. Put Grace back on."

Roman handed the phone back to Grace. She went out into the hallway to finish the conversation.

"Chet and Susan send their love." Jasper picked up the Bible. "Are you becoming interested in something other than art?"

"Grace gave it to me." He hesitated and then decided to confess. "I have no doubt Jesus exists. Not after what I went through."

"And what was that?"

"I doubt you'll believe me. So far, Grace is the only person who does."

"Try me."

Roman told him the whole story. He couldn't tell if Jasper believed or not. He waited, but Jasper just stood there, grim and silent. "Are you going to say something?"

"I'm glad it wasn't me on the receiving end of that lesson."

"The last person I told thought I needed to talk to a psychiatrist."

"I'm a Christian, have been for years. I stopped going to church after my wife died." His mouth tipped. "Went back when I got cancer."

"How is it I never knew this about you?"

Jasper sat in the chair by the window. He stretched out his legs as though making himself comfortable. "You never asked, and anytime I brought up spiritual matters, your eyes glazed over. There's a time for everything under the sun, Bobby Ray. The time never seemed quite right with you."

"I'm still having nightmares."

Jasper gave a slight laugh. "Not surprising. I may have nightmares just hearing about your experience."

"I'm still trying to figure out why Jesus rescued me." He expected Jasper to make a joke.

"Apparently, He's not done with you."

Roman had the same feeling, but he had more questions than answers. "Any idea what He'd want from me?"

"You're asking the wrong person. All I can tell you is faith is just the beginning of a long, difficult journey."

Grace returned briefly and said she'd leave them alone to talk. Roman told her to stay. They weren't talking about anything she didn't already know. She said she had things to do since he'd received word he'd be sprung from his prison tomorrow. "Okay, okay." He waved her away.

Jasper raised his brows. "Has Grace been with you the whole time?"

"Where do you think she'd be?"

"Home. It's only an hour away. The girl has a life of her own, you know."

"It was her choice."

"Really?" Jasper drawled, a cool smile of reprimand.

Roman frowned. Had he made her promise

to stay? He thought about Grace missing time with her baby. "I could send her home, but she doesn't have a car."

"Loan her yours. You can arrange a limo ride home. Or don't you trust her with your keys?"

"I trust her with my life."

"Then give the girl a break."

"She'll probably call Brian Henley."

Jasper gave a soft laugh. "The fact that Grace stayed with you through all this should tell you something. The girl cares."

Roman liked hearing that, but how deep did her feelings go? And how long would they last?

Jasper brought their conversation around to spiritual matters. They fell into an easy exchange as Jasper told him about his childhood, his parents' religious beliefs that built a foundation for his own, his wife's faith. He even told Roman what to expect if he ever decided to set foot inside a church. Roman couldn't picture himself doing that anytime soon. Jasper said it was a good place to learn. It'd be easier to take that first sojourn into foreign territory with someone he knew.

"Someone like Grace, for example." Jasper gave him a taunting smile. "Who knows? She might take you to Brian Henley's church. Pastors know a whole lot more about Jesus and the Bible than I do."

"I'd rather figure things out on my own."

"You've always done things the hard way, Bobby Ray."

Grace came back before Jasper left. Jasper said he'd stay in touch and probably come down for a visit when Roman was back home. He wanted to make good use of the nice guest room again. He kissed Grace's cheek before leaving.

Roman decided to take Jasper's advice and let her know she was free to leave if she wanted to. "You should go home too, Grace. There's nothing for you to do, but sit around and wait."

She looked taken aback. "All right." She took the BMW fob from her purse and put it on his tray stand.

"That didn't come out right." He'd meant to sound self-sacrificing, not dismissive. "Keep my car." She'd been using it to get back and forth from the hotel. "Pick up your son. Go home. Take a few days off." That brought a look of surprise and relief.

"Are you sure?"

He realized how thoughtless he'd been. "You've been babysitting me for days, when you should've been with your son. I'll call a limo service when they check me out of this hotel."

"Do you need anything?"

Roman said he was fine, then missed her the minute she walked out the door.

Grace sent a text to Roman. Let me know when you're close. I have your house key.

Her phone beeped with a new message just as she finished changing Samuel's diaper. Roman. Be there in five.

She pulled Samuel's blue- and white-striped onesie down and closed the snaps. "Come on, little man." She swept him up and planted him on her hip.

A black Lincoln Town Car pulled around the circle and stopped beside the main house. Her heart quickened when Roman got out. She met him on the front walk, noticing how he relied on the cane. "It's good to have you home." She passed by him, heading for his front door, keys in her hand. Unlocking the door, she handed over the fob and house key. His fingers brushed hers, and she stepped back, holding Samuel closer. "It just occurred to me there's probably nothing edible in your refrigerator."

"I can always microwave a frozen dinner. It'll probably taste about as good as hospital food."

Grace couldn't help herself. "You can come over for dinner, if you'd like."

He grinned. "I knew if I sounded pathetic enough, you'd invite me. What time?"

She gave a nervous laugh, wondering if she

was about to make a mistake. "Whenever you're hungry, I guess."

"I'm hungry now."

Something in his tone made her put up her guard. "You'll have to watch Samuel while I fix something." She figured that would make Roman run for the hills.

"As long as I don't have to change his diaper." Roman closed the front door and walked alongside her. The cottage felt smaller the moment Roman walked in. He left his cane by the door. She put Samuel back on the blanket she'd spread on the carpet and strewn with toys. "Keep an eye on him. He can cover territory faster than you might think." Roman sat on the edge of her sofa and leaned forward, seeming to take his duties seriously. Grace hesitated. "I haven't started dinner, but I could make you a sandwich to tide you over."

"What I'd really like is a cup of your coffee." He picked up a stuffed rabbit and jiggled it. Samuel reached up and grabbed hold. "Is he trying to eat it?"

"Everything goes in his mouth right now. He's teething."

"Teething?"

"Don't worry. He hasn't drawn blood yet."

Samuel sent the rabbit flying, surprising himself. Limbs stiffening, he screamed. Roman looked on the verge of panic. Grace took pity. Turning Samuel on his stomach, she pat-

440

ted his bottom. "Go get it, little man." Calm again, Samuel pushed himself up. "He's fine." Grace returned to the adjoining kitchen. "I guess you haven't been around babies that much."

Roman gave a hard laugh. "I've done everything possible to avoid ever having a kid."

Well, that told her more than she wanted to know. "How very responsible of you," she muttered as she measured coffee.

"He's sort of cute."

Sort of cute? "Gee, thanks." She poured water into the machine. "I happen to think Samuel is the most beautiful baby ever born." Opening a cabinet, she took down a Raiders mug. "But then, I suppose every mother feels that way." Samuel rolled over and managed to grab the rabbit. "He's also very smart."

Roman was still stationed like a bodyguard on the edge of the sofa. "If you say so." Samuel lost interest in the rabbit and rolled over again, grabbing hold of the hem of Roman's jeans. He started to fuss. Roman looked distressed. "Should I move him?"

"If you want."

"It doesn't matter what I want. What does he want?"

"He wants you to pick him up and hold him."

Roman made a couple of tentative moves before he took firm hold and sat the baby on his lap. They stared at each other. When Samuel swung his arms around, Roman laughed. "I think he's throwing punches at me." He pretended to dodge. Samuel let out a baby giggle, which made Roman laugh.

"You'll have to put him down if you're going to have coffee."

Roman put Samuel back on his stomach and placed the rabbit just out of reach. "Go for it, buddy."

Grace handed Roman the mug of fresh brew and busied herself taking out sandwich fixings. She thanked God the man didn't have a clue what she was feeling. Everything had been fine until he died on the sidewalk, and her world turned upside down. She didn't want to love him. She'd just be hurt again, far worse this time than ever before. She felt a blush coming and tucked a strand of hair behind her ear. Turning away, she opened the jar of peanut butter. *Get a grip, Grace. Don't forget who you're dealing with here.*

"I haven't thanked you properly for saving my life."

She faced him. "I didn't save your life. God did."

"Yes, I know Jesus saved me, but He used you to do it." He looked grim. "You did CPR on me. Remember?" He rubbed his chest. "My chest still aches."

"I'm not surprised. A man helped me. And then two paramedics worked on you, and then a surgeon. You had a lot of hands on you, Roman."

"Yours were the first."

Why did he have to look at her like that? Her insides felt warm and soft. "Well, I'm glad you're alive."

"That makes two of us."

Roman hadn't moved, but he felt closer. His gaze traveled over her face, lingering on her mouth. Samuel started to cry. Thankful for the distraction, Grace went to check on her son. She bent down and munched at his tummy, making him laugh before she scooped him up.

Roman returned to the sofa. Leaning forward, knees apart, he held the mug in both hands and watched her pour formula into a bottle. He looked so pensive, but then considering what he'd been through, he did have a lot to think over. She warmed the bottle in the microwave. "Did you sleep any better last night?"

"No."

Grace came back with Samuel on her hip and handed Roman the bottle of warm milk. He looked surprised, then worried. "You're sure you trust me?"

"I only have two hands, and you're both hungry." She gave him what she hoped was an encouraging smile as she relinquished her son. "Be brave, Roman. Cradle him in your arms, give him the bottle, and you'll be just fine."

Roman did what she told him and gave her a smug look. "I think I have the hang of it."

All that male confidence needed a reality check. "I should warn you: what goes in one end comes out the other." He uttered a short, suitable word. She smiled slightly. "Precisely."

Grace prepared chicken parmigiana and slid it into the oven. She started water heating for spaghetti and cut squash, sweet peppers, and onions for roasting. Setting the table for two, she looked over and saw Roman stretched out on the sofa with Samuel lying on his chest, both sound asleep. Heart aching, Grace sat in the rocker and watched them.

Oh, Lord, don't let me make another mistake, please. I don't want to be like my mother and pick a man who'll destroy me. Patrick came close. And the other . . . I can't blame anyone but myself for the choices I've made.

Samuel stirred. She carefully lifted him away, not wanting to disturb Roman. Holding her son close, she studied the man occupying her sofa. Roman had been tormented by nightmares at the hospital. He'd talked in his sleep and cried out at times. Now, he looked so peaceful.

Roman awakened to the sound of running

water. He sat up, rubbing his face. He'd slept deeply, without dreams for the first time since he'd had the near-death experience. Grace stood at the kitchen sink, giving Samuel a bath. Towel draped over her shoulder, she looked at him. "You're awake."

"I didn't mean to go out like that."

"You were exhausted." She gave a nod. "Your dinner is on the table. You might have to microwave it." Samuel splashed, and she laughed.

The meal smelled and looked good. "You've gone above and beyond duty taking care of your boss." He pulled out a chair and sat, feeling more at home here than anywhere else.

"It's no more than a friend would do." Grace pulled the stopper and let the water drain. Wrapping the towel around Samuel, she lifted him from the sink. "Come on, little man. Let's get you ready for bed."

Roman took a few bites, relishing the home-cooked meal. He noticed the time on the microwave and groaned inwardly. Grace didn't seem upset, but what woman wants a man to come over so he can spend three hours sleeping on her sofa? He called out to her. "I'll take dinner over to my place and get out of your way." He pushed the chair back.

She came back, Samuel riding her hip, his hand clutching the front of her blouse. "You can finish dinner before you go." When Samuel started to fuss, Grace bounced him and kissed him on the top of the head. "I'd better get him settled."

"Thanks for dinner, Grace."

"You're welcome. I think you'll sleep better now that you're home and fed."

By home, she meant the big house, and he knew he wouldn't. He finished dinner, rinsed his plate, and put it in the dishwasher, seeing the irony that he knew how to keep things neat and tidy in someone else's house, but not his own.

Collecting his cane, he closed her door on the way out. He stood on her stoop and let his eyes adjust to the night. Crickets chirped and fell silent as he walked along the pathway. He'd left the front door unlocked. Flicking on the lights, he came into the foyer. He left them on and switched on more in the living room. He turned more on in the hall. His footsteps echoed. He'd left his bed unmade. When had he become such a slob? He looked around his stark, black-and-white, ultramodern bedroom and decided he'd sleep better in the guest room.

Wide-awake now, Roman went back to the living room. The silence unnerved him. He turned on the television. Pulling his black book out from under the couch, he sketched the prostitute's house in Bodie. Flipping the page, he drew his mother. One drawing flowed into another: Reaper lying in a pool of blood, White Boy falling. The images darkened, and he filled several pages with demonic faces. Realizing what he was doing, he shoved the book back under the leather couch.

He hadn't seen Jesus' face. All he saw was light.

Raking hands through his hair, he stood and limped to the windows, where he looked out at the night sky. He saw darkness everywhere. Grace would see the stars. He felt seven years old again, abandoned, scared. He'd never felt safe in the apartment when his mother was gone. Even less so when she brought men back. That last night, she'd left him alone and vulnerable. He'd clung, and she'd pushed him away. He'd watched out the window, just as he was doing now. He moved back from the blackness.

Jesus. Jesus.

Roman sensed monsters lurking just beyond the veil, so close, still intent on pulling him away from the One who'd saved him.

29

The week passed slowly without Grace coming to work each day. Roman gave her some space. It was the least he could do, after everything she had done for him.

Late Saturday night, his phone beeped an incoming message. Grace. Would you like to go to church with me and Samuel tomorrow?

Roman's first inclination was to say no, but he remembered Jasper's advice. Best to go for the first time with someone he knew. And he'd have more time with Grace. He thumbed a response. What time? Her answer came quickly, and she wished him a good night.

Roman drove to Van Nuys, Grace in the front passenger seat and Samuel strapped into a car seat behind him. The parking lot filled; a multitude migrated toward the open doors, where greeters handed out programs. Roman had never felt comfortable in a crowd.

Grace turned to him. "I'll take Samuel to the nursery and be right back." She nodded toward a set of open double doors into what looked like a small stadium. "We usually sit on the right side about halfway down."

He felt a moment of panic as she disappeared into the throng. Who had she meant by "we"? He spotted her again, weaving her way through the crowd like a salmon going upriver, and then she was gone. Others moved around him like he was a rock in the stream. He tried to get out of the way, but felt himself swept along in the tide. Once through the doors, Roman slipped out of the stream and stood close to the wall.

The sanctuary looked like a concert hall, complete with a band setup onstage. A large screen hung behind them, high enough for everyone to see announcements rolling one after another: a women's Bible study on Wednesday nights, choir auditions and practice times, men's ministry events. A mission team was heading to Zimbabwe for two weeks; volunteers were needed for the Sunday school classes.

What was taking Grace so long?

Maybe he should have stayed home and watched a few church services on television before he ventured into the fray. He might have had a better idea what to expect.

"Hey, you!" Shanice appeared, grinning at him. "I didn't expect to find you here."

"That makes two of us."

"Are you here all by yourself? And why do you have a cane?"

"Torn muscle." He shrugged, not wanting to talk about it. He looked over Shanice's head toward the back doors. "Grace is around somewhere. She said she was dropping off Samuel in the nursery, wherever that is." Must be Timbuktu, considering how long she'd been gone.

"You look ready to bolt." Shanice's dark eyes danced with amusement. "Never been in a church before?"

"No." And this just might be his last time.

"It can be pretty overwhelming. Come on." She took him by the arm. "We'll take good care of you until Grace catches up." He spotted Ashley and Nicole. They must be the rest of the "we" Grace mentioned. He looked around for exit signs. Shanice almost pushed him into the row of seats. "Just do what everyone else is doing and you'll fit right in with the crowd."

Roman had never been good at that.

A man came out center stage and shouted for God's people to praise the Lord. Everyone surged to their feet. Roman stood uneasily. Lyrics replaced announcements on the screen. Everyone was singing. Loudly. It was a giant karaoke bar, but no one needed a few drinks to loosen up. This gang was already bouncing and clapping.

Jasper had told him about choirs and pastors in black robes, silence and decorum. He hadn't said anything about shrieking electric guitars, synthesizers, drums, or singers who sounded like rock stars. The place shook with the music. Shanice leaned toward him. "Don't you sing?"

"Not even in the shower."

By the third song, most people had their hands in the air, some jabbing a finger at the ceiling like football fans rooting for their home team. Grace slipped into their row. Shanice made room for her. She said something in Grace's ear before they switched places. Grace scooted in beside Roman. She smiled at him and then joined in the singing. Her voice wasn't as strong or trained as Shanice's, but he liked it better.

After half an hour, Roman figured singing was all that went on in church. He read the lyrics carefully and began to enjoy how a couple thousand voices could blend together. Just when he was getting comfortable, the music ended and another man came onstage and invited everyone to pray. Roman looked around as he listened, taking in the worshipful attitude of so many.

When the prayer ended, a rippling sound surrounded him as everyone took their seats. He sat, tense and watchful. The overhead screen posted an outline. Grace opened her Bible. He'd brought the one she gave him, but didn't have a clue where to look. She took it and found the place quickly, pointing out the passage to him. Roman read the chapter,

451

closed the Bible and put it aside, and focused on the speaker. The preacher talked about guarding your heart because it set the course for your life. Roman knew all about guarding his heart. He'd been doing it for years.

The sermon ended too quickly for Roman. He wanted to hear more, but the band came out again. A last song, another word from the pastor, and it was all over. "I'll get Samuel and meet you out front." Before Roman could stop her, Grace slipped out and joined the throng heading for the exit. Nicole sat texting. Ashley looked around and then intercepted a man in a business suit. He looked happy to see her.

Shanice grinned at him. "You survived. What do you think of church?"

"Not what I expected."

"Is that good or bad?"

"I don't know. I was expecting formality and tradition and a list of everything you have to stop doing."

She laughed. "There are all kinds of churches, Roman." Someone caught her attention and gave her a hug. Roman noticed plenty of public displays of affection, all circumspect, and hoped no one would attempt to hug him.

Shanice introduced him to several people, including a man who immediately invited him to a men's breakfast the following Saturday. Roman said thanks, he'd think about it.

He couldn't imagine anything worse than having breakfast with a bunch of strangers.

"There are a wide range of choices, if you want to get involved," Shanice told him as they made their way to the double doors. "We have baseball and soccer teams, and there are plenty of guys who like to play tennis and golf."

Golf? Roman gave her a dry smile. "Anybody do parkour?"

"Is that why you're limping?" When he stayed silent, she gave a slight shrug. "Well, you'd be surprised. I know two stuntmen who go to church here. So, where did you learn it? Training for *American Ninja Warrior*?"

"I picked it up in the neighborhood I grew up in, in San Francisco. A matter of survival."

She raised her brows. "I thought you were some aristocrat's brat who grew up with a silver spoon in his mouth."

"Seriously?" Roman laughed. "You couldn't be more wrong."

"Well, homeboy, we were neighbors. I grew up across the bay, in Oakland. Plenty of drugs and gangs there, too." She gave a grim laugh. "I always picked a boyfriend big enough to beat up anyone who tried to mess with me."

He knew there was more to that story. "Parents?"

"My father's serving time at Chowchilla. My mother was one tough mama who made sure I finished school and went on to college.

How about you?"

"Not so lucky."

Grace joined them, Samuel riding her hip like a cute little monkey. Shanice grinned. "Roman's still here. I thought he was going to bolt for the door before the service even got started, but he stuck it out like a good soldier." She took Samuel and buried her face in his neck, blowing raspberries against his skin while he squirmed and laughed.

"Roman drove, so I won't make it to lunch today."

Shanice handed Samuel back. "I'll call you later. We'll make time this week." She squeezed Roman's arm. "It was good to have you here, Mr. Velasco."

Grace kept Samuel at the cottage until his bedtime. Bundling him up, she took him back to Burbank. Selah came out the front door the moment Grace pulled up to the curb. She didn't even greet Grace as she opened the door, unbuckled Samuel, and lifted him from his car seat. "I've missed my Sammy." Jostled awake, he cried. *"Ay, mi corazón, al fin estás en casa."*

Selah slammed the car door. Glaring at Grace, she spoke in rapid Spanish. She reverted to English. "I was worried! I thought you'd had an accident! Don't keep him so late." She didn't give Grace a chance to speak as she hurried up the walkway and went

454

inside the house. The front porch light went out.

Grace got back in the car and sat for a moment, fighting tears. She felt wrenching loss after having had a whole week with Samuel, knowing it would be Friday before she would see him again, and then only for two nights. She hadn't had any luck finding suitable, affordable childcare, even after months of looking. Was she being too particular, demanding too much in the way of recommendations? Was she afraid to hurt Selah, who had been so supportive over the last year? Selah hadn't been concerned about Grace's feelings this evening. She had looked at her like an enemy, spoken harsh words, some of which Grace understood. *Ungrateful. Irresponsible.* She cried most of the way home.

Unlocking the cottage door, Grace dumped her purse and keys on the table. The empty crib made her cry again. She got ready for bed. An hour passed, then another, and she still couldn't sleep. She got up when the digital clock glowed 12:34.

Pulling on a thick terry-cloth robe, Grace went outside. The pavers felt cold against her bare feet. She inhaled the crisp night air. The lights were on in Roman's studio. Apparently, he was having a sleepless night, too. Wrapping her arms around herself, she looked up at the stars, flung diamonds on black velvet. She wanted to pray, but didn't have words for what she was feeling, what she needed to ask.

My son. Lord, my son, my son.

Wiping tears away, she sighed. The chill had begun to penetrate, driving her inside. She sat on the sofa and read her Bible until her eyes grew heavy. Rather than face the empty crib in the bedroom, she pulled the blanket off the back of the sofa and covered herself. The pillow smelled faintly of Roman's aftershave. She dreamed of him and awakened breathless. Disturbed, she lay awake again.

Oh, Lord, help.

Grace inhaled the strong scent of fresh paint when she entered the main house the next morning. She made coffee, filled a mug, and headed for the studio. Roman stood at the back wall, making wide sweeps with a paint roller, covering whatever he'd painted there recently. "Good morning. Have you been up all night?" She felt her cheeks warm, wondering if he would ask how she'd known he'd been up at all.

"Had to get something off my mind." Roman made one more broad sweep before dumping the roller into a rumpled tarp. Vibrant colors and shapes bled through the muddy beige. She tried to discern what he'd hidden.

"I saw you on the patio around midnight. You're not sleeping any better than I am."

She didn't look at him. "What were you painting?"

"Nothing worth talking about."

Nothing good, by the tone of his voice. "Could you paint Jesus?" She offered him the mug of coffee.

"I didn't see His face." He took the mug, his fingers brushing hers. "It's the others I remember clearly."

Grace worked in the office until noon. When Roman didn't come down, she took a sandwich and iced tea upstairs to his studio. He sat, one hand buried in his hair, the other tapping a pencil on a blank sheet of paper. She set the plate and glass on the stand beside his work area. He glanced at her, and she noticed the shadows beneath his eyes. "Talia called. She has some prints for you to sign."

He tossed the pencil into a tray. "How many?"

"Two hundred. She set the price at one thousand each."

"How much would you pay for one of them?" She didn't want to answer. He lifted a brow, his mouth curving in a sardonic smile. "Don't look so guilty, Grace. I wouldn't hang one on my wall, either." He swiveled on the stool. "Problem is, I've lost my momentum. I don't have a clue what to draw or paint right now."

"It'll come to you."

He gave a bleak laugh. "Maybe God has a problem with my work, too."

"Maybe He has something else for you to do."

"Such as?"

She wished he'd stop looking at her. "I don't know. Ask Him."

"I don't know how."

"You just talk to Him. I do it all the time."

"I don't hear you talking all the time."

"You don't have to pray out loud." She looked at the blank sheet of drawing paper. "Hector told me when he painted pottery, he'd start with an ordinary shape. A cactus, for example, or boulders." Roman had plenty of those on his property.

"As you know, cacti and boulders aren't my thing." He looked her over. "I'd be more inspired if you posed for me."

Her mouth fell open. He must be kidding. "Very funny. If you want a model, I have a file of letters from a dozen beautiful women very willing to do that."

"I'm not asking you to take your clothes off, Grace. Just sit for an hour. It might get me started on something other than what I've been doing." He nodded toward the wall he'd buffed that morning.

Grace's whole body went hot. She couldn't sit for an hour with him looking at her. She shook her head, mortified at the warmth that spread up her neck into her cheeks. "If you need inspiration, try what Hector does. Start with a line."

Roman smiled slightly. "Okay. Give me a line." He handed her the sketchbook and a pencil. "Let's see if it inspires me."

Grace went over to the windows and tried to match the horizon. She put the sketchbook and pencil on his worktable. "See what you can do with that."

He gave a dry laugh. "I should've known you'd want a landscape."

She stopped in the doorway and faced him. "It doesn't matter what I want, Roman. But maybe working on a landscape rather than painting whatever it is you hid on that wall would help you sleep at night."

"And what about you?" He looked at her intently. "What's keeping you awake at night?"

Her heart pounded. "Nothing you can fix."

Roman saw Brian sitting on the patio wall Tuesday afternoon, obviously waiting for Grace. He stood when she came down the path, leaned in, and kissed her cheek. Roman ground his teeth and moved away from the window. They'd probably be heading off to whatever quiet, romantic restaurant Henley had picked for the evening.

He didn't like the kind of heat building inside him. What right did he have to feel hurt or angry?

Think about something else. Don't speculate on what might be happening over there right now.

Picking up the sketch pad, he focused on the simple curves Grace had drawn. He imagined shapes forming, muted colors, shadows. Grace wasn't going to get a landscape out of him. He'd give her something else to think about. Sitting at his drafting table, he used her line to begin his work.

Sunset was a blaze of bright orange and golds, high streaks of purple that suited his mood. Everything seemed quiet at the cottage. Maybe Grace and Prince Charming had gone out for dinner while he was sketching. A light was on, but then she might have left it so she wouldn't have to walk into a dark house.

Driven by curiosity, Roman went downstairs. Pain radiated from his calf as he went out the front door. Henley's tan Suburban was still parked at the cottage. Roman muttered a foul word under his breath. So much for chaste kisses.

He had to get out of the house, or he'd do something stupid. Grace didn't belong to him. She could be with whomever and do whatever she wanted. What could be better for a girl like Grace Moore than a youth pastor?

Burning up inside, Roman went back to his studio walk-in closet, where he kept all his paint supplies. Grabbing a backpack, he stuffed in a couple cans of spray paint and a hard hat with lamp. He might not be able to climb ladders or do parkour anymore, but there were places that screamed for a piece of graffiti. He did an online search of pedestrian tunnels in Los Angeles County, pulled up a map, studied it briefly, and made a quick plan.

The sun had gone down by the time he headed for his car. The lights inside the guesthouse were now on. Maybe Prince Charming was spending the night. Roman shifted gears and roared up the driveway. Rocks flew from beneath his tires as he pulled onto the canyon road.

It didn't take long to reach his first destination — a supermarket parking lot. Shrugging into his backpack, he limped toward a bus stop. He had the feeling someone was watching him. Just nerves. The bus arrived. He took a seat in the back, emotions churning, trying to think about something other than Grace in the arms of another man. His calf hurt, and he stretched out his leg. It took thirty minutes to get to his second destination. He winced as he went down the steps. The bus pulled away. He crossed the street and started walking. A few blocks, that's all, but every step shot pain up and down his leg.

He should've brought his cane. After a block, he was sweating. Maybe this wasn't a good idea. He sat at a bus stop. When one came, the doors swishing open, Roman waved it on. He couldn't sit here all night.

Gritting his teeth, he stood and kept going.

The tunnel was deserted. Most avoided pedestrian tunnels after dark. Sometimes the homeless used them for shelter. This one was vacant and cleaner than most. Roman slipped off the backpack and pulled out his supplies. He put on the red hard hat, pressed the lamp light, and went to work. The scent of Krylon filled the tunnel, the only sound, the hiss of spray paint. He had flashbacks of hell and worked faster. Anyone who walked through here would see creatures glaring at them from both sides and above. He finished one, then another farther down. He planned six in all. Flames around the end of the tunnel would complete the work.

He thought he heard footsteps and froze, a can of spray paint in his hand. A late-night pedestrian? Homeless person looking for a place to spend the night? Quickening his pace, he pulled another can of paint out of his backpack, then another, shifting from hot red to orange and licks of yellow, lines of black. Tossing the cans into his backpack, he took off the hard hat and shoved it in. He zipped the pack closed and straightened. A man stood midway in the tunnel, watching him. Roman's pulse shot up. "How long have you been there?"

"Long enough." The voice was deep. "I couldn't believe my luck when I saw Roman Velasco get out of a car at the supermarket. I've had my suspicions about you. We met once, at the gallery in Laguna Beach. I doubt you remember."

Roman didn't, but he knew who the man was.

Roman limped toward him, the backpack held tightly in one hand. He could use it as a weapon. "You're the cop who was asking questions."

"The flock of blackbirds you painted gave you away. My wife keeps an eye on what's happening in the local art world, and she's been interested in you. She's the one who received the brochure from the gallery in Laguna Beach. The minute I saw that painting, I knew I had you."

"Is that so?"

"Think you can get past me? Outrun me? I don't think so. Not with an injured leg."

The man stood taller than Roman, with broader shoulders. He'd know how to block a blow and take a man down.

Roman knew he was facing jail time. Assaulting a cop would just add more. "Okay." He shouldered the backpack. He'd pushed his luck for years. Tonight, it had run out. "Let's go." He could imagine the headlines. He could imagine Grace's shock and disappointment, and Jasper's and the Mastersons'.

What would they think of him? Part of him was relieved it was over. The other part wanted to run. Problem was, he couldn't run fast enough.

The cop stood aside. They didn't speak as they walked. "LAPD has a file on your work. I've done some digging on Roman Velasco. Not your real name." He knew about Bobby Ray Dean. He knew about Sheila Dean and how she died. He even knew a few details about Roman's European activities. "You've been building a reputation for yourself."

Roman tripped and uttered a soft curse as pain shot up his leg. He stopped and bent over to rub his knotted calf.

"Have you had your leg checked out?"

"Yeah. It's not going away."

"Got your wings clipped. Surprised me when you picked a tunnel. You've always liked heaven spots. Is that how you injured yourself?"

"No." Roman glanced at him, curious. "What do you know about heaven spots?"

"Did a little graffiti in my time. Not like yours. Bubble letters. Sloppy. Pointless." He laughed low. "You're something of a legend, you know?"

"I get buffed just like everyone else."

"That last piece, across from the bank. It's still there." He chuckled. "I dropped in at the restaurant in that building, asked about it. The proprietor takes great pride in having the Bird's work on his wall."

Roman felt a flicker of pride and then the heavy weight of regret that he hadn't quit before ruining everything he'd hoped to gain. "You'll get a lot of street cred for netting the Bird."

"I've thought about that many times."

The squad car came into view, parked at the curb. At least the cop hadn't cuffed him. Roman thought about running again. But where would he go? The officer knew who he was, where he lived. Roman opened the door, tossed his pack onto the seat, and slid in. Leaning his head back, he uttered a soft curse. He had only himself to blame. He closed his eyes and waited for the pain in his leg to ease.

It wasn't the long drive Roman expected. The cop pulled into the supermarket parking lot and stopped next to Roman's car. Roman stared at him in the rearview mirror. The cop smiled slightly.

"I was off duty. Was picking up a few things on the way home." He turned and looked at Roman. "The Bird is done flying, isn't he?"

Roman had forgotten to sign the piece in the tunnel. He wouldn't be going back to lay claim to it. "Yeah. He's done."

"Have a good night, Mr. Dean." He got out and opened the door for Roman.

"Thanks." Roman grasped his backpack and slid out. The police car pulled away.

Another second chance.

Grace had been nervous since Brian called, asking if he could bring takeout for dinner so they could talk. Did he want their relationship to become more serious? Her friends thought he was the perfect man for her. And Brian did have all the character attributes she wanted. He was a man of faith, kind, considerate, employed. She'd never felt the flutter of physical attraction, but as Brian had pointed out, friendship was a good foundation for marriage.

Brian had arrived early and waited on the back patio. He stood and kissed her cheek before retrieving a brown paper bag from his car. "Italian." He held up the bag. "I went to Trattoria. Fettuccine Alfredo, tossed salad, garlic bread, and tiramisu for dessert." They'd had dinner at the small restaurant the week before she and Roman went on the road. How sweet that Brian remembered what she'd ordered. More desirable attributes. Brian was thoughtful and had a memory for details. Patrick would've bought Thai food on her credit card.

Brian followed her inside the cottage. He seemed pensive. "How's Roman doing?"

Why did Brian have to bring him up? She was trying hard not to think about the man who lived right next door. "He's not sleeping, and he doesn't know what to paint." She found herself talking about the back wall in the studio. "I don't know what he paints, but he seems to use that space to get rid of frustration." Brian said he probably had a lot of things to process after what he'd been through. Grace's thoughts kept circling Roman. "He went to church with me. He'd never been in a church. He looked so uncomfortable, like he was on another planet."

Brian chuckled. "Well, Scripture does say we're not of this world, and Jesus had to smuggle in the Kingdom of Heaven down here."

They talked about the youth group and how some teens who'd never been introduced to church found it a strange environment, too. That's why Brian went to them first, so when they did come into a service, they had an idea what to expect. "They're more comfortable in a converted supermarket than the traditional church." The group was growing faster than Brian had anticipated. He was teaching the book of Mark.

Why wasn't it this easy to talk to Roman?

She knew the answer.

Brian helped with the dishes. She made decaf to go with the tiramisu. Brian sat at one end of the sofa closest to the swivel rocker where she sat. She remembered Roman stretched out right there, Samuel draped on his chest as they both slept. Her heart beat a little faster.

"What are you thinking about, Grace?"

Roman, of course, but she wasn't going to confess to it. She didn't want to think about another man tonight. She shouldn't be thinking about him at all. "Nothing important." She shook her head, trying to push Roman from her mind. "You said there were things you wanted to talk over with me." Brian had covered a lot of topics, but still seemed to have another on his mind.

Brian nodded slowly. He set his coffee mug aside and leaned forward, his hands clasped between his knees. "We need to talk about where our relationship is going."

She hadn't expected him to be so blunt. "I think that's up to you."

"We're both looking for permanence. Isn't that so?"

Grace felt a sudden misgiving, a reluctance she hadn't felt with Brian before now. "Yes." She could hear the hesitation in her voice.

"We like each other." Brian spread his hands. "We can talk about everything. We share the same faith. We're both striving to be disciples of Christ."

She felt inexplicably nervous, wishing he'd stop.

"Even with all that going for us, there's something missing." His smile was apologetic. "From what you've told me about your marriage, I'm not sure you know what I'm talking about."

Grace had never seen Brian so embarrassed. She knew what he was trying to say. "No spark."

He nodded. "If that's all you have, it's not enough to build a marriage, but if you have everything else, it makes it that much better."

Grace felt the prick of hot tears. What if you felt that spark for someone who was inappropriate? What if you could barely catch your breath when you were with a man who didn't know how to love, didn't want to love anyone? What then?

"I never meant to hurt you, Grace."

"It's not you, Brian." She shrugged. "I've felt that spark. I just wish it was with the right man."

"Someone other than Roman Velasco, you mean."

Her face went hot. "Why would you say that?"

"I knew the minute I saw you at the hospital. A woman doesn't get that upset over a man unless she's in love with him."

She almost wept. "Is that why you're saying this now?"

"No." He put his palms together, avoiding her eyes. "The thing is I met someone . . . I'd like to get to know her better." He raised his head. "And you know her."

Everything became clear in an instant. "Shanice."

Brian looked surprised. "How did you know?"

She smiled slightly. "The way you two were talking in the hospital waiting room." She'd sensed at the time something had happened between them, but she had forgotten all about it. She laughed. Oh, the irony. "I'll remind her that she's the one who picked you out."

"For you."

She leaned forward and took his hand. "She thought you were a good prospect."

Roman cleaned up before Grace arrived the next morning. When she brought his coffee to the studio, he told her Jasper was coming for a visit this weekend. He'd called late last night after Roman had dragged himself home. Grace's face lit up like Christmas was just around the corner. "That's great! I'm planning a barbecue on Saturday. You and Jasper are welcome to join us."

Roman had a sick feeling in the pit of his stomach. He didn't have to wonder if Brian Henley would be at the party. "You can tell Jasper when he gets here. I may have other plans." He wondered at the flicker of confused disappointment.

Roman stayed in the studio the rest of the day, making sketches of the hills, his mind still on what had happened the night before. He hadn't even asked the officer's name. Talia might have his card. Or Grace would have made a note in her organizer. Better not to ask. He refocused on the figure he was sketching. He smudged a black line, softening it. He studied the curving lines he'd added. Would Grace see what he was hiding in this picture?

Grace returned. He ignored her until she cleared her throat. He didn't look at her as he covered his work. "What's up?"

"I'm sorry to break your concentration, but I have a few messages to give you before I leave." Roman held out his hand as she came closer. She glanced at his drafting table. "Something new?"

"I've been inspired by your line."

"May I see?" She leaned forward.

He inhaled the fresh, sweet scent of her. Was she wearing perfume? Or did she always smell this good? He imagined burying his face in the curve of her neck. Other images teased him, and he planted his hand on the sketchbook. "Not yet." His voice came out rough. She glanced at him, and he saw her pupils dilate. His heart pounded like he'd been on a long run. "Back off."

She did. "Have I done something wrong?"

"No. I'm just trying to . . ." To what? Protect himself?

"I didn't mean to pry."

"I'm glad you're interested." If that look had been a hint of what she was feeling, why was she spending so much time with Brian Henley? She was close enough that he could touch her. He made a fist and pressed it against his injured leg.

"Is your leg hurting you?"

"It's something I'm going to have to live with. A reminder of what happened." He was afraid of how much she mattered to him. She'd be walking out of his life soon. "I'll have to find a good masseuse." He gave her a teasing grin, trying to lighten the tension between them. "Unless you want to volunteer."

"Very funny." She stepped away.

He spoke before he thought better of it. "We're back to the old routine, aren't we?" Not that he wanted it that way. He missed the closeness they'd shared on the road and in the hospital, but feared it, too. He wanted to reach out and take her hand, but didn't.

That road trip had turned his life upside down and inside out. He got into the car the first day thinking it would be good to get to know his personal assistant on a more personal basis. How many other lies had he told himself? He'd left full of pride and purpose, thinking he could manage his own life on his own terms, and returned physically broken, spiritually awakened, and mentally confused.

She took another step back. "Well, I'll see you tomorrow."

Roman nodded. He could almost feel the

walls going up, not just his, but hers. Maybe they weren't so different. He could tell her the truth — that he didn't have any answers about anything anymore, that seeing her with another man made him physically ill, that he wanted more, but was afraid to think about how much more he wanted.

30

Grace put Samuel in the playpen and gave him his Baby Einstein piano toy. Ashley arrived with a big bowl of homemade potato salad, a tray of brownies balanced on top. "I was in the mood to bake last night. If I don't get these brownies out of my house, I'll eat every one of them."

Nicole arrived red-eyed and pale. "I need to borrow a bowl." Shanice came in on her heels with a big pot of Boston baked beans.

Ashley looked through the open doorway to the patio. "Where's Charles? I thought he was coming today."

"He had to work." Nicole ripped open a package of salad, dumped it into Grace's bowl, took a bottle of raspberry-pecan vinaigrette out of her bag, and plunked it on the table.

Nicole gave Shanice a fierce look. "And before you say a word, I already know if I had any brains, I'd quit and find another job."

Shanice's eyes widened. "I didn't say anything."

"No, but you were thinking it."

Shanice put her pot on the stove and faced Nicole. "All I've ever said is guard your heart. I've had mine broken a few times. We all have."

Nicole wilted into a chair. She looked ready to cry. "He's an important man doing important work, and I feel important when I'm with him."

Shanice gripped Nicole's shoulders, leaned down, and kissed her cheek. "You'd be important without him, honey."

"I'm just an office worker, Shanice."

Grace felt Nicole's pain. "So am I."

"You don't understand. I'd do anything for Charles. Anything!"

Grace understood all too well, wanted to warn her friend. "I did everything for Patrick, Nicole, and none of it mattered to him. It's hard to think clearly when you're vulnerable and want something so much."

Brian came in with a case of sodas and a man Grace hadn't met. "Nice afternoon for a barbecue." He gave Grace a quick kiss on the cheek. "This is Nigel Campbell, one of our hardworking deacons. You'll have to do the honors. I've only met Miss Tyson." Brian gave Shanice a nod. Shanice ignored him as she gave Nigel a quick greeting and went back to stirring the beans.

Grace introduced Ashley and Nicole. The minute Nigel spoke, Ashley's face lit up. "You're a Brit!"

Roman and Jasper came down the cobbled pathway from the main house and Grace went outside to welcome them. Jasper carried a big watermelon. Roman had a six-pack of Heineken beer and a bottle of champagne. Roman followed Grace inside, where Shanice and Brian stood on opposite sides of the table, the air vibrating with tension. Setting the beer and champagne on the table, Roman extended his hand to Brian. "Henley, right?"

Smiling, Brian shook his hand. "Looks like our prayers were answered. This is Shanice. She was at the hospital, too."

"Grace said you came. Thanks for looking out for her."

Jasper winked at Grace and leaned close. "He's on his best behavior today."

Grace put the beer and champagne in the refrigerator. Samuel was pounding on the toy piano, and Jasper went over to have a closer look. "And who is this little fella?"

"My son." She lifted Samuel and sat him on her hip. "Samuel, this is Mr. Hawley, Mr. Velasco's friend."

Brian plucked Samuel away. Holding him up, he jiggled him until he laughed, then laughed with him.

■ ■ ■ ■

Roman watched Brian with Grace's son. The baby obviously knew him, and Henley was comfortable handling him. Brian carried Samuel back to Shanice, and the two of them talked in low voices. Roman watched the interchange, wondering if Grace noticed. She didn't seem bothered that her boyfriend was showing considerable interest in her friend. Shanice took Samuel from Brian and joined Roman. "What are you working on? Another mural?"

"Something new. Grace's idea. Hoping to keep my mind off the trip to hell."

"Thankfully, that's a trip I'll never take, though I deserve it." She blew a raspberry against Samuel's neck.

"I thought he was yours. You were holding him the first time I met you."

Shanice laughed. "You mean the day we were all checking you out to make sure you didn't have dishonorable intentions toward Grace?" She lifted Samuel to her shoulder. "I grab this little guy every chance I get. No guarantees I'll ever have one of my own." Her eyes lingered wistfully on Brian. "He's pretty special."

"Are you talking about the baby or Brian Henley?"

Shanice looked embarrassed. "I meant

477

Samuel, of course, but Brian's pretty cool, too. Nicole, Ashley, and I picked him out for Grace." She explained about the matchmaker website and how many men they'd considered before deciding Brian was the perfect guy for Grace.

It must be nice to have friends who cared enough to search for a prospective mate. Charcoal already started, Mr. Perfect put sodas into an ice chest outside while talking with Ashley and Nigel. Samuel had fallen asleep on Shanice's shoulder. Grace took hamburger patties and bratwurst from the refrigerator. He caught her looking at him and felt a twinge of satisfaction. At least her eyes weren't glued to the man who had built the fire.

"Nice gathering."

"I'm glad you came." Grace slipped an apron over her head. "You didn't seem overly enthused when I invited you."

"I wasn't sure I'd fit in." He'd decided this was his backyard, not Brian Henley's.

Brian came in for the platter of meat. "Charcoal is ready."

They all sat outside to eat, and Roman listened to the easy conversation rolling around him, answering questions when they were directed at him. Nicole said she had to leave and Grace walked her to her car. When she returned, Shanice asked if she'd gotten anywhere with Nicole. Grace shrugged.

Jasper told a couple of stories about working with a pain-in-the-neck kid at Masterson Ranch, leaving no one to wonder who he meant. Roman was less than happy about it, until others volunteered a few of their own stories of youthful pranks. Brian admitted he and a couple of high school friends stuck wet cotton balls all over the principal's car during a Midwest winter. "It was three weeks before the weather warmed up enough to get them all off."

Roman laughed. "Did you get away with it?"

"My conscience beat me up so much I confessed."

Shanice faced Roman. "I want to hear what happened when you were resuscitated."

Apparently, they all knew. "Grace did CPR."

Grace shook her head. "There was a man who helped me, and then the paramedics. Tell them what happened, Roman."

Was this why Grace had invited him? Roman didn't like being the center of attention. "I didn't believe there was a hell until I went there." They all stared at him.

"That's it?" Shanice protested. "That's all you're going to give us? Come on! We want to hear everything."

Jasper chuckled. "Better do it. I have a feeling that girl doesn't give up."

Roman told them about the demons, the

tunnel, the stench, the screams. He looked at Grace. "You and I had just been talking about Jesus. I wouldn't have thought to scream His name otherwise." Her face softened.

"Did you see Him?"

"What?" He faced Ashley. "I saw light and felt a hand grab hold of me. I didn't see a face, but I know who it was." He looked at Grace again. "I have no doubt Jesus saved me, but I don't know why He bothered."

Brian leaned forward, hands clasped between his knees. "He loves you."

Roman gave him a mocking smile. "You think so?"

"God's love and Grace's prayers." Shanice patted Roman's knee. "Whatever the reason, it's clear God's not done with you yet."

Jasper had said the same thing. "Well, you all know the Bible better than I do."

They sat around the fire pit as the sun went down. Ashley had brought fixings for s'mores. Brian talked about camping with the Boy Scouts. Somehow, sometime during the evening, Roman stopped hating the man and felt absorbed into membership of this small group. These people talked easily about Jesus and the power of God.

Grace went inside to put Samuel to bed. Roman thought about following her. Brian was looking at him as though he knew what Roman was trying to hide.

Everyone helped clear the bowls and platters and gather the paper plates and cups. Pitching in, Roman took out the garbage. When he came back, Brian announced he had to leave. Church came early in the morning, and he'd better be wide-awake and ready to teach his band of little brothers and sisters. He extended his hand to Roman. Prince Charming had a firm grip and looked him straight in the eyes. "Let's get together for lunch sometime and talk." He produced a card. "My number."

Roman didn't want to like him. He tucked the card in his shirt pocket and watched Brian approach Grace. No kiss this time, but they had an audience. They stood close, talking quietly. The intimacy between them stung Roman. They embraced briefly. Brian and Nigel left. Ashley followed soon afterward.

Shanice sat with Roman on the wall. "Beautiful night, isn't it?" She tilted a look at him. "Please be careful with my friend."

"I haven't done anything to earn a warning."

"It's the way you look at her when she's not looking that concerns me."

Had anyone else noticed, other than Jasper? "Maybe you're the one who should be careful."

Shanice didn't pretend not to understand. "Brian, you mean. Believe me. I'd never do anything to hurt Grace. I've done enough damage already." She stood and said she hoped she'd see him in church the next morning. He said he'd mention it to Jasper. As Shanice walked away, he wondered what damage she'd done and what it had to do with Grace.

Dirty dishes stacked and set aside, Roman poured Jasper a second glass of Napa cabernet. They'd gone to Grace's church together. Roman had been waiting to hear Jasper's opinion, but he seemed unusually quiet. "What did you think?"

Jasper shrugged. "Different from what I'm used to, but good sermon. I didn't see Grace."

"She was there with Shanice and the others. They go out for lunch every Sunday." Roman had sat on the opposite side of the auditorium, where he couldn't see her, knowing he wouldn't be able to concentrate if she was anywhere close.

Jasper leaned back. "Great steak, by the way. You haven't lost your touch, Roman. If you ever decide to give up art, you can always go to culinary school and open your own restaurant."

"This is the first real meal I've cooked in months, unless you count a ready-made dish popped into the microwave. Grace usually starts something before she heads home."

"How are things between you two?"

"She's doing a great job."

Jasper gave a soft laugh. "That's not what I was asking, and you know it."

"It's none of your business, but we're going nowhere."

"Because that's the way you want it?"

"Not exactly."

"What exactly?"

Roman downed his wine. "You know my history with women."

"There's a big difference between having sex and having a relationship, my friend." Jasper's expression softened. "This is a new thing for you. Listen up. Here's rule number one. You don't hook up with a lady like Grace Moore. You spend time with her, see where things go."

"It might be easier to keep things as they are."

"Easier?" He shook his head. "You've always had attachment issues. That's part of your history, too. It's not easy to go through life without love. It's lonely. It's painful."

"How would you know?"

"Observation."

Roman felt uneasy under his mentor's perusal. He stood, glaring down at him. "I like Grace. A lot. More than any other woman I've ever met. That doesn't mean I'm in love with her."

"I remember how you were with Susan."

Roman swore. "I was a teenager, and just like every other guy who lived at the ranch!"

"I know. You all fell in love with her for a while. You're looking for what Chet has with Susan. You might just get it."

Hope was deadly. "They're one couple in a thousand."

"Depends on what territory you're occupying." Jasper set the wineglass aside. "You don't go into a relationship thinking about odds. And if you aren't in love with Grace, I'll eat my socks."

Roman stood at the glass wall. Was Grace back from lunch yet? What did women talk about when they got together for lunch?

Jasper joined him. "I've been in your shoes. Falling in love is terrifying. You don't know what's up or down, and half the time you feel inside out." He gripped Roman's arm. "Love is worth it, Bobby Ray. It's the best part of being human." He smiled. " 'Faith, hope, and love — and the greatest of these is love.' It can last forever."

Roman shook his head. He knew Grace felt something, but did she feel enough to last? She didn't know him as well as she thought, and he was afraid if she did, that would be the end of any possibilities.

"Be honest with Grace. Tell her how you feel."

"What if I'm not ready?"

"Then be a stand-up guy and leave her alone. One way or the other, you're going to have to make up your mind."

Roman didn't see Grace after she brought his morning coffee. He had completed several pages of sketches for the new painting, based on Grace's line. Setting up a tinted canvas, he penciled in the layout. Glancing at the clock, he was surprised it was eleven thirty. Most days, Grace checked in midmorning with messages.

The house was quiet. Roman headed down the hall to the office. Had she gone grocery shopping? Was she off somewhere on errands? She usually informed him when she was leaving the house. Maybe she was having lunch at the cottage.

Grace sat with her elbows on the desk, hands over her eyes. Her posture told him she was upset. "Grace?" She started, but didn't turn to face him. Roman entered the office. "What's wrong?"

"Nothing. Everything's fine." Her tone said otherwise.

"Okay," he drawled. "What happened? Brian break up with you?" He could only hope.

Wiping her face quickly, Grace turned. "Brian and I are friends. That's all." Her eyes were red and puffy.

"You were hoping for more."

"I always hope for too much," she muttered

and looked back at her desk. "No messages this morning. A few e-mails you might want to read."

Roman didn't move. "What are you hoping for?"

She looked at him, sorrow seeping into her eyes. "Wisdom. Sometimes you have to end a friendship so you can move on."

Had Shanice come clean about her attraction to Brian? "Your best friend?"

"One of my best. I trusted her." She shrugged. "Sometimes people aren't who you think they are." She gave him a beseeching look. "But I don't really want to talk about it."

"Well, if you change your mind, I'm here." He'd never made such an offer before and realized he sounded like Jasper. He winced inwardly, knowing he was ill-equipped to ask the right questions and give sage advice. Especially to a woman.

"Thanks, Roman." She smiled, her eyes moistening. "God is going to have to work this out."

Grace stopped by the studio an hour later to bring him a sandwich. When she approached the easel, he shook his head. "No peeking until it's finished."

"Am I going to like it?"

"Depends on whether you see what's in it."

"You're being very mysterious." She

thought for a moment. "Ah. Hidden pictures."

"Actually —" he wiped his hands on a stained towel — "it's my first landscape."

She chuckled. "I'll believe that when I see it!"

That evening, Grace spooned chicken salad onto a plate, made herself a cup of tea, and checked Facebook on her phone. There was a trending article about the graffiti in a pedestrian tunnel in LA. The writer didn't want the graffiti covered. Though it lacked the distinctive signature of the Bird, it might have been done by the longtime infamous and unidentified West Coast graffiti artist.

Something clicked inside Grace. There was a link to a related article, this one including a picture of a demon's face. Several citizens had been interviewed, all saying they didn't like walking through that tunnel with grotesque faces and flames at the end. "It feels like you're walking into hell."

Again, that click.

Opening her laptop, Grace did a search on the Bird. Numerous hits came up, including speculation about work in Europe. People had been trying to figure out the Bird's identity for more than a decade. One article reported that his signature, *BRD* in black letters made to look like a blackbird in flight, always appeared in the lower left corner of his pieces. Grace's heart began to pound. She remembered the living room wall at the Mastersons'.

Grace pulled up images of the Bird's work. A man mooning a surveillance camera. Petroglyphs of women in high-heeled, red-soled shoes carrying shopping bags and strutting along the walls of a subway tunnel. A pregnant girl wearing a Save the Whales T-shirt as she opened the front door of a Planned Parenthood clinic. Two peace protesters in a street brawl. A priest with his foot planted on a treasure chest. She scrolled down to the demon faces in the pedestrian tunnel.

Clicking on one photo, she sent it to Roman's office e-mail address, intending to print it out in the morning.

Lord, I know it's Roman. What do I do with this information?

Grace barely slept. When she entered the main house the next morning, heavy metal music blasted from the bedroom housing Roman's exercise equipment. Curious, she went down on her knees and pulled the black sketchbook out from under the couch. Flipping through the pages quickly, she found the last pages covered with demon faces. She shuddered as she put the sketchbook back.

She went to the office, where she did another computer search, printing out articles on the Bird and pictures of his work. Putting all the papers into a file folder, she headed down the hall to talk to Roman.

She froze in the doorway, seeing Roman straddling the weight bench, his biceps and back muscles bulging, his skin glistening. She took a slow breath and tapped on the door. He didn't hear her over the rock music as he continued repetitions with the metal cable pulley system. He might be the one sweating, but she was beginning to feel the heat. She walked over and shut off his music.

"Hey! You're early."

"I'm on time."

He wiped his face with a towel, wincing when he lifted one leg over the bench and stood. "What's up?"

His discarded T-shirt lay on the floor. She was afraid to look him in the eye, worried what he'd see. "Can we talk?"

"Can we? I hope so." He flipped the damp towel around his neck. "We did a lot of that on the road."

The scent of healthy male sweat only served to make her more nervous. She wasn't sure where to direct her gaze. Something about him roused dangerous sensations inside her. She should've stayed in the office instead of rushing down here to ask if he was the Bird. She should've waited until later, after he showered and dressed and went to work in his studio. Did she want to know more about him?

Roman swiped the T-shirt off the floor and

pulled it on inside out. "Is this better?"

"Yes. Thank you."

His breathing hadn't eased. She noticed the pulse in his throat. Was it from his workout, or was he feeling some of what she was? She had to break the tension. "Never mind. It can wait." She turned and headed for the door.

"How about this evening?"

Confused, she looked back. Was he asking her to stay late?

Roman rubbed the towel over his damp hair. He tilted his head, studying her. How much of what she felt showed right now? She wanted him to touch her, but if he reached out, she'd run. He came closer, holding the two ends of the towel he'd hung around his neck. "Take the day off, Grace. Let's talk over dinner. Six o'clock. I'll cook."

Dinner after work hours? "I don't know if that's a good idea."

His hands tightened on the towel. "We haven't really talked since we got back from the road trip."

They'd talked, but she knew what he meant. They had stopped digging around inside one another. It was an opening she needed. "All right."

"We can put *everything* on the table." His mouth tipped slightly.

"Everything?"

He walked around her. "You can tell me

what has you so riled up." He glanced at the file in her hand. "I'd better get cleaned up."

Grace didn't breathe normally until Roman went into his bedroom and closed the door.

What *everything* had he meant?

31

Roman made a grocery list before driving to Malibu. He wanted to make sure he had everything he needed to impress Grace. He bought fixings for spinach and pear salad and beef Stroganoff. He'd noticed she didn't drink alcohol, so he opted for a bottle of sparkling grape cider. Susan Masterson said every woman loved chocolate. He picked out a small mousse cake from the bakery. He also picked up a flower arrangement with two candles.

It had been a long time since Roman spent all afternoon in a kitchen preparing a special meal, not since the last Christmas at Masterson Ranch. That had been his way of saying thank you and good-bye at the same time.

The evening was warm. Grace liked the view. The patio table would be the perfect place for an intimate dinner for two. At five, Roman showered and shaved. He pulled on a dark-blue T-shirt, black jeans, and wove a leather belt through the loops. She'd wonder what was wrong with him if he dressed up any more than that. He came out of his bedroom and opened the sliding-glass door to the patio. His pulse picked up speed as he saw Grace making her way toward the house.

She came in holding his contribution to the barbecue — the bottle of champagne in one hand, the Heineken six-pack in the other. The manila folder was tucked under her arm. "I thought I should return these." She headed for the kitchen.

Roman caught the subtle hint of perfume as she passed. A positive sign. He followed her. "I noticed you and your friends don't drink." She looked great in black skinny jeans and her lightweight pink sweater. She put the champagne and beer in his refrigerator and moved around the long counter away from him. Roman met her on the other side, plucked the file folder from her hand, and tossed it on the polished granite surface. "We're not working tonight."

"I just need to talk to you about something I saw —"

"Whatever it is, Grace, let it wait."

She looked back at the kitchen. "Something smells very good."

"Wondering where the take-out boxes are? There aren't any. I figured it was about time I fixed you dinner." He nodded toward the sliding-glass doors. "It's a nice evening. We'll eat on the patio." He watched her take in the table set for two, the wineglasses and bottle chilling in a bucket of ice, the flowers and candles ready to be lit after the sun went down.

Her expression held something akin to fear. "What is this?"

Roman hadn't expected a grown woman to panic, especially one who had been married. "Take it easy, Grace. I miss having dinner with you. We talked on the trip. We get back here, and we're back in the rat race. I thought it'd be nice to spend an evening together, reconnect the way we did on the road." *Shut up, you moron. You sound like a used car salesman.* He was feeling a bubble of panic himself.

She took a noticeably shaky breath. "Okay. What can I do to help?"

"Nothing. Everything is ready. Are you hungry? We can eat right now."

"Yes. Let's eat."

She sounded like she wanted it over and done with.

Dinner didn't go as Roman had planned. Grace barely took a bite. Conversation felt stilted, her mind elsewhere. He forgot to light the candles until dinner was over, and then it was too late. So much for ambience.

They both cleared the dishes. She edged him out of the way, rinsing and putting them in the dishwasher as though working for him again. His emotions flared and frayed. Angry, he tapped the file folder. "Is this what's been on your mind since you walked in the door?" He wanted to rip it in half without even seeing what was inside.

She closed the dishwasher with a bang. "Yes." She came around the counter and walked past him. When she got down on her knees and reached under the couch, Roman's stomach clenched. He knew what she had in her hand before she stood and faced him.

Immediately on the defensive, he clenched his teeth. "That's none of your business."

"I'm sorry, but I've seen you shove this under the couch, and I was curious. And then when I saw the photos online —"

"What photos?"

She didn't answer. Opening the book, she found what she was looking for and brought it to him. She put the sketchbook flat on the counter in front of him.

Roman glanced down. "The demon faces from my nightmares. What about them?"

Grace opened the folder and pulled out computer printouts of several pictures. He couldn't read her expression when she looked at him. Disappointment? Fear? Confusion? "Are you the Bird, Roman?"

Roman felt exposed, vulnerable, ashamed. "It's just something I've done over the years to deal with . . . whatever." He took the file and closed it. "Just forget about it. It's got nothing to do with you."

"It says in one of the articles the police have a file on you. You could be arrested."

He could tell her about the police officer who let him go. Instead, he felt cornered, defensive. "Thinking about turning me in?"

"No, but this tells me I don't really know anything about you."

"You know what's important." *Not everything, not yet.* "You know me better than anyone else on the planet, including Jasper." *Take a risk,* Jasper had told him before leaving. *Stop letting fear and anger rule your life. Stop allowing the past to rule your future.* How much of what the Bird had done had come out of the helpless frustration he'd always felt, beginning with the night his mother walked out the door?

Grace looked on the verge of tears. "Who are you, Roman?"

Roman could hear Jasper's voice. *Let the walls down, Bobby Ray. Let her in.* "I don't know." He waited for her to say something that would crush the heart of him, but her face changed. She looked at him with compassion.

"You're an artist." She spoke softly, with certainty. "I know that much about you."

He was afraid to ask, but needed to know. "What are you going to do with what you know? About the Bird."

"It's your secret, not mine."

"It's ours now. Maybe you'll feel better if I tell you I can't fly anymore. I can't outrun anyone. The tunnel was the last piece I'll ever do."

"Because I know?"

"Because I got caught that night. I saw everything I've worked for going up in smoke, and then he let me go." He uttered a curse. "Everything has changed, Grace."

"A near-death experience will do that to a person." She touched his arm.

Maybe there was hope. "Yeah, but I'm not talking about that. It was coming on before that. I wanted more."

"More of what?"

"Life." He was close enough to touch her and did. Her breath caught. The skin of her throat felt like warm silk. "You want more, too, don't you?"

She didn't deny it, but she took a step back. "I work for you, Roman. We're friends. Two people saved by God's grace. That makes you my brother in Christ."

He wasn't going to let her get away with that. "I'm more than your boss or your brother, and you know it. I see it in your eyes every time you look at me." When she turned her head away, Roman cupped her face. "Keep looking at me, Grace."

"This isn't a good idea."

It was the best idea he'd ever had, and he wasn't backing down. "The night you kissed

Brian, I got the feeling you two were checking to see if there was any chemistry. Let's see about us."

Roman expected sparks, not a conflagration. Grace stiffened at first; then her body relaxed. He slipped an arm around her and pulled her closer, deepened the kiss. She tasted so good, he wanted more. She responded, and his body caught fire. When she pulled back, he didn't want to let her go. She uttered a soft sound, and his arms loosened. Her hands clasped his shirt, her forehead resting against his chest. Her hair smelled like sunshine and spring blossoms. He ran his hands down her arms. They'd gotten their answer.

"I can't . . ." Her voice sounded choked with tears. "I can't do this, Roman."

"We're only kissing, Grace. I'm not going to do anything more than that until you're ready." She was still close enough for him to breathe in the scent of her. He could hardly draw breath, he wanted her so much. *Slow down, Bobby Ray. Give her time to catch up.* His hands moved to her waist, then down to her hips.

"Please." She sucked in a breath. "Don't."

Which was it? When she drew back, he let her move away. He'd never had to coerce a woman, and he wasn't going to now. With a little patience, they would get to where they both wanted to go.

Grace sank onto the couch. Her hands shook as she covered her face. "I have secrets, too, Roman."

"I'm not looking for confessions, Grace." Roman kept his distance until he had full control. Sitting on the coffee table in front of her, he took her hand. He lifted her chin. Her flushed cheeks and dark eyes told him everything he needed to know. "We have our answer, don't we?" They were going to be good together — very, very good. "I think we should take our friendship to the next level." He kissed her palm.

She relaxed slightly, her expression bemused, but hopeful. "What level do you mean?"

Roman held her hand between his. Was she shaking, or was he? He couldn't remember ever being this scared, but her breathless silence reassured him. "More intimate."

She looked momentarily confused; then understanding came. She slipped her hand from between his. "By intimate, you mean sex." She spoke in a dull tone.

Why did she look so hurt? "I'm not suggesting a one-night stand. We can get to know each other better, see how things go."

Grace stood and moved away from him. "I'm such an idiot!" She covered her face. "I'm a complete fool!"

Maybe the evening wasn't going to end the way he hoped. "It's the smart thing to do.

Make sure we're compatible. We'll take our time and decide how far we want to go with this."

She turned on him fiercely. "You want as little of me as you can have!"

"What are you talking about?" Didn't she understand how he felt about her? "I want *everything*!"

"Everything? No, you don't! You want the easy part. You don't want the hard stuff, the things you can't survive without real love, without God in the middle. You want my body, for sex, sure. But you don't want the rest of me. The baggage I carry, the issues, the struggles, the insecurities, the pain. And you certainly don't want Samuel!" She tried to step around him.

Roman blocked her way. Her anger roused his own, adding heat to frustration. If she wanted to let it all rip, so could he. "I'm not a youth pastor who'd make the perfect father. I didn't even know mine. What do you want from me, Grace? Tell me!" When she started to cry, he felt ashamed. He put his hands on her shoulders, his voice softening. "Tell me."

She shook his hands off, raised her head, eyes fierce. "I want a man who wants more than a friend with benefits!"

"Okay. Move in with me. We'll work everything out."

"It's the same thing!"

"You're in love with me, and you know it."

"Yes, I love you, but that doesn't mean I have to do anything about it!"

"What about Patrick? Didn't you start that relationship in bed?" The words sprang from nowhere, and he knew he'd said the worst thing possible. He expected to feel the palm of her hand across his cheek. Instead, she stepped back, gaping, eyes flooding with tears.

"Yes. I suppose you could say that." Her voice was quiet again, trembling, rational. "And you know how well that turned out."

Roman caught her wrist. "You just admitted you're in love with me, and now you're leaving? Make me understand the logic."

All the steam went out of her when she looked at him. Tears spilled down her cheeks. "Why bother? You wouldn't understand. You don't want anything more from me than Patrick ever did." Her voice broke. She yanked free and left him standing in the entry. She slammed the door as she went out.

Grace sobbed all the way back to the cottage. She was shaking, still pulsing with the emotions he'd stirred in her. How could she have allowed herself to fall in love with Roman Velasco? She'd known the minute she met him that he was trouble. She should have run that first day. She never should have given in to temptation and rented this cottage.

She couldn't work for him anymore, not

under these circumstances. If Roman came over right now, she'd weaken. She'd let him in, hoping he'd say he loved her. How easy it would be to convince herself everything he suggested would be fine. Wasn't everyone doing it? Who got married anymore? A few more kisses would end whatever resistance she had. She'd never felt knee-weakening, heart-pounding desire for anyone before Roman, not ever. If he touched her again, she'd let him stay.

She'd let passion rule once before and paid the price. She was still paying.

Trembling, Grace phoned Shanice. "Can I come over and spend the night with you?"

Shanice expelled a foul word. "What'd Velasco do?"

"He kissed me. That's all. But I've got to get out of here. Now."

"Are you all right to drive? You sound —"

"Yes! I can drive!"

"Okay. Grab what you need and come. We'll talk when you get here."

Grace pulled her suitcase from the closet, tossed in several changes of clothing, toiletries, and her Bible. She packed her laptop and books in her backpack. Grabbing her keys, she went out the front door, locking it behind her. She'd have to come back and box everything else. Or could she arrange for someone to do it for her? Grace didn't want to come within a mile of Roman Velasco. She couldn't trust herself.

Angry, confused, Roman paced. Pain shot up his leg. Raking his hands through his hair, he wondered what he'd done wrong and how he could fix things. Why had he thrown Patrick in Grace's face? What did she mean that he was exactly like her ex-husband? Grace just didn't get it. He'd never asked a woman to spend an entire night, let alone move in with him. That should count for something.

He'd wait a few minutes to let her cool off. Then he'd go over and talk with her. Maybe if he told her she didn't understand how deep his feelings ran. Maybe she needed to know she meant more to him than any woman he'd ever met, and he wanted her in his life, for however long these feelings lasted.

He'd give her some time to think. Maybe a night to sleep on the idea. Talk again in the morning.

Do you really think the girl is coming back, Bobby Ray?

Roman headed for the door. He limped along the walkway and saw taillights leaving the driveway. Without the leg injury, he would have run after her. He exhaled a four-letter word. Where would Grace go? Wherever her son lived during the week, probably. Where was that? Burbank! Where in Burbank? Maybe she'd stay with a friend. Which friend? Shanice? Doubtful. Or was it? He couldn't remember her last name. He killed the urge to get in his car and follow her. She'd be long gone by the time he reached the road. Even if he did catch up, chasing her would only endanger her and make everything worse.

Think!

Roman pulled out his phone and texted her. Don't run and hide. Talk to me. He knew she wouldn't read it until she got to wherever she was going. He pocketed the phone and looked out into the darkness.

Grace had to come back. *Calm down, Roman. She still works for you. She'll cool off. She still lives in your cottage. Everything she owns is in that place. She's not going to leave it all behind. You'll have a second chance.*

Roman closed his eyes, struggling with the tsunami of emotions. He'd forgotten how much love hurt, and now the tide of pain was rolling in and over him, pulling him under. "Jesus, help me."

He spent the rest of the night in his studio blasting the back wall with spray paint.

Grace cried all the way to North Hollywood. She managed to dry her tears before she reached Shanice's Magnolia Boulevard condo. Shanice came out the front door of the complex and embraced Grace on the walkway. "Oh, honey, you're shaking." She grabbed Grace's canvas suitcase. "We'll talk inside."

A warm breeze whipped palm branches overhead as Grace went up the stone steps and into the white plaster building with a red-tiled roof. An elevator took them to the third floor. Shanice quickly unlocked the door and let Grace in. Sinking onto the couch, Grace pulled several tissues from a box on the coffee table. She was already having second thoughts about leaving the cottage. What if she went back tonight? Would Roman knock on her door and apologize? What if he did? Would that change anything? *Oh, God, why did You put me there if it was going to end like this?*

Shanice put the suitcase down and sat with her. "What happened?"

Facing the truth, Grace started to cry again. "He wants a friend with benefits."

"Did you — ?"

"No! We only kissed, but . . ." She looked at Shanice.

"Oh."

Grace blew her nose. "He made dinner, a really nice dinner, and set up the table on the patio. He chilled sparkling cider. He even had candles."

Shanice gave a soft laugh. "Well, that dirty dog."

Grace hiccuped. "It's not funny."

"Oh, honey, I know. Anyone with half a

brain can see you're in love with the guy. I thought maybe he felt the same way, but never mind. Roman Velasco looks like the whole package — good-looking, rich, single. But he's damaged goods."

"So am I."

"Aren't we all?"

Grace yanked out two more tissues. "I love him, Shanice. And now, I have to quit my job. I can't live in his cottage. I have to move. I can't see him again. If I do, I'll give in, just like I always do." She wrapped her arms around herself and rocked. "I should've run the day I met him. I thought I was immune. I thought I'd learned my lesson about men. And then I move in right next door!"

"We all thought God put you there." Shanice took her hand. "You haven't done anything wrong."

"This time. He makes my knees weak."

"You had the good sense to get out of there."

"Yes, but what am I going to do now? Go back and live with the Garcias? Selah wants Samuel. She's pushing hard to keep him, and I can't let that happen. I don't know what I'm going to do. I'll be unemployed again. I don't have a place to live. I don't want to give up my son." Grace sobbed. "I can't bear it."

Shanice put her arm around Grace. "You don't have to give him up. You can stay here."

"What about your roommate?"

"She moved out a few days ago."

"But I should just let the Garcias keep him! I'm such a mess. Samuel deserves a good, full-time mother, and Selah loves him so much. Samuel should have a father, and Ruben is a good one."

"Stop punishing yourself, Grace. You made one mistake. You need to think this through rationally. You've been beating yourself up since —"

"I just want to do what's best for my son."

"Listen to me. What's best for Samuel is to be with his real mother full-time." Shanice squeezed Grace's hand and stood. "I'm going to fix some chamomile tea." She went into the adjoining kitchen. "You're staying with me until we sort things out. As for Selah, that woman is putting you through hell. You can pick up Samuel tomorrow and bring him back here. You're his mother, Grace."

"And then what?"

"I'll muster the troops. Ashley and Nicole and you and I will all put our heads together and come up with some options."

Grace felt steadier until her phone pinged with a text message — the second one Roman had sent — and her heart began racing again. Shanice looked over her shoulder, but didn't say anything. Afraid she'd weaken, Grace deleted both texts. Her phone was almost dead, and she'd forgotten to pack the charger. A quivery warmth spread at the thought of going back, a telltale understanding of what would happen if she did. She turned off her phone and threw it in her purse.

Roman didn't sleep all night. He'd gotten up periodically and gone to the studio to see if Grace had come home. The lights stayed off in the cottage. Her car wasn't in the garage the next morning. He drank all six bottles of Heineken and half the bottle of champagne, hoping he could drown the hot lump of pain in his throat. He passed out on the couch and dreamed of the Tenderloin. *Hey, Bobby Ray. Did you think you'd be any better as Roman Velasco? You're still the same bastard son of a ghetto prostitute, not even a father's name on your birth certificate. Stick with your own kind.* The Tenderloin morphed into hell, with monsters wandering the streets and climbing the walls he'd blasted with cans of Krylon. *Welcome home, Bobby Ray.* Mocking laughter surrounded him, jeering grins and grotesque faces. *Welcome back.*

Roman awakened late in the afternoon, hair stiff with dried paint, mouth dry, head pounding, sick to his stomach. He checked his cell phone. No response from Grace.

Depression hung so heavy he felt the crushing weight of it. *Just end it,* a voice growled.

Roman tried to pray, but the voices kept taunting him. *Even the demons believe in Jesus, Bobby Ray. And you know where they are. You know where you belong.*

His cell phone rang, and he grabbed it, not even checking the ID. "Grace? Where are you?"

"It's Brian."

Roman felt the hard kick. "Is she with you?"

"No. She's staying with a friend."

Emotions in turmoil, Roman wanted to make demands, but knew he had no right. "She's safe. She's okay."

"Safe, yes. Okay? No more than you, by the sound of your voice."

"You're the kind of guy she's looking for. Someone stable, all together."

"She's in love with you."

Why did love have to mean loss? Roman's eyes felt like they were filled with salted sand. He rubbed them. *Don't cry. A man doesn't cry.* The silence stretched.

Brian sighed. "I'd say you're in new territory, my friend. I'm here, if you want to talk. Day or night."

Brian sounded like Jasper. When had talking ever done any good? Roman didn't trust himself to speak. He touched the button to end the call and tossed the phone on the coffee table.

32

Grace called the Garcias. Thankfully, Ruben answered. He didn't seem surprised to hear from her in the middle of the week, nor that she needed to speak with him and Selah as soon as possible. "You've made your decision." He sounded relieved. "Come this evening after seven. It's important the whole family be here."

Shanice asked if Grace wanted her to come and lend support, but Shanice wouldn't hold back if Selah resisted. The last thing Grace wanted was to hurt the family who'd helped her through the most difficult time in her life. But she wasn't going to make her child the sacrifice.

Selah opened the door and embraced her. "I know how difficult this has been for you, *chiquita.* I knew you'd eventually do the right thing." She released Grace and stepped back, her smile beaming. "Ruben and the children are in the living room."

No one spoke when Grace came in. She

felt outnumbered with Ruben, Javier, and Alicia all seated in the living room. The atmosphere felt heavy with tension. Only Selah looked happy, excited. "We've been looking forward to this for months." Selah waved her toward the couch. "Please, sit."

It might have been wise to bring Shanice as support. Insides quivering with nerves, Grace perched on the edge of a chair. She swallowed hard, trying to find the right words.

Selah clasped her hands in her lap, cheeks flushed, eyes bright. "We can have the papers —"

"Selah." Ruben spoke firmly. *"Permítele hablar."*

Grace didn't know an easy way to tell Selah. "I'm keeping Samuel. I'm taking him with me tonight." Selah looked confused and then shocked. Grace went on quickly before she could speak. "I can't begin to tell you how much I appreciate all you've done —"

"You can't take him!" Selah's eyes darkened in anger, even as the color drained from her cheeks. "This is his home. He belongs here with me!"

"Grace is Samuel's mother, Selah." Ruben put his hand firmly over his wife's. "You and I have talked about this many times."

Selah yanked her hand free. "I'm as much his mother as she is." She glared at Grace and looked ready to fight.

Alicia surged to her feet, startling everyone.

"You're more his mother than you are mine!" She burst into angry tears, stepped around the coffee table, and fled down the hall. Stunned, Grace winced at the slammed door.

Ruben, furious, jerked his head at Javier. "Get your sister. This is a family matter." When they both came back, Ruben stood. *"Siéntate!"* A rapid-fire conversation in Spanish took place before Alicia obeyed.

Ruben took his seat, calmer now. "Tell your mother how you feel, Lici." He spoke gently, but with insistence.

"She won't listen. She never listens." The tears came again, but all defiance was gone.

"What's wrong with you?" Selah demanded, her anger shifting from Grace to her daughter.

"You care more about Sammy than you do about me or Javier."

Selah waved a hand, dismissing the accusation. "That's not true! I do your laundry. I fix dinner every night. I drop you off at soccer practice and pick you up. You've been spoiled."

Alicia's young face twisted with hurt. "When was the last time you came to one of my soccer games, *Mamá*? You used to come."

"I don't have time."

"*Papá* makes time. He comes when he doesn't have to work late. But you? You never have time anymore. Sammy is always your excuse. It's too hot. He needs to play, and he can't do that in a stroller. He needs a diaper change." Her voice rose. "It's always about what the baby needs."

Angry and defensive, Selah looked between her children. "I'm always here for you! You're both almost grown up already. You don't need me anymore."

"You used to sit and talk with me after school every day, *Mamá.*" Alicia leaned forward, hands fisted in her lap. "All you care about is Samuel, and he isn't even yours!"

Selah looked as though she'd been slapped.

Ruben turned to his son. "What about you, Javier? Do you have something to tell your mother?" When Javier shrugged, Ruben told him to speak up.

"I'm graduating in June and —"

"Yes," Selah interrupted, impatient. "And you'll go off to college and have a life of your own."

"I'm not going to college next year, *Mamá.* I'm enlisting in the Army."

Selah stared at him, then shook her head. "No, you're not. That's not even funny. Tell him, Ruben!"

"He's eighteen. He can speak for himself." Ruben leaned back in his chair, his hands gripping the arms, the only sign of his tension.

Javier leaned forward. "The Army will pay my way through university, *Mamá.*"

"You'll go to the junior college and work."

She turned away from Javier and faced Grace again. "We have other things to talk about tonight."

"More important things than your own children!" Alicia started to rise again, but one look from Ruben had her sitting. She turned her face away.

Javier shrugged. "Maybe she'll believe me when I get on the bus to boot camp."

Alicia erupted again. Selah grew defensive.

Grace didn't want to be in the middle of their family crisis. Maybe caring for Samuel had been Selah's way of fighting off the inevitable loss of her own children. They all began talking in Spanish at once. Grace got up quietly and walked down the hall. Samuel awakened when she lifted him. "Mama . . ."

Her heart melted. *Oh, Lord, thank You. He knows I'm his mother.* He rested his head on her shoulder and fell back to sleep. She had reached the front door when Selah came into the foyer.

"You can't take him."

"*Mi amor!* Stop this!" Ruben grasped her arm. "Samuel is her son. We agreed to help —"

She wrenched her arm from Ruben's grip and took a step toward Grace, arms outstretched. Grace spread her hand on Samuel's back and backed away. Ruben caught Selah by the shoulders. "Go," he ordered Grace as Selah became hysterical.

A wave of grief overwhelmed Grace. Maybe if she'd tried harder, or worked things out differently, this family wouldn't be suffering now. "I'm sorry, Ruben. I'm so sorry." She fled, Selah crying out behind her. Opening the car door, Grace fumbled with the straps to secure Samuel in his seat.

"Grace, *espera.*" Ruben came down the walk. Selah stood on the threshold, arms wrapped around herself, sobbing.

Closing the car door, Grace stood in front of it. "You're not keeping him, Ruben. I'm sorry Selah is so upset." She started to cry. "Samuel is my son, and I'm not giving him up. I told you both at the hospital, right after he was born."

He held up his hands. "It's all right, *chiquita.* I knew this day would come. I warned her. She knows a child belongs with his mother."

Looking past him to Selah, Grace shook her head.

"My wife has been living a dream. She's awake now." Sorrow etched his kind face. "You have a good job and a beautiful place to raise your son." When he held out his arms, Grace went into them.

Grace thought better of telling him she had no job or home and no idea what she was going to do in the days ahead.

Grace had left all of Samuel's things at the

515

cottage, and taken nothing from the Garcias. She stopped at a Walmart and picked up what she needed for a couple of nights before going back to Shanice's. While Samuel slept, Grace composed a letter of resignation and apology to Roman. She told him she fully understood as per their rental agreement she would have to forfeit the security deposit and last month's rent she'd paid.

When Shanice got up the next morning, Grace held up the envelope. "My letter of resignation and the key to his house. I'll drop it off when I go back and get Samuel's things and a few more of my own."

"Nothing doing, girlfriend." Shanice plucked the envelope from her hand. "You're too vulnerable. I'll take care of it."

Grace wanted to argue, but Shanice was right.

"Call the church, honey. See if any of the men who help people move are available this weekend."

Samuel secure in his car seat, Grace drove to a public storage facility and rented a unit large enough to store her furniture until she had a place to live. The church administrator called back in the afternoon. Four men had volunteered for work Saturday morning.

Shanice returned with everything Grace needed: playpen, baby clothes, baby food, diapers, and toys. The crib would have to be taken apart and packed, but Grace loved having her son snuggled against her at night.

"I gave Velasco the letter and told him everything would be cleared out this weekend."

"Did he say anything?"

"He took the letter, heard me out, and closed the door."

Hot tears filled Grace's eyes. "Well, I guess that's that."

Shanice sighed. "You don't have to go, Grace. We can take care of everything."

"I'll go early and do the packing."

"I can go with you."

"I'll be all right." She gave Shanice a weak smile. "I'm not the naive girl I was."

Shanice looked dubious, but didn't argue. "I'd offer to keep Samuel, but I think you're safer if he's with you."

Grace understood all too well.

Early Saturday morning, she headed to Topanga Canyon with boxes and tape. She alternated between fear and hope she'd see Roman. When she unlocked the cottage and walked in, she found a large manila envelope that had been slid under the door. She stepped around it and put Samuel on the living room rug with toys from her tote bag. Inside the envelope was the rental agreement, *Canceled* written in dark, bold letters across the front page, a check reimbursing her security deposit and last month's rent paperclipped to it. In a white legal envelope, she found another check for two months' salary, and a formal letter of recommendation. *Efficient . . . personable . . . trustworthy . . . quick learner . . . hard worker . . .*

Heartsick, Grace sat at the table, the papers in her lap. Clearly, Roman agreed all ties needed to be severed. She just hadn't expected to feel so shattered. Covering her face, she wept.

Oh, God, why did You bring me here? Why did I ever meet Roman Velasco if all he'd do is turn my life upside down and inside out? Help me understand!

Samuel grabbed hold of her jeans and cried. Wiping tears away, Grace lifted him and held him close. This was no time for a pity party. She needed to remember the good things that had come out of her relationship with Roman. They'd had a wonderful four days together on the road. He hadn't died in Santa Clarita. He'd met Jesus. She couldn't allow herself to sink into an abyss of regrets again and play the *if only* and *what-if* games. She thought of Selah and her dreams. Now, she had to put down her own.

Setting Samuel on the rug, Grace put everything back in the manila envelope, folded it carefully, and tucked it into the tote. Time to pack and move on.

After reading Grace's carefully worded letter

of resignation, Roman knew whatever chance he had with her was over. He watched her arrive early Saturday morning. His heart squeezed tight when she appeared on the path, Samuel riding on her hip, and several flattened boxes tucked under her arm. She didn't look up. When she disappeared inside the cottage, Roman moved away from the windows. He tried to concentrate on the painting. Giving up, he went back to the windows. Two men carried a sofa out of the house. Two more toted a mattress. Grace didn't have much, so the work was done and everyone was gone before noon.

Roman stood at the easel for the rest of the day. The landscape Grace had started with a single line was coming together. Every time he looked at it, he saw Grace. That had been the point, hadn't it? He'd intended to show her, see if she noticed what he was hiding in the scene.

The phone rang. Roman answered without looking at the ID, hoping against all odds it was Grace. Maybe they could talk, work things out. Unfortunately, it was Hector. His *compadre* had learned enough English to be understood, and wanted Roman to see the mural he'd just finished at a Mexican restaurant on Olvera Street. Roman needed to get out of the house and said sure, he had time, plenty of time. He headed downtown.

As soon as Roman walked in the door, Hector called out and wove his way through the tables packed with patrons, a wide grin on his brown face. *"Amigo!"* He waved his arm toward the wall. "What do you think?"

Roman liked the vibrant colors, the mountains in the background, Mexican workers toiling in fields, a beautiful Latina carrying a basket of white lilies, children in colorful costumes dancing in a circle. He nodded. *"Buen trabajo, amigo."*

Hector laughed. "You speak Spanish!"

Roman forced a smile. "You just heard the extent of my vocabulary." Other than *gracias* and a string of curses best forgotten. A plump redhead made her way toward them. Roman recognized her from the picture Hector had shared in San Diego. "Your girlfriend?"

"*Mi esposa.* Two weeks ago. Vegas. No questions asked." Hector put a possessive arm around her as she looked at him with adoring eyes. "Tracy, meet Roman Velasco, *el patrón.*"

"A pleasure." Roman shook her hand.

"Hector has talked a lot about you."

Roman winced. "I'm not an easy boss."

Hector wasn't finished dispensing news. "We're expecting a *bebé.*" He looked proud and happy. Feeling an odd pang of envy, Roman congratulated them.

"Come." Hector waved him over to a vacant table. "Dinner is on me."

The guacamole and chips were fresh and delicious, the salsa hot enough to make

Roman's eyes water. For a small girl, Tracy had a big appetite. Hector chuckled and said she was eating enough for twins. Roman ordered a combination plate of chiles rellenos, enchiladas, refried beans, and rice. Hector talked about the importance of family and friends. Other mural projects had come his way. He'd be able to support a family now, but assured Roman he never forgot *un amigo.* "Anytime you need me, I'll be there."

Roman told him the mural in San Diego had been his last. "I'm working on canvas now." The landscape would keep him occupied for a while. What then? And when he finished it, would he sell it? Doubtful.

The waitress cleared plates and brought back coffee and flan.

"Bring Grace next time you come down. She'll want to see the wall."

"Grace quit."

Hector's brows shot up. "You let her?"

"Wasn't my call."

"But you still see her. Yes? She lives right next door."

"She moved out. This morning, as a matter of fact."

Hector looked angry. *"Eres estúpido o no más obstinado?"*

Tracy blushed. "Hector said —"

Roman held up his hand. "I think I got it." Was he stupid or just obstinate? Why not be honest? "Let's just say I took a shot, and she

521

dodged the bullet."

"You just give up?"

Roman turned the mug of coffee and didn't answer.

Hector shook his head. "She was good for you, *jefe.*"

"Yeah." Roman lifted his mug. "But I wasn't good for her." He looked at the gold band on Hector's finger. "Things don't always work out the way you hope."

Dinner over, Roman didn't feel up to Topanga Canyon and drove to Laguna Beach. Talia's gallery was closed. Just as well. She'd want to know what he was painting. If he told her, she'd want to sell it, sight unseen. He headed north. He stopped in Malibu and walked the beach. He sat, forearms resting on his knees. The moon shimmered white light on the sea. He thought of the light that had surrounded him, the firm grip that had pulled him up from the abyss.

Jesus, why did You bother saving me?

Angry, Roman pulled out his phone.

Jasper's voice was groggy from sleep. "Everything okay?"

"I took your advice and suggested Grace and I move to the next level."

"Oh." Silence. "And?"

"She quit. She moved out of the cottage."

Blankets rustled and Jasper sighed deeply. "Start at the beginning."

"I made a nice dinner, set everything up on

522

the patio. She likes the view." Roman's eyes felt gritty. He stopped talking and tried to breathe.

"Did you make a pass?"

"I kissed her. She said she loved me. I asked her to move in —"

"Move in?"

"She didn't like the idea of being friends with benefits."

Jasper groaned. "Bobby Ray, when I said 'settle down,' I didn't mean ask her to shack up with you. I meant marry her."

"Who gets married these days without trying each other on?" He thought of Hector and Tracy, already pregnant.

"Try each other on? You mean like a change of clothes." Jasper sounded angry now. "You want a relationship that lasts? You *commit*. You want to play house and screw around? Go back to the club and find another one-night stand."

Roman could feel Jasper's disappointment, but it wasn't close to his own. How many times had he risked his life climbing to high places to blast a wall, but he didn't have the guts to risk his heart. He thought he could protect himself from the pain, but it was here, full-on, deep-set, like claws trying to pull him under.

"Bobby Ray." Jasper's tone had softened. "Call her. Apologize. Ask if you can start over."

"It's too late."

"You won't know unless you try."

"She's not picking up."

"Be strong and courageous. For once in your life, come out of the shadows."

They talked for over an hour. Roman stayed on the beach all night and watched the sunrise. "Jesus." The light and colors brought back the relief and wonder of being pulled up out of hell and feeling life come into him again. "Jesus." Roman wanted to pray, but didn't know how. "Jesus." He looked at the sunrise and remembered the power that lifted him from death to life. "Jesus, help me."

When Roman returned to Topanga Canyon, he went into the cottage. Grace had left the key on the kitchen counter. No note. Wrenching pain filled him. Alone, in silence, he admitted what he'd known for a long time. He loved her. Until this moment, he hadn't been able to admit it, let alone say it to her. If he said it now, she wouldn't believe him.

He'd spent three years looking for his mother before finding out she'd died the night she left him alone in the apartment. Only then had he given up. Was that when he gave up on loving anyone more than himself? Roman walked back to the house and sat on the edge of the leather sofa, head in his hands.

One person might tell him how to build a bridge to Grace. Brian Henley answered on the third ring. "I've been hoping you'd call. I just got home from church."

"Can we meet for coffee? I need some light on a few things."

"We all do."

They set a time and place.

33

Roman entered Common Grounds and spotted Brian Henley seated at a table in the corner. Laptop open, he raised a tall cup of coffee in greeting. Roman nodded in acknowledgment and got into line. He'd expected Brian to suggest a Starbucks downtown, not a place in an industrial park filled with blue-collar workers.

Roman relaxed. He was back in the old hood. A tattooed, male barista took orders while a girl with flaming-red hair and piercings in her nose, her lip, and the tops of her ears worked the machines.

Sluggish from lack of sleep, Roman ordered three shots of espresso in a tall, regular coffee. The two baristas moved like dancers, working around each other with tango precision. They had to, considering the number of clients. Most customers collected their orders and left. A few stayed, occupying the half-dozen tables.

Brian closed his laptop when Roman slid

into the seat facing him. Tucking the computer into a worn backpack, he looped the straps over the back of his chair. He picked up his cup of coffee and gave Roman his full attention. "Glad you didn't back out."

"I had my moments." The coffee was hot and rich. Still not as good as Grace's. "You hang out here a lot?"

"It's close to work and a good place to meet new people."

This clean-cut guy wanted to meet ghetto rats? A teenage girl with dreadlocks came in and called a greeting. Brian knew her name. "Does Shanice know you're meeting chicks at a local coffeehouse?" He meant it to be rude.

Brian just smiled. "She's got nothing to worry about." He grew serious. "You look tired."

"Too much on my mind."

"Hell or Grace?"

"They kind of go together, don't they?" Roman gave a bleak laugh. He wanted to ask if Brian had learned where she was staying, but knew he wouldn't get an answer. "She's probably told you the whole story by now."

"She didn't volunteer, and I didn't ask. You talked about your near-death experience in hell at the barbecue. That's something I won't forget."

"I hadn't planned to talk about it at all." Roman spoke dryly.

"Hard thing to keep locked up inside your-self."

"I know Jesus saved me, but from where I'm sitting, things are worse, not better."

"Okay." Brian nodded. "Maybe you're trying to hold on to old ways. The question is: are you willing to give Jesus your life?"

Frustrated, Roman leaned in, teeth clenched. "What does that mean?"

"Stop living by your own rules."

Roman had read enough of the Bible Grace gave him to know about rules. "Yeah, well, the Bible is full of commands. Most of them don't make a lot of sense to me."

Brian leaned forward, too, holding Roman's look. "Here's the good news, Roman. We're under the new covenant, the one Jesus paid for with His own blood. When you say yes to Jesus, He gives you the Holy Spirit. The next time you read His Word with that in mind and some prayer, you'll begin to understand. The Spirit is going to teach you and show you how it applies to your life. You'll start recognizing God's voice. You'll know where you've gone wrong and how to get right with God. You follow His lead. Your life begins to change from the inside out."

Roman shook his head. "You make it sound easy."

"Simple." Brian leaned back, never breaking eye contact. "Not easy."

"You seem to have it all together, Pastor."

Brian's mouth curved in a wry smile. "Hardly." His phone buzzed. "I need accountability as much as any man, maybe more." He checked the message and tucked the phone back in his pocket. "Pastors tend to be targets for the enemy. You met a few of Satan's helpers. Destroy a shepherd, and a whole flock can be lost."

Curious, Roman shifted the conversation away from an experience he didn't want to think about, let alone talk about. "How did you end up as a — what did you call it? A shepherd?"

Brian talked about his childhood in the Midwest, his farming family, growing up in the church, the pretty girl he met at a Christian event and married while at Bible college and lost all too soon.

The easy rapport surprised Roman. He found himself talking about growing up in the Tenderloin, shoplifting from corner markets so he had something to eat, his mother's disappearance, moving from one foster home to another. "Jasper says I have abandonment issues."

"No big surprise there."

Roman finished the last of his coffee. "I never had a father."

"You always had a Father. Now you can get to know Him." Brian's phone signaled another message. He checked it.

Roman glanced at the time and said a foul

word out of habit. "We've been talking for two hours."

Brian laughed. "Good to know we can. I've got to get back to church." He stood and shrugged on his backpack. He stopped on the sidewalk. "How about next week?"

Roman was surprised the pastor was willing to go another round with him. "Sure. You name the time. I make my own schedule, but you have a job."

Brian walked backward, facing Roman. "I'll check my calendar and call you."

"You need a ride?"

"I'm two minutes away. The church is a block down on the right."

Roman didn't see any steeple. "That's an industrial building."

"Yeah!" Brian grinned. "Low rent, plenty of space. Hey, do you play basketball? The youth group is playing tonight."

"No basketball." Roman sighed. "I used to do parkour." Stretches and strengthening exercises had brought a lot of pain, but no improvement to his leg. It was a constant reminder he hadn't imagined his trip to hell.

"Why don't you come and look around on Sunday? No shirts and ties here. Service at ten." Shifting his pack, Brian jogged across the street and disappeared down a driveway.

The meeting hadn't gone as Roman expected. He'd felt at ease, as though nothing he might say would surprise Brian Henley.

Maybe pastors had heard it all.

With the encouragement of her friends, Grace decided to launch an online business. She wasn't convinced it would be enough to support her and Samuel, but it was a start.

"Good grief, girl." Shanice was her biggest cheerleader. "High school honor roll, scholarship to UCLA, promoted from receptionist and secretary to office manager at a public relations firm in under four years! You have a lot going for you. You've got all kinds of marketable skills, honey. All you need is a little confidence. I tried to tell you that when you first lost your job."

Grace's friends had taken on the project at their most recent Sunday lunch.

Ashley suggested a website. "We need a good name for it. You can link it to a blog about a single mom with a baby making it in the world. That would help drive traffic to your site."

Grace gave a soft laugh. "I haven't made it anywhere yet."

"You will. God isn't going to let you down." Ashley stirred her coffee. "It's the journey people want to read about."

"You can offer several different services." Shanice jotted notes. "You know how to write a good résumé. That's a marketable skill right there. You helped your husband write his term papers, didn't you? You could offer online editing. And tutoring."

"Did you ever write slogans for that PR firm?" Ashley made herself comfortable on the sofa.

"Sometimes." Harvey Bernstein had often asked her to help with brainstorming. She'd come up with a few one-liners still seen on billboards.

"Sometimes start-up companies need people to write slogans. They pay good money for them."

Her friends' confidence in God's provision and in her skills bolstered Grace. She designed VirtualGrace.biz with free graphics. She listed her qualifications and services offered and wrote her first blog post.

She called Harvey Bernstein with her plan. He kept his eyes on the game and knew several people who might need her assistance. He even told her what prices she should charge. "These are up-and-comers who will expect to pay more, and you're worth it. I just pulled up your website. Great job, Grace. That'll get you work as well." Harvey had always been an encourager.

The first inquiry came from the son of a friend of Harvey's who had a start-up tech business and needed a brochure. He told her she'd been highly recommended, and sent his business plan and pictures.

Her first blog, "Sifting through the Rubble," drew attention as well, especially after

Shanice shared it with everyone she knew — old friends and new, church members, business associates at two studios. Ashley passed along the post to fellow teachers and administrators. Grace hadn't expected her confessional to be of interest to anyone, but comments and e-mails poured into the website, most from women, half of them mothers. A few offered practical advice.

Selah kept calling. They had talked twice since Grace took Samuel, and both had been distressing conversations. Grace stopped answering. She hoped Selah would come to accept that her time with Samuel, while greatly appreciated, was now over. This was the tenth voice mail in two days. *I know you've received my messages, Grace. Considering all I did for you, you could at least give me the courtesy of returning my calls. I want to know that Sammy is all right.*

"Enough!" Shanice tossed the magazine she'd been reading on the coffee table. "Do you want me to call her back and tell her to stop harassing you?"

"She loves him, Shanice. I should've left their house when I first had Samuel instead of allowing her to feel false hope."

"You told her. She just didn't want to listen." Shanice sat on the sofa next to Grace and put her arm around her. "Oh, honey, don't feel so guilty. Samuel is your son, not hers."

"I don't know how to make it easier for her."

"You told Selah when you moved to Topanga Canyon you intended to have Samuel full-time as soon as you could arrange for proper childcare. It's been two weeks, and she's still calling. Maybe you should change your phone number."

"I know, but it feels so final."

Shanice gripped her hand. "Don't start lying to yourself. You've been hoping Roman would contact you again. And if he did, what would you do? Move in with him the way Nicole has with Charles? You saw how unhappy she was the last time we saw her. Is that what you want?"

"No." Right now, she didn't care about anything. She was miserable and aching to see him again. *Be honest, Grace.* In her current emotional state, Roman could easily make her forget her moral decision. A few more kisses like that one and she'd give in to what he wanted rather than what God wanted for her.

"Little boys want their toys, honey."

Grace looked at Samuel playing contentedly on the floor and remembered the day Roman had come over to the cottage exhausted after nights without sleep. They'd talked, and he'd held Samuel on his knee.

He'd stretched out on her sofa, Samuel on his chest, and both had fallen asleep. She sat, looking at them for the longest time. Samuel needed a daddy. Had she been hoping Roman would want to fill that role?

She had to stop thinking about him! She needed to concentrate on moving forward, starting over again.

Shanice had given her strength over the last two weeks, but Grace didn't want to outstay her welcome. Shanice had a life of her own, and Brian wanted to be part of it. Whenever he called, Shanice looked guilty, as though she'd done something terrible to Grace rather than merely invite her to have a girls' night out. Grace was responsible for what happened, not her friend. And then, in the aftermath, she'd delayed moving ahead because she lacked faith. Now she realized the cost to Selah and her family. She didn't want to make the same mistake again.

"I'm going back to Fresno, Shanice."

"To your aunt's?" Shanice's eyes widened. "But she wouldn't even speak to you —"

"I'm not planning to stay. I'm only going for a visit. If she'll let me. It's time, and she and I need to talk."

"What if she slams the door in your face?"

Grace gave a soft laugh. "Aunt Elizabeth would never be so rude."

"Why are you going to her when she wouldn't help you before?"

"I just want to talk with her about a few things." When her aunt had left Memphis, she'd abandoned everything and everyone she knew. Maybe Aunt Elizabeth could tell her how she'd done that. Grace also wanted to know why.

"You'll come back after that?" Shanice looked hopeful.

If she stayed in Southern California, temptation would pound on the door of her mind and heart. How many times in the last two weeks had she thought about driving to Topanga Canyon? She'd been looking for an excuse to see Roman again. But she knew what would happen if she did.

Twice in the last week, she'd picked up her son and pulled out her car keys intending to go. And then she'd heard that still, small voice warning her. *Don't go back, Grace. Trust Me.*

"As long as I'm here, I'll be tempted to contact Roman. And I'd be a fool if I did. My mind tells me he wants all the physical benefits without any responsibilities, but my heart is deceitful." She lifted one shoulder in bleak admission. "At least Patrick put a ring on my finger while using me. Roman wasn't even willing to do that. Though I guess I should give him credit for his honesty."

"Brian met with him at a coffee shop." Again, that faint stain of guilt on Shanice's face.

"How did it go?" Grace regretted asking

and held up her hands. "Never mind. I don't want to know." She stood, grimacing. "I'm going to call my aunt. Pray for me."

When Aunt Elizabeth answered, Grace asked if she would mind having company for a few days. Aunt Elizabeth sighed. "I take it you've made a difficult decision."

"Several." Grace ran her hand over Samuel's head.

"When shall I expect you?"

"Tomorrow afternoon, if that's convenient."

Roman managed to cross the racquetball court fast enough to send the ball zinging toward the back wall. Brian missed it and let out a groan of defeat. "Mercy! I surrender." He bent at the waist, hands on his knees, and gave a wheezing laugh. "Even with a bum leg, you're more of an athlete than I am." Breathing hard, he straightened. "And here I thought artists spent all their time standing around painting."

Grinning, Roman bounced the ball up and down. "Depends on what kind of painting we're talking about. A tagger has to be fast on his feet or he'll end up cuffed and in the back of a police car."

"Are you still doing graffiti?"

"Not anymore."

A couple of young women stood at the window, watching. One had dark hair like Grace. Turning away, Roman retrieved his bottle of water and drank deeply. He couldn't get through an hour without thinking about her. It'd been a couple of weeks, and he still felt crushed and broken inside. If she loved him, why the silent treatment? He'd put out the olive branch the first few days, hoping she'd pick up or text back or call or write or *something* so they could talk things out. Clearly, that wasn't going to happen.

Brian picked up his towel and wiped his face. "She's hurting, too."

Roman didn't have to ask who he meant, but wondered how Brian knew he was thinking about Grace. Was the pain etched on his face? He'd been trying to push it down, keep it out of sight. How long before it eased? How long before he could get through a single day without feeling like his heart had been ripped out of his chest?

"I want you to think about something." Brian looped the towel around his neck and grabbed the ends. "The way you're feeling now could give you an inkling of what God feels whenever we brush Him aside. Our Father sent His Son to pay the price for our sins, Roman. And Jesus suffered and died willingly out of love for us. Everything you and I have ever done wrong in this life was paid for on the cross." He let out his breath. "We ought to love Him more than we love anyone else." His eyes were filled with compassion. "You want to get things right, my friend? Stop obsessing about Grace. Make Jesus your first priority."

The words sank deep and brought up the memory of power surrounding him, a power that sent demons screaming into the darkness. Roman remembered the warmth and light encompassing him, lifting him, all because he'd cried out the name of Jesus. Would he have known to do that if Grace hadn't been talking about Jesus moments before his heart stopped? Had that been an accident of timing, or God's planning?

His throat felt tight. His eyes burned.

Jesus, I'm sorry. I know You want more from me than what I'm giving.

Brian kept repeating the message. Roman felt it squeezing through the cracks in the wall he had built around his heart. Maybe it was time to stop putting all his hope in Grace instead of the One who reached down and pulled him up into the light.

Grace might not love him, but God did. Always had. Always would. And it would be a whole lot safer giving his heart, soul, and mind to Jesus than to a flesh-and-blood woman.

Selah called Grace again the next morning. She left another message, this time apologizing for her previous outburst, but asked tearfully if she could see Sammy, just for an hour or two. Grace called Ruben at his work number. "Selah and I both need your help." She told him what had been going on for the past two weeks.

"I didn't know, Grace. I'm sorry. Things have been difficult at home. Alicia is acting out. I called our priest. Father Pedro wasn't surprised to hear from me. We set a day and time for family counseling. I haven't told Selah yet, but she's going. We're all going."

"I'm so sorry." Grace pressed cold, shaking fingers against her forehead.

"This isn't your fault, *chiquita*. Selah was struggling before we met you. I thought helping you have your baby would help her."

Grace informed him she intended to change her cell phone number and would be moving out of the area in the next few days.

"Selah will be heartbroken when she realizes she's driven you away."

"There are other reasons, Ruben."

"Eres como mi propia hija." Ruben spoke in a choked voice. *"Dios te bendiga."*

No one had ever considered her a daughter before or offered such a blessing.

Grace had everything she needed in her suitcase, backpack, and a couple of boxes when Shanice came home at noon. She packed the car while Shanice sat on the sofa with Samuel in her lap. She looked teary-eyed when Grace was ready to say good-bye. "I'm going to miss you, girlfriend. You have no idea how much." She lifted Samuel over her head and jiggled him. "And you, too, punkin." She handed him back to Grace.

"I'll stay in touch."

"Any idea where you'll end up?"

"Not yet." Grace had some ideas, but she needed to do more research. And Aunt Elizabeth would undoubtedly have ideas as well. Her aunt had never withheld personal opinions, and looking back, Grace wished she'd listened. She could have saved herself so much grief. "Thank you for everything, Shanice. VirtualGrace.biz wouldn't exist without you."

"You just needed to remember who you are and who's on your side. God's going to take care of you, honey. Just stick with Him."

Roman sat at his drafting table, the Bible from Grace open in front of him. He finished reading the story of Elisha, a successful farmer who demolished his plow and killed his team of oxen as a sacrifice so he could follow Elijah and serve God. Roman felt something shift inside him. *Okay, Lord. I get it.* Give up one life and start another. Get rid of whatever held him back.

Leaving the desk, he went to the windows and thought about the discussions he and Brian had been having about priorities. Roman had been surprised how comfortable it was to talk with Brian. He didn't ask questions the way Jasper did, wearing him down, wearing him thin. Silence didn't bother Brian. He made it easy to tell the truth. They had become friends because of it.

He might be standing at this window right now, looking out, but inside, he was still running scared. *Lord, I've read enough to know You're calling me. Okay. I'm listening. I'm done trying to figure everything out by myself. Go ahead and do what You will. I'm tired, Jesus. I just want to rest.*

Afterglow, his best work, was still on the easel. He looked at it every day, seeing the woman who had inspired it. Had it become an idol? Maybe it was time to give it to Talia, let her sell it. Or give it to Brian to give to Shanice so she could give it to Grace. It only seemed right to give her the painting. She'd inspired it.

I'm still trying to find a way to get to her, aren't I? I love her, Lord, but I was too much of a coward to tell her how much.

Brian assured him the pain would lessen with time. He needed to get his priorities straight. His life depended on God, not a woman.

Roman slid open the glass doors. Sunset in the canyon. Grace would have loved the western sky streaked with purple. Lighting the wood in the fire pit, he sat and watched the sun go down. He'd taken this view for granted, but Grace was right about it. The colors were never the same. *God's good night,* she'd called it.

Stars appeared, one by one, until thousands scattered across the dark canvas. *And I call myself an artist?*

His cell phone rang — Brian. Roman answered. "Hey."

"How are you doing?"

"I'm better than I've been." He could tell something was up by Brian's tone. "Any other reason for the call?"

"I just got off the phone with Shanice. Grace left this afternoon."

Roman felt the hard punch in his stomach. "Left for where?"

"Shanice said she headed north, and even Grace wasn't sure where she'd end up. She wants Samuel to grow up somewhere other than Los Angeles."

How far north did she intend to go? She could end up in Oregon or Washington. Alaska? Roman closed his eyes.

"I'm sorry, Roman."

"Yeah." He looked out over the canyon. "That's life."

"Why don't you come on over to my place tomorrow. We can talk." He gave Roman the Vermont Square address. "Call Uber. You can't leave that fancy car of yours on my street. How about eleven?" He chuckled. "Or is that too early for an artist to be up?"

Roman stayed outside, his emotions spiraling down until he hit rock bottom. He couldn't see any way up except one. *Jesus, grab hold of me again.* Closing his eyes, he imagined himself reaching up. He felt the weight beneath him, sucking him down in a vortex of grief.

And then the whisper came, a thought not his own filling his mind.

Let go of her and walk with Me. One step at a time. One day at a time.

Simple. Not easy.

Let her go and put your hope in Me.

Shivering with the encounter, Roman took his cell phone from his pocket. Hand shaking, he tapped Photos. He thumbed through the pictures of Grace he'd taken on the road trip. How many times had he done this over the last two weeks? If he couldn't have Grace, he could at least look at these pictures and imagine what might have been.

Let go, God said.

One by one, Roman deleted the pictures. When he got to the last one, his thumb hovered. He remembered the moment he'd taken this shot. Grace had been standing on a high place above the Dardanelles. She'd looked back over her shoulder, beckoning him to follow. And he had. She'd been a girl in love with life, and maybe, for a few minutes at least, a woman in love with him. Better to remember her like this than the last time he saw her; tears running down her pale cheeks, eyes full of hurt and disillusionment. He could almost hear her voice. *I love you, Roman.*

A soft breeze whispered through the chaparral. *I love you more.*

He felt the warmth of that declaration, the deep yearning to get closer to the eternal One. He could, if he stopped hanging on to someone who didn't belong to him and never had.

Roman filled his lungs with the cool night air and touched the screen softly.

Grace disappeared.

34

Aunt Elizabeth opened the front door. "Oh. I thought . . ." She looked ready to cry as she stepped back. "Never mind. Come in. Where's your suitcase?"

"In the car. Along with a playpen and —"

"Let me take him while you bring in whatever you need." She plucked Samuel out of Grace's arms.

Astonished, Grace watched her aunt carry her son into the living room. She'd never held him before and had barely glanced at him the one time Grace brought him here.

Grace put the playpen and suitcase in her old bedroom and peered into the living room. Aunt Elizabeth had Samuel perched on her knees facing her. She was talking to him in a soft, affectionate voice as he flapped his arms like a happy bird.

"Thank you for keeping him occupied." She reached for Samuel, but Aunt Elizabeth shifted him.

"He's fine where he is."

Grace sat on the edge of the sofa, hands on her knees. "I thought you didn't like him."

"I thought you were going to give him away. I didn't want to become attached." When Samuel squirmed, she gave Grace a questioning glance.

"He wants to be on the floor. He's crawling now. I'll keep an eye on him so he doesn't break anything."

Aunt Elizabeth put him down. "I'll save you the trouble." She got up and went around the room, picking up the breakables and putting them on a high shelf.

What had happened to bring about this change? "You were so angry when I told you I was pregnant."

"Of course I was. Should I have been happy about the circumstances of his conception?"

Grace stared at her. "I was afraid you'd want me to have an abortion."

"Grace." Aunt Elizabeth's tone softened. "You've always been a people pleaser. Frankly, I expected your friends to talk you out of having a baby."

She spoke quickly in their defense. "My friends were the ones who suggested the pregnancy counseling center."

"Yes, I know that now, and I imagine the family who took you in had plans of their own for Samuel." She raised a brow in challenge.

"Selah still wants to adopt him." Samuel

slapped his hand against the sliding door to the garden, leaving a sticky handprint on the pristine glass surface. She rose, knowing how her aunt liked everything clean and neat. "I'll get the Windex."

"Sit down. Don't worry about the window." Aunt Elizabeth chuckled when he slapped it again. "It's double-paned safety glass. He can't break it. I'd say Samuel is going to be an outdoors boy." She glanced at Grace. "Speaking of boys, how is Roman Velasco?"

Grace knew he'd come up in conversation sooner or later, just not this soon. "I don't know. I quit and moved out of the cottage a couple weeks ago."

Aunt Elizabeth's mouth curved in a rueful smile. "He wanted to be more than friends."

"He wanted to be friends with benefits."

"I'm glad you passed on it. Most relationships that start out that way don't end well." Aunt Elizabeth shook her head. "A pity, though. I liked him."

Grace lifted her chin in surprise. "You did?"

"Yes, I did. Unlike Patrick Moore, who never cared enough to consider your feelings about anything, Roman was very defensive of you. He thought I was treating you badly." She shrugged. "Which, of course, I was. Roman Velasco also couldn't take his eyes off you, another thing that set him apart from your ex-husband. The man loves you, Grace."

"Not enough."

"He's an idiot, but then most men are, where women are concerned. I imagine you were something new to him, a girl with moral values and faith. What do I tell him when he calls?"

"He won't." She imagined Roman back at a nightclub, picking up some pretty blonde on the make, just like the one who had come on to him at the gallery. He'd be careful, of course. He'd want someone who knew the rules. She kept telling herself she was glad any chance of a relationship was over, but her heart beat faster at the mention of his name.

Aunt Elizabeth studied her. "Well, we don't have to talk about him until you're ready. We have plenty of other things to discuss. The past, for one thing." She stood. "Why don't you set up the playpen in the kitchen so we can keep an eye on this little wanderer while I finish getting dinner ready?"

Grace did as her aunt suggested. Samuel wasn't particularly pleased to be caged. She put an activity center in the playpen to keep him occupied. Aunt Elizabeth stood at the kitchen sink, peeling potatoes, rousing memories from Grace's childhood. She'd come into this house traumatized and grieving.

As an adult, Grace could understand and forgive her aunt's inability to show compassion to a traumatized child. Aunt Elizabeth had been grieving, too, and angry over the circumstances of her sister's death. But as that child, Grace had lived in constant fear. Not just when she moved in with Aunt Elizabeth, but well before that, when she witnessed her father's rage, and when her mother taught her to play hide-and-seek. She'd learned to hide from so many things. Was she hiding now?

Aunt Elizabeth spoke over her shoulder. "Your hair looks nice down around your shoulders." She cut the peeled potatoes, dumped them into a pot, and added tap water. She dried her hands, added salt to the water, and put the pot on the stove. She faced Grace and leaned against the sink counter as though bracing herself. "You're very quiet."

"Just remembering things from the past." Grace regretted saying that when she saw the pain flicker in her aunt's eyes.

"Nothing good, I imagine." Aunt Elizabeth slipped her hands into her apron pockets as she looked away. "I've done many things I regret, Grace, and most have to do with you." She let out her breath. "You were only seven when I brought you home with me. And I took out all my bitterness on you."

"I can understand why."

Aunt Elizabeth sat at the kitchen table and put her hand on Grace's arm. "We need to talk about the past."

"About my mother."

"Yes, and your father." She gave a gentle

squeeze and lifted her hand away. "But the trouble didn't start with them."

After dinner, Aunt Elizabeth had to go to a deaconess meeting. Grace bathed Samuel in the kitchen sink and dressed him for bed, then held him close as he drank a bottle of warm milk while she prayed over him. She sang a favorite hymn softly and watched his eyelids grow heavier until he couldn't hold them open anymore. Lowering him carefully into the playpen, she covered him with his favorite silky-edged blanket.

Filled with an aching tenderness, she sat on the edge of the twin bed and watched her son sleep. He looked so peaceful, so content. Her little boy had nothing to worry about because he trusted his mother. *Lord, I want to be that trusting of You.*

Nothing was happening the way she expected. Aunt Elizabeth wanted to talk about the past, but later — tonight when she got back, or tomorrow. Would she change her mind? Grace had questions to ask about the past, and she wanted to borrow some of her aunt's courage in setting out for another place, a new beginning. Aunt Elizabeth had done it successfully, leaving family and friends in Memphis and moving all the way across the country. What had it taken to do that? Had Elizabeth Walker set off on a grand adventure, or had she run away?

Samuel shifted. Grace readjusted the blanket. She remembered her first night in this room, how terrified she'd been. Night after night, she'd hidden herself away, just wanting to feel safe, praying Mama would come for her and tell her it was all right to come out.

And then the angel had come and her fears had gone away. She felt the wonder of him, her precious secret that she'd shared with Roman. He knew demons existed. Did he believe God sent angels?

The garage door whirred. Aunt Elizabeth was home. Grace leaned over the playpen and put her hand gently on her son's chest. "You're safe in this room, Samuel. I had a friend who watched over me. God is watching over you, too."

Grace went into the kitchen just as her aunt opened the side door from the garage. Aunt Elizabeth looked resigned. "I thought you might be up."

"How did your meeting go?"

Aunt Elizabeth set her purse on the table and removed her coat. "We all have our job assignments. I'll put my things away and then we can talk."

"Should I fix tea?"

"That would be nice." Coat draped over her arm, she picked up her purse. She stopped in the doorway and looked back. "Why don't we both put on our pajamas? It might help to be comfortable while having our conversation."

They sat in the living room in wing chairs facing each other across the coffee table, like girls at a slumber party, sipping tea and pretending to be adults. "Where do I start?" Aunt Elizabeth sounded weary, perplexed. "When you went away to college, Grace, I missed you. You probably won't believe that, but the house felt empty." She set her cup and saucer on the coffee table.

"I spent more time at the office, if you can believe that. I practically lived there. It was hard coming back to an empty house and knowing it was going to stay that way. I didn't think you'd come home, even for holidays. I was alone again. I thought that was the way I wanted it. The thing is, I couldn't stop thinking how Leanne would feel if she knew I'd treated you more like a ward of the court than my niece." She met Grace's look with difficulty. "Your mother would've been hurt and disappointed."

"You took me in, Aunt Elizabeth. You didn't leave me in foster care." She would have been passed around, a few months here, a year there. Who knew what could have happened under those circumstances? Grace thought of Roman and the childhood he'd had.

"I have many regrets, Grace, but the biggest of all is not raising you with the love you so desperately needed. And deserved."

Grace saw the cost of that confession and felt her heart softening. "I understood why you couldn't love me. Every time you looked at me, you saw my father, and he —" She shook her head, unable to say the rest.

Aunt Elizabeth put fingertips to her brow. "I'd forgotten you overheard that conversation." She lowered her hand and raised her head. "I said lots of things I shouldn't have said. I was so angry. It started long before Leanne died, though that exacerbated things. My anger goes back to childhood." She put her hands on her legs as though bracing herself. "One of my first memories is seeing my father kick my mother in the ribs when she was on her knees scrubbing the floor." She closed her eyes. "I must have been only four or five, because Leanne hadn't been born yet."

Grace felt the hot rush of tears and didn't say anything.

"My mother never argued with my father. She never said a word against him. She taught us to obey, too. We learned early to discern his moods and stay out of his way. Mama had another baby a few years after Leanne. A little boy. He was blue. Something about his blood not being oxygenated. Cyanosis, I think they call it. I looked it up once."

She took up her teacup and saucer, sipping slowly, eyes dull. Her hand shook when she put them down again, calmer. "My father blamed my mother when the baby died, of course. The sad part is she believed him. She felt she deserved the beatings." Aunt Elizabeth fisted her hands, her voice lowering, tight and strained. "I tried to stop him once, and he almost killed me."

She shook her head. "Back in those days, people didn't talk about abuse. It was a family matter, best kept secret. I got a job as soon as I was old enough, just to get out, just to save enough to leave home. Of course, my father expected the lion's share of my earnings, but I found ways to squirrel money away. I stayed away so much, I didn't know what else was going on when I wasn't there."

She closed her eyes for a moment before going on. "Mama was sick. We never knew what was wrong with her because she wouldn't go to the doctor. I think she saw an end to her misery and welcomed it. Who would blame her?" She sat for a long time, silent.

"And my mother?"

Aunt Elizabeth pressed her lips together, face pale. "I came back for her after Mama died, hoping she'd come with me. She insisted Daddy needed her. He hadn't been well. I could see he wasn't. Maybe he was sorry for the way he treated our mother. Maybe he was looking hell in the face. I don't know. I didn't care." She rested her head against the back of the chair. "I went to see her as often as I could. Leanne would call, and we'd talk. Dad didn't make her life easy.

Everything that ever went wrong in his life was always someone else's fault." She gave Grace a sad smile. "Your mother was a good caregiver." The curve of her mouth turned bitter. "As for me, I stood over him once, near the end, and said if it was up to me, I'd leave him in his chair and let him rot in his own feces."

A cold chill prickled Grace's skin.

Aunt Elizabeth's expression wavered between shame and guilt, anger and regret. "Leanne became like our mother. I became like Dad." She looked at Grace, her eyes growing moist. "I just didn't use my fists."

Grace moved to the sofa and sat on the edge so she could take her aunt's hand. "I love you, Aunt Elizabeth."

"I know you do. God knows why. You are like your mother. She could forgive anything." She turned slightly, her hands around Grace's, holding on firmly, expression intent. "We need to talk about your parents. What do you remember about that night?"

"I didn't see anything that happened. Mom said we were going to play hide-and-seek. I heard Mom talking fast. Daddy shouted at her. Something crashed, and I heard Daddy sobbing and saying, 'Leanne' over and over. Then I heard him coming. I thought he was looking for me, so I didn't dare move. He opened the closet door and threw boxes off the high shelf and then found a gun. He saw me then. He pushed the clothes aside and stared at me. He didn't say a word. He closed the closet door. I just huddled there, waiting in the dark. And then . . . I heard the shot."

She shook her head, remembering bits and pieces of that awful night.

"Everything was confusion after that. I was too scared to move. I heard a loud crash and men's voices. The lights came on and a policeman found me. I ended up with the nice couple who kept me a few days." When Grace had first met the Garcias, she'd thought of that kindly couple. "And then you came."

Aunt Elizabeth's hands loosened. "I'm so sorry all that happened to you, Grace. I didn't make things any easier by talking about your father the way I did. Life was hard enough on you without having me play jury and judge. Whatever happened that night caused your father to take his own life. He could have taken yours as well, but he didn't."

Grace felt the tears coming and held them back.

Aunt Elizabeth lifted a hand and tucked a curl behind Grace's ear. A nervous gesture. "Brad and Leanne loved each other, maybe too much, maybe in the wrong way. Relationships don't always make sense. What happened was a tragedy. But when God offered me a gift, instead of receiving you in gratitude, I held on to my anger. I'm an architect when it comes to building walls. The only person I've ever allowed close is Miranda Spenser." Her mouth tipped in a wry smile. "She came from the same kind of background, but didn't allow it to embitter her." Aunt Elizabeth patted her hand. "I tried to give you to her once, as though you were an unwanted puppy someone dumped on my doorstep."

Grace wasn't surprised. "When?"

"The day after I brought you home with me. Miranda said no, of course. She said I needed you." Her eyes glistened with tears. "I was so angry. She and Andrew have always wanted children. I couldn't understand why she wouldn't take you. But she was right. I just didn't learn fast enough. Life would've been so much better for you and me if I had let down my guard."

"You are now."

Aunt Elizabeth gave a bleak laugh. "High time, don't you think?" Her voice thickened with emotion. She looked tired, but also relieved. She ran her hands over her lap. "I know you came to talk about other things, but can we wait until morning? I'm exhausted."

When they both stood, Grace stepped forward and embraced her. Her aunt's arms came around Grace, and they held on tightly to each other for a moment. Aunt Elizabeth withdrew, letting out a soft breath. "I hope you plan to spend a few days."

"Three at least."

"Thank you." Aunt Elizabeth cupped Grace's cheek. "You've always been a sweet girl, just like your mom."

Roman had been sitting in Brian's living room for hours. They'd talked about many things, but eventually Brian got Roman talking about life as a tagger in the Tenderloin.

"I had a crew. There were always guys who wanted to come along for the kicks. Some watched; some helped with the ropes. I had one dude, Lardo, strong as a linebacker, who got me up and onto a roof before the cops spotted me." He felt the push inside to go deeper, pull up the pain by the roots. He finished his soda and crushed the can in one hand. He didn't want to think about Lardo or what had happened to him.

Agitated, he stood, mangled can in his hand. He didn't have to tell Brian everything. "Where should I throw this?"

"Recycling is under the kitchen sink." Brian didn't press.

Roman threw away the can and came back. He looked at Brian, measuring his expression. Brian looked back at him. Roman sat. "I always picked heaven spots."

"Heaven spots?"

"High buildings, structures — the higher, the better."

"Sounds dangerous."

"That's the point. The bigger the risk, the more street cred. I did one piece on the Bay Bridge. Almost ended up in the bay. I hit a couple of five-story buildings. No problems. And then I picked an overpass, made the stencils, had my gear, and posted my crew. High risk of being seen, so I had two spotters. Then White Boy showed up. I wasn't as close to him. He was a tagalong. Couldn't shake him." He shook his head. "I didn't need or want his help, someone who couldn't do any better than bubble letters, but down he came on his own setup."

Emotion gripped him, and he rubbed his face before looking at Brian again. "White Boy didn't know the difference between dynamic and static ropes from the junk he stole out of a hardware store. He had a can and was coming down to spray. I told him I'd kill him if he did." He heard the faint echo of White Boy's laughter. *You gotta reach me first.* "I had an empty can and threw it at him. He dodged. That's all it took. His rope slipped. He lost hold." Roman's eyes burned. He swallowed convulsively before he spoke. "He fell."

"You think it was your fault."

"I don't know, but I felt responsible."

Roman still dreamed about the broken body in a spreading pool of red. A car caught White Boy's body in the headlights. The driver slammed on the brakes, but went over White Boy before the vehicle came to a screeching, spinning halt. Other cars stopped, people getting out to stare at the dead boy shattered on the pavement. No one looked up to see the other one in the black hoodie. Bobby Ray Dean climbed fast, rolled over the wall above, kicked out of the harness. Lardo and the others scattered. Bobby Ray ran until he couldn't run anymore, then slid down against a wall and sobbed.

"I have nightmares sometimes. I hear him screaming on the way down. I see when he hit." Roman felt hot tears welling. Was White Boy one of those lost souls in hell now? "I never used a crew again. I always worked alone. And I went higher and did bigger pieces."

"Sounds like you had a death wish."

Roman's mouth twisted in a bitter, self-mocking smile. "Maybe, or maybe I thought I could be faster than a speeding bullet and leap tall buildings in a single bound." He did learn how to make it across narrow alleys to lower roofs on the other side. He'd had plenty of practice street running as a kid, escaping foster families and outrunning police and social workers. He knew how to hit the ground, roll, and use the momentum to keep going. He used obstacles to propel himself. San Francisco's city streets had been his playground.

How many times had he heard a siren whoop and seen red lights glowing on building walls, a searchlight scanning the heights for him? The night White Boy died, Bobby Ray Dean had run until he felt like his heart would explode.

He told Brian more about White Boy, a year younger, who wanted to be like Bobby Ray Dean, who loved the adrenaline rush of taking risks, painting high places, using parkour to outrun the police or rival gang members. Elbows on his knees, Roman rubbed his face. "There wasn't even an obituary for him." His voice was rough.

Brian leaned forward, his eyes full of compassion. "What was White Boy's real name?"

Roman raised his head slowly. "I don't know." He couldn't see Brian's face through his tears.

"But you didn't quit after that?"

"I did more. I blasted the hood with it. It was the only time I felt alive and in control."

Bobby Ray continued to tag for the gang, but spent more time on other pieces, his own ideas, his own voice. He painted a red-faced devil around the front door of an apartment house. The entrance swallowed people going in and vomited them out. He painted a chef roasting rats over the garbage cans in the alley of a famous steak house. He turned an air-conditioner grille into a grinning monster. "My gang tags got buffed within a few days.

My other pieces lasted longer."

The crushing irony was that the night White Boy plummeted to his death, the Bird flew. BRD wasn't just Bobby Ray Dean's initials anymore. He became the Bird. The half-finished piece he'd painted that night was in a heaven spot. It would have cost the city big money to have it buffed, so it stayed.

"Where are Reaper and Lardo now?"

"Dead. Killed at a party. Couple of older guys came in looking for Reaper's brother and figured one was as good as the other." Roman rubbed the back of his neck. "I was supposed to be at Reaper's that night, but I was doing some stupid project for my history teacher. Playing the game, trying to get through high school."

Had he refused all opportunities for a higher education out of penance? "I went a little crazy that night and blasted Turk Street with red paint. Cops caught me and I ended up in juvie."

"Anyone try to bail you out?"

"Are you kidding?" Roman gave a dark laugh. "The foster couple I'd been living with was glad to be rid of me. The court decided I needed a change of scenery and sent me up to Masterson Ranch. Talk about culture shock." He shook his head. "They boarded horses and had a hundred head of cattle as well as half a dozen boys. I wasn't co-operative. I did everything I could to get

563

kicked out."

"That's where you met Jasper Hawley."

"Yeah. He looks mellow, but he's persistent."

"He got to you."

"He's a hard man to shake. He's still keeping tabs on me. Calls me one of his 'lost boys.' "

Brian smiled. "I thought he was your father when I met him."

"Really? How's that? We don't look anything alike."

"He loves you like a son."

Roman didn't want to think about that. He hadn't wanted to love anyone until he met Grace. People died. People left. "He always seems to call or show up when I'm in crisis mode. I don't know how he does that." Considering the disappointment in Jasper's tone during their last conversation, he figured Jasper had finally given up on him. He hadn't expected it to hurt so much.

"God nudges people." Brian opened a cabinet. "Most people just don't pay attention." He measured coffee and put the basket in the coffeemaker, filled a carafe, and poured it into the reservoir.

"I've told you more than I've told anyone." Including Grace.

"I'll hold it in trust." Brian considered him for a moment. "God has had His hand on you for a long time, my friend."

"We'll have to agree to disagree on that one."

"Maybe you need to go back and look at everything with new eyes. From where I'm sitting, God saved your life several times, not just that one time in Santa Clarita." His expression was intense, as though he were trying to drill through steel. "Jesus came to set you free, Roman, not remind you constantly of where you missed the mark. We're saved by grace . . ."

His fleshly mind went to Grace, God's instrument to keep him alive and give him one more chance to get things right. And he'd insulted her with a naive offer of what he considered a relationship. No wonder she ran.

He'd let her go, and now here he was thinking about her again. He refocused on what Brian was saying and knew what he meant. God's grace covered it all.

Brian laughed softly. "I can always tell when you're tuning me out."

"I hear you. I'll think about it." Maybe he should go back to the Tenderloin. He had unfinished business there.

Brian rubbed his hands together. "Could I talk the Bird into doing some flying for me? Graffiti is the kind of art that appeals to my parishioners."

Roman remembered the police officer in the tunnel. "I'm not blasting walls anymore. Gave my word."

"I'm not suggesting anything illegal, Roman. It'd be in the open, no black hoodies necessary."

"What are you talking about?"

"Something conspicuous on the wall facing the street. I want people to know there's a church in the industrial park. Of course, I need to get permission from our landlord, but he's a cool guy and a Christian. I think he'd go for it."

Ideas flashed like a slideshow in Roman's mind. Every time he read the Bible, he remembered paintings he'd seen in cathedrals and museums across Europe, others only in his head. He felt a spark and sensed the Holy Spirit bringing it to flame.

What do you say, Bobby Ray Dean? Want to do a little art for Me?

Roman laughed. Graffiti for God? What an outrageous idea! He itched to have a pencil in his hand.

Brian grinned. "Looks like you're already thinking about it."

35

Grace sat at the kitchen table, her laptop open, editing a business brochure. She peered out the window. It had been an hour since her aunt had taken Samuel out in the stroller. She'd never known Aunt Elizabeth to take a neighborhood walk, let alone ask to have responsibility for a baby.

The front door opened. "We're back!" Aunt Elizabeth called from the foyer. "I didn't give Samuel to the gypsies." She appeared in the kitchen doorway, cheeks flushed, smiling, Samuel perched happily on her hip. "Half a dozen neighbors wanted to know what I was doing with a baby. I told them I found him in the supermarket and couldn't resist tossing him in the basket." She chuckled. "I never knew I had so many nosy neighbors, but then again, I haven't taken a walk around the block in years." She looked over Grace's shoulder at the computer screen. "What're you working on?"

"Editing a brochure for a new business

venture."

"How did you get the work?"

"Harvey Bernstein has sent a few jobs my way." Her aunt had never met her boss at the public relations firm.

"Looks good. Then what will you do?"

"I have three other projects lined up, and Jasper Hawley has connections with several high schools in the Sacramento area. He's recommended me as an online tutor. I had my first inquiry this morning. I'll meet Kayden and his father on Skype during Samuel's nap time."

Aunt Elizabeth patted her shoulder. "I think you're going to do very well, Grace."

The unexpected compliment and pat on her back made tears well up. She had tried for years to win her aunt's approval. "I hope so." She saved the file and closed the laptop. "I can take him." She reached out for Samuel.

Aunt Elizabeth shifted away. "He's fine where he is." She took an arrowroot cookie from the box and gave it to him.

"He's going to get messy with that. Your blouse —"

"Don't worry about my blouse. It's washable silk." She leaned against the counter. "You young people seem to be creating your own careers these days."

"Sometimes out of necessity. Thankfully, I'm not doing this completely on my own.

Shanice and Ashley helped create the website and have been posting about it on social media."

"How much will the tutoring job pay?"

Jasper had suggested charging forty dollars an hour, but Grace felt more comfortable starting at thirty. If she helped Kayden, she would have one reference and hopefully begin building from there. She grinned at her aunt. "I'll have to keep a spreadsheet of my income so I won't get in trouble with the IRS."

"You bet you will." Aunt Elizabeth laughed. "I won't have my niece become a tax dodger." She shifted Samuel to her other hip. "You always were a good tutor, Grace. You helped Patrick Moore earn that college scholarship, didn't you? He never would have made it out of high school, let alone through UCLA, without your help."

She might not have received the credits, but she had learned a lot through the various classes Patrick took. "He tried."

"Did he?"

"He was good at some things, Aunt Elizabeth."

"I suppose that's a healthy way to look at an unhealthy situation, but what about your dreams, Grace? You put them on hold to help him. When is it your turn?" Aunt Elizabeth put Samuel on the floor and took some wooden spoons from a drawer. He banged them on the polished wood.

"I dream I can make a decent living at home so I can parent Samuel full-time."

"And you'll do it. You've been successful at everything you tackled."

"Except marriage."

"Oh, for heaven's sake, stop kicking yourself. Patrick was never a husband. He was a big boy looking for a mommy to take care of him."

Grace had been reluctant to bring up Patrick, but now her aunt had thrown that door wide-open. "I'd like to know how you were able to take one look at him and have him all figured out."

Her aunt gave a dismal shrug. "I worked with his father. Or I should say I watched how his father worked. He charmed others into carrying his load and took full credit for the work done. And then he got the accolades, promotions, and raises."

Grace wondered at the bitterness in her aunt's expression and tone. "Did he do that to you?"

Her aunt gave her a catlike smile. "He tried. Then moved on to others I admired. Charm always sends up a red flag for me. Patrick's sudden interest in you screamed of selfish motives."

"I guess I should have known better. Why would the most popular guy in school pick a nerd as a girlfriend?"

Aunt Elizabeth's eyes went dark and hot.

"The nerds of yesterday are the CEOs and entrepreneurs of tomorrow. You studied hard. You went out looking for work as soon as you were old enough for a permit. You had goals and dreams. Those are admirable qualities, Grace. You never used people."

It was the first time Aunt Elizabeth had defended her, and it put Grace in the odd position of defending her ex-husband. "It wasn't Patrick's fault I was so blind."

"You were young and naive in high school." Aunt Elizabeth sat, back rigid, facing Grace. "You weren't blind at UCLA. You saw. You knew it was no accident when he bumped into you on campus. And he just happened to need tutoring? When you mentioned you'd seen him, I could hear the doubt in your voice. You smelled a rat, but you wanted to hope. Who doesn't? Especially when the guy looks like a Greek god."

Grace blushed. "He didn't have to marry me."

"It was a good investment, wasn't it? Dating can be very expensive." Cynicism dripped. "Two can live as cheaply as one." She huffed. "He had everything he wanted — a pretty girl to bring home the bacon and cook it, then do his laundry and homework, and be a sex partner when he was in the mood. I doubt he was even a good lover. Too selfish. You were always careful with money, so I imagine whatever savings you had went into his

571

pocket. He liked to ski, as I remember. An expensive hobby. He managed to go to Big Bear half a dozen times, didn't he?"

The truth didn't hurt Grace as much as it had when Patrick walked out on her. She had suffered more from guilt and hurt pride than a broken heart.

"I know I disappointed you, Aunt Elizabeth. I'm sorry for being such a fool."

Her aunt's expression softened. "I share the blame. If I'd brought you up to know your worth, you might not have sold yourself short. Sometimes women love too much and lose themselves completely."

Like my mother, Grace thought, thankful that her aunt didn't say it.

Aunt Elizabeth put on the teakettle and got out two cups and saucers. Samuel had lost interest in the spoons and crawled toward the door to the garage. "Good thing I don't have a doggy door or he'd manage to escape. I wish I had one of those jumper things you could hang in the door."

"I have one in the trunk." She'd been sure her aunt wouldn't want it attached and possibly scratching up the lintel.

"Well, what are you waiting for? Go get it."

Grace came back inside and installed the gently used doorway jumper. Samuel squealed in delight when he saw it. She fitted him into it, and he bounced happily. Aunt Elizabeth laughed. "Doesn't take much to please that boy." She leaned down. "Careful you don't bounce too high, Rapscal. You might just bump your head."

"Rapscal?" Grace couldn't believe her aunt had given her son a nickname.

"Douglas called him that."

"Douglas?" Grace didn't remember anyone by that name.

"Retired grocer. Widower." Aunt Elizabeth waved her hand airily. "He bought the house next door." She set two cups of tea on the kitchen table. "He's fixing the place up. Ruby Henderson let it go after her husband died. She moved into an assisted-living facility and put the house on the market last year."

Suppressing a smile, Grace looked at her aunt over the rim of her teacup. "Is Douglas nice?"

Aunt Elizabeth gave her an annoyed stare. "We were talking about the men in your life. I don't have any in mine." She looked pointedly at Samuel and back at Grace. "Did you ever track down his father?"

Grace felt the heat surging into her cheeks. "No." She and her aunt hadn't trod this ground before, and Grace didn't want it plowed. And she didn't want to admit she had never tried.

"I'm not reprimanding you, Grace, but have you ever thought about it?"

"Yes, and decided it was a terrible idea." She stared into her cup of tea, not wanting to see what her aunt might be thinking. "We barely talked." She didn't remember anything about him.

"Why did you go to that club in the first place? It was so . . ." She shook her head. "Out of character."

Grace sighed. "I don't know. I was depressed and lonely. Shanice loves to dance. Patrick and Virginia's baby was due that week."

She'd been working every day, coming home to an empty apartment at night, taking online classes, keeping busy so she wouldn't think about her empty life. She wondered if she'd ever fall in love with a man who would love her back. Shanice said, *Come on, girlfriend, have a little fun for a change.* Why not? Everyone else seemed to be doing it.

The club had been packed, the sensuous beat of the music loud, people dancing like pagan worshipers. She'd been shocked at first, but wanted to fit in. So she pretended she could be as cool as anyone else. Before that night, she'd never had more than one glass of champagne, and that was in celebration of Patrick's graduation, but Shanice ordered her a sloe gin fizz. It tasted good and went down easily. It also went to her head.

One drink would have been more than enough to keep her high for the evening, but she paid for another. She danced alone, moving to the music, and then found herself in a man's arms. She didn't even look up at him. It was fun to dance with someone who knew how to lead and exciting to feel the rush of heat and fast pounding of her heart. She'd never felt anything like this with Patrick.

When the man asked if she wanted to leave, she knew what he meant. Pushing down all sense of right and wrong, she said yes. They barely spoke on the drive to his condo. He asked why she'd come to the club. She said she wanted to have fun. He asked if she knew the rules. She shrugged and said sure, doesn't everybody? One night, no strings. She hadn't thought about the rest.

Aunt Elizabeth touched Grace's hand. "Please don't cry. I shouldn't have brought it up."

Grace wiped tears from her cheeks. They sat in companionable silence, Samuel bouncing happily a few feet away, thankfully oblivious to adult misadventures and catastrophes.

"What about school, Grace? Do you want to go back?"

"I've been thinking about it."

"You had your sights set on clinical psychology, didn't you?"

To figure herself out? "I'd need a master's to do anything with it, and an internship somewhere. That would all take too long. The subject still fascinates me, but I don't think I could stay detached from patients. I'm too much of an enabler."

"I'm glad you recognize that. It means you can change the pattern. So? What else interests you?"

Art, music, Bible studies, anthropology, sociology, biology, but she'd learned where her skills lay. "I'd major in business administration, marketing, accounting."

"All very practical." Aunt Elizabeth looked pleased. "Seems a perfect fit, too. You're already in business. You could go back to UCLA. You finished that last semester on the dean's list, didn't you? You might even qualify for another scholarship."

"Possibly, but I don't want Samuel to grow up in Los Angeles. I've been doing some research online. Merced has a UC campus. The town has a population of less than a hundred thousand, and the rents are certainly lower than what I was paying. I could afford a one-bedroom apartment." First thing she'd do was find a good church. "There's another nice thing about Merced." She gave her aunt a hopeful smile.

Aunt Elizabeth set her teacup back in the saucer, but didn't raise her head. "What's that?"

"It's only an hour away from Fresno."

"Oh." Her aunt's smile trembled. "Enough distance so you'll have a full life of your own, and still close enough to be part of mine."

"My thoughts exactly."

Grace stayed two more days before heading

north.

Saturday night, Grace made online reservations for an affordable Merced hotel and set up Monday appointments to see available apartments in her price range. She and Aunt Elizabeth attended the early service. Miranda had been by the house to visit twice, and declared herself in love with Samuel. She met them at the sanctuary door and took him from Grace's arms. "He'll be with me in the nursery. That way you can relax and enjoy the service."

"Now, wait just a minute." Aunt Elizabeth looked annoyed to have Rapscal snatched away.

Miranda just laughed. "I'll give him back, Beth. It's only an hour. Honestly, you could learn to share." And off she went.

Grace hadn't been inside this church since Patrick left her. She'd been embarrassed to face these friends after the collapse of her marriage. What must they think of her?

"You needn't worry, Grace." Aunt Elizabeth gave her an understanding glance. "The only difference between most of the people inside these walls and the outside world is we know we're sinners. Chin up, my girl."

My girl. Her aunt had never called her that before. She had the feeling if anyone did slight her, ask a nosy question, or make a cruel remark, that person would come up against Elizabeth Walker's slicing wit.

Pastor Andrew greeted her with a welcoming hug. "Miranda told me you're moving north to Merced." He recommended an independent Christian church. "An old friend of mine just retired and turned the pulpit over to a millennial on fire to reach his generation. Give it a try." He had written all the needed information on the back of his card. "And keep in touch." He gave her a fatherly kiss on the cheek.

There were new faces among the familiar. "The congregation's growing."

"Trouble in one of the larger churches," her aunt told her. "The new pastor swept house over the last two years. Anyone who questioned his authority and message was pushed out the door. They came and settled here. I went once to hear the man preach. Dynamic speaker, a leader of men, but Jesus had left the building. The lady over there, Charlotte, has started a women's Bible study. And that gentleman over there, Michael, now teaches a couples' class. Remember how they had to draft you to teach Sunday school? Well, we now have several seasoned teachers who delight in Miranda's Sunday school program. What that congregation lost, God planted here. He gave us the people we needed."

This church felt as much like home as the bigger, more charismatic one she'd attended in Los Angeles. She knew God would have a church home for her in Merced. She'd already packed the car, intending to leave early, until Aunt Elizabeth asked her to come to church with her. Grace hadn't been sure she would be welcome after such a long absence and since her divorce. She should have known better.

"Thank you for making me go," Grace said on the drive back to the house.

Aunt Elizabeth looked over. "The longer you stay away, the more excuses keep you away. There might be a few people who think they're holier than thou, but the rest love you and wanted a chance to let you know."

When Grace pulled in next to the curb and stopped, her aunt opened the door. "Have a safe trip."

Grace spoke quickly before her aunt could escape. "I love you very much. Thank you for the last few days."

Her aunt's shoulders drooped slightly, and she didn't look at Grace. "Call me when you get settled in your new home." She got out of the car without a word or look for Samuel. Grace leaned down and watched her aunt walk up the path, open the front door, and close it behind her. She wondered if she'd ever understand Elizabeth Walker.

It was an easy one-hour drive to Merced. The hotel was far less impressive than the one Roman had booked on the trip they took, but it was clean, close to the freeway, and offered a complimentary breakfast. Grace took Samuel for a long ride around town, wasting gas but getting acquainted with the streets, parks, UC campus. She ate at a small café, Samuel in his car seat next to her.

Back at the hotel, she settled Samuel in the playpen while she worked at her computer. Later, she tucked him into bed with her. Facing so many changes in her life, Grace had trouble sleeping. What was Roman doing right now? Working in his upstairs studio? Out at a club? He'd probably hired her replacement within days. She looked at the digital clock. Two in the morning.

Samuel awakened with the dawn and wanted to play. Grace dragged herself out of bed and got ready for the busy day ahead.

The first apartment would have worked perfectly, but the manager said the landlord was unlikely to rent to an unemployed, single mother. He asked if she qualified for welfare. She told him she had an online business. Questions followed, and she answered honestly.

The manager shook his head. "A start-up, you mean, and we all know how few last. Good luck, Ms. Moore. You're going to need it."

Grace stopped by the church Pastor Andrew had recommended and talked with the secretary, Marcia Bigelow. She was friendly and encouraging. "We have a Wednesday morning Bible study with childcare. Most are older ladies, but we sure would like to have a younger one join us." Grace thanked her for the information, doubting she'd have time for the weekly morning class.

The next day was long and without result. Two apartments had already been rented before she arrived for her appointments, and the manager of the third complex looked her over and asked if she had a significant other. She avoided answering, but felt uncomfortable as he showed her the apartment. "You'd be right down the hall from me. Any problems turn up and I'd be at your door in a heartbeat." She left.

Wednesday morning, Grace scanned the classifieds on the *Merced Sun-Star* website and jotted down possibilities. She made one more call, and the manager vented about college kids and parties. Yes, he had an apartment available, but he'd already had several calls before hers, and she'd have to wait her turn. Four o'clock was open. "Fill out the application online."

Sitting on the hotel room carpet, Grace prayed while playing with her son. She felt the nudge to attend the morning Bible study and glanced at the clock. She'd be late, but better to slip in quietly than sit here and obsess about things over which she had no control.

A circle of twelve women sat on folding chairs. The instructor smiled when Grace walked through the door. "Hello! Are you Grace Moore? Marcia said you might stop by. Welcome."

Several women turned simultaneously, and one stood, practically glowing with pleasure. "A baby!" The others laughed as the dark-haired lady led Grace to a clean, well-equipped preschool classroom. "I'm Lucy Yeong, and this is . . . ?" Grace introduced Samuel, who barely looked at Lucy and squirmed to be put down among the colorful shoe box–size blocks. "He'll be fine," Lucy assured Grace. "I've raised four of my own and have ten grandchildren."

Grace joined the other ladies. Anna Janssen, the instructor, introduced herself and had the ladies each do likewise. "We'd just started, Grace. Ephesians, chapter 5. Would you like to read the first two verses?"

It didn't take long to find out these older women knew a lot more about God's Word than Grace did and had been putting it into practice for decades. The discussion was lively, sometimes serious, other times filled with laughter. Anna reminded Grace of Miranda Spenser. Age didn't matter; Grace felt right at home with these women. When it came time to end in prayer, Anna asked if there were any specific needs. Grace said she was looking for an affordable apartment.

Dorothy Gerling asked to talk with her after class ended.

"What about a house? We have a two-bedroom bungalow for rent. Our daughter was living in it before she enlisted in the Air Force. George and I have been debating whether to rent or sell." Grace told her how much she could afford to pay. "That sounds fine to me, but let me check with George."

Grace went to reclaim Samuel from Lucy Yeong, who looked as infatuated as Aunt Elizabeth had. "He's adorable. I hope you're coming back on Sunday. I'm in charge of the nursery."

Dorothy peered in. "George says yes. Would you like to take a look right now? I have time, if you do."

Post–World War II bungalows lined the street, some overgrown, some neat and simple. Dorothy met her on the sidewalk. "There's been a real turnover in this neighborhood over the last five years. Elderly owners are dying or selling to the younger generation. Lots of diversity here."

It was affordable housing in a far-from-affordable world.

The Gerlings' bungalow sat on a corner lot. The lawn was recently mowed, and neatly trimmed shrubs wrapped around the front. Dorothy said they had hired a gardening service to maintain the place, so Grace wouldn't have to worry about yard work.

Dorothy unlocked the front door. Grace followed her into a cozy, furnished living room. Both bedrooms were also furnished. "We remodeled the bathroom last year." A new sink, cabinets, shower, and tub. The kitchen was small but functional with a table against the windows looking out onto a huge backyard.

"You and Samuel would be perfectly safe here. Just keep the doors and windows locked and get to know your neighbors."

Grace had already noticed the Neighborhood Watch sign on the other corner. Her years in Los Angeles County had taught her to be careful.

"This used to be the garage." Dorothy went through a side door from the kitchen and two steps down. The room would make a good office. A door opened into a single-car garage that would easily accommodate her Civic.

"No air-conditioning, unfortunately. It would cost too much to put it in, but they built these houses so people could open their windows in the morning and evening and let in the cool, fresh air. And there's a nice covered patio out here." Dorothy opened the French door to the outside. "It's lovely in spring and summer. Alison loved to sit and read in that swing."

Grace gasped as she got a good look at the fenced and hedged backyard. In Los Angeles, builders would have put up another bungalow. A lawn covered the first two-thirds of the backyard. The back had empty vegetable boxes and a small garden shed. The white picket fence behind that separated the property from a single-lane road.

"That's a nectarine tree over there," Dorothy pointed out. "I still do canning. I'll come over when the fruit is ripe. You can keep as much as you want, of course."

"It's so beautiful, Dorothy. Are you sure you want to rent it for so little?"

"I'm delighted, Grace. An unoccupied house can be a problem for the neighborhood. And there are young families moving in now. I'm sure when you take Samuel out in the stroller, you'll meet other mothers your age." She looked around. "Besides, I'm not ready to sell this place. Alison might change her mind in a few years and decide to come back to Merced. George says I'm dreaming, but I guess I'm just not ready to let go yet."

"Do you want me to sign a rental agreement?"

"I suppose they do that sort of thing these days, but I think I can trust you. How many girls with a baby show up at a Bible study a couple days after they move to a new town? A check for half a month's rent now, since we're already two weeks into August. Then the full month's rent will be due on the first each month. How's that?"

"An answer to prayer." Grace put Samuel

down and let him explore the living room while she took her checkbook from her shoulder bag.

Dorothy chuckled. "It's been a long time since I've spent time with a baby. Alison is our only child. She was engaged last year, but they broke it off. Alison has always had a mind of her own, and a lot of men are put off by that." She took out a notepad and began writing.

"Thank you so much, Dorothy." *Father, forgive me for having any doubts about Your provision.* "God is good."

Dorothy glanced at her with a wide smile. "All the time." She tucked Grace's check carelessly into her purse, tore off the notepaper, and handed it over. "Our address and phone number, in case you have any problems with plumbing or the stove or gophers in the back lawn. Whatever. Just give us a call and George will be over like a flash. He loves to fix things."

"If it's all right, I'd like to stay for a little while."

"Of course." Dorothy handed her the key. "The house is yours now."

Grace saw her out the front door, thanking her again, before closing it. She covered her face, overwhelmed with what had just happened. "Thank You, Jesus. Thank You, thank You!" Laughing, she scooped up Samuel and kissed his chubby cheeks. "What do you think

586

of your new home, Rapscal? Isn't God good to us?"

Setting Samuel down again, she called Aunt Elizabeth. "Guess what? Samuel and I have a two-bedroom house! Would you like to come up this weekend and see it?"

Aunt Elizabeth didn't speak for a moment, and then answered in a husky voice. "Yes. I'd like that very much. All I need is an address."

"East Twenty-Second Street." Grace laughed. "Hold on. I have to go outside to tell you the number. I forgot to look."

36

Roman saw no point in keeping a big house on a mountaintop when he was spending so much time at a church in the valley. He decided to clean out the detritus of his life and put the place on the market. He filled plastic bags with spray cans and tubes of old paint and had the pile taken to a toxic waste company.

It took three days to whitewash his studio walls, obliterating all signs of his work. A flooring company refinished the hardwood. A two-bedroom apartment was available in the complex where Brian lived. Roman applied online and got it.

He left most of his furniture in the Topanga Canyon house. The real estate agent, who specialized in selling luxury homes, had said the house was perfectly staged. Modern. Minimalist. "The furniture might just sweeten the deal. If not, we'll sell it for you."

He had his books, clothing, the bedroom

furniture Grace had picked, and a fresh start ahead.

"Must be nice to have freedom enough to do whatever you want." The real estate agent had looked envious.

Free? This was just the first step out of the cage he'd built around himself. Right now, he wanted to get as far away as possible from the life he'd created and live the one God had planned for him. And that seemed to be enlisting a group of ex-gangbangers into helping him paint graffiti on a church wall. Settled in his apartment with one bedroom dedicated to drafting table, art supplies, and books, Roman set to work on the drawings for the church mural. The project kept his mind off Grace. He'd handed over the landscape to Talia, giving her permission to sell it. When she asked what he planned to do next, he said it wouldn't be anything she could put on a gallery wall.

As ideas took form on paper, his focus and excitement for the work grew. He'd be doing this piece in the open with a crew to help, but the rush he'd always felt doing graffiti was returning, keeping him going. He worked until his shoulders and back ached. He stood and stretched, pacing until the pain diminished, then went back to work. He didn't feel driven; he felt inspired. This was something new.

Brian came by to see the progress. "I saw

your other work at the gallery show, but this is something else!"

"Yeah," Roman agreed without arrogance. He studied the painting. It looked like someone else's work, not his own. God was in this, and Roman felt exhilarated, excited, *alive.* Art had always been his means of expression, a way to pour out his wrath and frustration, but this work had a whole new dimension. He knew the One who had inspired him and why. This universal Christ triumphant hadn't come out of his mind, but had been planted by the Lord.

Praise God, all you people of the earth. Praise the Lord!

How many years had he been searching for something to fill the void in his life? He'd tried everything — wandering, work, women. He'd fallen in love with Grace, but now he wondered what would have happened if they had gotten together. He'd still have been hungry for more.

Grace knew the Lord and loved Him. She had tried to take Roman by the hand and bring him to the altar, but he'd resisted, even after his near-death experience in hell. Why had he been so stubborn?

Maybe Grace had to be out of his life in order for him to get right with God. As long as she'd been around, his thoughts focused on her. His desire had clouded his thinking, distracted him from heeding the call of God.

She had already fully committed herself to living for the Lord. He hadn't yet made that life- and soul-altering decision. Now, he understood.

I still love her, Lord. You know how much. You hear my prayers in the middle of the night. But, oh, God, as much as I love Grace, it doesn't compare to what I feel in Your presence. I sense You all around me and inside me. You are enough. More than enough.

Roman knew only too well that God had the power to stop and start a heart. The life of any man or woman rested in the palm of His scarred hand. It took a trip to hell to teach him Jesus was the Way, the Truth, and the Life.

Prayer had become a constant, mindful conversation for Roman. Mostly one-sided. After so many years of silence, Roman couldn't stop talking inaudibly to the One who truly listened, the One who heard beyond the words to the motivations deeper than Roman himself could analyze.

Change me, Lord. Put a new heart in me. Make me the man You intend me to be.

Roman had stopped praying Grace would call or write or pass along a message through one of her friends, and begun praying God would watch over her and Samuel, provide for their needs, protect her, guide her, bless her. *Oh, God, please keep her away from guys like me. She deserves so much better.*

Brian put a hand on his shoulder. "Are you okay? You seem a little out of it today."

"I'm more in it than I've ever been."

He tacked the drawings up on the wall and studied them. He wasn't using transfers this time. He'd use narrow-stream, gray spray paint for the outlines and assign areas for his crew to fill in. No ropes and harnesses, either. He'd keep everyone safe on two rented, rolling mechanical lifts.

Brian looked worried. "How much will that cost?"

"It's on me. So are all the materials. Just got the call this afternoon that my house sold."

He'd come alongside Brian with the youth group. They were a tough, motley crew, eager to get started, especially the ones who'd repented of tagging buildings. They were itching to get their hands on cans of spray paint and not have to worry about being busted by the cops. Roman didn't miss the irony of his situation: the loner organizing a youth group project, the reformed-and-redeemed graffiti artist doing his work in the daylight for anyone to see, and on a church, of all places. God sure had a sense of humor.

Roman power-washed the wall and let the kids prep it with white paint. It was a day-long job with two lifts, gallons of white paint, and sprayers. The next Saturday, Roman got there early, intending to have all the sections drawn before the crew of teenagers arrived, but fifteen showed up hours before they were scheduled. Parents came and others he hadn't seen in church.

"You couldn't have picked a better day." Brian lifted his chin at the clear, cool fall morning. The mechanical lifts were in place, along with the paint supplies.

Roman had a bad case of nerves. "Everyone's early. I didn't expect a crowd."

"Yeah, well, nothing we can do about that. Everyone wants to see how you do what you do. Where are your drawings?"

Roman tapped his forehead. "It's all right here, my friend." He looked up at the massive canvas and envisioned the lines and shapes already burning into place. Might as well get started. Stepping into the lift, he pushed the button to raise the platform. Grabbing a can of gray spray paint from a box, he tried to block out everything but the vision God had given him. He shook the can, pressed the button, and made the first wide curve. A fountain of energy welled up inside him and began to overflow to those waiting to do their part.

Crew members sat and watched. After a few minutes, Roman forgot they were there. He worked for three hours straight, moving the machinery, emptying cans of paint. When he tossed the last can into the box and pushed the button to lower the lift, everyone erupted in cheers.

Realizing they were cheering for him, Roman went cold. "*Stop!* Listen to me!" When he had everyone's attention, he pointed. "This wall is a testimony to the power of Jesus Christ. *It's all about Him.* If you came to work, here's what you're going to do." He gave out instructions, tossing cans of paint to each and telling them where to start and where to work. "Okay, crew. Let's blast this wall for Jesus."

An hour later, Brian and Roman stood across the street, watching. "Wow!" Brian shook his head, amazed. "It'll be done before the day is over."

"Not completely. Once the kids have everything filled in, I'll do the finish details. Hector has a crew lined up to do the protective coat." He saw one boy ready to move on to another section. "Hey, Bando!" Limping across the street, Roman pulled another color out of the supply box and showed him where to work next.

Cars passed by. A few drivers stopped to watch. The crowd grew. A patrol pulled over, and officers got out. Roman recognized one. His stomach dropped, and his pulse picked up speed. The cop headed straight for Roman.

"Are you in charge here?" The policeman who had caught the Bird doing his work in the tunnel looked at the wall.

"Yes, sir."

"Impressive piece. Sort of in-your-face, don't you think?"

Roman didn't see the need to answer. The officer looked around. "You got permission this time." He smiled slightly. "Nice to see all these kids working on something constructive." He winked at Roman. "Have a good day." He went back to his patrol car. He and his partner got in and drove off.

Brian laughed. "You look pale. Were you expecting him to arrest you?"

"It crossed my mind."

The next morning, Roman was less than pleased to find a TV crew on-site when he returned to do the finish details. His work crew was also there. Contemporary Christian music blared, a few kids doing hip-hop moves in the driveway. One did a backflip from a standing position. A reporter approached. Roman dodged the microphone and stepped onto the lift. He pretended not to hear the questions called up as the machine rumbled into action. It was going to be hard enough to concentrate with a dance contest going on without adding reporters to the fiasco. His phone vibrated. When he saw Brian's ID, he answered. "Tell them to leave."

"They want to know why Roman Velasco is painting graffiti."

"I'll talk when the project's done. Right

now, I have work to do." He shut off his phone. A prickling feeling made the hair rise on the back of his neck. The Bird's wings had already been clipped. Now, it seemed the Bird would be cooked. How much jail time would he be serving for all the identified pieces he'd done over the years?

That thought sent a shudder of fear through him, but he shook it off. He needed to concentrate and finish this masterpiece. No use worrying about the consequences now.

Whatever happens, I trust You, Lord.

Grace loved her new home. Samuel slept with her for the first few nights until she put his crib together and transferred him to his own room across the hall. She didn't get much sleep the first night, listening to his screams of protest that turned into pitiful wails. She moved her bed so they could see each other. He finally wore himself out at one in the morning.

Samuel took his first steps at ten months. He toddled around the house and climbed on furniture. One tumble off the sofa taught him to turn over on his stomach and slide down until his feet touched the carpeted floor. Most of the time, he played contently in the office, toys strewn all around Grace's computer desk. His inner clock told him when it was time for Mama's full attention, and he could be quite vocal in claiming it.

Word spread, and VirtualGrace.biz quickly brought in more clients. Grace had enough work to meet expenses and put some into savings. When more requests showed up in her e-mail in-box, she made priorities and set boundaries: God first, Samuel second, work third. She got up early every morning to read the Bible and spend time in prayer. That quiet time steadied her for the rest of her busy day.

Samuel always awakened by six. Every morning after breakfast, when weather permitted, Grace strapped her son into a jogging stroller she'd bought off craigslist and took him out for a mile run. She often thought about Roman doing his weight-machine workout. She had to get some exercise when most of her day was spent at a computer. She found a bicycle at a thrift store, and every clear afternoon before Samuel's nap time, she strapped him into a bike seat, and took him on a thirty-minute ride. She also took breaks so he could play in the backyard. When it rained, Grace played with Samuel on the rug.

She met Angela Martinez over the side fence. Angela and her husband, Juan, had a nice yard, too, but the back third was taken up by a garage for Juan's truck, trailer, and John Deere mower for his landscape maintenance business. Angela was a homemaker, rearing three active children: eight-year-old

Carlos, five-year-old Juanita, and two-year-old Matías. Angela had plenty of sage parenting advice. Juan asked if he could prepare the soil and seed Grace's vegetable boxes. Both families would benefit from an eventual harvest. George and Dorothy Gerling thought that was a great idea and gave permission.

Aunt Elizabeth came up in November to celebrate Samuel's first birthday and surprised Grace with a sizable check. "I don't know what he needs or likes at this age. You use the money however you want."

Grace hugged her aunt. "It'll start his college fund."

A delivery truck showed up, along with Dorothy and George announcing they'd bought Samuel a red race car bed. George went right to work assembling it. "Every boy dreams of race cars."

Dorothy put on sheets stamped with little cars and a matching bedspread. "I couldn't resist!" She left a spare set for Grace. They couldn't stay long. George had a golf outing with buddies, and Dorothy had a book club meeting.

Aunt Elizabeth was painfully polite until they left. "What a waste of money!" She stood with hands on her hips looking at the new bed as though she wanted to dismantle it with an ax. "Don't they have grandchildren of their own to spoil?"

Samuel clearly liked his big-boy bed, though

Grace intended to keep him in his crib a while longer. He could spend nap time in the race car. "They have one daughter, single and in the military."

"Oh." Aunt Elizabeth's shoulders relaxed. "Well. No wonder." She sighed. "At least there's a nice, thick rug on the floor and the bed isn't so high he'll fall off and fracture his skull." With that grim blessing, she swung Samuel up into her arms. "Come on, Rapscal. Let's play with the Duplo blocks I brought you."

Aunt Elizabeth called, upset, a week later. "Did you give the Gerlings my address? They sent me an invitation for Thanksgiving."

Grace confessed and waited for Vesuvius to erupt. When her aunt didn't say anything, Grace sent up a silent prayer before searching for a concession. "If you'd rather it was only the three of us, that's fine. Your place or mine. I just don't want another Thanksgiving to go by without you."

"On that we certainly agree." The long pause made Grace bite her lip. Her aunt sighed. "It was actually a very sweet invitation."

"Then you wouldn't mind?"

"I'll let her know I'd love to come." Her tone was tinged with slight sarcasm. "I hope she doesn't put oysters in her stuffing."

Thanksgiving Day with Dorothy and George turned out to be very pleasant.

Christmas was fast approaching, and Grace found herself thinking more about Roman, wondering how he'd celebrate the holidays. She'd thought time and distance would diminish her feelings. Most days she was working so hard, she didn't think about anything but Samuel and what needed to be done to provide for him.

Evenings were different, and nighttime, the hardest. She had vivid dreams about Roman and sometimes awakened in tears.

Today was one of those days when she couldn't get Roman out of her head. Samuel toddled over and wanted to climb onto her lap. She worked that way for a while and set him down to play again. A few minutes later, he came back. Grace closed her laptop and lifted Samuel. "Okay, little man." She kissed his warm neck and breathed in his sweet, baby scent. "How about a bike ride, Rapscal?" He loved bike rides and flapped his arms, making her laugh.

Closing the garage door, Grace pocketed the remote and set off down the street. They wore matching neon helmets, the only brand-new things she had splurged on so far. By the time they returned, she was tired and Samuel was sleepy from the cool wind in his face. She put him down for a nap in his race car bed and was intending to go back to work when the phone rang.

"Hey, girlfriend!"

"Hey, back atcha." Grace laughed. In addition to frequent texts and e-mails, Shanice called every few days to check on her.

"How are things going?"

Sprawled on the sofa, Grace sighed. "Right now, I'm done in. I just took Samuel out for a bike ride."

They carried on their usual friendly conversation for fifteen minutes before Shanice admitted she had another reason for calling. "I wanted to talk to you about Roman, honey."

Grace's heart started to pound. "What about him?"

"Well, he's not the man I met in Topanga Canyon, that's for sure. He and Brian have become good friends. Roman sold his house and moved into the apartment complex where Brian lives. He just finished a project for the church. You should see it, Grace. It's drawing a lot of attention. Some reporters showed up, and there have been a couple articles on the piece. Check it out on YouTube. It's amazing!"

"I'm glad to hear he's doing so well." Grace tried to keep her tone neutral, despite the wild beating of her heart and the surge of hope she needed to crush.

"Do you want me to tell Roman where you are?"

"Did he ask you?"

"No, but I'm sure he'd like to know."

Grace closed her eyes tightly, unable to speak for a moment. "I think it's better to leave things as they are." If Roman loved her, wouldn't he have asked about her by now? She left Los Angeles months ago.

"Are you sure, honey? He might have reasons for not calling you."

Just as she had reasons for keeping her silence. *God, am I doing the right thing? I don't know anymore.*

"If he does ask, can I tell him? I have no doubt he's a Christian now, Grace, or I wouldn't bring him up at all. I know how much you grieved over the guy. You still love him, don't you?"

It wasn't really a question. "All the more reason to keep my distance, Shanice. Roman never said he loved me." Grace put a shaking hand to her forehead. "Can we not talk about him? Please. I've been trying hard to move on."

"Doesn't sound like you're having much luck with that."

How could she forget a man like Roman Velasco? Or was he Bobby Ray Dean now? Was he still the Bird, out painting walls at night? Roman Velasco, Bobby Ray Dean, or the Bird, she was still in love with him. "Keeping busy helps."

They talked for a few more minutes and ended the call.

Samuel came toddling into the living room

and climbed up so he could sprawl on her chest. She remembered how he'd slept on Roman this same way at the cottage. *Lord, how long before this ache goes away?*

That night, Samuel snug in his crib, Grace lay wide-awake. At midnight, she gave in to temptation, went to her office, and opened her laptop. She did a quick search on You-Tube and found Roman's most recent work. She drew in a soft breath when she saw Jesus on the back of a white stallion. The clouds painted at the building foundation line made the church look like it was floating. The wall was magnificent, but it was the man obviously avoiding the camera who held her attention. She pulled up other YouTube clips. Seeing him, even on a computer screen, increased her painful longing. She switched to Google and found a recent newspaper article. Talia Reisner must have supplied the reporter with a public relations package.

Images produced a screen full of pictures of Roman Velasco: at the gallery opening, working on the San Diego mural, in a night-club, dancing with a beautiful blonde. She closed her laptop. Covering her face, she cried. *God, make these feelings go away. Please.* She took a Tylenol PM and went back to bed. Lying on her side, she looked across the hall at her son sleeping peacefully in his crib. Roman had been clear about what he wanted and didn't want.

I've done everything possible to avoid ever having a kid.

It wouldn't be wise to open the door to Roman again. Samuel needed a man who would love her unconditionally . . . and love her son no matter how he was conceived.

37

Now that the project was done, Roman found himself inundated with interview requests. He agreed to meet Tuck Martin, a freelance reporter, at Common Grounds, and asked Brian to join them. Talking about Brian and the crew was easy. Roman wanted them to get the credit they deserved. Martin was more interested in Roman's personal history, life, and career as an artist. Roman stopped talking.

Brian smiled at Martin. "Roman is a little reticent about his personal life."

"I gathered that." He looked at Roman. "Is there a reason?"

Roman wished he hadn't agreed to this. "Too many people have an unhealthy interest in other people's business."

"I've done considerable research on you, Mr. Velasco." He talked for the next ten minutes while Roman squirmed. Tuck Martin had managed to dig out information from public records and interviews with retired social workers. He'd spent several hours with Talia Reisner and got an earful about Roman's temper, bohemian ways, and reputation as a player, which led Martin to the nightclub Roman used to frequent and a few other shorter interviews with women he'd hooked up with. Jasper Hawley and the Mastersons were noticeably absent from Tuck Martin's list, nor did he mention Grace Moore.

Roman pushed his chair back. "Seems to me, you have more than enough information to write your story already."

Brian gave him a look that reminded Roman of Jasper Hawley. *Hear the man out.*

Roman remained seated. "Just what are you after, if that isn't enough to write a juicy piece for *People* magazine?"

"I'm interested in the man behind the art." Martin leaned forward. "A year ago, you were a loner living the good life on a mountaintop, and now, you're down in the flatlands working with a crew of gang kids and painting a masterpiece on the wall of a church that meets in an industrial park." He gave a soft laugh. "How did that happen?"

What could Roman say? "People change directions all the time." He felt Brian's glance.

Tuck Martin looked unconvinced. "Why did you bring a pastor to the interview?"

"He's a close friend." He jerked his chin at

Brian. "He's the one that came up with the idea."

Brian shook his head. "I just offered Roman the wall. He and God did the rest."

Tuck Martin gave Roman a wry look. "Do you agree with that statement? You think God had something to do with it?"

"Yes and yes."

"Are you a Christian?"

Roman gave him a sardonic stare. "Don't I look like one?"

Brian laughed. "A young disciple."

"How did that come about?" Tuck looked at Brian for an answer.

Brian tilted his head toward Roman. "Ask him what happened in Santa Clarita."

When Roman didn't speak up, Brian rose. "I'm going to get another cup of coffee. Need anything, gentlemen?" When neither answered, he strolled away. Roman knew what Brian wanted him to do, and he knew what response he'd get.

"I had a heart attack, died on the sidewalk, and went to hell. Jesus got me out."

Tuck Martin laughed. "Yeah. Right." He grew serious again. "Great joke, but now, I'd like to know what really happened."

Roman just looked at him.

Martin frowned and searched Roman's face. "You weren't kidding, were you?"

"Never been more serious in my life." Roman lifted his coffee, thinking he'd said more than enough, until he felt the nudge to go on. "I didn't believe in God. Strike that. Maybe it's closer to the truth to say I hated Him. I'd just had a heated conversation with a Christian. We'd called a truce and pulled in to have lunch. I dropped dead on the sidewalk." He shuddered. "Looking back, the timing seems providential."

Martin's mouth twisted in a cynical half smile as he leaned back. "Tell me what it was like in hell."

Roman measured Tuck Martin's expression. "Someday you'll see it for yourself."

"Is that a polite way of telling me to go to hell?"

"Reject Jesus, and that's where you'll end up."

"You'd allow me to put that in my story."

"Can't stop you now, can I?"

Brian came back as Tuck Martin turned off his recorder and dropped it in his backpack. "Do you know what he just told me?"

"I hope so." He looked at Roman with approval. "Your NDE."

Roman shrugged. "He doesn't believe me."

"It was a good thing Grace was with him in Santa Clarita, or he'd be dead. She knew CPR."

"Grace?" Tuck Martin's interest returned. "Talia Reisner said you had a personal assistant who lived and traveled with you."

Roman felt a rush of protective anger.

"Grace didn't *live* with me. She had her own place." He wasn't about to tell this nosy reporter she lived next door in a cottage he owned. "She's as straitlaced as they come. And if you insinuate anything else in your article, I'll rip your head off."

Martin drew back.

"Sorry, Mr. Martin." Brian chuckled. "Roman is a new Christian."

Martin held up his hands. "I wasn't meaning to insinuate anything. Ms. Reisner spoke very highly of Ms. Moore. She said you needed a keeper, and Grace was organized, efficient, and a delight to know."

Roman glared at him. He knew what the next question would be.

"I'd like to talk with her."

"I'll bet you would," Roman growled, wishing again he'd never agreed to this interview.

Brian glanced at Roman and then back at Tuck Martin. "Grace moved out of the area."

Roman watched Tuck Martin closely and saw reporter instinct rising up like sludge in a clogged drain. When he looked at him, Roman stared back, letting the anger show. *Ask about Grace again, and you are going to regret it.*

Martin's brows flicked up. Face relaxed, expression enigmatic, he leaned back and settled in. "There are plenty of bestselling books out there about near-death experiences in heaven. A couple of movies, too. I don't

609

remember any about hell."

Roman returned Martin's cynical smile with one of his own. "It's not an experience I want to remember. Why would I want to write about it?"

"You could hire someone."

"Like you?" Roman snorted. "You don't believe me."

"I might if you talked about it a little more."

Brian sat quiet, clearly observing them.

Martin kept pushing. "You should warn people, don't you think? Isn't it your Christian duty?"

Roman gritted his teeth to keep from telling Martin where he could go and what he could do with himself once he got there.

Brian rescued him. "They've been warned. It's all written in black-and-white. Most people like believing they can be good enough to get in the gate. Truth is, none of us are. Jesus holds the key."

"That's the party line."

Brian leaned forward, hands loose around his fresh cup of coffee. "Before you go, can I ask you a question?"

"I grew up in a 'Christian' home." Martin's face hardened. "I've seen religion firsthand."

Roman watched, amazed at how easily Brian could get people to talk. Maybe it was the way he listened, full of compassion without judgment or condemnation. Turned out Martin was from a hardworking, middle-class Christian family, but not the loving kind Brian had. Tuck's father had been controlling and intolerant of anyone who didn't share his views.

"He made sure I was sitting in the pew every Sunday. In suit and tie." He shrugged. "Haven't worn a tie since I left home."

"How's your relationship with your father now?"

Tuck shook his head. "He's the same, just older and tired. He mellowed once Mom died. Still goes to church. My sisters and their families go, too. I love my father, but we disagree on just about everything. I see him once a year, and we stick to safe topics." He gave a bleak laugh. "Fishing. That's about it."

Brian, a fisher of men, told him there was a big difference between religion and faith.

Tuck Martin's phone rang. Apologizing, he checked the display. "Forgot the time. Gotta run." Roman and Brian stood. Tuck shook hands with both and thanked them for their time. He looked at Roman. "Working on anything else?"

"Nothing I plan to show or sell." Roman felt Brian's glance. They were best friends, but that didn't mean he had to tell Brian everything.

Tuck shouldered his pack. "I've done more talking this morning than both of you put together."

Brian smiled. "Maybe you needed to." He

took out a card and handed it to him. "Anytime."

Brian tapped on Roman's door that evening. "Thought you might be up."

Roman went back to the sofa, stretched out his legs, and put his feet on the coffee table. He turned off the basketball game. "How'd the board meeting go?"

"Long. Like the day. I'm exhausted." He stood in the living room.

Roman knew something was on his mind. "So, what're you doing here? Sit down or go home and get some sleep."

"I won't be able to sleep until my curiosity is satisfied." He tipped his head. "I'd like to see what you're working on."

"It's not finished."

"I'm not a critic."

Roman shrugged, and they went into the second bedroom. Sketches littered the drawing board. A large canvas sat on an easel. Brian had to move to the other side of the room to see it. "Oh, my." He spoke softly, in reverence. "She's beautiful."

"I could use more light." Roman felt edgy, exposed. "This would've been better done at the place in Topanga Canyon." *And with the right model.* He joined Brian and studied the painting with a critical eye.

A young woman, advanced in pregnancy, wearing Judean clothing, stood with one hand spread over the top of her swollen belly, the other cupping beneath as though holding the unborn child in tender embrace. Her expression revealed wonder and fear.

"What do you call it?"

The Indwelling.

"She looks like Grace."

Roman's heart leaped, but he didn't say anything. He'd been praying just before Brian knocked on the door. If God wanted him to search for Grace, three people had to bring her up without any encouragement from him. And now, here was Brian, a few minutes later, doing exactly that.

Number one.

Roman was afraid to hope. Hope hurt.

Brian frowned. "You haven't mentioned her in months."

"Nothing to talk about."

"You still love her."

"Leave it alone, Brian." Roman went into the living room and turned the basketball game back on. Brian sat in the easy chair as though he intended to stay awhile. Roman gave him a mocking smile. "I thought you were tired."

"I can get her address from Shanice, if you want it."

Temptation rose quickly. He caught himself before he gave in. "It's better if I don't know." If he knew where she was, he might not be able to wait for God's timing.

"Why not, Roman? You're not the man you were."

"I'm not the man she needs."

Brian laughed and shook his head. "Listen to you, playing the martyr. If all you want is a roll in the hay, then, yes, I agree. Leave her alone. But you want more, don't you?"

"I've laid out my fleece." Brian would understand. The Old Testament prophet Gideon had laid out a fleece twice to be certain God was speaking, that what he heard wasn't just his imagination. Roman knew asking for three confirmations was pushing it, but he wanted to discern whether it was God nudging him or his own sinful heart leading him on. *I need to be sure, Lord. I know what I want, but there are plenty of days when I still don't know what's right.*

"Okay." Brian stood. "I'd better get to bed or I'll be too tired to face tomorrow. I've got counseling appointments all morning, so I won't make lunch." They'd been meeting every Wednesday for months. Brian opened the door and then looked back at Roman. "You mentioned going to San Francisco after you finished the wall. Still planning on taking that trip?"

Something else God had been pressing him to do. "I've been thinking about it."

"Whatever it is that's holding you back, remember, you already survived it."

"That doesn't mean I want to relive it."

After Brian left, Roman watched the basketball game — or tried to. He kept thinking about going to San Francisco. Would he ever be completely at peace unless he went back to the Tenderloin and took a slow walk through his past? *What good is it to remember the bad stuff, the shame, the anger that got me into so much trouble? Why do You keep pushing me to do this? What do you want from me, Jesus?*

Go with open eyes, Bobby Ray. Look for Me.

The hair stood on the back of Roman's neck. He knew that still, small voice. When the suggestion came from Brian, Roman ignored it. Now, it was a command.

I know what happened there, Lord. I've confessed it. Why do You keep hounding me about it?

Roman wanted to go on making excuses, but he knew he wasn't going to find any peace in disobedience. Rubbing his face, Roman leaned back. *Okay, okay. I get the message. Just don't expect me to be happy about it.*

Grace left the UC Merced campus in high spirits. Her meeting with the dean of admissions went far better than expected. Her UCLA transcripts had been transferred. The dean was impressed. She could qualify for financial assistance, and the education and sociology departments had test programs for children. Samuel would make a good guinea pig, but he'd miss his playtime with Matías. The two little boys got along better than brothers.

On the drive home, she thought about how much time VirtualGrace.biz demanded. A scholarship was one thing; financial aid in the form of a loan was another. She'd be reducing her income by cutting back on work hours, and she'd also be taking on school debt. It was all well and good to dream about returning to college, but she needed to think about whether now was the right time. Samuel was changing so quickly, she didn't want to miss a minute with him. Dorothy had volunteered to babysit, but three mornings a week and two nights away was too much time. Her education could wait until Samuel was old enough for preschool.

But then, she might decide to homeschool him.

Grace gave a soft laugh as she parked in front of the bungalow. "I guess I'm supposed to wait, Lord." With so many questions and conflicting emotions, she didn't want to plow ahead. All things in God's perfect timing. Now didn't seem to be it.

Aunt Elizabeth came up to spend the weekend. Chuckling, she put her overnight case on the dresser. "I can't believe I'm going to be sleeping in a race car bed!" It was a full-size twin bed and comfortable.

"Samuel won't mind." Grace kissed his neck as he rode her hip. "He's going to sleep with Mommy."

Dorothy and George invited them for Saturday brunch. "We're leaving for San Francisco on Monday."

"Another cruise." George sighed dramatically. "She goes online, finds deals, and drags me along."

"Quit pretending you don't love it." Dorothy laughed, admitting she loved cruises on Princess ships and jumped on last-minute, low-cost bookings. "It's just ten days this time, down to Mexico and back."

George winked. "She won't have to cook."

Aunt Elizabeth smiled. "Well, before you book another trip, Dorothy, I'd like you to come to Fresno. We can have lunch. I want you to meet my friend Miranda Spenser. You two have a lot in common."

Grace was surprised her aunt was willing to share.

"I'd love that!" Dorothy went to get her day planner. As they decided on a date, Dorothy came up with another idea. "Why don't I bring Samuel with me?"

"Miranda would love to see him."

Grace wasn't ready to relinquish him for a daylong excursion to another town, nor did she want to hurt feelings. "I'm sorry, ladies, but my son is too young to be hanging out with older women."

Dorothy and Aunt Elizabeth laughed, and didn't press.

As they all chatted and enjoyed the afternoon, Grace thought over the past few months and counted blessings. God had provided all her needs. She had a livelihood, friends both new and old, and a church family. Aunt Elizabeth was now involved in her life in a loving, nondictatorial way. Only one thing kept Grace from feeling at peace: Roman Velasco. He'd changed a great deal, if the most recent feature article was any indication. He had told the reporter about his new life, his work, and even his near-death experience in hell. Pastor Brian Henley had been at the interview and was quoted several times. Shanice had told Grace the two men had become close friends.

Perhaps her love for Roman was the cross she'd have to bear. Or so she'd thought since moving to Merced. *Move on, Grace. Stop asking what-if.* But now, she felt the nudge to rethink her decision. Maybe it was time to call and talk to him, wish him well. His phone number came to her immediately, warm tingling temptation at a touch of her cell phone screen. And then what? Closing her eyes, she prayed. *Should I call him, Lord? Should I open the door?*

Silence. She didn't expect to hear God's

voice, but she wanted to feel right about it. When she didn't, she knew the answer.

Wait.

Roman awakened when his cell phone vibrated on his bedside table. Groggy, he reached for it, knocking it onto the carpeted floor. Caller ID, Shanice. She wouldn't call unless it was an emergency. Coming fully awake, Roman grabbed it. "Brian okay?" His voice sounded hoarse from sleep.

"Brian's fine. He's with a grieving family at the hospital, and can't go with me to a nightclub to help a friend. He said to call you."

"What's the problem?"

"My ex-roommate, Deena. She checked herself into a six-month recovery program a while back, and then found out yesterday that her fiancé is cheating on her. She's gone AWOL. She called me from a club. I've got to get her out of there before she does something she'll regret. I've already gone down that road and don't want a repeat scenario. Can you go with me?"

"Where are you now?"

"I'm pulling up in front of your apartment."

"Okay, but only if I drive." She sounded so uptight, he didn't think she should be behind the wheel.

"Fine, but hurry up! Please."

It took him five minutes to dress. He used

the stairs instead of waiting for the elevator and jogged to the car, where he found Shanice already buckled into the passenger seat. The engine was running and waiting to be put in gear when he opened the driver's side door.

"Thanks, Roman. Brian said you'd come through for me."

"Where are we going?"

"After Dark. I can give you the address."

He muttered a foul word under his breath. "I know where it is."

"Oh." Shanice looked at him. She winced. "Unhappy memories?"

"Just a reminder of who I was not so long ago."

"Well, don't feel like you're the Lone Ranger. Three years ago, you would've seen me there every Friday and Saturday night. Brian knows, in case you're wondering. I like to have fun. The band is awesome, and I love to dance." She gave him a wry look. "Is that why you were there?"

"I can dance, but no, that's not why I went to that club."

Roman felt her studying him.

"You went to hook up." She looked straight ahead. "I imagine you had your pick of willing women." She didn't say anything for a minute, then glanced at him. "Was Grace the reason you stopped going?"

I asked for three, Lord, and here's Shanice

bringing up Grace. One more, Lord. Oh, Jesus, please, one more. "No. I stopped going before I met Grace." He merged onto the freeway and accelerated, slipping easily between cars until he reached the fast lane.

"What made you quit going?"

"I wanted more than what I found there." They drove for ten minutes in silence. Pulling off the freeway, he spotted a familiar parking structure, turned in, and pulled a ticket from the machine.

"I brought Grace here once," Shanice confessed.

Roman laughed in disbelief. "What'd you do? Gag her and drag her?"

Shanice didn't laugh. "Almost. I never knew her husband, Patrick. I met Grace after her divorce. She came to an evening Bible study. Nicole, Ashley, and I already had the Sunday-after-church brunch going and invited her to join us. Ashley went to the club with me occasionally. She likes to dance, too, but wasn't always asked. Anyway, Grace never went. All she did was work — six days a week — and church on Sundays. She didn't have a life. I thought she needed to loosen up and have some fun." She looked away. "I'm an idiot."

Roman spotted a parking space and whipped in. He wanted to hear more, but Shanice was already getting out of the car.

The club hadn't changed. Though the faces

were different, it was the same scene — men on the prowl, women on the make. Couples danced to the steamy beat, looking like they were having sex standing up and fully clothed. He couldn't imagine Grace in a place like this.

"There's Deena." Shanice nodded toward the bar and wove her way toward a girl with two guys hovering. Roman followed, ready to step in if there was a problem. Shanice said something to the two men that had Deena protesting, and the men backed off. Shanice leaned in and talked to Deena, who was clearly arguing. Seeing it would take Shanice time to convince her friend to leave, Roman sat at the bar and ordered a Coke.

An attractive blonde slid onto the stool next to him. Her black dress was short, tight, and riding up on her shapely thighs. The low top made her chest look like a baby's bottom. She smiled at him. "Finally, a man who looks interesting."

Roman got up and stood beside Shanice.

Deena looked at him. "Oh, wow! Who are you?"

"Deena, this is my friend Roman Velasco. He's here to help me get you home safely."

"Okay." She gave him a bleary-eyed, sloppy smile. "I'll go anywhere with him." When she started to stand, she sagged slightly and Roman slipped an arm around her to keep her upright.

As soon as the three of them made it out the front door and into the cool night air, Deena groaned. "I'm going to be sick." She bent at the waist and threw up on the sidewalk. A car honked as it went by, teenage boys hanging out the windows, laughing and making cruel comments.

Deena moaned. "Oh, I wanna die . . ."

"Yeah, I know the feeling, honey." Shanice took over and guided her to the parking lot, where she vomited again, this time in a garbage can. The two women talked in low voices. Deena started to cry, and Shanice put an arm around her. He felt a sense of déjà vu.

His mother often drowned herself in booze after a night of streetwalking. She'd cry and mumble to herself. Sometimes she smoked pot until she was too mellow to care about anything, including him.

Deena made it to Shanice's Lexus on her own feet. She kept crying and mumbling while Shanice buckled her in. Shanice wiped the hair back from Deena's face and told her to try to sleep. She'd be home soon. It took over an hour to reach Deena's parents' house, and the girl was sober enough to be embarrassed. She apologized profusely as Shanice helped her out of the car.

Roman got out. "You need a hand?"

"Better if I take her inside and talk to her folks. I might be a little while."

"I'm not going anywhere."

It was another hour before Shanice returned and sank into the passenger seat. "Thanks for coming with me, Roman. When she called, I took it as a cry for help." She put her head back. "I hate that place."

"What turned you off to it?"

"Grace." She shook her head. "I was telling you how I wanted her to have some fun? Well, I made her take her hair down that night. It was long then. And blonde. And I made her put on one of my slinky dresses." She glanced at him. "I dumped that part of my wardrobe after that night." She sighed. "We walked into After Dark, and Grace froze with her mouth open. I thought it was hilarious and half dragged her inside. She was so shocked and uptight, I said I'd get her a drink. Of course she protested. She doesn't drink, you know. I lied and said I'd get her something harmless. One was enough. She looked more relaxed than I'd ever seen her."

Shanice leaned back. "Some guy asked me to dance, and off I went. I checked on Grace once, and she still had that sloe gin fizz in front of her. Or so I thought. I didn't know she finished the one I bought her and ordered another. She seemed okay sitting at a table by the back wall, watching the action. I'm ashamed to say I forgot all about her for a while. When I did remember, she wasn't there. She wasn't in the ladies' room, either.

I looked all over and couldn't find her. I was more ticked off than worried. I figured she called Uber and went home." She covered her face. "I wish."

Roman knew something bad happened that night, but was afraid to ask what.

"I called her the next day, intending to tell her it wasn't nice to leave without telling me. I could tell she was crying. I asked what was wrong. She couldn't even talk. I left work and went to see her. It took a while, but she told me everything. She was so ashamed, and it was my fault. I should've been watching out for her instead of off having a good time."

His hands shifted on the wheel. "Did someone rape her?" He could feel the heat of anger rising.

"No, thank God. She said she felt good and started to dance. By herself. A man took her in his arms and danced with her. When he asked if she wanted to leave, she said yes. He took her to a condo in Malibu. You can guess the rest."

Roman's hands tensed on the wheel.

Shanice looked straight ahead. "She didn't ask his name. She said they barely talked. She couldn't even remember what he looked like. Tall, dark hair, strong. When he went into the bathroom after they had sex, she threw on her clothes and left." Shanice started to cry. "That's the last time I went to After Dark. Until tonight. I didn't want to be reminded of what a lousy friend I was that night."

She wiped away tears. "I told Grace how sorry I was. I should've stayed with her. Her self-esteem was in the basement. Of course she blamed herself." She looked out the car window. "She would've been safer with her hair up. Men seem to go for blondes. And that black dress."

Roman remembered how beautiful Grace looked the night of his Laguna Beach art exhibit.

Shanice sat up straighter in the passenger seat and looked at him, eyes glittering in the dim light. "Would you like to know why Grace bleached her hair? Her husband said she'd be pretty if she were a blonde. Can you believe that? As if she isn't already beautiful inside and out. But you know Grace. She wants to do her best at everything she does, and of course, she wanted to be a good wife. So, she gave him what he wanted. Not that it made any difference to that jerk."

Roman winced, seeing himself as he'd been.

"She told me she has terrible judgment when it comes to men." She gave him a wincing look.

"Including me, you mean." His heart was pounding hard and fast. "Sounds like she's right." He glanced at Shanice. "Did she ever go back to After Dark and try to reconnect with the guy?"

"Are you kidding? No!"

"Just wondering. She had a relationship with someone after her divorce, didn't she?"

"A boyfriend, you mean?" Shanice shook her head. "Not that I know about, and I'd know." She shifted in the passenger seat, facing him. "I don't get it, Roman. Why is it some people can get away with everything, and then along comes someone sweet like Grace, and she can't even act out one time without paying the full price."

Roman glanced at her. "What price?"

She gave him a pained smile. "Samuel."

Roman felt like she'd punched him in the stomach. "I thought she and her ex —"

"He didn't want children. She lost a baby once, and he actually celebrated. He didn't want the responsibility." Shanice looked at the street ahead. "She didn't tell us for three months. She could've had an abortion. A friend even suggested it."

He went hot. "You?"

"No, but I'm not saying who. Grace thought about giving him up for adoption. It was agreed that Selah and Ruben Garcia would take him, but the minute Grace held Samuel, she couldn't go through with it. It's been an emotional tug-of-war from day one. When you rented her the cottage, she saw a way out of her situation, and then, of course, that changed. I just wish she hadn't left LA. I miss her." She met his gaze briefly. "She wanted her son to grow up in a safer place."

"She needed to get away from the Garcias. And me." Roman pulled alongside the curb and put the car in park, leaving the engine idling. "Anything else you want to tell me about Grace?"

Shanice looked apologetic. "I think I've said too much already."

He waited a moment longer and saw she meant it. "I love her, Shanice." He wanted to ask how to find her. *Jesus, I want to get things right. Oh, God; oh, God.*

Shanice's eyes glistened. "I know you love her, Roman. And I'd give you her address if I hadn't given my word."

He got out of her car. Shanice came around to the driver's side, but didn't get in. She put her hand on his arm. "I'm sorry. I shouldn't have even brought her up tonight. I don't know why I did. It wasn't my right to tell you her story."

"No, it wasn't, but I'm glad you did." He thought he'd felt pain enough, but he hadn't known the half of it.

Shanice slid into the driver's seat and Roman closed the door. She lowered the window. "Please don't think less of her."

"Don't worry about that." Roman leaned down slightly. "When you talk to Brian, tell him I'm going to be gone for a while."

"How long?"

"I don't know."

"Where are you going?"

"San Francisco." He'd already packed and planned to leave the next morning. "Tell him I'm taking care of unfinished business. He'll understand."

"Safe travels, Roman." Shanice drove away.

Roman entered his apartment and tossed his keys on the coffee table. Sinking onto the couch, he put his head in his hands. "Jesus." It was a soft, broken cry. Shanice talked about the men in the club, and he saw himself — callow, callous, a user. If Grace had stayed at the cottage, he'd have had no qualms about seducing her.

A blonde. In a black dress. Just his type.

"Jesus." Roman's voice came out in a broken rasp, hanging between self-disgust and despair . . . and anger, too. *God, You should have left me in hell. It's what I deserve.*

Saved by grace, Brian had told him more than once.

Grace.

Leaning forward, Roman wept.

38

Grace sat outside beneath the covered patio with her aunt while Samuel toddled around the backyard. She'd already plucked one wiggly worm and glossy snail from his fist, thankfully before he popped them in his mouth for a taste. He headed for the big red ball, accidentally booting it. With a squealing laugh, he went after it.

Aunt Elizabeth chuckled. "He'll make a good soccer player." She sipped her green tea.

It was a little chilly outside, but Samuel needed running room. He'd been cooped up in the house for the last week while rain pattered the roof.

"What's on your mind, Grace?"

What always seemed to be on her mind lately: Roman. She didn't speak his name aloud. "Nothing but the usual." She couldn't bring herself to talk about him. Not with her aunt. Not with anyone. How long was it going to take to get over him?

"Is your business going all right?"

"It keeps me very busy. Jasper referred another student. Thankfully, because one of my clients no longer needs my services. He got an A on his final."

"Just like Patrick." Aunt Elizabeth grimaced. "Sorry. I didn't mean to bring up the past. What about your social life?"

"Church on Sunday and the ladies' Bible study midweek."

"Have you met any eligible bachelors?"

"I'm not looking for one."

"Because you're still in love with Roman Velasco."

Grace wasn't going to lie. "There's nothing I can do about that."

Samuel pounced on the ball, and it shot out from under him like a rocket. Grace and her aunt laughed. Samuel let out a screech of surprise and propped himself up on his arms. He got to his feet and went after the ball again.

"Nice to see he doesn't give up." Aunt Elizabeth set her teacup on the saucer.

"Not when he wants something."

"What about you, Grace? Why don't you just call Roman and see what happens?"

"I know what would happen, and I'm not taking the risk. Besides, you've done without a man all your life. So can I." Regretting her angry outburst, Grace stood. "Would you like more tea? I'm getting more coffee."

"You can't even bear to talk about —"

"If Roman wanted to pursue a real relationship, he'd find me."

Aunt Elizabeth set her teacup and saucer on the end table. "And how on God's green earth is he supposed to do that? You changed your number and moved to Merced. You swore me and all your friends to secrecy. What's the man supposed to do? Hire a private detective? Hunt you down like one of the FBI's ten most wanted?"

"Has he called you?"

Aunt Elizabeth didn't speak for a moment. "No."

"He's never asked Shanice either. So there's the answer."

Aunt Elizabeth wilted slightly. "I didn't know." She looked away. "I thought . . ." She shook her head. "Never mind what I thought. It's none of my business, and I'm sorry I butted in." Her expression turned to one of pain and concern. "I just want to see you happy."

"I'm fine. Really, I am."

"No, you're not. You've lost weight. And you don't look like you're sleeping very much."

Grace came back and sat. She watched Samuel wrestling the red ball into submission. "I don't want to do anything that's going to hurt Samuel."

"Like introducing a man into his life who

may not be the marrying kind."

"Precisely."

Aunt Elizabeth didn't say anything for a long time. Samuel sat and rubbed his eyes. Grace got up and went to him. Lifting him, she hugged him close. "Nap time, little man." Aunt Elizabeth followed Grace inside and stayed in the kitchen to wash the few dishes. Grace sat in the living room rocker, Samuel snuggled in her lap, his head resting against her chest. She loved this time of day, loved the feel of his little body loosening and warming in her arms as he fell asleep.

"He looks like an angel." Aunt Elizabeth sat on the couch. "You're a good mother, Grace."

"I'm trying my hardest."

"Maybe you're right. Maybe it's better to leave things as they are."

Grace wanted to believe that.

Roman slept for a few hours and left around noon to drive up the Pacific Coast Highway. He needed time to think before he arrived in San Francisco. When he reached the city, he didn't check into a hotel on Nob Hill or downtown, though he could easily afford either. He went to the Phoenix in the old hood. A last-minute cancellation had opened up a room. He took that as a sign God was with him.

Still wide-awake after midnight, he decided

to take a stroll down memory lane. Nighttime had been playtime when he was a teen. Shrugging into his leather bomber jacket, Roman went for a walk through the Tenderloin.

It hadn't improved much. The homeless population had grown. Trash still spilled over cans and alley Dumpsters. New graffiti marked walls. Some tough-looking kids came down the sidewalk toward him. Roman took his hands from his jacket pockets and stared the leader in the eye. The group passed by without a word, two looking back at him. Roman kept going until he came to the overpass where White Boy died. He looked up at the concrete arch, letting himself think about his erstwhile friend, and made peace with the place before he walked on.

The apartment house where he'd lived with his mother looked the same. The right kind of graffiti would improve the place. The third-story window was dark. How many hours had he spent looking out and waiting for his mother to come home?

You know I love you, baby. I always come back, don't I?

The nightclub where she worked had a new name, but was still in business. Sleazy music oozed out the front door. Steeling himself, he went inside, but got no further than a podium occupied by a middle-aged man in a cheap suit. "Twenty bucks will get you inside." The man looked Roman over. "A hundred will get you more." Roman didn't take out his wallet. The smell of booze hung in the place, and one glimpse of an expressionless girl gyrating on the stage turned his stomach. A man at a table by the stage stood and tucked money in her G-string. Roman went back outside.

Gulping cold, moist coastal air, he walked away.

He spent another two hours wandering the streets, thinking about his mother. *Be honest. Look to Me.* Understanding bubbled to the surface. He'd loved his mother. And hated her — for what she did to make a living, for leaving that night, for breaking her promise. He'd never wanted to admit those feelings, but now he felt them like an open wound that still bled and left him raw with pain. He knew what God wanted him to do — to confess what he'd kept locked inside for so many years.

I am the Healer.

Instead of the shame Roman expected, he felt the old pain soften into understanding. His mother had been a child when she got pregnant and gave birth to him, barely an adult when she died. To his knowledge, she never had friends or family to help her. She'd been abandoned long before he came along. Whatever the circumstances, Roman knew something else. She hadn't thrown him away. She kept him close. She loved him.

Still walking, Roman suddenly remembered the landlord in the apartment building talking with the stranger who'd grabbed him. What had he said? It all came back, as if it played out in front of him. The man had given the landlord a wad of money and then followed Bobby Ray up the stairs. *You're coming with me.* Bobby Ray had fought, instinctively sensing something wrong, terribly wrong. The would-be abductor started carrying him down the stairs. Then Bobby Ray's second-grade teacher had shown up with a police officer. The man let go of him and disappeared like a rat down a hole.

The hair on Roman's neck prickled as he experienced an epiphany. He'd only been seven, but he'd felt the evil in the man's intentions. Even after that narrow escape, he'd kicked and clawed to get away from the policeman, who put him in the back of a squad car. He hadn't seen them as rescuers. They were both enemies who wanted to take him away from his mother. He'd cried and screamed curses on the teacher, who sat next to him in the squad car. He'd kicked the back of the police officer's seat all the way to the station, where he was turned over to a social worker from CPS.

Lord, how many years have I carried all that hatred around and let it shape my life?

Sitting in an all-night café, Roman asked God what he should do next. He got an

636

answer as the sun came up. Exhausted, but resolved, he went to the elementary school and asked for the names of the second-grade teachers who'd been there the year he was seven. He recognized the name of one and asked where he might find Morgan Talbot.

"Mr. Talbot is still here. He's on break right now."

God's perfect timing. "Could I speak with him?"

The secretary made a call to the teacher's room. A few minutes later, Mr. Talbot entered the office. Roman recognized him immediately. Talbot's hair was now gray, not red; his shoulders stooped slightly, and he wasn't nearly as tall as Roman remembered. He'd seemed a giant to a seven-year-old boy. Talbot's eyes were still kind.

"You probably don't remember a seven-year-old kid named Bobby Ray Dean."

"I remember." His smile was wistful. "You were the first boy I had to turn in to CPS. I'm sorry to say there have been others since."

"I don't imagine it gets easier."

"No. It doesn't."

"Maybe it'll help to know you saved my life that day." Looking back now, Roman saw how God sent Talbot at the exact time Bobby Ray Dean needed rescue. "The landlord had just sold me. If you and that police officer had arrived five minutes later, I would've been gone and probably long dead by now."

He felt gratitude well up inside him, not just for Talbot, but for God, who sent him. He held out his hand. "I'm late in saying it, but thank you, sir."

Mr. Talbot's eyes moistened, and he shook hands with Roman. "I was just doing what was right." He cleared his throat. "The officer was my cousin. He's retired. Living in Montana now."

"How about you? Are you retiring soon?"

"He'd better not." The secretary spoke up from behind the counter. "He's the best teacher we have."

Talbot apologized and said he needed to get back to the classroom. Break would be over soon, the children lining up. He paused in the doorway. "You were very good at art, as I remember."

"I make a living at it. Under a different name. Roman Velasco."

"Didn't you just do a big project in Los Angeles?" The secretary intruded again. "Something on the side of a church building. I saw it on Facebook."

Roman addressed Talbot. "If you're interested, you can see it online. The work wouldn't exist if you hadn't done what was right."

"I'll look you up." He smiled. "Thanks for coming by, Bobby Ray. It's nice to know one of my pupils is doing so well." He went down the hall, his back a little straighter.

"He needed to hear that." The secretary nodded. "Most students remember the upper-class teachers in high school and forget all about the ones they had in the first few years, the unsung heroes who teach the basics."

Outside, Roman took out his phone and called Jasper Hawley. He told him he had time on his hands and would like to come up and see him, and Chet and Susan. "Unless you already have plans over the next few days."

"I'm in Portland right now, but I'll be back day after tomorrow. Something happen, Bobby Ray?"

"Just taking another look at my life from a new perspective."

"It's about time."

Roman had other things he needed to do, and he might as well get one errand done before he headed back to the hotel for some much-needed sleep. He went to the coroner's office on Bryant Street to find out everything he could about the circumstances of his mother's death and where she had been buried. The clerk told him the medical examiner's office retained dental records, tissue samples, a full body X-ray, and DNA of everyone brought into the morgue. His mother had died of an overdose of heroin. Her body had been cremated, her remains placed in storage. Roman filled out all the necessary paperwork and paid the fees to have her ashes released to him.

"It's been over twenty-five years. It might take a few days to find her."

Roman gave his contact information. He went to the wharf for dinner and then back to the hotel. He slept for eighteen hours without dreaming and awakened fully rested. Instead of wandering the Tenderloin, he went to Golden Gate Park and imagined how much Grace would love it. He drove to Cliff House for a late lunch. His phone vibrated. The medical examiner's office. "It usually takes a lot longer than this, but we found your mother's remains."

God seemed to be moving things along.

Roman pulled into Masterson Ranch the next day. Gibbs and DiNozzo barked from the front porch. Chet came out of the barn, and Susan down the steps of the house. She got to him first and hugged him. "Nice you came back so soon."

Chet laughed. "We were worried you'd wait another decade before visiting again."

Roman said he'd like to stay a couple of days this time, if they had room. They told him he could stay as long as he wanted. They all sat in the kitchen and talked around the table for two hours before Roman asked them if he could spread his mother's ashes in the hills above their house.

Susan looked at Chet, tears in her eyes. Chet nodded. "We'd be honored, Bobby Ray."

They told him he could stay in his old room, but he'd have to share it. They only had four boys right now, but the one living in his room was another tough case just like him. Roman met Jaime Lopez when everyone gathered for dinner. He recognized himself at fifteen: angry, broken, no family, no future, no hope. All that had changed on this ranch with these people, and would for this boy, too, if he cooperated. Roman told Jaime as much after lights-out.

The next morning, at dawn, Roman took his mother's ashes up into the hills. He found a beautiful old valley oak with outstretched branches and a view of the ranch. In spring, these hills would be covered in green grass, golden poppies, and purple lupines. He opened the box and carefully spread her ashes.

"I love you, Mama. I forgive you." When he finished, the tears came from down deep. "Forgive me." He'd hated her, blamed her for dying and leaving him on his own. It had taken him all these years to see and confess it to her. He had carried that anger around like a heavy shield to protect himself against ever loving anyone again.

It took dying before he could learn to live.

It was sunset before Roman returned to the

house. He took his place at the dinner table and listened to the conversation going on around him. He volunteered to do the dishes and then joined everyone in the living room for the house meeting. When asked, he talked about his time at the ranch. "The program works, if you work it." Chet and Susan told the boys about his success as an artist. They all knew about the piece he'd done on the church.

Jasper came late. "Two trips up here in six months. That's a good sign."

Chet and Susan turned in for the night, leaving José in charge. Roman sat on the porch with Jasper. Neither Chet nor Susan had mentioned Grace. Considering how well they'd all gotten along, he'd hoped they'd bring her up. And now, here was Jasper talking about every subject except the one Roman wanted most. Several times, he had to clench his jaw so he wouldn't ask. That wasn't part of the bargain he'd made with God. *Three people, Lord.* He needed one more. His heart squeezed tight with pain. *I guess You're saying no.* He looked out at the stars and let her go again.

"Time to head for home." Jasper put his hands on his knees and stood. "Walk me to the car." Roman fell into step beside him. Jasper opened the car door. "Don't stay away too long, son."

"That works two ways. You have my new

address, but you'll be on the couch again. No fancy guest room."

"Not a problem." Jasper studied him. "You're not going to talk about Grace, are you?"

Roman's heart jumped. Number three. God was answering his prayer. "I've been waiting for you to bring her up."

"Are you going to see her?"

"I'd be on her front doorstep if I knew where she lived."

"You haven't talked to her at all?"

"Figured that was the way she wanted it after she quit and moved out of the cottage. Have you seen her?"

Jasper hesitated. "No, but I've talked with her several times. She's got her own business now. VirtualGrace.biz. I've referred several students to her. One landed on the honor roll after she worked with him."

"Can you give me her address? I'd like to make amends in person."

"I can, but I won't. Better if you contact her first. Give her the choice."

It wasn't the answer Roman wanted, but he understood. "That makes sense."

As soon as Jasper drove out of the yard, Roman took out his phone and found Grace's website. He tapped Contact, thumbed a short message, said a quick prayer, and touched Send.

Sighing, Roman looked up. All he had to do now was wait . . . and hope she'd respond.

39

Grace couldn't sleep. After an hour of trying, she decided to get some work done and check her messages. She made coffee and stepped down to her small office. One of her students had sent a term paper for her to edit. She redlined problem areas and wrote comments in a sidebar before sending it back. That done, she responded to another student's question.

It was after two in the morning when she checked her website e-mail. Her heart leaped when she recognized Roman's address. The message had been sent at 10:20 that evening. The subject line read *Request*. She positioned the cursor and then lifted her hand away as though about to burn herself. Was she opening herself up to more heartache? *Think before you do anything, Grace. Think!* She could delete his message without reading it and pretend she never received it. No, she couldn't. She'd been praying for weeks. This might be God's answer. She just hadn't expected to feel such a jumble of emotions when it came.

Oh, God; oh, Lord . . . She didn't even know what to ask now.

Pushing her chair back, Grace went up the steps into the kitchen. She poured herself another cup of coffee, then just as quickly poured it out. The last thing she needed was more caffeine. Her pulse was already racing. She went back to her desk. Sitting straight, hands fisted, she stared at the screen. *Don't be such a coward! Just read it,* she told herself fiercely. She opened the message.

Grace — I'd like to talk to you in person. If you're willing, name the time and place. I'll be there. Roman.

Should she meet him? Why was she even asking that question? She knew this day would come. Hadn't she been praying about it? She just didn't feel ready. *Will I ever be ready, Lord?* She didn't want to hope for anything.

Multiple possibilities popped into her head. She could meet him in a coffee shop. That would be neutral and safe. She could leave Samuel with Dorothy or Angela. She cast aside one idea after another, sensing all the while what God wanted, if she had the courage for it.

Oh, Lord, help.

Taking a deep breath, she let it out slowly as she tapped Respond.

I live in Merced.

Merced was a long way from Los Angeles. Roman would undoubtedly decide she wasn't worth the drive. Heart still thumping, but feeling justified, she went back to work on another project. It'd be hours before he read the message, and she doubted he'd answer.

A window in the lower right corner of her computer screen popped up with a ping, showing she had a new message from Roman. What was he doing up at three in the morning?

I'm at Masterson Ranch. I can be in Merced in a few hours. Just need an address. Why are you up so early?

She tapped Respond.

Couldn't sleep. Have work to do. What about you?

I haven't slept well for months. That's one of the things I want to talk about with you.

She didn't know what to make of that and leaned back in her chair.

Another message popped up.

Sorry. That probably came out wrong. Don't worry, Grace. I promise to keep my hands to myself.

She hesitated so long, another message popped up.

Please. Talk to me.

Please was a word she'd never heard him say. She typed her address and set two o'clock for their meeting time. She sent it before she could change her mind, and then hoped the appointment wouldn't work for him.

His response came quickly.

Thank you. See you at 2.

Roman packed his duffel bag, set it by the front door, and went into the kitchen to tell Chet and Susan why he was leaving a day early. He could smell the coffee and bacon. Chet stood at the counter talking to his wife as she speared slices of sizzling meat and turned them over on the griddle. Chet noticed him first. Glancing over her shoulder, Susan smiled. "Good grief, you're up early."

"Sorry to be cutting the visit short, but I'll be back. I contacted Grace. We're meeting this afternoon in Merced."

Chet's brows rose. "Sounds serious."

"As serious as it can get. I'm hoping she'll

hear me out."

Susan opened her mouth to say something, then closed it again. She gave Chet a look and focused on the bacon. Chet poured a mug of coffee and handed it to Roman. "Jasper told us things didn't go well between you two. That's why we didn't bring her up."

"I behaved like an ass. She had the good sense to quit and leave. I owe her more than an apology."

"She's agreed to see you. That's good news."

He'd have to wait to find out.

The house was already hopping. All four boys were up, had showered, and came into the kitchen hungry and talking, except for Jaime, who jerked his chin at Roman in greeting. Susan told Roman to sit down. "You're not traveling on an empty stomach. And if your meeting isn't until this afternoon, you have plenty of time for breakfast." She served him scrambled eggs, bacon, and toast and put the platters on the table for the rest to pass around, family style. Roman seldom ate a full breakfast and had to restrain his impatience to get on the road.

Once the boys were fed and on their way to morning chores, Roman felt free to leave. Chet and Susan walked him to his car. "You want a little advice about women?" Chet patted Roman's shoulder. "Take it slow and easy."

Susan gave an indelicate snort. "If I'd waited for you to propose, I'd still be living with my parents in Texas."

"I proposed."

"You said you had something to ask me in a few years. I said, 'Why wait?' "

Chet smirked at her and winked at Roman. "Like I said. Take it slow and easy. The girl will let you know what she wants and when she wants it."

Susan punched him in the arm.

Driving out of the yard, Roman looked in the rearview mirror. Chet had his arm around Susan as they both waved. Susan leaned into her husband.

Lord, that's the kind of relationship I want.

Grace tried to work, but she couldn't concentrate. Desperate to do something to curb her tension, she cleaned house while Samuel played contentedly with blocks on the living room rug. It stopped raining long enough to take Samuel out for a walk around the block. She wanted him tired and sound asleep when Roman came. Samuel toddled along happily for a while, but he soon started fussing and wanted back in the stroller. She went on ahead, encouraging him to chase her. He enjoyed that for half a block and then sat in the middle of the sidewalk in protest. When they returned home, she fed him lunch and put him on the carpet to play. He wanted to be held. Giving in, Grace rocked him. She almost fell asleep in the chair. Settling him in his race car bed, she kissed him and carefully closed the door.

She had time to brush her teeth and take a quick shower, but no time for makeup. A touch of lipstick would have to do. She brushed her hair hurriedly and raked her fingers through it. Staring at herself in the mirror, depressed, she looked pale, shadows under her eyes and wild-eyed on top of it. *Calm down, Grace. Breathe!* She drew in her breath, letting it out slowly. It helped relax her. She prayed and felt prepared. Until the doorbell rang.

Rubbing damp palms against her jeans, Grace took another deep breath and released it before opening the door. Roman stood on the other side of the screen door, and her pulse rocketed. So much for moving on. *Oh, Lord, help me.*

Roman felt all the old fears rise when he walked up the path to Grace's front door. Love had always been the enemy, the emotion to avoid. In the past months, Brian had helped him see more clearly what Jasper had tried to get across for years. Just because one person let you down didn't mean everyone would. And, in truth, Roman had let Grace down because he'd lacked the courage to step up and be the man God intended him to be.

That was then; this is now, he reminded himself. *I behaved like a child. God, make me the man You want me to be.*

He stood at the door, heart in his throat, and pressed the doorbell. *Lord of mercy, help me say what needs to be said. And if it's Your will . . .*

The door opened. Grace appeared, and all thought left him. He could hardly breathe. If he'd ever had any doubt about being in love with this woman, it was gone now. She looked younger, more vulnerable, her dark hair longer, down around her shoulders. She was wearing the pink sweater, white blouse, and jeans he remembered. She'd lost weight, but then, so had he. He couldn't tell what she was feeling, but he sensed wariness. Considering what had happened between them the last time they were together, Roman understood her distrust. She inhaled sharply, and his heart pounded harder. It helped to know she was nervous, too, afraid how this time together might go. Seeing that made him calmer. Roman knew how and where he wanted this meeting to end. Or rather begin.

Unlatching the screen door, Grace pushed it open a few inches. "Come in." She stepped back. To give him room or to keep her distance? She didn't meet his gaze, but offered her living room with a tense gesture. The sofa was pale turquoise with yellow pillows. She'd hung up the hand-lettered art-work, which he now recognized as a quote from Psalms, and the pictures of Jesus.

Where two or three gather together as my followers, I am there.

"Please. Sit." Grace's voice trembled slightly. She cleared her throat. "I'll make some coffee."

Roman felt as much at home in this house as the cottage. It wasn't the furnishings or decorations. It was Grace. Instead of sitting, Roman followed her and stood in the kitchen doorway, watching her. The faint flush in her cheeks had disappeared. She was pale now. Was she afraid of him? He hoped not. She almost dropped the canister and gave him an embarrassed glance. He didn't have to ask if he was making her nervous, and he didn't want her to be. How much of what he felt showed in his face? Too much, apparently. He had to stop drinking in the sight of her.

Take it slow and easy, Chet had said. But not too slow, according to Susan.

Roman tossed all his experience with women. None of it applied. If he didn't say something soon, he'd have another heart attack. He smiled at her, hoping to get them both over a rough start. "I've missed your coffee." He could stand all day and watch her. She was more beautiful to him than anything he'd ever seen. But she might relax if he looked at something else.

The view from the kitchen window showed a large lawn and vegetable garden. "Nice place for Samuel to play." Grace said yes. She took an unsteady breath as she spooned coffee. Then she started to talk. She told him about Dorothy and George Gerling, her landlords, and Juan and Angela Martinez and their three children who lived right next door. Juan planted the vegetable garden, and Angela gave her parenting tips, and little Matías was Samuel's first good buddy. She was rambling, a sign she was still nervous. He noticed she'd filled the coffee filter to the brim. She uttered a soft gasp and spooned coffee grounds back into the canister.

Roman wanted to put his arms around her and say, *It's okay, Grace. I'm just as scared as you are.* He tried to relax, but his pulse galloped, his breath high and tight. He breathed in and out slowly before he spoke. "Where's Samuel?"

"He's down for a nap." Grace barely glanced at him, her attention caught by something on the kitchen table. Roman looked down at a blue-trimmed plate, and understood. There were the things she'd gathered on their road trip: five smooth stones, a pinecone, and a pair of acorns linked together by a single twig.

Picking up the acorns carefully, Roman held them in the palm of his hand. "You didn't throw them away."

Blushing, Grace turned her back. "Why don't we sit in the living room?" She filled two mugs with coffee and left him standing alone in the kitchen. Roman replaced the acorns on the plate. Strange how something so small and ordinary could fill him with so much hope.

Grace occupied the rocking chair, leaving him the whole sofa. She held her mug cupped tightly in both hands, a talisman. His was on the coffee table, a sizable barrier between them. He sat, but didn't touch the mug. He hadn't come for coffee.

"I came to apologize, Grace." Something he'd never done before. "I didn't treat you with the respect you deserved, and I'm sorry for that." Pressing his palms together between his knees, he leaned forward, sending up a shotgun prayer. *God, help me.* "I was afraid to tell you how I felt about you." She looked away, and he held off saying the rest, waiting for her to face him again before he went on. "I was in love with you then, and I'm in love with you now." He'd never said those words to anyone and he saw the walls going up.

"I don't want that kind of love, Roman."

"I'm not finished."

Lips parting, Grace's eyes filled. She almost spilled her coffee. "I'm not sure I can listen."

"Please?"

Setting the mug on a small lampstand table, Grace put her hands on her thighs before she looked at him in anguish. "Why did you come, Roman?"

"I laid out my fleece, and God said yes." Why should she believe him? *Just say the rest, Roman.* "I came to ask you to marry me."

"What?" She drew back, shocked.

"You heard me." He knew what he was asking. Brian had given him a copy of the standard wedding vows once. Roman had some sense of the depth of commitment it would take for a relationship to last for the long haul, through all the challenges life would throw at them, not to mention the issues and personality traits they would each bring along. He knew it wouldn't be easy for either of them. God knew what childhood issues and adult issues they had. Even with all that, they had God's promises to stand on. *Nothing is impossible for God.* "Just to be clear, Grace, I want to love, honor, and cherish you for as long as we both live."

Bowing her head, she clenched her hands in her lap. She shook her head. "I know what you think about women, Roman. The ones you meet in clubs. You don't know as much about me as you think you do." Tears spilled down her cheeks.

"I know you went to After Dark and met a guy, and Samuel is the result."

Sucking in a breath, Grace stared at him, her cheeks blooming red and then going white. "Shanice told you?"

"Not as a betrayal. It all came out when I went with her to pick up a friend at After Dark."

"Oh." Grace covered her face.

Roman's heart ached for the fear and uncertainty she'd suffered because of one night of forgetting herself. She had fought to keep her son, and now carried the responsibility alone. How many other women would have taken a different path? Thank God, Grace followed Him and not the crowd. "What Shanice didn't know is I could be the guy she was talking about."

Grace lowered her hands, frowning. "Why would you say something like that?"

"It's not impossible. I used to hang out at After Dark regularly. I had a beach condo in Malibu around that time. I remember a girl with long, blonde hair who left in the middle of the night while I was in the bathroom. I don't want to sound arrogant, but that had never happened before." The few women he'd brought to his condo had been sent home in a cab — usually before they were ready to leave.

Another sin I confess, Lord. I treated women the way men treated my mother. "I'm not the man I used to be, Grace, but I'm still a long way from the one I want to be."

"Women are held to a higher standard than men." Her mouth tipped in a sad, knowing half smile. "Especially by men."

Was she remembering the self-righteous remarks he'd made in Bodie? "You're right, and it's wrong. I've lived as a hypocrite for a long time." He'd condemned a long-dead woman for being in the life his mother had lived, remembering how he'd suffered right along with her. He'd never seen Grace angry until that day. She hadn't realized she was showing compassion for his mother. What did he know about what happened between his mother and father, what the circumstances were? What right did he have to judge anyone?

Grace's expression was enigmatic. "Is that why you came? Because you think you could be Samuel's father?"

"The girl I met told me she wanted to feel something." Roman saw the flicker in her eyes. "I wanted the same thing. And I'm not talking about sex, Grace. I'm talking about connecting with someone emotionally." He'd never understood the pent-up longing until Grace showed up and their relationship progressed. "I'm not explaining very well." He tried to gather his thoughts. "It only took a day to understand you were never coming back to the cottage, and I'd blown everything with you. It took me months to work through all the reasons you had to leave and what I needed to do to get right with God." Again, that flicker. He'd been saved when she left, but he hadn't been a Christ follower. And that made a fundamental difference in who he had been and who he was now.

They sat facing each other, the coffee table between them. Roman didn't look away. "You admitted you loved me that night. You left because you wanted a man willing to commit, not a boy who wanted everything on his terms."

"If we're being honest, I left because I knew if I stayed, I wouldn't be strong enough to say no a second time."

"You did the right thing in leaving, Grace. I wouldn't have left you alone." He thanked God she hadn't waited. Where would they be right now if she'd weakened? They'd be living together. She'd never have felt secure and cherished, and he'd still be the same arrogant, self-centered jerk he'd been then. If Grace hadn't fled, he might never have felt the need to examine his life and realize he had to let God change him from the inside out.

Grace looked troubled. "How could Samuel be your son, Roman? You said you've always taken precautions to avoid fathering a child."

How many other callow things had he said in his lifetime? "I had a standard." He gave a bleak laugh. "Not much of one, I'll admit. I didn't want to be like my father: get a girl pregnant and walk away." Hardly an excuse, but the truth. "My mother never told me who he was, left that line blank on my birth certificate. Maybe she didn't even know, and I have no way of finding out."

Throat constricting, Roman struggled with a tide of emotions. "Crazy as it sounds, I missed my father. I know that might not make sense to you, but I needed him." Over the last few days, his eyes had been opened. "Jasper tried to fill the gap, but I wouldn't let him. Chet tried, too. I had walls up. When I accepted Christ, I found my Father. But there's still that flip side. I still wonder." He was silent a moment, praying. *Jesus, help her understand what I can't explain to myself, let alone another human being.*

Time to put all his hopes on the table. "I love you, Grace. I want to marry you. I don't know Samuel yet, but he's your son, and that's enough reason for me to love him." Grace's brown eyes softened. Was that love or compassion? "I didn't tell you all that so you'd feel sorry for me."

"I don't."

"A boy needs a father."

Her eyes filled. "So does a girl."

"Maybe that's why God sent the angel to you." His heart beat faster at the warmth in her expression. "If you say yes, we'll go through premarriage counseling." Shanice had told him about Patrick. "We'll both do our own homework. If we keep Jesus front and center, we'll make it through whatever this life throws at us." His palms felt moist.

He hadn't thought to ask if she had met someone else. Another Brian Henley type who would be perfect for her instead of someone like him. "You told me once that you loved me. Do you still love me, Grace?"

"I've been trying very hard to get over you."

"Any luck with that?"

"None." Her lips tipped up.

Roman let out a breath. "Thank You, Jesus."

Grace laughed softly. "I never thought I'd hear you pray."

He hadn't realized he'd spoken aloud. "That makes two of us." He felt steadier inside, seeing a future and a hope opening in front of them. Her defenses were coming down, and his body was fast remembering the kiss they'd shared in Topanga Canyon. The rush of heat was coming on, and he wanted Grace in his arms right now. He put his hands on his knees, intending to make that happen, when he felt a check in his spirit telling him to wait. Better not to test his control . . . or hers.

Lord, I don't deserve anything, but here You are again, showing me mercy and unfailing love.

"Mama?"

Roman turned and saw Samuel standing in the doorway, cheeks flushed from sleep, dark hair damp and matted. The last time Roman saw Samuel, he'd been a baby learning to crawl. Now a little boy stood on his own two feet, rubbing sleep from his eyes. Love swelled inside Roman until his eyes burned. Whether he was Bobby Ray Dean's son or not, he could be. And he would be.

Clearing his throat, Roman spoke gently. "Hey, there, little man. Do you remember me?" Samuel looked at him in bewilderment. Why would this child remember? Roman had barely spent time with him. That was going to change.

Grace rose and went to Samuel. Lifting him, she perched her son comfortably on her hip and sat on the couch beside Roman. "Samuel, this man wants to be your daddy."

Samuel looked up at Roman, eyelids drooping. Leaning against his mother, he went back to sleep.

Roman grinned at her. "He didn't say no." Was Grace going to say yes? "I guess he doesn't have a problem with it."

She laughed softly, eyes shining as she ran her hand over Samuel's hair in a loving caress. She looked at him. "Neither do I." Reaching up, she drew Roman's head down and kissed him.

When her lips parted, Roman deepened the kiss. The old Roman would have put the child to bed and kissed Grace until neither cared whether they were married or not. The new man wanted God's blessing and Grace's trust. He wanted her to know he'd cherish her, not use her. And right now, with her hand on his chest, he wanted her too much.

Capturing her hand, he straightened, then brushed her hair back over one shoulder with a trembling hand. Her flushed cheeks and darkening eyes drew him in, and he couldn't help but kiss the racing pulse beneath her ear.

She drew in a soft breath. "I should put Samuel back to bed."

Tempted to agree, Roman knew it wouldn't take much more to cross the line.

"Safer for both of us if you keep him right where he is." He cupped her cheek.

"Okay." She let out a soft sigh.

"Was that relief or disappointment?" Roman couldn't resist one more kiss, just to find out. And that kiss led to another until they were both breathless and trembling.

"I'd better move." Grace took the rocking chair on the other side of the coffee table. Shifting Samuel in her arms, she settled more comfortably. "Are you heading back to Los Angeles this afternoon?"

"I'm staying in the same hotel you and I stayed in on our road trip." He'd checked in before coming to see Grace. "It'll serve as home base until I find a house."

"A house? You want to move to Merced?"

Laughing, Roman shook his head. "I don't know yet, but I didn't just stop by on my way back to LA to say, 'Hey, by the way, I'd like to marry you.' I'm sticking around until you do."

Samuel awakened again, groggy and grumpy this time. Grace stood. "He needs another hour, at least."

Roman followed and stood in the doorway as she settled him. He grinned as he backed out so she could close the door. "A race car bed?"

"Gift from Dorothy and George. Aunt Elizabeth sleeps in it when she comes to visit."

"Does that happen often?" She hadn't moved, and the hall felt too small for the two of them. He glanced into the other bedroom with an inviting queen-size bed. He closed the door. Out of sight, out of mind. He hoped.

"She's coming tomorrow to spend the weekend."

"She'll want my head on a platter."

Grace looked back over her shoulder with a grin as she returned to the living room. "Actually, she's been rooting for you." She lifted his mug. "Your coffee's cold." She picked up hers as well. "We can sit in the kitchen and talk." Pouring two mugs of fresh coffee, she set them on the table.

They sat facing each other. Roman imagined sitting together like this for decades to come. "Mmmm. I really have missed your coffee."

"It's a poor reason for wanting to marry a girl."

"Just one of many good ones." He looked

at her for a moment, thankful she didn't seem nervous about his perusal now. "I've missed you." More than he could express, and far more than he'd thought possible. The old, niggling fear rose that even the best things in life don't last forever. "Until death parts us" meant one of them would go before the other. He and Brian had talked about that. Each day was a blessing from God, to be lived to the fullest, without fear.

"Don't buy a house yet, Roman."

"I'll rent until we decide what we want to do. Unless you want to move back to Southern California. How do you like it here?"

"I like it very much, but you're a big-city boy."

"Am I?" He'd grown up in the Tenderloin, bounced from youth hostel to hostel in Europe, had a Malibu beach condo and a fortress in Topanga Canyon. Now, he lived in a two-bedroom apartment in a rough neighborhood in LA, not a place he wanted to settle his wife and child. But then, what did he know? Where they would live was just one of the many things they'd have to work out together.

Roman stretched out his hand on the table, palm up. Grace let out a soft breath of surrender and slipped her hand into his. "I guess it doesn't matter where we live, as long as we're together."

It would be easy to accept her surrender,

let her give in, but Roman wanted Grace secure and content, as well as happy.

"It matters, Grace." He lifted her hand and kissed her palm. "We'll wait for God to tell us where He wants us."

EPILOGUE

Talia's Laguna art gallery buzzed with activity, patrons, journalists, and collectors viewing Roman's work, as classical music played softly in the background. Waiters moved among the guests, offering champagne, sparkling cider, and hors d'oeuvres. Grace stood beside Roman as he answered questions about his art, marveling at the ease with which he moved conversation from his work to the work God had done in his life.

Talia had been on her A game, sending out engraved invitations to wealthy art patrons and collectors for the grand opening of Roman's first show in over three years. Of course, Talia had widened her net through social media for the continuing show over the next two days. Roman's paintings would all be sold by then, but would remain on the walls over the weekend so people could enjoy what would soon be hidden away in someone's mansion. Advance orders for reproductions and signed prints would be available.

This was the second art show Grace had attended. What a difference from the first, when Roman had been edgy, angry, eager to take flight. His work had changed drastically, as well. He no longer attacked a line of canvases. He spent weeks making sketches and taking long walks with Samuel until the work came together in his mind. He painted one canvas at a time, each different in style — impressionist, fauvist, and one large, realist work Talia declared a masterpiece titled *World Changers.* Roman had even included several pieces of graffiti.

Several people stood in deep conversation with Talia near *World Changers,* among them a movie star and a businessman who'd made the cover of *Forbes* magazine. Competing buyers, no doubt. Art could be a good investment, something to tuck away and sell later if fame dimmed or stocks went down. Roman's painting was nothing short of glorious, and though Grace understood the realities of making a living, she still prayed *World Changers* would end up in a public place where many would see how the disciples might look in current times — an interracial group including an accountant, a college student, a gangbanger, a middle-aged fisherman; men who might be enemies if not for their shared faith in Jesus Christ.

The last three years had brought major adjustments in Grace and Roman's lives.

After three intensive months of premarriage counseling, they'd felt equipped to wed. Brian officiated, Shanice at Grace's side, Jasper at Roman's. Two months later, Grace confirmed her pregnancy. Roman attended Lamaze classes and coached her in the delivery room seven months later. He was the first to hold their daughter, Hannah. Grace had never seen him weep tears of joy.

Others wanted to get close enough to speak with Roman, so she withdrew. Roman gave her a questioning look, and she smiled to reassure him. Rather than avoid the guests as he once had, Roman stood among them, answering questions. He looked comfortable in his skin, handsome, though still averse to formality in black jeans, leather boots and belt, an open-neck white shirt, and a black leather jacket. He told Grace the only occasion important enough for a suit was a wedding: theirs first, and then Brian and Shanice's, where she had been matron of honor and Roman, the best man.

Friends had come in support of Roman's opening: Brian and Shanice with their year-old son, Caleb, riding on his mommy's hip; Aunt Elizabeth looking elegant in a black dress and heels; Jasper and the Mastersons; Ashley and her new husband, a fellow teacher with two teens. Even Dorothy and George Gerling had made the trip down. Grace had accepted Angela and Juan's offer to keep

Samuel and Hannah for three days. Roman had wanted to bring Samuel along, until Grace explained an art show would not hold the interest of an energetic four-year-old, and Hannah would miss her big brother.

Tuck Martin was talking with Roman now, another journalist involved in their conversation. Where once Roman had been reticent to share anything about himself, he now spoke freely about God and how Christ had become the center and purpose of both his life and his art. Some invented other explanations about Roman's near-death experience, but his transformed life testified to the truth of it.

Grace often marveled at the changes in her life and Roman's. They talked about moving back to Los Angeles, but for now had decided to stay in Merced. Roman knew what it meant to Grace to stay the course at UC Merced and earn her degree. She was taking it slow, making Samuel and Hannah her first priority.

Needing space for Roman to work and with a new baby on the way, they had bought a house on the outskirts of town. Roman converted an upstairs rec room into his studio and made the attached RV garage into a man cave complete with a sound system and a variety of gym equipment. Samuel loved hanging out with Daddy, and, equipped with a safety harness, he could climb to the top of the rock wall, snap on the ceiling loop, and bungee jump. Roman laughed at his squeals of excitement as he bounced up and down until Roman caught hold and unhooked him for another climb. Roman's injured leg kept him from running, but he worked out daily and had the upper body strength to climb with Samuel or go up a salmon ladder or across a cliffhanger bolted into the side wall.

When their pastor felt called to teach at a Midwest Christian college, a pastoral search committee started looking for a replacement. They wanted a pastor who could teach the Word, encourage the aging congregation, and reach the younger, unchurched, and lost generations. Roman knew Brian's congregation was merging with Victory Outreach and texted him about the opening in Merced. Brian said he and Shanice would pray about it. A short time later, they came up for a visit and attended church with Roman and Grace. A couple weeks after that, Brian submitted his résumé, was invited to preach, and soon after, they offered him the senior pastor position in Merced. The Gerlings gave them the bungalow, rent-free, until they could find a home. Brian wasted no time in drafting Roman into ministry. The two men helped an InterVarsity Christian Fellowship group on the UC campus. They also found local hot spots that attracted high school students. Roman's man cave became a favorite meeting place; Samuel, the youth group mascot.

Grace felt Roman's arm slip around her. "I see someone I want you to meet." He excused them and led her to a middle-aged couple who had just come through the front door.

The man saw Roman coming and held up his hands in surrender. "Sorry to crash your party. Don't call the cops on me."

Roman laughed. "Hope you left your hand-cuffs at home. Grace, this is the police officer who busted me in the tunnel." He winced as he faced the man again. "Never did get your name."

The man winked at Grace. "He was too nervous to ask. LeBron Williams, and this is my wife, Althea, your number one fan."

Althea held out her hand. "I've been hop-ing to meet you for years."

"Stop gushing, honey. You'll embarrass the man."

Althea rolled her eyes and addressed Grace. "I kept an eye out for the Bird's work. We kept the secret until he did that interview."

LeBron snorted. "She's been bragging on me netting the Bird ever since."

"I could've killed him when he came home and told me he'd met you, and didn't even have an autographed slip of paper to show for it." Althea shook her head and gave her husband a teasing smile. "LeBron used to do a bit of graffiti back in the day." She looked at Roman. "He took me to see the mural on that industrial building. And we've been down the art walk several times. Are you planning to do another?"

"A wall. In Oakland. Spring break. Already have site approval and a crew lined up." Roman looked at LeBron. "There's always room for another worker. All you have to do is color inside the lines." Grace asked for their contact information and told Althea she'd send all the details.

The woman looked like she'd been handed two tickets for an all-expenses-paid, around-the-world cruise. "We'll be there!"

"Just the way I want to spend Easter. Back in the hood." LeBron grinned. "Come on, honey. The man has to mingle." He shook Roman's hand again. "Keep up the good work, Mr. Velasco."

Another art critic wanted a word with Roman. Grace wandered the gallery and ended up at *World Changers* again. "It's magnificent." Shanice stood beside her, having handed off Caleb to his daddy.

"It's so different from what he was painting when I met him." But then, so was Roman. So was she.

God had been drawing them to Him from the time they were children, both desperately in need and longing for a father. Long before they knew Him, He'd been at work in their lives. The Lord had promised those who believe that He would take away the stony, stubborn heart; give them a tender, responsive heart; and put His Spirit in them so they could follow Him.

How many times over the last three years had Grace watched Roman in wonder as she witnessed the fulfillment of that promise? She had seen that same astonishing transformation in others as well. Shanice, once a party girl, now a pastor's wife; Aunt Elizabeth, embittered and cynical, unable to love, now at peace, an affectionate aunt and granny, unafraid to open her heart to others. Grace's own life had begun with a childhood of fear and violence, and an aunt who couldn't bear to look at her, but felt duty bound to fulfill a sister's wishes. The nighttime visitor had opened her heart to the Lord, though it had taken a painful journey to learn He was trustworthy.

Shanice studied the painting. "The longer you look at it, the more you see. Everyone is calling it a masterpiece."

"It is wonderful. It's the best work Roman has done so far." An overwhelming joy filled Grace. "But it's just a shadow to the real one." Roman would understand what she meant. "It isn't what Roman's done, Shanice. It's what God has done in Roman." She took her friend's hand. "It's what God has done in my life and yours, and Aunt Elizabeth's and so many others we know." Tears filled her eyes as Grace felt the future open before her, like a door to life and hope and the never-ending life Jesus offered them. "We're all God's masterpiece, created anew in Christ."

Shanice squeezed Grace's hand. "For His good purpose."

"When I look at this painting, I'm amazed at what God has done." Grace glanced over her shoulder at Roman and Brian, in conversation with Tuck Martin. Roman caught her look and smiled at her before refocusing on the two men talking.

Even here and now the Lord was working on another masterpiece.

A NOTE FROM THE AUTHOR

Dear Reader,

Writing *The Masterpiece* has been a long journey. The characters and story have morphed several times, as seems always to be the case when I write a novel. The questions that started the project had to do with how childhood trauma can impact an adult life. It seems our culture is filled with damaged people from broken homes and relationships. I wanted to explore two individuals and how traumatic childhood experiences impact their adult thinking and behavior. Can they have a normal life? Can two broken individuals find wholeness together? With Christ, all things are possible, but what if faith is lacking?

Grace came to faith at a young age, but Christians aren't perfect. We're in a spiritual battle all our lives with an active, cunning adversary: Satan. I wanted readers to see how easily we can fall into traps and be seduced by worldly philosophies. Even when we are saved by grace, we suffer consequences. God comforts us, loves us, and shows us the way to walk through this life.

Roman had to learn the hard way. Some people have to go to hell before they can see or hear the truth.

The prevailing cultural view seems to be everyone will go to heaven no matter what they've done or not done or what they believe. Advocates of this belief say God is love, and there is no hell. In truth, Jesus talked more about hell than He did about heaven. Research showed me there are near-death experiences that are not full of light and joy, but are horrific and terrifying.

It is absolutely true God is love, but a text taken out of context is a pretext. God is also **just**. He is **holy**. He is **righteous**. Sin brought death to Adam and Eve — and to all of us. This life is not all there is. The wages of sin is death, and hell comes after. God sent His only begotten Son, Jesus Christ, to pay the price for our sins, in blood, so that we can be saved out of death into life eternal in heaven with Him — if we believe in Jesus' work on the cross. It is a matter of choice. Believe and be saved. Reject Him and spend eternity in hell. Jesus has done everything needed to keep us safe, to give us a future and a hope. Jesus did not come to enhance our lives. He came to *save* us.

This is one of the reasons I wrote *The Masterpiece*. It isn't only about two broken people trying to find wholeness together. It's about where wholeness can be found for each and every one of us. In Christ Jesus. No place else.

If you want to know why you are here, what you were meant to do, where to find love that lasts forever, and what the meaning of life is, seek the Lord. He has all the answers you need. "For we are God's masterpiece. He has created us anew in Christ Jesus, so we can do the good things he planned for us long ago" (Ephesians 2:10).

Francine Rivers

DISCUSSION QUESTIONS

1. What were your initial impressions of Roman? Of Grace? Did your impressions change throughout the story, and if so, how and why?

2. When Roman offers to let Grace live in the guest cottage, she struggles with whether to accept. She tells her friends she's been praying about it but hasn't felt like she's received a clear answer, except that other opportunities she explores don't seem to come to fruition. If you were Grace, would you have taken that as a clear answer from God? Have you ever been in a similar situation? How did you ultimately make a decision?

3. At the end of chapter 5, Grace has conflicting thoughts when she finds out about Patrick's betrayal. What did you hope she'd do? Why?

4. What do you think it means that Grace

notices details in Roman's work that no one else sees?

5. Grace remembers that Patrick "hadn't forced her to give up anything, but he'd known how to make her feel guilty enough to surrender all her dreams so he could attain his." Are you or someone you know being manipulated by false guilt? Why is this such a convenient tactic for manipulation — or even to make us doubt our own actions and decisions? How can we combat it?

6. When Grace asks Roman what he believes, he says, "We're born. We survive as best we can. We die. End of story." Have you ever felt that way, or known someone who did? How did Roman's response make you feel? Sum up your own beliefs in a short statement like Roman's.

7. Susan tells Grace that if Roman can't let go of his past, he will never reach his full potential, and Grace knows the same applies to her. What elements of their pasts do each of them need to let go of? How do we see this happening in the story? Are there things in your past that you need to let go of?

8. After Roman and Grace visit Aunt Eliza-

beth, Grace shares her experience about an angel visiting her as a child, which opened her heart to the Lord. Have you or a friend ever had a supernatural experience like this? If you're comfortable doing so, share it with the group.

9. Roman did not have a supernatural experience as a child, or anything that specifically pointed him to Christ. Are there indications that God was indeed looking out for him, just as He was looking out for Grace? Can you look back on your own life and see ways that God was guiding or protecting you, even without supernatural intervention?

10. Grace wonders why she couldn't see the truth about Patrick, and in chapter 26, Aunt Elizabeth comments to Miranda that Leanne couldn't see the similarities between her husband and their abusive father, either. Why do you think that is?

11. When Roman asks why he didn't know Jasper was a Christian, Jasper responds, "You never asked, and anytime I brought up spiritual matters, your eyes glazed over. There's a time for everything under the sun, Bobby Ray. The time never seemed quite right with you." What are some reasons for waiting until someone is ready to

hear the gospel? What are some reasons for sharing the truth, whether a person seems ready or not? How can we know which is best?

12. Jasper tells Roman, "Faith is just the beginning of a long, difficult journey." How does this play out in Roman's life after his near-death experience? In what ways have you seen the truth of this in your own faith journey?

13. After Roman's near-death experience, he is left with a chronic leg injury that the doctors can't explain. How did you feel about this element of the story? Why do you think the author chose to include it?

14. What is Roman's intent when he suggests to Grace that they become "more intimate"? How is this different for him from the casual hookups he's had until now? Why is it still not enough for Grace?

15. Aunt Elizabeth tells Grace, "I'm an architect when it comes to building walls." The same could be said of both Grace and Roman, as well as many people in real life. In what areas do you build walls? What are some ways you've found to begin to tear them down, either in your own life or the life of someone close to you?

ABOUT THE COVER

The Lord has ways of putting people together in times of need, and while working on *The Masterpiece*, I needed to talk with a real-life graffiti artist. When painters came to work on our house, I met a young man who had been a gang tagger in the Bay Area as a teenager, but graffiti had been a passing phase in his life, and I was looking for someone dedicated to the art form.

Along came a couple from Monterey who contacted me through my website, asking if I'd be willing to meet with students from the Czech Republic, many of whom had been reading my novels. Rick and I said yes, and arranged to spend the weekend. The Wongs hosted a luncheon gathering at their home for a Q & A. During the conversation, students asked me what I was writing. I gave them a brief synopsis of this novel. Before we left, the Wongs told me they had a friend in San Francisco, Cameron Moberg, a Christian who also happened to be a graffiti artist.

I fired off an e-mail. Would Mr. Moberg be willing to answer some questions? Cameron said yes. I checked out his work online and found it stunning. The more I learned about this young man, the more he seemed to be living out my protagonist's journey. Especially

CAMERON AND FRANCINE

the epilogue. I sent pictures to friends at Tyndale. Cameron now has fans at the publishing house. They contacted him about using his artwork on the cover of *The Masterpiece,* which was exactly what I hoped would happen.

Unfortunately, Cameron and I didn't have time for a face-to-face meeting before he headed off for a project in Australia. The final manuscript was in the hands of my editor before Cameron and I were able to get together. But eventually Rick and I invited Cameron and his family for a Saturday afternoon picnic and swim. As soon as I opened the front door to greet them, I felt like I'd known the family for years. I think that's the way it is when we meet Christian brothers and sisters, whether in the neighborhood or on the other side of the world. We are immediately connected. We have Jesus in common. We are family.

It was a hot day. We enjoyed hot dogs, watermelon, and watching Cameron and Crystal's two boys swim. We older folks sat in the shade and chatted. We certainly didn't lack for conversation, and I felt the Lord in our midst. When Cameron suggested Rick and I come down and have a lesson in graffiti painting, I said yes. I couldn't wait to get my hands on a few cans of spray paint and have the opportunity to experiment.

ORIGINAL GRAFFITI ART USED ON THE COVER

Check out Cameron's work online at www
.camer1.com.

ABOUT THE AUTHOR

New York Times bestselling author **Francine Rivers** had a successful writing career in the general market for several years before becoming a born-again Christian. As her statement of faith, she wrote *Redeeming Love,* a retelling of the biblical story of Gomer and Hosea set during the time of the California Gold Rush. *Redeeming Love* is now considered by many to be a classic work of Christian fiction, and it continues to be one of the industry's top-selling titles year after year.

Since *Redeeming Love,* Francine has published numerous novels with Christian themes — all bestsellers — and she has continued to win both industry acclaim and reader loyalty around the world. Her Christian novels have been awarded or nominated for many honors, and in 1997, after winning her third RITA Award for inspirational fiction, Francine was inducted into the Romance Writers of America's Hall of Fame. In 2015, she received the Lifetime Achievement

Award from American Christian Fiction Writers (ACFW).

Francine's novels have been translated into over thirty different languages, and she enjoys bestseller status in many foreign countries.

Francine and her husband live in northern California and enjoy time spent with their grown children and grandchildren. She uses her writing to draw closer to the Lord, and she desires that through her work she might worship and praise Jesus for all He has done and is doing in her life.

Visit her website at www.francinerivers.com and connect with her on Facebook (www.facebook.com/FrancineRivers) and Twitter (@FrancineRivers).

The employees of Thorndike Press hope you have enjoyed this Large Print book. All our Thorndike, Wheeler, and Kennebec Large Print titles are designed for easy reading, and all our books are made to last. Other Thorndike Press Large Print books are available at your library, through selected bookstores, or directly from us.

For information about titles, please call:
(800) 223-1244

or visit our website at:
gale.com/thorndike

To share your comments, please write:
Publisher
Thorndike Press
10 Water St., Suite 310
Waterville, ME 04901